The Institute

Harry Backhouse

DEDICATION

To Mary and Bernard, for always having faith in me.
To my mother, for never giving up on me.
To my father, for being the role model I aspire to become.

CONTENTS

ACKNOWLEDGMENTS

Front cover photo by Staff Sgt. Steve Cushman.
Back Cover Photo from the Photograph Collection (COLL/3948), Marine Corps Archives & Special Collections.

THE INSTITUTE

1 - PROLOGUE

Cold.

Icy, bitter cold.

The Royal Scots expected this when they came to Norway. They used to believe that the weather was a far worse threat than the enemy.

Tales were told of men going to sleep and being found as cold as ice and dead to the world.

But now, tales were different.

They told of danger hiding in every blizzard, tales of huge monster-like men who could not be killed.

These 'monsters' were Russian soldiers, rumoured to have been genetically enhanced to adapt to the cold Norwegian climate. The Royal Scots were wary of facing them.

Their current mission was to escort a convoy of vehicles carrying oil – a simple enough task for experienced combatants like these. The route had always been deemed as relatively safe, and normally wouldn't have required an escort.

However, the Western Alliance was worried. There was supposedly a new Russian commander that had been brought in, and the raids on Western bases had become much more frequent.

In fact, there were very few locations that were deemed to be safe nowadays.

The Royal Scots were led by Major Gregory Allerson. Known for his friendly attitude and aged looks, he was nicknamed 'Old Greg' by his fellow soldiers, despite only being in his forties.

Old Greg, a soldier for twenty years, prided himself on never having had a convoy destroyed under his command. The Royal Scots were said to be always cheerful when fighting, and had been called crazy by other regiments.

However, as they trudged through the blizzard that enveloped them as they escorted the convoy, they could find very little to be cheerful about. There had been a reconnaissance force sent ahead, but it had not reported back.

'Old Greg' would be glad to leave this place. This was to be his last mission, after which he would be retiring and returning to Scotland. He allowed his thoughts to wander.

He still remembered the day he had left his wife, Dorothy, to join the army for the first time.

Old Greg, as a regiment commander, was rarely able to take holidays. Unfortunately, it meant he could not see his family very often.

He hoped that one day he would be able to tell stories to his children and grandchildren, about how he had fought for the Western Alliance.

Allerson had a son, a child named William. He would be a young man now, maybe wanting to join the army himself. Greg smiled. It would be good to see him again.

A shout from the front of the convoy snapped him out of his daydream.

"Major Allerson sir! We've found the recon force!" yelled Private Wallace, a young man who had just joined the regiment. This was his first mission. He was a well built, rugged man with red hair and brown eyes. "They've been wiped out."

Greg walked to the front, finding it hard to believe what the soldier had said. The convoy had stopped suddenly. Despite his experience of war, what he saw still shocked him.

A line of corpses all lay out in the snow, blocking their path. Pools of blood stained the snow.

It was called, 'The Mark of Fenrir'. No one knew who was responsible, but Western soldiers had been the victims of guerrilla attacks, and mutilated corpses left in prominent positions, as a warning to any who found them.

When confronted with this sight, even the Royal Scots' morale took a hit.

"Alright, get 'em out of the way," Gregory Allerson ordered, steeling himself, as he scanned the nearby area.

Private Wallace and the rest of the men did so, and the convoy continued.

Allerson grimaced, keeping alert as he clambered back into the jeep.

Suddenly, the vehicles stopped again. At the front of the convoy gunfire was heard. Through the blizzard, Allerson glimpsed fast moving shapes. He could hear his soldier's screams of pain.

"Form a circle, protect the central tanker! Sound the bagpipes! We're not going down here!"

The soldiers immediately obeyed. The bagpipes sounded and Allerson stood upright. They always lifted his spirit, even in the direst of circumstances.

Then the screams at the front of the convoy were silent and the Scottish soldiers were still, looking out into the snowstorm. They switched on thermal vision, through one of the dials on their goggles and saw themselves surrounded by the glowing red silhouettes of their enemies.

"Open fire!" Allerson roared, and the Royal Scots let rip with their guns.

The enemy surged forward and the Scots got their first true glimpse of their terrifying foe. Huge wild eyed men, covered in hair and possessing sharp melee weapons. These brutes possessed immense strength and were very tough to kill.

Allerson picked his targets carefully. A well-aimed shot to the head could bring down one of them, but they moved with a speed surprising for their size.

These mutated humans possessed had sacrificed intelligence for savagery.

Suddenly, high-pitched screeching filled the air, sending the Scottish soldiers into panic.

"The Cry of the Wolf!" Private Wallace muttered to himself, terrified. "It means Fenrir himself is coming!"

Fenrir was the name given to the Russian commander, a rumour that they had heard from locals. Never having been seen by any who lived, his presence would be a death sentence to the Royal Scots.

The brutes were soon put down, and the Scots stood in silence and in fear. The bagpipes had ceased playing long before now.

"Careful now, lads," Allerson said, with a grave expression. "The convoy drivers are dead. We're going to have to fight until we can get this tanker moving."

The screeching got louder, as what sounded like wolves in the distance began howling. Gregory Allerson gripped his weapon tightly. *He would take out Fenrir*, he told himself. *He'd be a hero when he returned.*

If there was one thing he had learnt during his time with the army, it was that everything could be beaten.

"Thermal vision," he reminded his soldiers as he brought down his visor. The brutes were just a recon force sent to assess their strength and the next Russians would be the hunters, far more deadly than those they had just fought.

He scanned around still looking through his visor. There was nothing there.

"There's somethin' fishy about this, lads," Allerson said. "What's radar showin'?" he shouted.

"Nothing, sir, this damn blizzard is interferin' with it!" the radar operator replied.

Allerson swore. "Alright, try to get the convoy movin' again, find anyone else who can drive these. Willie, prep the snowmobiles in case we need to make a quick escape," he ordered a sergeant.

"But the oil, sir," Private Wallace said. "How will we protect it?"

"Laddie, I value the lives of my soldiers. If I can't get this oil back, I'll at least get back my men," Old Greg said, straightening up. "Do ye have a problem with that, sonny?"

Wallace shook his head, saluting.

"No sir!" he said quickly.

Allerson nodded, as he began making his way back to the front of the convoy.

One of his soldiers approached him, a young man of around twenty.

He cleared his throat then began speaking quickly.

"Major Allerson sir, we've-"

THUNK!

Allerson stared in shock as he saw a long silver arrow embedded in the man's throat.

The man coughed blood, and then sank to his knees.

This was enough to get Allerson out of his stupor.

"The hunters are 'ere!" he roared, and began sprinting back towards the snowmobiles.

The howling had resumed, but now was much closer.

"Mount the snowmobiles!" he ordered his troops, and they quickly unhooked them from the side of the tankers. The armoured vehicles at the front of the convoy had all been destroyed so they had no heavy weapons left.

There were enough snowmobiles for them all now that their numbers had been depleted so severely.

"Formation Bannockburn!" Allerson yelled, and the regiment spilt into three groups, and sped off down the front of the convoy.

So it wasn't wolves that were howling. It was the hounds of the Hunters.

Allerson gritted his teeth, the snowmobile vibrating as he floored the accelerator. He heard a bark beside him and saw a hound snapping at his heels. He drew his pistol and plugged a shot into it, ending the creature's life.

"Sharp right!" he heard a soldier ahead shout, and turned, just in time. Many were not so lucky, as they tumbled off the edge of a giant crevasse. He heard their screams and shouts as they fell.

It seemed that nature triumphed over both man and beast. Allerson kept going, increasing his speed. There were still about twenty snowmobiles with him.

By now, they were about two miles from their own territory, where the border patrol would pick them up. But before that, there was a forest they had to make it through.

He drove onwards, noticing that the snow was soft and deep here. The hounds eased off, but he didn't know why.

Suddenly, huge figures appeared from the snow in front of them.

They were Russian shock troops. More huge men, this time armed with shotguns and submachine guns.

It was an ambush. The Russians had planned it all.

Allerson turned his snowmobile, and faced to the side. If he could draw the attention of the men, some of his soldiers might have a chance of getting past. He increased his speed, driving sideways through the forest in front of the shock troops, firing his pistol behind him.

He could hear them pursuing him, and ducked as bullets whizzed over his head and thudded into the trees.

Allerson pressed on, focusing on avoiding trees and obstacles.

He could do this.

But from behind a tree emerged a figure that threw himself into Allerson, knocking him off his snowmobile.

He lay on the floor and reached again for his pistol, a high calibre .44 Magnum. Before he grabbed it, a huge foot stamped down crunching his hand.

He felt like his whole arm was on fire, but clenched his mouth shut to avoid crying out. He looked up at the brutish man staring down at him.

He could see the glint in its eyes of a predator that knows its prey is helpless.

Allerson smelt its rancid breath on him, and struggled violently, but it was futile.

He glared in defiance. The Russian pulled out a long, serrated knife. There was a savage grin on his face.

* * *

Once the battle was over, Allerson's corpse lay in the bloodstained snow, his eyes glazed.

About twenty metres away lay Private Wallace. He had been flipped from his snowmobile and lay motionless in the snow. He was alive, but barely. Once a new recruit with his whole career ahead of him, he had now seen more of war that he ever wanted too.

Eventually, he forced himself up and staggered towards the border, the Western Barracks at Oslo, as the rest of his comrades lay dead around him. He felt a gut wrenching desire for revenge, but he was helpless on his own. His mission now was to report the annihilation of his regiment and let the Western Alliance know just what they were up against.

2 - **THE SELECTION**

"Officially, war was declared in 1964 when the Russian Federation, in conjunction with other satellite states, invaded West Germany without provocation. Other attacks were made at the same time, both in Asia and the Middle East, as the Russians sought to expand their sphere of influence.

Subsequently, the United States of America proclaimed themselves 'Protectors of Liberty', and established the Western Alliance – a coalition of capitalist countries which included the British Empire, France and West Germany.

The war continued, extending to different theatres and, in the years that followed, Europe became a battleground."

- A.G. Phelps, a Modern History of the World

* * * * *

Michael Bakerson, a brown haired sixteen year old, stood still, watching the man on the stage. He bit his lip nervously. Today was the day. The day where his entire future would be decided. He fidgeted, imagining the worst that could happen.

Last month, Michael had taken the preliminary examinations needed for admission into The Institute. Applicants' backgrounds were thoroughly examined, with many tests and interviews.

Some of the tests were similar to those required at an ordinary school. Tests like Mathematics, Problem Solving and Logical Reasoning. Others were different. Like ones for teamwork, physical fitness, combat skills.

The Institute was no ordinary school.

It was a military academy located in what had once been called London, where the next generation of soldiers would be trained to fight in the war. If you lived there, you would receive free food, healthcare and shelter, as well as being equipped with technology to enhance you as a soldier. You would receive citizenship as a member of the Western Alliance. It was tough to get in, and every young person aspired to go there.

For Michael, it was an impossible dream. He lived in the south of Independent Britain, one of the many poor nations in this modern world. Geographically, Independent Britain consisted of the areas which had once been Northern England and Scotland, yet these countries no longer existed. Its capital was in Edinburgh, yet this was far removed from Michael's village.

Michael lived in the area which had once been called Manchester, which was now as nameless as the village he lived in. Most inhabitants of Independent Britain lived in small isolated communities. For Occupied Britain, as the South of England was now known, it was a different matter. The military owned area was akin to a huge training ground for the soldiers of the Western Alliance.

Food was scarce, and the only way people could survive in the village was through subsistence farming. That was how almost everyone lived here. For farmers, modern technology was a rarity and people would resort to old-fashioned methods to get food from the land. The other legal way of life was to become a miner, where the risk of death was high. The alternative was to live as a brigand. Living as a brigand was illegal, as it meant crossing the border into Occupied Britain to get meat. The journey was long, but apparently wildlife still existed in the hills of a place which had once been called Wales. Michael had only tasted meat once and even that was only a scrap, but it was delicious.

Apparently, meat had once been a plentiful resource all over the world, but as the war progressed, the military began placing taxes on meat, and used it for themselves. In fact, the military had taken a lot more than meat from the people of Britain.

He remembered back to a particular lesson in his school at village, where his teacher had taught them about how the world had come to be what it was.

There had been about thirty children in their class, and they all listened intently as their teacher read out from a thick, leather bound book, with the imaginative title of 'A Modern History of the World'. They were all around thirteen years old, so mature enough to understand the textbook.

Michael smiled to himself as he thought about the heroism of the Western forces. How they had persevered, innovated and used resources in ways never before imagined. And now, he might be joining them.

The Institute was where soldiers were trained before going into real combat, the first rung on the ladder. The largest military facility in Europe, located in the centre of Occupied Britain.

Or he might be failing and being forced to become a farmer or miner, having to toil long hours just to feed himself. All of that depended on what happened in the next few minutes.

His sister squeezed his hand reassuringly. She was fourteen years old, and called Jane. She possessed deep blue eyes, like all of his family, and was never seen without a smile on her face. Michael smiled back. Almost the whole village was here, supporting their loved ones in the hope that they might be lucky enough to be selected. Michael's village had only managed to get a person into The Institute four times in the past.

It was a cool day in late spring. The sky was a typical grey, and there was a slight breeze blowing through the air. A smell of straw hung about the area. The village was a circular layout, with their simple homes scattered around in no particular order. It was fairly large in Michael's opinion, but he had been around long enough to know it inside out. His favourite part of it was the bridge over the river than ran along at the outskirts. He enjoyed standing out and gazing into the distance, looking towards what lay ahead.

The stage was a rudimentary wooden platform that had been set up at the edge of village to welcome the military guests that were coming. It had clearly been used before and weathered by the elements, but still somehow stood its ground.

He looked around and saw the tell-tale sandy hair that belonged to his best friend Steve. Steve was shorter than Michael and had dark brown eyes and handsome features. Michael and Steve had always been friends. Their friendship had begun when they were young.

It had begun in their first day at school. Michael, back then only four years old, had run in excitedly, but had tripped on the tree stump and had fallen. Steve had been the first one to his aid. Michael had been grateful, and the pair had instantly got on. They had similar interests and worked well together. Whereas Michael was smarter, Steve was stronger, and there was plenty of mutual respect between them. If anyone could get into The Institute, Steve could.

The man on the stage cleared his throat. He had an eye patch over his left eye and had short black hair. He had a ruddy complexion, but there was an of air calmness about him that made him seem like a man you would not want to cross. He seemed slightly wary of the flimsy wooden stage, as though he suspected it might break down.

The man wore khaki army uniform, more for tradition than anything else. A reminder to the people of the majesty which had once been the British Empire. Now though, that was merely a memory. The soldiers who fought for the Western Alliance all wore temperature regulated black combat gear.

The man looked around, and then began speaking.

"Good moo-erning, ladies and gentlemen, lads and lasses," he announced in a thick Scottish accent. "Right now I'm here to inform ye of who from yer village has passed the tests that all ye youngsters have all been working for, during the last month or so. But first, let me inform ye that at least one of ye lads has passed the test, so because of that, I will go through the introduction about why this opportunity is the best one ye will ever get at this place."

The man cleared this throat again, and then continued.

"The war has been raging for many years, but we are closer to victory than ever before. The Western Alliance is triumphing against the Russian brutes through superior technology and strategy. The reason why we are doing so well: our soldiers. The Russians inject their soldiers with chemicals and genetically modify them, cloning a generation of physical giants of great strength and durability. To counteract this, the Western Alliance has created The Institute, the largest military training complex in Europe. This is the place for which we search the country, finding the best and brightest to recruit and train. There is no limit to the amount of places at The Institute; we will take anyone who is good enough.

But to be good enough, ye have to be damn good. The Institute will train ye to use the most powerful weapons we have at our disposal, to fly a Z-56 fighter plane, to man an armoured mechanised walker, and to be able to safely disable a bomb that could take out half a city. We do not look for the physically able, that is the Russians' job. We look for the ones with the true grit and determination, as well as the brains to be able to use our equipment. And we believe that anyone who has passed here today might just have what it takes.

I will now read out which of ye candidates have passed," he finished.

The whole crowd was completely silent. In the past there had only been four people from his village to make it to The Institute, the last one being many years ago. It was a shock to have someone make it in after so long. Who would it be? Would it be him? The officer cleared his throat. "The lucky applicant who has got into The Institute is … Steven Green!" he announced. Michael smiled and cheered, along with the rest of the people there. He looked across at his friend Steve, who seemed stunned. Steve walked over to the stage, shook the hand of the officer, and then stood on the stage, still reeling from the surprise.

Michael was pleased for him, yet could not help feeling a pang of envy. Steve would get to join the army, but Michael would have to live out his life in this village. He would now have to become a farmer, or a miner. He didn't want that. This had been his chance for a better life, yet it had been snatched from him and given to his best friend. He sighed to himself.

Well, if anyone deserved it, Steve did.

However, it seemed the man on the stage had not finished. He would now make a speech congratulating Steve on his achievement. The officer cleared his throat once again.

"Very well done to you Steven, and welcome to The Institute." Michael almost rolled his eyes. "Now, the second candidate who has passed the test is ...

Michael Bakerson!" he announced and once again, the whole crowd cheered.

3 - CHOSEN

Michael froze. Everyone was looking at him, smiling. There had to be some mistake. There had never been two people from his village in The Institute. He was stunned. He had actually made it?

He had made it into The Institute.

Michael broke out into a huge grin. He had made it into The Institute!

He walked up slowly, the message still not quite sunk in. He wouldn't have to be some farmer; he had a chance at last to have a better life. And he would take it with both hands.

He walked up onto the stage, people patting him on the back as he passed. This was a record, the first ever year where there had been two people from the village to make it. His name would go down in history as being one of them.

The man with the eye patch smiled as he shook Michael's hand.

"Well done, son. Ye passed by the most," he said gruffly. Michael stared at him in wonder. He had passed by the most, out of everyone in the country. This was incredible.

"Just joking!" the man boomed, chuckling as he patted Michael on the back, hard. Michael laughed nervously along with him, but was still surprised by the remote possibility.

"My, my kiddie, ye are gullible," he said to him. "But ya did do well, sonny. Ye should be proud of yerself. There ain't many who get into The Institute, and ye better make the most of it. My name's Sergeant Raines, by the way, but you can call me sir," he grunted. He seemed cheerful enough.

"Thank you ... sir," Michael said, anxious to please him. He had heard first impressions counted for a lot.

Raines smiled, and then addressed both him and Steve. "I will see yous tomorrow morning, here at dawn. Ye don't need to bring anything, as all will be provided for at The Institute. Just don't come stark naked like one lad did over in Ireland," he said with a wink. Michael couldn't tell if he was joking or not.

"Anyway, have fun, have a last meal or something. Tomorrow will be a big day. First impressions count for a lot at The Institute," the Sergeant said, then strode off back to the military vehicle he had arrived in.

Michael watched as it drove off into the distance towards the border of Occupied Britain. He let out the breath that he didn't know he had been holding. He had done it. He had actually done it. He still couldn't believe it.

He turned around, and found himself and Steve surrounded by people, most of whom they had never met.

His mother rushed up to him and embraced him. "I have ... never ... ever been so proud!" she gushed out, whilst crushing his ribcage.

Michael, finding it hard to breathe, just nodded. He looked over at Steve. The two of them had never been particularly popular, but now they were heroes.

Steve in particular seemed overwhelmed, though mainly from girls who had never paid him any attention before but now were worshipping him.

Good for him. He deserved it.

Michael walked forward through the crowd, as people congratulated him. However, he noticed that some people - particularly ones his age - seemed muted in their excitement. He could sympathise with them. He remembered what he had felt when he thought only Steve would be getting through.

Jealousy. Envy.

He sighed in relief. At least he had made it.

Michael finally made it out of the stage area and into the huts where everyone resided. He noticed his father standing near their hut, and walked over to him.

"Hi, Dad," Michael said brightly. "You okay?"

His father looked at him strangely.

"I suppose you're so proud of yourself now, boy?" he said stiffly. "Glad to be out of this poor little village? Getting free at last?"

Michael opened his mouth to protest, and then closed it.

His father was ... right.

"John!" his mother scolded, having caught up with them. "This is Michael's big day, don't you dare ruin it for him," she glared at Michael's father.

He shot an angry glance at Michael, then strode off.

His mother smiled apologetically at him. "Sorry about father, sweetheart. He's not himself today. You go enjoy yourself," she said.

Michael blushed a deep shade of crimson. "Mum," he said. "Don't ever call me sweetheart," he implored, embarrassed and thankful that none of his friends were nearby.

She winked at him. "Sure, dear," she said, then went off in the direction his father had gone.

Michael turned around, and saw that the initial buzz after the selection had faded, and most people had gone back to their daily lives.

He couldn't really blame them. For most people, the next time the brigands came back with stolen produce would mean more to their lives than this particular Selection. Their lives were tough enough to get by without distractions. Tonight there would be a small celebration, where hopefully the brigands would be able to secure some meat for everyone to share, as was the custom on the annual Selection day.

He made his way towards the bridge by the river, and he realised that it would be the last time he could ever be there. He listened to the steady flow of the water as it continued to flow. He looked out across the farms to the familiar sight of treetops in the distance. He watched as a bird circled through the sky.

It was only now that Michael really clicked that The Institute meant almost nothing here. Sure, for the lucky few it would be the event of a lifetime, but for everyone else, the river would keep on flowing. Life would continue.

He noticed Steve catch up to him, and they grinned at each other, elated.

"This is awesome!" Steve enthused.

"I know, right?" Michael said. "Out of everyone, it was us two who made it."

"It was always going to be us, we're just that good," Steve joked.

"We must have been." Michael said thoughtfully. "Wonder what it'll be like."

"You worry too much Mike, just do what I do. Never think more than twenty seconds ahead," Steve said with a wink.

Michael rolled his eyes.

"Did you see Bloor's face?" Steve asked him with a smirk.

Michael shook his head. "Nope," Bloor was widely recognised as the bully of the village. He was the physically biggest of all the boys, and made particular mockery of Steve because of his height.

"Aw, it was great. He looked like some alien had got in," Steve described smugly.

"Which was true," Michael interjected teasingly, nudging him.

"You shouldn't be so harsh on yourself," Steve countered with a grin.

Michael grinned, and looked out into the woods beyond the farms.

"I wonder what the people there will be like," he mused once again.

Steve shook his head. "As long as there are girls there, I really don't mind," he joked, "but come on, let's get some food."

Steve turned and began walking back towards the centre of the village. He glanced back, for the final time, at the bird that swooped down back to its nest.

"We'll be finally free," he whispered, almost to himself.

4 - **TIME TO LEAVE**

The next morning, Michael woke up early. Last night, he had had one of the best meals of his life, even eating a whole leg of chicken by himself. It had been delicious. Everyone had been happy, and even his father was enjoying himself. It was still dark, and Michael reckoned he had about half an hour before sunrise. He got out of his bed and put on some clean clothes. He wanted to make a good impression.

He wandered over to the other side of the hut where his sister Jane was sleeping. She looked so peaceful. He realised that he wouldn't have long left with her. He felt sad, despite the opportunity. He would have to say goodbye to so many things. He blinked the tears out of his eyes.

He left their hut and began walking to his grandfather's house. Unlike most of the village, Grandpa Ted still lived in a house. Apparently, everyone had once lived in them, but after the Second Blitz of 1965 most had been destroyed. The Western Alliance had promised to rebuild them, but they never did. Ted's house was one of the few that had survived and he still lived there.

Michael went inside, closing the door behind him. The door was always unlocked, as Grandpa firmly believed that he had no right to lock his door on anyone but rather extend his hospitality to everyone.

Michael heard Grandpa Ted's voice boom out through the old house. "Welcome, my boy. Come in, come in!" he roared cheerfully. How Grandpa Ted knew it was him, Michael never knew. Michael smiled and went into the kitchen. The familiar smell of old leather boots greeted him.

"Hi, Grandpa." Michael said, awkwardly standing in the doorway. Grandpa Ted looked up from the book he was reading. He was an elderly person, and quite thin. His skin was slightly browner than everyone else's, 'Too many years in the sun.' Ted always told them. He had no hair left, and must have been older than eighty. His eyes were bright and inquisitive, not affected by the years that had taken their toll on his body. He leapt up from his chair with surprising energy for a man of his age, and embraced Michael tightly.

18

"You are so tall now, Mikey-boy," he said. That was his nickname for Michael. "You will make a fine man one day."

Michael smiled awkwardly, not sure what to say.

"Sit down," his Grandpa instructed him.

Michael did so.

"Now, Mikey-boy, today will be a very important day for you. You will have to say goodbye to us, and welcome the possibility of never seeing us again. You may die in your first battle. You may never make a battle," Grandpa told him. He had always been straight to the point, never beating about the bush.

Michael stared at him, shocked. He had never considered it that way. The Institute had always been an opportunity in his eyes.

Grandpa Ted looked at him seriously. "Michael. You know me. I will never pull wool over your eyes. I will always tell you what I think is right," he said.

"You know, I had a friend once. He volunteered for the army. We were best pals. He made it in. I didn't. We were the kind that always looked out for each other. Like you and young Steven. When he joined the army, I wished him well. He thought it was the opportunity of a lifetime. An adventure. He said he would come back whenever he could. I thought he would too.

Three years later, he did return. It was on injury leave. I was so pleased. But he was different. He was a changed person. He was cold, distant. He rarely spoke to anyone. He was violent, and quick to anger. He grew bored of the village life. He left after a month, desperate to return to combat. I was gutted. He had meant a lot to me. I never thought anything could separate us, but war had. The army doesn't turn boys into men. It turns men into machines."

Michael stared at him. "Why are you telling me this? It's what I've been wanting my whole life," he said, confused. Surely this was what Grandpa wanted?

Grandpa held up a hand to stop him. "Michael, all I am doing is trying to warn you. The army might be right for you. Just *don't let it corrupt you*," he cautioned.

There was a long silence. Eventually, Ted placed his hand on Michael's shoulder. "Hey, I'm not trying to ruin it for you, Mikey-boy. Today is a big day for you. Remember, whatever you do, I will be proud of you," he said with a smile.

Michael nodded. "I know. Thank you, Grandpa. I'll miss you," he said, standing up.

His grandpa stood up too and they hugged tightly. Michael felt emotions well up inside of him. He didn't bother to hold them in. He loved Grandpa so much, but this could very well be the last time he saw him.

Despite Grandpa Ted's lively outlook, Michael knew this was a façade. When he was younger, he had once sneaked up to the side of Grandpa's house to surprise him. However, as Michael glimpsed through the window, he saw his grandfather coughing dreadfully.

Michael assumed he had a cold, until he glimpsed the handkerchief in his hand. It was stained red.

At the time, Michael knew little of the significance of this, but as he matured, he realised his grandfather did not have long left to live. Coughing blood was serious, but there was nothing anyone could really do about it.

He let tears flow down his face. Grandpa Ted did not break away, but held Michael there until Michael had finished.

When Michael turned and left, he felt slightly abashed at crying. But as he stepped through the threshold of the house, he was filled with emptiness. He walked back to his hut.

As he walked through the village, he looked around. He noticed the Cuttings, a middle aged couple who had always been friendly to Michael. When he was younger they used to give him small woodwork toys to play with on his birthday. He waved to them and he passed their hut, and they waved back brightly.

He continued walking until he reached his hut. His mother was up, and they smiled at each other. He then went into his part of the hut. On a small wooden table that Grandpa Ted had gifted him, he had all of his possessions. There were some small woodwork animal toys that he played with, including a rhino which was his favourite animal.

There was a small pile of books that he had read over twenty times each. He had salvaged them from the remains of the library that was about a mile away from their village. There was also one comic book there, named 'The Invincible Iron Warrior'. He smiled fondly as he ran his hands over the worn pages. He loved this comic, a superhero who had managed to fight against his oppressors using technology - just like the Western Alliance did.

Twenty minutes later, Michael was waiting at the edge of the village with his mother and sister. His mother was in tears. She hugged him tightly. "Mikey, please try and come back when you can," she urged. Michael hugged her back.

"Don't worry, Mum, I will," he reassured her.

"And remember to wash regularly," she reminded him.

Michael smiled. "Sure I will," he said.

"And remember to cut your nails if they get too long," she told him.

"Mum, I will be fine!" Michael said, breaking the hug but with a smile. "You can trust me," he grinned.

He faced his sister. "Hey sis, you be okay without your big brother to look after you, alright?" he said, teasing her.

She hugged him. "I'll be fine," she said with a smile. "Don't die out there."

Michael hugged back. "I'll try not to. Now, we might not see each other for a while, so take care of Mum and Dad for me."

She grinned at. "Mike, I'll be at The Institute next year with you, just you wait," she said with a smirk.

Michael grinned. He wouldn't bet against it. Jane was smart, he had no doubt she would make it.

"Jane ... I'll miss you," he got out, avoiding eye contact. His chest felt tight.

"Hey, be confident," she reassured him. "And the next time I see you, you better have a girlfriend," she teased.

Michael smiled despite himself. "Well, I'll try," he joked, hugging his sister for one last time.

He heard the rumblings of a truck in the distance. He wasn't taking anything with him except from a pocket watch, a souvenir from his mother. Inside the watch, there was a picture of his family all together, smiling happily.

Michael looked around, wondering if he would see his father there, but he was nowhere in sight. He wished he could have said a proper goodbye, but it was too late now. He gulped down his emotions, knowing that they would not help him now. He breathed a shaky breath, trying to remain calm.

He was incredibly nervous, and fidgeted while the truck came closer. It stopped and Michael walked over towards it. Steve arrived by his side, having said goodbye to his family.

"You know Mike, your sister's fit." Steve said with a smile. Michael rolled his eyes punched Steve's arm lightly.

"Shut up," he said, but not too annoyed. He and Steve were too good friends to stay annoyed for long.

Steve winked at him. "I will really miss her," he said in mock sadness as they reached the truck. Sergeant Raines stepped out.

"Good moo-erning boys," he said, seemingly happy to see them. "And prepare yerself for a four hour journey in the back of a truck to The Institute," he said, abruptly dropping his cheerful manner.

"Get in," he ordered, jerking his thumb to the back.

Michael and Steve walked round. The back of the truck was bare and empty. They climbed in and tried to get comfortable.

Raines began driving back without warning, and suddenly they were speeding off down the road. Neither of the boys had ever been in a truck, and they stared out the back at the signposts whizzing along. There were no other vehicles on the road whatsoever.

At one point, they passed through a place full of huge, tall buildings, similar to Grandpa Ted's yet much larger.

A city. He remembered Grandpa Ted had told him they were called. They used to be everywhere, but as time wore on, more and more were damaged by air raids. Eventually, the government stopped funding repair programmes, instead putting their money into constructing missile bases and military fortresses.

The truck journeyed onward and though Michael was fascinated with the new sights on the road, the rhythmic movement of the truck as it rolled along the smooth surface combined with the early time of day made him drowsy. His eyes drifted shut, and soon he was fast asleep.

5 - **THE ARRIVAL**

Michael woke with a start, freezing cold and completely soaked with water. He sat bolt upright, and his eyes adjusted blurrily to see the grinning face of Sergeant Raines in front of him. He looked to his left and saw that Steve was similarly drenched.

Sergeant Raines chuckled. "You two laddies sleep like the dead. Anyway, get up. We're 'ere," he ordered. Michael immediately leapt out of the truck, the fact he was covered in water already gone from his mind.

He was here at last.

Their truck was parked in a huge complex with hundreds of other vehicles. He could see all sorts of vehicles: jeeps, cars, tanks and trucks. Michael looked around in awe. It was incredible.

The layout of The Institute was interesting: it comprised of a gigantic high street stretching many miles, with the various buildings and sectors all coming off from the side. The street was very long and about fifty metres wide. In it were various people walking around. Michael noticed an aged man with a short grey beard pass him. He couldn't possibly still be in employment, could he?

"Outta the way!" he heard a gruff voice yell from behind him, and he moved to the side as a large lorry trundled past him. Michael stared in amazement at the size of the vehicle. It was like a moving house.

He turned and continued walking down the high street. He looked to his right and saw several nice-looking houses, whilst on the left side there were several tall office-like buildings. They seemed to be made of black glass, which Michael presumed was so people couldn't look in. He looked past the houses and saw several firing ranges in the distance with some military looking vehicles.

It was understandable that they were further away - they clearly couldn't risk a stray artillery shell landing near the buildings.

The ground they walked on was a dark grey coloured cobbled stone that was worn down from use. This was probably adapted from an old street in London.

"Follow me," Raines instructed them, as he led Steve and Michael down a path into the busy central courtyard. Most of the people around them just wore normal civilian clothes, there were very few in any form of military gear. The only ones who did wear them were black-clad bored looking patrols that wandered around.

Sergeant Raines forged ahead, and Michael hurried after him. They walked down the high street, and Michael looked around at the various buildings. There were houses here similar to Grandpa Ted's as well as very tall office blocks. He led them into a building with a sign above that said the 'Initiation Centre'. They arrived in a sort of reception area, where there were many cubicles to the side.

Raines told Steve and Michael to get in a cubicle each. Now Michael was alone in a room with only a screen in front of him. As the cubicle door slid to a shut, he looked at the screen and was shocked to see the words upon it.

'Please remove ALL clothing in preparation for a full body scan.' it read.

Michael took off his t-shirt and his shorts, and finally, after much hesitation, took off his boxers. Standing there in embarrassment, he watched the words change.

'Please do not move while the full body scan takes place.'

Michael did so, and then a blue light flashed around the cubicle for several seconds. Immediately afterwards some clothes slid out in a tray from a wall. The tray contained several sets of boxers, grey t-shirts, grey shorts, grey trousers and grey socks. Michael sighed and put them on. To his utmost surprise, they fitted perfectly and were actually quite comfortable.

He looked at the text on the screen.

Subject: Michael Bakerson

Height: 185 cm

Weight: 70kg

Suggested Size: Medium

He raised his eyebrows, impressed. They got all that from one short scan? Wow.

Please exit the cubicle.

Michael did so, carrying his old clothes in his hands. Steve was also out there. When Sergeant Raines saw them, he nodded towards them.

"Your rooms are numbers 33 and 35 on floor four. Take the lift up there. Training starts tomorrow, at eight o'clock. Be there and don't be late," he said, striding off.

Steve and Michael looked at each other with raised eyebrows. Michael shrugged.

"Let's go, then," he said before entering the lift, Steve following behind him. He pressed the number '4' button and waited while it moved up. It was an odd sensation as the floor moved yet Michael's body remained stationary.

Michael glanced at Steve. "You nervous?" he asked his friend.

Steve shook his head. "Nah. We've already made it in," he stated confidently.

"I am." Michael admitted. He always found it difficult out of his comfort zone, and he had very little idea at what they would face.

Steve smiled slightly. "Stop worrying, Mike. Seriously," he reminded him.

Michael smiled to himself. "Yeah ... well, I just don't want to mess up," he remarked.

Steve laughed. "I think the only one in danger of messing up here is me."

Michael smirked. "True," he reasoned teasingly.

When the lift door opened, they were in a long corridor. They made their way down, keeping an eye out for their rooms. Whilst they walked down, a boy strode out of one of the rooms. He looked at Michael and Steve with a bored expression then went into a room with its door marked 'Common Room'.

"Shall we go in there?" Michael asked nervously.

"Why not?" Steve said, his eyes glinting with excitement as he pushed open the door.

They entered a huge room which had many tables and chairs. It was crowded, full of people talking, engrossed in their own conversations. They all seemed to be around Michael's age. He noticed many girls and was surprised. He knew girls from his village had applied to The Institute as the opportunity was open to everyone. However he had never pictured many of them actually being here. In this room though, the numbers of each gender seemed pretty even.

Most people ignored Steve and Michael, so they just walked around and found an unoccupied table. They looked at each other, grinning.

"This place is awesome." Steve enthused. Michael just smiled, unable to believe that they had finally made it. To others, it might seem like this place was nothing special, but it was to him. This is what his whole life had been building up towards.

"Excuse me," he heard voice next to him. Michael looked up and saw a beautiful brown haired girl standing next to him.

"You're new here, right?" she said, looking from him to Steve and back.

"Erm, yes." Michael said, his mouth suddenly feeling dry.

She flashed him a brilliant smile. "Welcome to The Institute. My name's Sophie. I hope you like it around here."

Michael was about to reply when, suddenly, a large burly boy came butting in next to Sophie. "Sophie, you flirting with the newbies? I thought you'd stopped that now," he said.

Sophie gave him a look of mock hurt. "Raymon, I was trying to begin a long and meaningful friendship," she said, and winked at Michael.

"Sorry boys, I've got to go," she said, then strode off, arguing with Raymon.

Michael felt slightly dejected. He noticed a boy sitting by himself at one of the tables. He had light brown hair and wore thick glasses. He went over sit next to him, beckoning at Steve to come with him. The boy glanced up nervously, and then looked back down at whatever was in his hands.

Michael sat down next to the boy and saw that he was tinkering with some electrical device. "What's that?" he asked the boy quietly.

"N-nothing," the boy stammered, hiding the contraption in his pocket. He then seemed to reconsider, and brought out the device. "I-it was a television remote, but I've reprogrammed it," he said quickly.

By now Steve had sat on the other side of the boy.

"What does it do?" Steve asked him. The boy shrugged.

"I don't know," he said quietly.

"Shall we find out?" Steve asked him.

The boy smiled nervously, then pressed the 'On' button at the top of what had once been a remote. There was a flicker of bright blue light inside it, and then a small bang as the device exploded, showering them all with sparks. The acrid smell of smoke wafted up towards them.

They all looked at each other, then Steve's mouth started to twitch. Michael and the boy smiled, and soon they were all laughing out loud at the minor explosion.

Suddenly the boy stopped laughing as he looked up fearfully. Michael and Steve followed his gaze to see Raymon towering above them. He was flanked by two other tall, burly boys who looked like some monstrous Russian mutations gone wrong.

"So, nerd-face has found himself some friends. Must be the first time that's ever happened to him." Raymon sneered and the two large boys laughed.

Steve stood up from his chair and looked at Raymon with annoyance.

"Who the heck are you?" he demanded.

Raymon raised an eyebrow. "Me? I am Raymon Collins, son of Alfred Collins," he said that name like it was supposed to mean something.

"Is that supposed to impress us? Who's Alfred Collins?" Steve asked him.

Raymon laughed. "Who is Alfred Collins? What dung heap did you come from? Wales?" he scoffed. He bent down towards Steve.

"For your information, Alfred Collins is the one who finances this military Institute and the one you owe for being here." Raymon said with an air of cockiness.

Steve smirked. "So you think you're above everyone else just because of your daddy? Mate, you've got a serious lesson to learn. We all took the same exams to get here, so we're all equal," he said.

Raymon laughed harshly. "Actually, little know-it-all, some of us didn't need to take exams as we didn't come from some grotty little village. Now, shortie, I don't like your attitude. I think we'll need to fix that, won't we? I'd say in the toilets, him and nerd-face," he sneered, narrowing his eyes. His two cronies laughed and cracked their knuckles.

Michael saw anger flare up in Steve's eyes and knew that Raymon had gone too far. Steve would never back down now.

One of the large boys began advancing on the small boy. Michael calmly blocked his path, standing in the thug's way. If he couldn't stop Steve fighting, he may as well help him. The brute stopped, his tiny brain figuring out what to do. Then he seemed to reach a decision and tried to swat Michael out of the way.

Bad move.

Michael ducked the hand and punched the boy in the gut. He heard muffled shouts next to him, telling him that Steve was fighting as well. The brute recoiled, and then charged in again. Michael sidestepped him, then elbowed him in the ribs. The large boy grunted in pain, but then backhanded Michael in the side of the head, knocking him to the ground.

Michael was dazed. He could hear the dim chanting of the other people in the background.

"Fight! Fight! Fight!"

He hoisted himself to his feet. He could see the brute smiling cockily as he lumbered towards him. Blood pounded through his head as Michael readied himself. He would show this thug. He noticed that the boy seemed to favour his right arm when he threw a punch. He also observed that he seemed to be protecting the side where Michael had elbowed him earlier, presumably still in pain.

Michael would have to use that to his advantage. The brute finally reached Michael and swung a punch at his head. Michael quickly ducked under it.

"Fight, fight, fight!"

Michael would have to make sure that the boy did not land a hit. He was quicker and more agile than the bigger boy. As the boy made a lunge at him, Michael noticed him take a step forward with his left foot.

Now was his time to strike. Michael ducked under the lunge and swung a punch at the boy's injured left side. It made contact. With him off balance, there was no way he could stop himself from toppling over without squatting down, lowering his centre of gravity.

Pressing his advantage, Michael attacked. He swung a vicious punch to the boy's face, making contact with his nose and knocking him to the ground.

Michael stood over his opponent, triumphant. He felt proud. He had beaten someone who must have been at least a foot taller than him.

Michael looked up and realised that the crowd were a lot quieter now. He looked behind him and saw the boy's terrified face. He slowly turned to face Sergeant Raines standing right in front of them.

"Bakerson, Green, Collins, Brooke and Gilmore, would you please follow me." Raines ordered, referring to Michael, Steve, Raymon and the two boys they had fought. Michael looked at Steve, who had no visible injury, and at the brute he had been fighting - Gilmore, who had a black eye. Brooke, the thug whom Michael had been fighting, had a bleeding nose that looked as if it was broken.

Michael originally felt quite pleased, although as they followed Sergeant Raines that feeling deteriorated rapidly, transforming into something along the lines of dread.

Sergeant Raines led them into a small room that had his name on the door in gold-coloured lettering. Inside the room was a large desk with a wooden chair behind it. The boys stood nervously as Sergeant Raines sat behind it.

"Right, let's get this speech over with," he said wearily. "So, you boys are new here. I'm reminding you that fighting is not allowed with yer teammates outside of sparring classes. I saw the CCTV and I know what happened. You boys will be punished for this severely, so I strongly suggest never fighting again. We're all on the same side here, whether ye like it or not. Save your fighting for the battlefield."

He cleared his throat. "Yer punishment will be extra physical training each morning from six until seven for one week," he said, looking at Steve and Michael.

He then turned on Gilmore, Brooke and Raymon. "You three seemed to start it, so I'm giving you the task of cleaning out the ditches at the back of the field," he said.

Raymon Collins protested. "But sir, they started it! They attacked us!" he complained.

Sergeant Raines looked at him. "Collins, ye don't seem to know your place here. I'm in charge. Ye raise your hand to speak and ye call me sir. Is that understood?" he said sternly. Raymon lowered his head, but he glared at Steve and Michael.

"Yes, sir," he muttered quietly.

"What was that?" Sergeant Raines asked.

"Yes, sir." Raymon said clearly.

"Well, then, that's fantastic, isn't it?" said Raines cheerfully, though there was a deadly glint in his eyes as he surveyed Raymon. "As you were wondering why ye got the punishment, I recall it was three of you against two of them and you were threatening to stick their heads in a toilet. Yes, the cameras have sound so I suggest you watch what you say." Raines said.

"You three, leave," he said to Gilmore, Brooke and Raymon Collins. Steve and Michael looked at each other worriedly as they waited.

"Right, you two." Sergeant Raines said. "I saw what ye did back there and it was bloody decent. You stepped in the save the wee lad. You actually managed to teach those brutes a lesson. Well done. I reckon we might make soldiers outta you someday, provided you keep your temper," he said, looking at Steve.

"Physical training won't be so bad. It'll build you up, give ye a bit more chance if you ever have to meet them again. But I won't let you off again. You keep your heads down and work hard. I don't want to have to speak to ye again, but if I do, it'll be a lot worse than physical training. Ye can go now." Raines said.

Michael and Steve started walking out.

"Boys?" Raines called after them.

They looked back and he actually smiled.

"Good luck." Raines said.

6 - **HANS SIGURD**

As Michael walked out of the office, he couldn't believe his luck. He had been caught fighting and hadn't been kicked out of The Institute. He had learnt a lesson though. He wouldn't fight again in a hurry.

Physical training, he hoped, would not be so bad. He could have got a lot worse a punishment, like Raymon had.

"Nice one on that Brooke," Steve said. "You beat him pretty hard."

"But you took on two of them and still managed Gilmore a black eye." Michael said, impressed.

"To be honest, Raymon didn't do much. I think he relies on his cronies to beat people up for him." Steve said thoughtfully.

"Still, I reckon we got off lightly. I thought we were gonna sent back for sure." Michael commented.

"Eh, well, no point thinking about it." Steve said shrugging. "Anyway, we better go and make sure that boy's alright."

"Yeah." Michael mumbled as they went back into the common room. This time went they went in, they got paid a lot more attention than last time. People were looking at them, whispering. Raymon was glaring at them angrily, but Michael ignored him.

They sat down on the table with the boy again, who smiled at them shyly.

"Thank you," he said.

"No problem, mate." Steve said. "They deserved it. Hopefully they won't bother you again. What's your name by the way?"

"Arthur," the boy said quietly.

Arthur smiled again. "So ... so we're friends then?" he said anxiously.

"Of course." Michael replied, smiling.

They heard a boy clear his throat in front of them. Michael looked up to see a tall, muscular blond boy standing in front of them.

"Excuse me," the boy said in a thick foreign accent. "Are you the boys that battled the Collins boy?" he asked.

Michael and Steve looked at each other. "Yes." Michael said.

The boy nodded.

"Well done. You taught him a lesson. My name is Hans Sigurd. I have come here from Norway. You seem like worthy people to make acquaintances with. I offer you my friendship," he stated, offering a hand for them to shake.

Michael hesitated, slightly suspicious, then shook it firmly.

"I'm Mike. This is Arthur and Steve," he said, gesturing to Arthur and Steve respectively.

Hans shook their hands in turn. "It is a pleasure to meet you. I have found it difficult to make friends here for the most part. Even in Norway, I was not a popular person. It is good to have some people here whom I can trust," he said in a heavy accent.

"Thanks." Michael said awkwardly.

The Norwegian sat down. "You are most welcome. Now, tell me of your lives." Hans said briskly.

"Well," Michael began. "Steve and I come from a village in the South of Independent Britain. We never really had much contact with the military until we got selected. We were the first people from our village for ages to be picked, so we were really lucky," he told them.

"I see." Hans said.

"What about you?" Steve asked him.

"I was born in the far north of my country, where it was very cold. Life was ... very tough there. Our village was running out of food. One night, a military patrol passed by us. I took my chance and climbed on top of one of their vehicles.

I was only eight. When they found me, one of the generals took pity on me. He raised me like his own son ... taught me English. I think of him as my father, as I never knew my real parents. They died when I was very young. My ... argh, what is it in English ... adopted father was killed one month ago, so the soldiers with him decided to send me here so I could become one of them. One day I will avenge him. I have seen a lot of fighting. I have seen the Russian scum first hand. I have even fired rifles, though not at the enemy yet," he sighed. "I long for the day when I can be a true soldier and erm, what is it ... utilise the technology here. I'll send the Russians to hell." Hans declared passionately.

"How did the Russians get so powerful?" Steve asked, visibly confused.

Arthur cleared his throat. "Well, after being established, the Western Alliance began seizing land for the war effort, starting with Western Germany, and then proceeding to take control of nations such as France and Italy. They took control of the Southern British Isles, Occupied Britain, transforming it into their main naval base in the North Sea.

As the war continued, it began to grow more brutal and bloody, as neither side could find a way to defeat the other. Both sides began developing weapons to try to give their side an edge. For the Eastern forces, mainly the Russians and Chinese, their breakthrough was in genetics. By modifying human DNA and fusing them with the genes of animals, they were able to develop enhanced soldiers through cloning. Weaknesses were eliminated, and the Russians began producing 'super soldiers'," he explained.

"How did we beat them then?" Steve asked. Michael knew the answer but he let Arthur answer.

"Well, as they were desperate, the Western Alliance launched 'Operation Firepower'. They began upgrading the strength their own soldiers, by giving them improved technology to give them an edge over their foes. It became a battle of brains against brawn, as US scientists developed new weapons to assist their soldiers.

The Western soldiers began using rapid dominance tactics to try to force a victory, using superior air power and artillery to crush the enemy's morale. We countered the Russians' genetic hybrids with their own technological innovations." Arthur told him.

"What are the Russians really like?" Michael asked curiously. He had heard that they were mutated, but nobody in his village really knew much about them. In Grandpa Ted's day, they had just been humans, albeit those of another country.

Michael was snapped out of his daydream when Hans began speaking.

"Beastly creatures, without a drop of humanity left in them." Hans said zealously. "The ones that fought against us were some of the worst, the men told me. Adapted to the cold, they were like Arctic bears. They would attack our camps in the blizzards, take us by surprise. I didn't really know what was going on is was so terrifying. Blurred shapes, snarling and howling. Father, they said, was taken by their leader, a creature they called Fenrir."

"Fenrir?" Steve questioned.

"A monstrous wolf from Norse mythology," Arthur said. "Supposedly, he was the slayer of Odin, the king of the gods."

Hans nodded. "No one has ever seen him and lived. Only glimpses through the snow. But the Russians vary. Some are pure animal, wolves and bears, yet some walk and can speak like men. They are a dangerous foe ... very frightening to me as a child," he recounted sadly.

Arthur spoke up. "They say the Russians have all kinds of animals. Twenty years ago, they launched a massive attack on the US mainland. The Western Alliance build machines, but they create abominations. Made with only the instinct to destroy. They had built genetically modified men who could breathe underwater and swim for miles. They swam across the Pacific Ocean in a huge swarm and attacked North America. They sunk most of our navy, but we eventually managed to beat them by electrifying the whole shoreline and pouring toxic waste into the seas. Now though, the war in the Pacific is mainly air-based as we use planes and hovercrafts against their recently created bird warriors." Arthur told them.

"But in Europe, the combat is mainly ground based. The Russian army mainly consists of brutish men that been genetically modified. That means some of them can have a poisonous bite, claws of their hands or even be capable of regeneration." Arthur explained.

Steve, Michael and Hans looked at him in complete shock.

"Wow. That's ... " Hans was at a loss for words.

But Michael was intrigued. "But how are their so many of them? Cloning must takes ages," he said thoughtfully.

Arthur nodded. "They're practically animals. They can reproduce," he answered. "This is why this war is a global disaster. It's not about defending democracy from dictatorship. It's about defending humanity from extinction."

They were silent as they processed this information. Eventually, Hans spoke up.

"So Artur," he asked, "Where is it that you come from?"

Arthur seemed to shrink back. "I come from London," he said quietly. "My family was quite well off, so I always had plenty of books to read and electrical devices to reprogram. I just like finding new information, I suppose. I kind of believe that innovation is the way forward."

Hans smiled. "We still need soldiers to protect our innovators," he said.

"That's more of a Russian way of thinking." Arthur commented with a slight smile.

Hans shrugged. "Norway is near Russia. Must be the cold that distorts our brains," he said, and they all laughed.

"Speaking of temperature, this country is so warm! How can you survive the heat?" Hans asked incredulously.

"Hans, this place is not hot at all." Steve deadpanned. "It's England, the home of rain."

Hans shrugged. "I prefer the snow," he said.

There was a silence as they sat together, content with each other's company.

"Anyway," Steve finally said. "Michael and I haven't checked out our rooms yet, we better do that and get some sleep. Goodnight guys."

Their rooms turned out to be quite lavish. They had an entire single bed to themselves with a mattress. This had been something neither Michael nor Steve had experienced before. They had their own bathrooms which contained a shower, a sink and a toilet, all luxuries to them.

Compared to their village, this was like paradise.

Michael smiled to himself. The Institute was a dream come true.

7 - **PHYSICAL TRAINING**

'BEEP! BEEP! BEEP!' sounded the screen on the wall.

Michael shook his head, not wanting to get up. He was too tired.

'ALERT! SUBJECT IS DESIGNATED AS HAVING PHYSICAL TRAINING SCHEDULED IN FIFTEEN MINUTES!' it said aloud in a robotic voice.

Michael sat bolt upright, remembering where he was. He was at The Institute. He also had the detention of physical training. He quickly washed his face and put on his standard grey clothes. He then went and read the screen.

ACTIVITY: PHYSICAL TRAINING

OVERSEERER: SGT. VELLON

FLOOR: 3

ROOM: GENGHIS 12

TIME: 06:00

ADDITIONAL INFO: 'You better not be late, garçon!' - Sgt Vellon

Michael put on his new watch which he had found on his bedside locker. As well as the time, the watch had many other features. Michael had fallen asleep whilst reading the instructions the previous night. Currently, the watch read the same message as the screen.

He hurried out into the corridor, which was deserted. At the end of it was the lift they had come up in. He entered and studied the different buttons.

BUILDING: RECRUIT FACILITY

1 - JULIUS

2 - SHERMAN

3 - GENGHIS

4 - WELLINGTON

5 - BOUDICCA

6 - MONTGOMERY

These were military commanders from history, Michael realised. So their floor, the boys' one, was Wellington, the famous British general who won the battle of Waterloo. That meant that the girls' dormitory must be floor five, Boudicca.

He pressed the button for floor three, Genghis. The door closed. When it re-opened on the floor below, Michael stepped out and searched for room 12. All the doors were closed. As he glanced through the glass panes on them, he saw various fitness suites and weights rooms. He opened room twelve and stepped inside. It was a sports hall.

A tall muscular man was waiting inside, staring at his watch. Steve was nowhere in sight. Michael cleared his throat.

"Sir," he began, but the man cut him off with a curt "Silence!"

Michael shifted awkwardly, but did not speak again. He did not wish to unnecessarily irk this man.

About a minute later, Steve arrived, clearly having just got out of bed.

"Morning, sir," he mumbled, stifling a yawn.

"Silence!" Vellon snapped once again in a heavy French accent. "You were forty three seconds late; therefore your punishment will be forty three press ups. Get to it! Now! Both of you!"

Michael was annoyed. Why did he get the press ups too? He hadn't been late. Then again, he didn't want to argue with Sergeant Vellon. Steve hesitated. "What's a press up?" he asked.

Vellon jumped to the ground and then demonstrated, pressing his chest to the floor while keeping his legs and feet off the ground and then straightening his arms.

"Now, do sixty press ups!" he ordered. Michael and Steve quickly got down and began trying to mimic his action.

The physical training session was hell. Sergeant Vellon made them run many laps around the hall with constant criticism, as well as forcing them to do a variety of workouts, making them completely and utterly exhausted. Michael's arms and legs felt like lead. By the end of it, he felt physically sick, but held it in, not wanting to incur Vellon's wrath. He and Steve staggered out of the sports hall when they were finally dismissed.

Michael returned to his room and had a long shower, then put on some clean clothes ready for the start of the main training. He hoped it would not be too physically demanding. Raines had told them it started at eight, so Michael waited for the message on his wall reminding him.

He had found a bottle of water and an energy bar on his table, along with a note reminding him it was important to stay hydrated. The bar was very dry, but was most likely packed with nutritious substances to help him recover.

Sure enough, the message came, with the annoying beeping that came through as well.

On the screen, it read:

ACTIVITY: BASIC TRAINING

OVERSEER: LT JONES

FLOOR: 3

ROOM: GENGHIS 12

TIME: 08.00

ADDITIONAL INFO: NONE.

Michael felt his stomach lurch. The same room? He hoped they weren't doing physical training once again.

When he got back down to Genghis, he found the corridor crowded with people. He couldn't see anyone he recognised. The door to the sports hall opened and everyone funnelled in. There was a buzz of conversation as everyone milled around nervously.

There was a temporary stage set up, with a large amount of officers. In the centre of the stage was a lectern, with a man standing behind. He looked like he was bored and would rather not be there. He was quite short with an air of cockiness about him.

He cleared his throat.

"Alright," the man said, in an American accent. "Settle down, boys."

The buzz continued until Sergeant Raines roared "SILENCE!", then the din ceased immediately and everyone gave their full attention to the man on the stage.

The man gave Raines a glance then cleared his throat again.

"Alright, boys, my name is Lieutenant Jones and I will be your commanding officer during your training. During this course you will all be placed into squads. You will be expected to work together in a team. Each squad will have a leader and a secondary instructor. You will show these the utmost respect, and obey them regardless. During you time at The Institute, your squad will be the most important people you know outside of your officers. These will be the people who you will have to trust in the field with your life. If you don't comply with our rules, you will be dismissed from The Institute," he said clearly.

"Right, let's get to it. The squads are as follows:

Squad 1, the Jaegers. These will be led by Sergeant Albrecht, with your assistant as Sergeant Blonsky.

Squad 2, the Spartans. These will be led by Sergeant Raines, with your assistant as Sergeant Vellon.

Squad 3, the Legionnaires. These will be led by me, with your assistant as Sergeant Blackburn.

Squad 4, the Immortals..."

The list went on, with more squads named after elite soldiers from antiquity. Praetorians, Jaguars, Companions and Varangians. Then, the names began being read out in alphabetical order.

"Adams, Paul ... Jaegers," Jones began, and a small boy went and stood next to an instructor.

"Bakerson, Michael ... Spartans." Michael breathed a sigh of relief and stood next to Sergeant Raines. He wouldn't want to be in Lieutenant Jones' team.

"Blackhurst, Thomas ... Companions," Jones continued, and a tall, muscular boy went to one of the instructors.

"Collins, Raymon ... Legionnaires." Michael noticed Raymon give an arrogant smirk as he strode over to Lieutenant Jones.

The list continued. Brooke was put in the Legionnaires, as was Gilmore. Sophie was put in the Jaegers.

"Green, Steven ... Spartans."

Michael grinned. Perfect.

The names continued to be read out, but Michael's relief soon turned into surprise as Arthur and then Hans were also placed in their team.

He gave Sergeant Raines a questioning look. Raines winked at him.

Michael smiled to himself again. Raines would be a good squad leader.

When the list was finally finished, there were about ten people in each of the eight teams.

Jones cleared his throat again.

"Alright, now that that's over with, we can get to business. As part of your training, some of you will be able to make it into the Coliseum and represent this Institute. For those of you who haven't heard of the Coliseum, it's the most important tournament for new recruits in the Western Alliance. Five military academies from around the Western Alliance compete in the toughest set of gladiator games yet, testing your training and proving which academy is best.

There's huge media coverage and the winners get advanced training with the latest military technology. The USA has won it every year except once when Canada hosted it in the coldest winter in thirty years. The USA is hosting it this year, so you lot have no chance, but if you somehow manage to pull this off, I'll get a promotion and be out of this stupid country," Jones said with a smirk. "The five regions involved are the United States, Canada, Occupied Britain, Australia and the Netherlands."

"You will be training in your squads initially, before our tests start. The best members will be put forward into the Coliseum tournament and have a chance to train in America. On the other hand, the reason the USA always win is that they

41

have the best facilities in the world, and they train with equipment none of you will ever get to even touch. Which is why you lot don't have a bloody chance," Jones said, once again looking bored.

"Raines tell 'em what they have to do," he instructed.

"Yes, *Lieutenant*." Sergeant Raines said, stepping up to the microphone.

"Right. During this course, you lads will be instructed in military strategy and tactics, as well as learning how to handle weapons that will be vital to yer survival in the war. Ye may think you've been incredible in getting this far, but let me warn you; The Institute is just the first rung on the ladder. You've got to be tough, disciplined and obedient, and be ready to push yerself to the limit.

Physical training will be on this floor, Genghis. Tactics and strategy will be in the Strategy Building, floor Napoleon. Equipment training will be located outside, zone Alexander. Vehicle training will be in zone Hannibal. The open water lake will also be used to toughen you up. That's all for now, your commanding officer can answer any questions you might have," Sergeant Raines finished and the Sports Hall descended into conversation once again.

"Spartans, follow me!" Raines barked and led them out into the corridor. Michael followed unsure of where Raines was taking them.

He took the squad lift to floor Montgomery, the rooftop, and then stepped outside. The wind was cold here, and it was very high up.

The squad stood alert, waiting for Raines to elaborate.

Raines looked at them all. "Ye all have to climb down to the ground, by yerselves. Don't take the lift. I'll see you when yer done. Off you go," he stated briefly, then walked into the lift and took it back downstairs.

8 - **THE DEEP END**

Michael stood there, shocked. There was a silence as Michael's squad, the Spartans, absorbed what Raines had just instructed.

Steve moved forward and peered over the edge. "It's pretty high, but we can go down on the window ledges," he said.

One of the boys in their squad shook his head. "No way! That's suicide!" he exclaimed.

Michael looked at him. He was small, weedy and his voice sounded whiny. He was most likely someone who had got in with his parents' money rather than his own capabilities. He also noticed as he glanced around that Arthur was looking very pale.

Michael took a deep breath. "What's your name?" he asked the boy.

"Tim," the boy replied.

"Well Tim, do you have any other ideas on how to get down without using the lift?" Michael challenged.

Tim opened his mouth, and then closed it again. He shook his head.

A girl spoke up. "I think you're right. We have to go down," she said boldly.

They turned to face her. She was tall for a girl, and had long blond hair and blue eyes.

Another girl nodded. "It's a test. He's throwing us in at the deep end to see how we react," she stated.

Michael spoke. "I agree. I think he's trying to build us as a team," he said.

Steve smiled. "Well, it makes sense. Spartans are meant to be brave," he said.

"Who are the Spartans, may I ask?" Hans questioned with his prominent Norwegian accent. He made all of his a's sound like 'ar'.

"Warriors from Ancient Greece, known for their military prowess and fearless nature," Arthur explained.

"So, how will we tackle this challenge?" Hans asked.

"Just do it," Steve said, and he began moving towards the edge.

"Wait! We need a plan," Michael said. "I think someone who is good at climbing should pair up with someone who is less confident at it."

He looked around. "What're all your names? I'm Michael."

"I'm Jenny," the tall blond girl said.

"Teresa," another girl said. She was quite small, though she had quite masculine shoulders. She had shoulder-length black hair and green eyes.

"I'm called Alexandra," the third girl said. She had auburn hair and was average height.

Hans, Steve and Arthur stated their names then their squad all turned to face their final member. He was a black-skinned boy who stood away from the group. He had a skinhead and looked very moody.

"What's your name?" Steve asked him.

"Why would you care?" the boy retorted.

"Because we're your team." Teresa said stubbornly.

The boy shrugged. "Joe," he muttered.

"Right then," Michael said, taking command. "I'd say that Hans, you go with Joe. Steve, you go with Teresa. I'll go with Tim. Jenny, you go with Alexandra. Arthur, you come last. Ready?"

They nodded. Hans and Joe set off down, climbing down confidently.

They lowered themselves from ledge to ledge. As Joe seemed intent on moving down as quickly as possible, Michael was sure he would fall sometimes. Luckily, he didn't lose his grip on the smooth stone window ledge.

Steve and Teresa went next. They were shorter than everyone else but still managed to make it down a decent way before Michael decided to set off.

He went down next, dragging Tim with him. It was high up, and his legs were shaking. Fortunately, the building had numerous windows due to the number of rooms and each window ledge was large enough to stand on.

Michael and Tim made it onto the first ledge.

Don't look down. Michael told himself. *One ledge at a time.*

He squatted down, placing his hands on the ledge and slowly lowering himself to the next ledge. He felt the strain on his arms but sure enough, he felt his feet reach the ledge. He let go and leant closer to the wall, pressing himself against the window. It was fortunate that the rooms were empty; otherwise he might have got in trouble for hanging outside a girl's bedroom. Thankfully he could lift easily his own body weight as well.

Tim, on the other hand, could not. His entire body was shaking as he squatted on the ledge, looking out over the gap in absolute terror. He was as white as a sheet.

"Tim..." Michael said slowly. "Come on."

Tim shook his head, but eventually knelt down on the edge of the ledge, still facing the window.

He began then lowering his feet down, keeping his elbows on the ledge above. He stretched his legs and nearly reached the ledge where Michael was standing.

"Easy now, come on," Michael encouraged. Tim then sank down so he was only holding on with his hands then attempted to throw himself towards the window as he let go with his arms.

Unfortunately, he did not have enough strength, and though his feet were on the ledge, his body weight caused him to topple backwards - away from the building.

For a horrifying second, Tim seemed to hang in the air as Michael watched, helpless. He saw the fear in Tim's eyes as his predicament dawned on them both.

Suddenly, time snapped back to normal as Tim fell - and Michael's instincts took over.

He shot out a hand and grabbed onto the top of Tim's shirt, then wrenched him towards the window, pulling him away from the drop.

Tim breathed frantically for a few seconds as he realised how close he had been to a severe injury, possibly even death. Michael gave him a smile.

"You okay?" he asked.

Tim nodded wordlessly, still in shock.

After a few moments, they continued clambering down without further incident. When they were past halfway, Michael heard Jenny shout from three ledges above them.

"Mike?" she called. "It's Arthur - he's not coming down!"

Michael silently cursed. "Alright, I'll - I'll come back up,'' he reassured them, then began lifting himself back up.

Though he tried not to show it, he was actually scared. It was a lot harder climbing up than it was going down.

"He's at the top, he won't come down," Alexandra informed him as he heaved himself passed her and Jenny.

"When you reach the bottom, tell Hans to get a rope thrown up here," Michael told her, then carried on climbing.

The ascent was a lot harder than it looked. His arms were shaking and he could feel his clammy hands turning numb. His breath grew more frantic and everything seemed to spin around him.

Eventually, after what seemed like hours, he reached the roof of the building where Arthur stood, talking to himself.

"There has to be another way, it's logical. There's always an alternative to physical prowess,'' he mumbled.

Michael stood next to Arthur. "Arthur, just grit your teeth and do it! Hans is getting a rope for us!"

Arthur looked at him. "That ... that would help,'' he said slowly. "Why didn't I think of that? I should have thought of that."

"Sometimes, you just have to go the simple route," Michael told him. Fear had clearly got in the way of Arthur's thinking.

He heard Hans shout below him, then caught the end of a rope as it was thrown up. Hans must have been strong to hurl it up to the roof.

Michael tied it around the chimney, making sure it was secure.

"Arthur," he spoke. "Just use the rope. You can do it."

Arthur nodded, taking a deep breath, then began slowly walking down, gripping the rope tightly. When Michael was sure the rope would hold, he began descending himself.

The rope burned his hands, but it was a lot easier than clambering down from ledge to ledge.

His breathing steadied as he got past halfway. He smiled. Their team might actually complete this task.

All of a sudden, he felt the rope moving and shifting, as though someone at the top was trying to untie it. Michael froze, fearing the worst. He gulped.

Then it happened. The rope slackened as though it had snapped - and Michael fell backwards into oblivion.

9 - **STRATEGIC PLANNING**

Michael hit the ground with a thump. He shook his head, dazed. It was a lot less painful than he had imagined.

He opened his eyes and saw his squad members standing around him, looking concerned. He then felt the ground below him move and he rolled to the side.

It was only then he realised he had landed on Steve.

"Steve, are you okay?" Michael asked him, worried

"Yeah, fine. You didn't fall from that high up. Why did you fall anyway?" Steve asked him.

Hans held up the rope. It was clear to see that it had been cut.

But who had cut the rope? The only people who had a grudge against him were Raymon, Gilmore and Brooke.

Had *they* actually cut it though? There was no proof of anything.

They heard Sergeant Raines clear his throat behind them. Michael and Steve quickly sprang to their feet.

"I have to say lads, I'm impressed. 'alf an hour is a record time for this task." Raines told them.

"Right lads, ye have a few hours until your next task, so 'ave some lunch. Meet me in the Strategy Building at one o'clock sharp," he said, and strode off.

Michael then realised he hadn't actually had breakfast.

"Lunch sounds good to me," he said.

For lunch, Michael bought a full English breakfast, which was delicious. It was the nicest meal he had ever had, made more enjoyable by the fact he could be with his friends. Last night there had been some sandwiches delivered to their rooms as they had missed mealtimes because of their fight with Raymon and his cronies.

The Spartans sat together at lunch, with the exception of Joe, who sat by himself.

"Why do you think he's so moody?" Teresa asked them.

"He seems a bit of a weirdo to me," Tim said.

Michael shot Tim an angry look. "How do you know what he's gone through?"

Tim just shrugged.

Arthur spoke up. "It's his colour. His people have always been persecuted. The instructors never usually let them in, he must have done exceptionally well on his tests."

Michael looked back at Joe, who glared at them then walked off.

"So, what task do you reckon Raines will be setting us next?" Jenny wondered.

"We'll find out pretty soon," Michael said

When their next task did come, they were waiting patiently outside the Strategy Building. Raines led them into a room which looked like some conference room on floor Napoleon. It had a large screen on the wall.

"Right," Raines said, looking around at them all. "Well done earlier. You've had a few hours break, but from now on there will be no stop to yer training throughout the day.

Every day, ye will begin with physical training then a teambuilding exercise. After lunch, ye'll have a lesson on tactics and strategy, which is where we are now, then ye will begin practicing with the equipment we have at our disposal here at The Institute

Every Sunday there will be a competition against the other squads. Ye will be judged on how you perform in these. At the end of your training, ye will be put in a field test," he explained. Michael could not help speculating on what this would involve.

"Now it's for military strategy and tactics." Raines continued. "Though it may not seem as important as running around and firing yer weapons at the enemy, it's by far the most important aspect of warfare. Without strategy, this war would already been lost.

Take the battle of the Ardennes, for example, 1968. The Polish planned to outflank our forces using a pincer movement with a holding force in front.

However, we 'ad a plan. We fell back, planning to fake a retreat, causing their flanking forces to break cover and try to run us down. They had to either fight us now or let us come back another day with a stronger force.

Then, our army turned and faced one of their forces, taking them head on.

We were able to split their army. We then advanced forward and were able to take advantage of them while they were a disordered mess. We had been outnumbered - but with superior strategy, we won, breaking the enemy morale.

As Sun Tzu once said, "*All warfare is based on deception*". This means making the enemy think you've got more or less soldiers than you actually have. Napoleon was a master at this, so we will be studying his battles and how we can use strategy in a more modern context."

Raines finished his speech and began putting them in pairs, giving them historical battles to study. Michael and Hans were given the battle of Cannae where Hannibal fought the Romans.

Surprisingly, their strategic training was very interesting and Michael left inspired.

The next part of their training was outside in zone Alexander, where they were supposed to be working with weapons and equipment. This was the part everyone was most excited for, as the main strength of the Western Alliance was their technology.

"I wonder which weapons we'll be using," Tim said.

"Raines mentioned something about fighter planes at our village," Steve commented.

"Don't be stupid, they wouldn't let us use fighter planes on our first day here," Teresa chastised.

"And Jones did say all vehicle training was in sector Hannibal," Michael said.

When Raines did arrive, he quickly put their excitement to rest.

"Before any of ye ask, we won't be firing any guns or using any military equipment today. First, you've got to know how to assemble, take apart and keep in pristine condition all the equipment you may be using," he said. "Now lads, let's get started! Everyone pick up an M18 assault rifle."

The equipment lesson turned out to be very boring. It involved polishing guns until they sparkled, which was a tiresome activity even at the best of times. But on a hot summer's day whilst the sun bore down on them, they were practically baking in the heat.

The afternoon wore on, and by the end of it, Michael was aching. The physical training from earlier was really taking a toll on him.

At last, the session finished and their squad was dismissed. They were all on their way to dinner, when a movement out of the corner of Michael's eye caught his interest.

It was Raymon Collins, and he was sneaking away from The Institute. Michael nudged Steve and pointed to him.

"Let's follow him," Steve said.

Michael had his doubts. "Are you sure? We'll be out of bounds then," he said nervously.

Steve raised his eyebrow. "When has that ever stopped us?" he asked Michael with a smirk.

Michael smiled slightly. "Good point," he told Steve. "Let's go."

10 - OUT OF BOUNDS

The only places where the recruits were permitted to go, with the exception of the outside pool and the lake, were the Strategy Building and the Recruit facility.

Raymon Collins was about to go outside this area.

Michael glanced at Steve as they crossed this invisible boundary. Should they be doing this?

Steve, however, looked resolute, so Michael thought it best not to argue and draw attention to themselves.

Raymon strode out onto a long wide road that ran through the centre of The Institute. Here they could see professional soldiers strolling around wearing casual civilian clothes but they all had that look in their eyes of veterans who had experienced war and suffering.

The same look Raines had, yet it was completely absent from Lieutenant Jones.

Raymon turned a corner; the duo followed after him.

Michael was nervous, but also strangely excited.

The military guards paid no attention to them, yet Michael and Steve still tried to keep out of sight in case Raymon looked back.

Raymon then entered a small house and closed the door behind him. Only high-ranking officers were permitted their own living quarters. Michael ducked behind a wall, and then peeked through the window.

Inside were Lieutenant Jones and Raymon, much to Michael's surprise. This must have been Jones' house.

Fortunately, the window was slightly ajar, so they could catch some of their conversation. Jones was careless.

"Are you sure this isn't bugged?" Raymon was saying.

"Positive," Jones drawled in his American accent. "Now get to it. What do you want?"

"Well I'm sure you have heard of my father, Alfred Collins, who finances this Institute. I want you to get me into the Coliseum games this year. In return, I'm sure he can guarantee you a promotion. Finally get you out of this country," Raymon said.

"I see. And if I don't?" Jones said coolly.

"Well, to say the least, you'd be demoted. In the right hands, money goes a long way," Raymon said.

Michael and Steve looked at each other.

"Alright, alright, no need for threats," Jones said quickly, and Michael could detect a trace of worry in his voice. "You can go now," he said, and Michael felt his stomach clench.

They would be discovered. They quietly snuck around the corner away from the front door. They heard it open, and Raymon's footsteps grew louder. Had he heard them?

Steve shuffled along and accidently bumped into a bush, which rustled.

They heard Raymon's footsteps grew closer, as he headed towards them. Then suddenly they heard a shout from inside of the house.

"I said go!" Jones yelled and Raymon walked away. Michael breathed a sigh of relief.

They waited five minutes before dashing off away from the building, which must have been Lieutenant Jones' residence.

When they were sure they had not been followed, they turned and looked at each other.

"I can't believe Raymon tried to do that," Michael said.

"I can," Steve said darkly. "Raymon's gonna pay."

"Should we tell someone?" Michael asked him.

"Who'd believe us?" Steve said. "We have no proof. It's our word against theirs."

Michael sighed.

"Let's just get back and get some food," he said.

Steve nodded. "Yeah."

They began walking back, and were on their way when they suddenly found themselves face to face with Sergeant Vellon.

"*Why* are you garcons not at dinner?" he inquired in his thick French accent.

Michael and Steve froze.

"Erm," Michael said, trying to find an excuse. They were in for it now.

"We were just looking around," Steve said.

The excuse sounded so lame, but Sergeant Vellon bought it.

"You boys need to eat. You are pathetic and weak, as you need to get stronger. Hurry up!" Sgt Vellon commanded and then walked off.

Michael carried on, relieved.

"He didn't seem to notice that we were in a restricted area." Steve commented.

"He must have had a lot on his mind." Michael mused. What was he so preoccupied with? Usually Vellon loved punishing recruits. It was unlike him not to reprimand them.

They made it back to the Recruit facility and had some food, sitting with their team in the food hall. Once again, it was delicious compared to what he was used to. There was meat here, sizzling bacon that made his mouth water just to look at. It was much better than the standard bread and rice meals he had had back at home.

"Where have you been?" Joe asked him.

Steve ignored the question. "It's good to see you're sitting with your squad, Joe," he said brightly.

Joe glared at him.

"Steve, stop it," Michael chastised. He changed the subject "So, whereabouts are you from?"

Joe narrowed his eyes. "Why would you care?"

"Because I'm on your squad," Michael replied.

Joe sighed. "Our family lived in the countryside after we emigrated from America. We live in Occupied Britain in Devon," he said in a bored voice. "Happy now?"

"Why did you emigrate?" Steve asked.

"My grandfather was a civil rights activist. They forced him to go," Joe explained.

"And are you going back for revenge?" Steve asked jokingly.

Joe didn't reply. Michael raised his eyebrows; was he serious?

He looked across at the other members of the table. Jenny, Alexandra and Teresa were all deep in conversation, while Tim was talking to Hans.

Michael smiled. For the most part, he had a good squad. He glanced across at the other table where Raymon and his cronies were talking and shuddered. He would hate to be in their squad; therefore he was grateful to Raines for putting him in the Spartans.

That night, he had a lot to think about as he lay down on his bed. Would Jones really crumble under Raymon's threat? Was his father that powerful? What was Sergeant Vellon doing earlier? And was Joe really trying to go back for revenge?

11 - **TAKEDOWN IN TRAINING**

The next few days, training continued. Early morning, Michael had physical training with Sergeant Vellon and Steve which still hurt like hell. After that, he would have to go through more physical training with the rest of his squad which caused Michael and Steve to be almost dead on their feet afterwards as well as soaked in sweat.

Before they even had time for a shower, Sergeant Vellon moved them on to hand to hand combat. As a soldier, most of the fighting would be ranged, but hand to hand combat was very important when your life depended on it. The Russians were a mainly close-quarters based army, with their hybrids usually clawing and mauling the Western soldiers.

The hand to hand combat lessons were very tough. They were in pairs and Sergeant Vellon taught them fighting techniques.

In their first lesson, Michael was paired up with Teresa. He thought he should probably go easy on her, seeing as she was a girl.

That was a mistake.

Teresa was tough - and she never went easy on anyone.

They were practising takedowns. Obviously it would be much different against the hybrids than against each other they could not let recruits actually train against enemy soldiers. However, the same techniques still applied.

"Arrgh!" Michael groaned, as Teresa took him down and smashed her elbow into his stomach. "That was unnecessary!" he complained.

"Yeah, well you're meant to be the tough guy," she taunted, placing her hands on her hips.

Michael got up and gritted his teeth.

"You asked for it," he said, and tried to focus on technique. They both squatted slightly, and faced each other.

During the lessons, Sgt Vellon would demonstrate techniques, and then the squad would keep practicing them until it became almost habit.

This particular move involved grabbing your opponent's tricep and taking their legs out from underneath them.

So far, Teresa had won every time.

This time Michael opted for a different strategy. Instead of going for her arm, as she expected, he lunged and grabbed her shirt collar. He then hooked his left leg around hers and brought her down.

He smiled, victorious. Though he hadn't noticed that when he had grabbed her collar, her shirt had ripped.

Fortunately, it was not badly torn and though it could probably be stitched back together, she wasn't happy.

Sergeant Vellon tapped him on the shoulder.

Michael gulped.

"You did not do the correct technique," Vellon said pointedly in his French accent.

Michael did not know what to say, so he remained silent, fear gripping him.

"But well done. Good initiative. I was wondering how long it would take for someone to figure out that variation. Of course, the Russians will not have collars, so I do not recommend you practice that," Vellon explained.

Michael breathed a sigh of relief.

"Teresa, please go and change your shirt. I will spar with Michael until you return," Vellon said with a smile.

Michael's relief quickly turned to dread as he faced Sergeant Vellon.

He would be lucky to leave here alive.

Training progressed throughout the week, yet the team were still not allowed to use weapons. They were all excited when it came to Sunday as they would be facing their first competition. It was their first chance to prove themselves to the instructors and compete for a place in the Coliseum.

"I'm nervous," Jenny said over breakfast.

"Same," Michael said. "I wonder what it will be."

"Do you think we will use weapons?" Steve asked.

"I doubt it," Arthur said. "We have been practicing hand-to-hand combat, so I imagine they will test us on that."

"Very true," Hans said. "In that case, the Jaguar and the Legionnaire squads will be our main threats."

"Don't judge a book by its cover," Michael warned. "Physical presence isn't everything."

"I'm just saying that strength makes you a better fighter," Hans pointed out.

"It all depends on the activity we will be doing," Jenny said.

After breakfast, they all waited outside. It was not a hot day or cold either, about nineteen degrees Celsius. Optimum temperature.

The recruits lined up in their squads, waiting until Lieutenant Jones arrived.

"Alright, lackeys," he said, scanning the various squads. "Today you will be put in a competitive match. The eight squads will be put into four teams of four. There will be fifteen flags placed around an area south of The Institute that you will have to capture. You have four hours. No weapons allowed.

The teams are as follows:

Team A, Legionnaires and Praetorians,

Team B, Companions and Jaguars,

Team C, Varangians and Immortals,

and Team D, Jaegers and Spartans. Now get in your trucks!" he barked, and each squad got in their own truck. Raines drove the Spartan truck.

So they were with the Jaegers on Team D. Michael smiled. That was Sophie's squad.

The trucks travelled towards their destination.

When they arrived, they found themselves at a forest. Raines addressed his squad.

"Right, lads, 'ere's some advice. Don't stray too far. Yer watches tell ye how long ye've got. Be back at the right time. Don't 'urt anyone too seriously. Also, ye should pick a leader. Good luck," he said.

The Spartans walked away together.

"So who should be our leader?" Michael asked.

They all looked at him as though it were obvious, with the exception of Joe, who looked at the floor.

"You," Jenny said with a smirk.

Michael frowned. "Why me?" he asked, although he was actually quite proud to be nominated.

"Well ... on the teambuilding exercise, you were a pretty good leader," Alexandra said.

"And you kicked Teresa's ass in training," Steve muttered, though they all heard him and laughed. Teresa punched Steve on the arm, hard. Michael still felt a bit guilty about that training session.

He felt pleased to be thought of as a good leader.

"Thanks guys," Michael said, smiling at them. "I'll do my best."

"So what now, Lord Michael?" Steve said, doing a mock salute.

"I'd say we discuss tactics with the Jaegers," he pronounced and walked over to where the Jaegers were standing. The Spartans stayed where they were.

The Jaegers were not the bulkiest of teams, but seemed to be relatively nimble.

Sophie turned and faced him. "So you're the leader, huh?" she said with a smirk.

Michael raised an eyebrow. "I could say the same thing about you," he said.

Sophie gave him a dazzling smile. "Well, I'm sure we're going to work together very well," she said, winking at him.

Michael didn't know what to say. He felt himself going red. He mumbled something, and then cleared his throat.

"What's your plan?" he asked her.

Sophie thought to herself. "Use the trees. Once we find flags, we should hide them up there. Stop the other teams nicking them."

Michael nodded. "We'll need at least four flags between the two squads to not lose the competition. So if we go for two for each squad, that should be good," he stated.

Sophie shook her head. "I want to win. Let's go for three flags each," she said.

Michael nodded. "Alright. We will go in two separate groups and search for them," he said.

"Why don't we put the fastest eight in the group to get the flags and the remaining ten to guard them once we've got some? Until then they can help us search," Sophie suggested.

"OK. Let's get to it," Michael said, and went back to his squad.

"So, boss, what's the plan?" Alexandra asked, eyebrows raised when he came along.

Michael rolled his eyes. "We are sending the fastest people to get the flags at the start," he said. "And don't call me boss."

She just grinned.

"Right, Joe, Jenny and Alexandra, you come with me. The rest of you will stay together and guard our flags when we get them. Until then you should search. Stay in a group. Steve's in charge," he told them.

Teresa glared at him. "You are not leaving me alone with all these boys," she stated, crossing her arms.

Michael sighed. "Teresa, you'll be with the Jaegers, too. You won't be alone," he said, then walked off with Joe, Alexandra and Jenny.

They met up with Sophie's group. "This is Dan, Oliver and Jane," she said, referring to the people with her.

Dan was a tall muscular boy, with big shoulders and dirty blond hair. He nodded at Michael. He seemed like the strong, silent type.

Oliver was the opposite. He was small, weedy and looked a bit like a rat. He had light brown hair and had freckles.

Jane had blond hair tied back in a bun. She was tall and quite bony, nothing like Michael's sister of the same name.

Michael nodded. "Let's do this."

"Alright lads," Lieutenant Jones said through a megaphone. "You will have four hours. Be back here then. If you are seriously hurt, press the alarm button on your watch and one of us will come and get you. There are cameras deployed around the woods so we can see what's going on.

The flags are in a five mile radius; your watch will beep if you are outside the zone. They are not hard to find, so I expect you to find them quickly. It's what happens once they have all been claimed which is when things will get interesting. This exercise is designed to test your tactics and combat skills." Jones cleared his throat. "The competition starts ... NOW!" he roared, and everyone sprinted off.

12 - **THE COMPETITIVE EDGE**

Everyone sprinted off into the forest. Within Team D, Michael and Sophie's faster group of eight ran ahead together whilst the rest of his team fell behind. After about ten minutes, his group stopped running and stood still.

Michael then looked to his left and saw a flag, the pole stood up in a clearing. It rippled in the slight breeze, as though inviting them to come and get it. Michael smirked, then walked forward and picked it up. The heavy metal pole was about four feet long with the plain red flag attached.

"One flag down, five to go," he said.

He grinned as Sophie walked up to him. "Well done," she said, making Michael feel quite pleased.

Michael then had an idea. "We can use these flagpoles as weapons. They'd be great," he said.

Sophie smiled, considering. "That's not a bad idea," she admitted.

The group carried on running, until suddenly they heard the shouts of another group. They stopped, and tensed themselves.

Then, out of the blue, they were attacked. Twelve people, whom Michael had barely time to recognise as a mix of Varangians and Immortals from Team C, charged out of the trees at them.

Michael swung the flagpole and hit one in the head. Another then tried to grab it, but Michael kicked him away. He was dimly aware of Joe fighting viciously to his right and Jenny and Alexandra taking on three of them on his left. He scanned around whilst they fought to protect their only flag.

He noticed in the distance there was a lone boy holding a flag, obviously staying out of the fight as he was trying not to lose it.

Michael shouted to Dan. "Take this!" and tossed him the flag. Dan caught it and swung it in a wide arc around himself, knocking a few people over.

Michael then sprinted off towards the lone boy, intent of seizing the flag for himself. The boy panicked and tried to run, but the flag weighed him down. He turned and tried to jab Michael with it, but Michael sidestepped him and grabbed the flag, wrenching it out of the boy's grip. The boy looked at him in fear but Michael ruthlessly jabbed the flagpole into his belly.

He stepped back, flag in hand, feeling triumphant, though a little guilty at the weaker boy's pain. He bent down and pressed the alarm button on the boy's watch, hoping that an instructor would come and get him.

Michael then looked around. He had ran away further than he had intended.

He was alone, not even able to hear the skirmish from which he had come. He would have to find his squad, although he didn't know which direction to look.

He decided to climb a tree. It was not too hard to get himself up, however it was difficult to balance the flag. Eventually he made it to the top and looked around. It was different up here.

The sun was shining and a cool breeze blew into his face. He could see the golden tops of the tall trees around and a hill in the distance.

He looked closer at the hill. There weren't many trees on it and he could see some sort of battle.

Part of Team B were on it, about ten of them. It was the first he had seen of them so far. However, he couldn't see the other half anywhere. Team B seemed to have about four flags, but were getting overwhelmed by an assault of roughly twenty five attackers.

That meant there must have been an alliance. An alliance between Team A and Team C.

Michael cursed. That was a lot of people his team would potentially have to compete against.

So the twelve that had attacked Sophie's and his team had merely been a scouting force.

Michael watched the battle. The Jaguars from Team B were fighting like lions, showing no mercy. They were all reasonably strong and they managed to use their flagpoles effectively.

He noticed their leader, Thomas, fighting three people at once. Those three people happened to be Raymon, Gilmore and Brooke, who all had flags of their own.

Michael began climbing down. He wanted to help Thomas and his team, but he knew he wouldn't be able to do much on his own.

He began jogging off, looking for his squad. He kept going for about ten minutes until he found the remainder of his team.

They were standing together, with many of his teammates on the lying on the ground. With a quick head count, there seemed to be about fourteen fully able with the remaining five or six injured.

When he came close, Steve turned around and spoke to him.

"Jenny's hurt. She's broken her ankle," he informed him.

Michael raced forward and saw that she was clutching her ankle in pain.

"What happened?" he asked as he knelt by her side.

"Stupid Team B attacked us. Then we met up with Sophie's group who were being pursued by Team C, and we beat them," Jenny told him whilst grimacing.

"There's been an alliance between the Team C and the Team A," Michael told them. "They're attacking the Jaguars now. There must be at least ten flags on the hill overall between the lot of them. How many do we have?"

"Three," Teresa said.

"I've got one," Michael told them. "So we won't come last. One team has to have less than us."

"But we want to win," Sophie reminded him.

He was determined. "That's right. We're going to help Team B. They have five flags, which means the other two teams must have five or six between them. We're gonna go for those first, which will take the pressure off Team B," he stated.

"Why don't we attack Team B?" Joe suggested.

"Because Raymon's an idiot and so are the rest of Team A," Steve said with a smirk.

Alexandra rolled her eyes.

"Boys," she muttered, nudging one of the Jaeger girls.

64

They both shook their heads.

Michael turned his attention back to Jenny. "Okay, have you activated your help signal on your watch?" he asked, concerned.

She shook her head. "I'm fine," she said, clearly determined to carry on.

Michael put his hand on her shoulder. "Jenny, I know you are brave, there's no need to prove yourself. But don't be stupid, you know you'll just hurt yourself more and be injured for longer," he said as gently as he could.

Jenny sighed and activated it. "Where are you going then?" she asked.

Michael stood up. "We're going to win this competition," he said resolutely.

13 - STRIVING FOR VICTORY

"Oooh, how inspiring," Steve snickered. Michael rolled his eyes.

"Team D, let's go," Michael said and they followed him. Even the Jaegers, the other half of his team, didn't question his leadership which he thought was strange.

They jogged over until they reached the hill. By then, some more people from Team B had joined the ones on the hill. The extra help could be just what they needed, though the odds were still against them.

But not anymore.

"Attack!" Michael yelled, and they charged towards Teams A and C. Michael sprinted through the brawl, ignoring everyone but his target: Raymon Collins.

Blood pounded through his head as he gripped the flagpole. He would really show him this time. He sprinted forward and jabbed the flagpole like a spear into the side of Brooke's ribs. Brooke grunted and collapsed, keeling over on the floor. Raymon then faced Michael and narrowed his eyes.

"You," Raymon said.

"No cronies to hide behind now," Michael taunted.

"I don't need any," Raymon sneered.

The rational part of his mind was telling Michael to back down as Raymon was quite clearly stronger than him, but once again, the bloodlust of the fight was with him.

Michael charged forward recklessly, but Raymon swung his flagpole at him. Michael blocked it, but only just.

The impact sent vibrations up his arm and Michael stepped back, wary.

He remembered what Sergeant Raines had said.

All warfare is based on deception. This was a completely different place to the strategy room, but concept was still the same, right?

Either way, it was worth a shot.

Michael put on a look of fear and Raymon bought it. Raymon grinned, stepping forward.

He swept Michael's legs away with his flagpole. Michael made sure to fall forward onto his knees, instead of onto his back. He also dropped his own flagpole as well. He wanted Raymon to feel certain that victory was his.

In the boy's eyes was the look of an animal that knows its prey is helpless: the brutish, primal instinct to destroy.

Michael, however, was in reality far from helpless.

As soon as Raymon was close, he sprung up, hooking his right leg around Raymon's and grabbing Raymon's pole with both hands.

Raymon had made a mistake in coming so close. The pole, much like a spear, was not built for very close quarters combat; there was no room to manoeuvre.

Michael powered upwards, pushing Raymon off-balance and using his momentum to bring the boy to the ground.

He now had the advantage. He pressed his knees to Raymon's chest then used his body weight to press the flagpole down onto his throat.

Raymon gripped the pole and tried to push it up, but Michael was weighing it down. The pole made contact with Raymon's throat and he began to struggle to breathe.

Michael smiled sadistically, blood still pounding in his head. The idiot deserved it.

Suddenly, everyone's watches beeped. "Exercise finished," they all said at the same time.

"Everyone, get up and line up in your goddamn squads!" Raines barked through a megaphone.

Michael got up, taking Raymon's flag with him. They all lined up.

"Ye stupid fools!" Raines yelled, his Scottish accent showing. "I know, yer all soldiers, but Jesus Christ, rein it in a little! Yer not bleedin' savages! Show some goddamn sense and don't bloody kill yer teammates!"

Raines took a breath. "Okay. Y'all lost some lads and lasses, so I'm not punishing anyone in particular. But next time, calm yerselves down!" he exclaimed, then handed the megaphone to Lieutenant Jones.

Jones grinned. "*Very* well done," he drawled in his American accent. "The raw aggression. The beasts inside of you. I *like* that!" he exclaimed. "That's what makes you soldiers, the love of violence! Our American military can harness that and turn you into fighting machines. That's what you want, right? To be given the chance to throw yourselves at the Russians!"

Most of the people nodded eagerly, but Michael didn't. He felt kind of disgusted. He didn't want to be some animal or fighting machine. He exchanged looks with Steve.

"Yeah, we've had a few injuries but they'll heal," Jones continued. "What counts is that you guys made it through. Now, for the scores:

Team B won, having six flags between them.

Team A were second, having five.

Team D were third, having three, and Team C were last, having two.

So congratulations to Team B, they certainly deserved it, especially with that sneaky stealing of the flags from the Team D!" Jones announced.

Michael felt terrible. He had assumed that his team, Team D, would win. He had got too caught up with his own personal duel with Raymon, he had not even realised that his team had had flags stolen from them. He had let them down.

He noticed Steve's shoulders slump and Alexandra sigh. Even Arthur wouldn't meet his eye.

Apart from the one flag he was carrying, the others were held by Sophie and Dan.

That meant his squad, the Spartans, was one of the worst. And he, as the leader, was responsible.

14 - RECOVERY

That night, Michael was disillusioned. The rest of his squad had gone up to the common room, but he decided to go on a walk. He decided to go to the Medical Centre to check up on Jenny and her injured ankle.

He walked out onto the street. It was early evening and the sky was overcast - the typical grey colour that always seemed to exist in England.

The Medical Centre was a hospital on the edge of the Recruit Area so Michael was allowed in. No one really paid him much attention. The receptionist, a bored looking middle aged lady, told him where Jenny's room was located.

He knocked uncertainly.

"Come in," he heard her call. Michael noticed her voice sounded tired.

Michael opened the door and saw her lying on her bed with her ankle and foot in plaster. She looked up slowly, as though she was expecting a doctor. When Jenny saw him, she brightened up considerably.

"Michael!" she exclaimed grinning, and then composed herself. "W-why are you here?"

"I was just checking up on you. How are you?" Michael asked, feeling quite hot.

"Apart from this stupid ankle, I'm fine. They've put a load of painkillers and stuff, so I don't feel anything," she said with a slight smile. "And thanks for coming."

Michael smiled, and pulled up a chair.

"Do you know how the exercise went?" he asked her, sighing.

She shook her head. "No, what happened?"

Michael grimaced. "We came third. I ... I messed up. We had four flags and I wanted the help Team B fight Team A and C. I lost focus. I went straight for Raymon and fought him. I didn't know what everyone else in the squad was doing. I guess I just got angry. You know, the heat and the rush of battle must have got to me. I beat him, and I ..," he faltered.

"What?" Jenny asked gently.

"I ... I almost killed him. Well, I mean, I would have stopped when he fell unconscious, but I was choking him and I just wasn't thinking straight," Michael admitted, looking at the ground. He felt incredibly guilty and regretted what he had done.

It was good to tell someone though. He hoped she wouldn't judge him too harshly, even though he felt he deserved it.

He was silent, not daring to look up.

"Michael," Jenny said slowly and gently. "You know what you did, and maybe it might have been wrong, but it was a fight and you were angry. You maybe should have behaved differently, but you can't change that now. The important thing is for you to learn from it and not beat yourself up about it."

Michael was about to reply, but then hesitated. She was right, really.

Had he honestly forgiven himself? No.

But how could he? He had almost killed someone.

True, that person was an idiot, but it was still unforgivable.

"Apologise," Jenny said, as though reading his mind.

Michael looked up. "You think Raymon would honestly accept an apology?" he asked, raising his eyebrows.

Jenny smirked back. "No. But it'd make you feel better," she said.

Michael smiled. "Thank you. You're good at giving advice," he said.

She shrugged. "Well, I'm just sensible," she said.

Michael raised an eyebrow. "And I'm not?" he joked.

"Yep," she said, grinning.

Michael laughed and shook his head.

"Well then, I should probably go say sorry. Thanks again Jenny, you're the best," he said, smiling at her and standing up.

"Erm, Michael," Jenny said awkwardly. Michael looked at her. "Thank you … for coming. I thought you guys would forget about me. I thought you'd be too preoccupied with your training," she confessed.

Michael smiled and squeezed her hand. "Hey, I'd never leave you. Training is important, but not as much as our friends," he reassured her. "See you tomorrow, Jenny. Goodnight."

15 - PROMETHEUS

Norway

"Sergeant Wallace, I have some news for you!"

The young red-haired man turned around to see his friend Jack Jennings, a Canadian man with youthful features and very light hair.

"Yeah?" he asked eagerly.

"We've got some intel on Fenrir," Jack said excitedly. "I thought you'd want to see it."

The recently promoted Wallace smiled. Ever since the massacre of his regiment whilst escorting the oil convoy, he had been keenly waiting for news of the Russian commander. He had sworn to avenge his comrades.

After Wallace had recounted to high command everything that had happened, he had been deemed as 'emotionally traumatised' and unfit to fight. He was the only survivor from the Royal Scots.

Despite that, he had been given a Medal of Honour and promoted to Sergeant. His job now was to inform soldiers who had recently arrived in Norway about the environment and advise them what to expect and how best to respond.

He currently worked in Base 16, a military stronghold in the city of Oslo.

Sergeant Wallace nodded. "I do," he replied, his Scottish accent prominent. "Where is it?"

"Follow me," Jack told Wallace. "We were able to intercept a transmission."

"A transmission? From Fenrir?" Wallace asked curiously.

"Yep," Jack replied, using the thumbprint scanner to access an intel room. This was an area where people worked at decrypting Russian communications and figuring out the locations of their armies.

Fenrir had been a top priority for a while now, especially after the massacre of the Royal Scots, but they were still no closer to finding him.

The room was full of people tapping away at computers who paid no attention to Wallace and his Canadian friend.

Wallace noticed a certain screen detailing the locations of the Russian attacks in the last three months. There were too many to count.

"Over here," Jack told Wallace. Jack worked as a reconnaissance officer, a scout in his division. It was his job to learn the latest information and brief his squad about the Russian army.

Wallace approached the computer screen the Jack was referring to.

"It's a transcript of an intercepted conversation," Jack explained.

It read:

- - -TRANSMISSION INTERCEPTED MID RECORDING - - -

FENRIR: Has The Institute been successfully infiltrated?

CONTACT: Yes, sir. They do not suspect a thing.

FENRIR: That better be so. I do not want any unnecessary complications.

CONTACT: There will not be sir. By the time my squad reaches the Coliseum, we will have access to the full database of Western Alliance intelligence.

FENRIR: I am aware of that. Are you sure that this line is secure?

CONTACT: I am. I encrypted this call myself.

FENRIR: It better be so. I do not wish for a failure, Prometheus.

CONTACT: Nor do I. I am fully confident in my success.

FENRIR: I will expect regular intelligence from you. End transmission.

- - - TRANSMISSION TERMINATED - - -

Wallace raised his eyebrows. "Is that it?" he asked Jack.

"Yeah, pretty good, isn't it?" Jack said enthusiastically. He made a lot of hand movements as he spoke.

"How?" Wallace asked sceptically. It didn't seem good to him.

"We've got bait. When the kids at The Institute finish training, we bring them here, lure out Fenrir and boom! We've got him!" Jack exclaimed, waving his hands dramatically.

"Right ... so you want to use lads who've just come out of training as bait for one of the most powerful military commanders in the world?" Wallace asked with a smirk.

Jack looked thoughtful.

"Yes," he replied eventually. "It will be worth it if we beat Fenrir."

Wallace snorted. "If? Fenrir might not even show up!" he exclaimed angrily. "I thought this was real intel, not some random conversation he had!"

"No, don't you see? They have a spy, but they don't know that *we know* they have a spy! We're a step ahead!" Jack enthused, waving his hands madly. "Plus, this is big news. We have to be far more careful who gets wind of information now. If The Institute has a mole, other places might too."

Wallace sighed. "Do we know who the spy is?" he asked Jack wearily.

Jack looked down. "No," he admitted quietly. "But it can't be that hard, right? I mean there's only about ...," he trailed off working out how many people at The Institute could possibly be entered into the Coliseum.

"A hundred?" Wallace stated, his eyebrows raised.

"More like eighty," Jack reasoned with a shrug.

"Exactly. So we're just gonna send eighty barely trained kids against Fenrir and hope that he'll reveal himself?" Wallace questioned.

"Well, no .... we would have to narrow it down. Find the recruits that are foreign, perhaps?" Jack suggested.

"That's a wee bit xenophobic. No, we need more info before we can act. There's still plenty of time until the Coliseum. Maybe we can find this mole before then," Wallace stated, preparing to leave.

"Why don't you go?" Jack asked him hopefully.

Wallace glanced back sceptically. "What?"

"Why don't you go to The Institute? You said yourself that you were sick of Norway. The change might do you good," Jack offered.

Wallace was about to retort, but he realised that it could be an opportunity to get away from this place.

He hated Norway.

"I ... that might not be a bad idea," Wallace remarked slowly. "What'll I say to the people 'ere, though? I might be viewed as abandoning them."

Jack shrugged. "You have a right to go and work at The Institute instead of here. What happened to your regiment wasn't a small thing," he reasoned. "You need a break from Norway."

Wallace thought back to what had happened to his regiment and a look of pain crossed his face.

Jack was right. Every time he saw the snow fall, he remembered the torrid blizzard which had taken away his regiment and his friends.

"Yer right," he said eventually. "I'm getting out of 'ere."

16 - THE SLOG

Occupied Britain

Monday. The worst day of the week. The day when Sergeant Raines decided to put his squad through the gruelling physical challenge nicknamed 'The Slog'.

It was already a muddy assault course, but would quickly turn into a swamp in wet weather.

As the Spartans stood huddled at the starting point, they were wishing they could be back in the warm common room by the artificial fire. As Jenny was injured, together were Alexandra, Michael, Steve, Teresa, Hans, Tim, Joe and Arthur.

Instead, Sergeant Raines and Sergeant Vellon had thought that this would be suitable punishment for their poor performance in the competition yesterday.

Sergeant Raines faced them. "Get to the end. Don't cheat. Don't fail. Ye have an hour," he instructed coldly, then walked off, leaving them in the rain.

Michael took a deep breath and looked at his squad. "Alright, let's do this," he said.

Tim protested. "This is stupid. You're the leader, you should do it. It's your fault we lost the mission," he complained.

Alexandra glared at the boy. "Tim, shut up!" she said angrily. "We're a team here."

Michael was surprised by Alexandra's defence of him and smiled warmly at her, grateful for the support. She returned it.

He turned to Tim. "Fine. Go in and explain that to Sergeant Raines. I'm sure he'll take your side," he said, annoyed. He didn't like Tim's pompous attitude and the fact that he had bought his way in to The Institute instead of taking the tests.

Tim sulked, shaking his head and looking down resentfully.

Michael often thought of himself as a nice enough person, but he thought he needed to be harsh with Tim here.

"We're a team," Michael said, addressing the group. "So we better act like it. I know I messed up the other exercise. And I'm sorry. So, I'm going to step down as leader," he announced.

Alexandra, Teresa and Steve immediately started protesting, but Michael held up his hand to silence them.

"Guys, I'm serious. I don't think I'm a good leader," he said.

Arthur cleared his throat. "I think that Michael should have a second chance before he decides whether to step down."

Hans nodded. "Next Sunday after the second competition we shall decide," he said, simply.

Michael nodded. "Alright. Well, if that's settled, let's stop standing in the cold and smash this course!"

The assault course, however, did not seem to agree with being 'smashed'. The first challenge was a three metre climbing wall. There was a small padded mat at the bottom to prevent serious injuries but you could still get a nasty bruise.

The handholds were wet in the rain, which made slipping a likely prospect. Hans fell, taking Tim down with him, but the second time up they all got through.

By now they were standing on a platform in front of a huge zip wire. It looked about four hundred metres long.

Michael didn't hesitate. He grabbed on to the small bar, which was shaped like a coat hanger with curved edges to prevent him from slipping off. He zoomed off, picking up speed. His arms hurt but he didn't dare let go. He gathered momentum as the ground got further away.

Suddenly, a searing pain struck his arm, almost causing him to let go. He looked across, and could see various soldiers on the ground below him armed with rifles and they were firing at him.

He gripped the zip wire more tightly, focusing on timing his landing perfectly. If he let go too early there would be a three metre drop at high speeds which would almost certainly seriously injure him. Let go too late and he would be thrown into a mud bath of a lake, making the rest of the assault course much more difficult.

He left go just before the drop ended, and he flew over it, skidding on the wet ground. He quickly stopped himself before he reached the muddy water.

He hoisted himself to his feet, and began scouting out the next activity whilst the rest of his team went on the zip wire. He inspected his arm. They must have used rubber bullets as it had not penetrated his skin, but it still hurt like hell.

Adrenaline stopped him from feeling too much pain, so he tried to keep moving and remain fired up.

Michael surveyed the next obstacle. It was a balance beam across a stretch of water. It seemed easy enough, but in this weather it would be very slippery.

Alexandra was the next one to arrive after the zip wire. She timed her jump perfectly as well. Michael walked over to her, pointing to the second exercise. "We can't go across standing up," he stated.

She nodded. "You go first. I'll catch you if you fall," she said with a smirk.

Michael rolled his eyes, and started towards the beam. It stood about two metres off the surface of the water. He bent low and wrapped his arms around the top of the beam, and hugged it tightly. Then he began slowly advancing, by gripping and moving with his legs. Progress was slow, but at least he didn't fall. He kept going for about ten minutes, making it past halfway, until he heard a small scream from behind him.

He looked behind him and saw Alexandra upside down below the beam. Hans was too far away to help, so Michael very carefully rotated himself around to face her. He slowly made his way over while she stayed there, very still. Her hair was hanging down.

When Michael reached her, her tried to reassure her.

"Don't worry Alexandra, you'll be alright. Stay calm," he kept moving until he had climbed over her.

He could see in her face she was scared, but she was trying to keep her cool. He couldn't blame her. The water below was probably as cold as ice.

He looked at her. "Okay, Alex - can I call you that? I'm going to grab your waist and pull you back up onto the top of beam," he said gently.

She nodded, and Michael, still gripping the beam tightly with his legs, wrapped his arms around Alexandra's waist.

He then gently began pulling her up, taking most of her body weight in his arms. He hoisted her up, and she heaved a sigh of relief when she was upright.

They stayed still for several seconds, Michael holding onto her to make sure she would not fall again. Her breathing calmed down, and she nodded.

"Thank you," she whispered quietly. "I can carry on now."

Michael let go, and she carried on going across the beam. Michael averted his eyes from looking at her as he followed, focusing on making sure he didn't lose his own balance.

After that exercise, they moved on to the next one. It was a very long track with metal poles spaced evenly at intervals either side of it. It looked suspiciously easy to make it to the end.

By this time, Hans and Steve were with them. Steve, never one to think about possible consequences, stepped forward to go on the path.

"Watch and learn," he said cockily as he swaggered forward to the track. Michael laughed.

Steve walked forward onto the channel as the rest of them held their breaths. He stopped, and nothing happened.

He turned around and faced them, spreading his arms out in triumph. "Piece of cake."

Then small shots whizzed through the air and pounded into him, knocking him straight to the ground.

Teresa, who had just arrived, let out a small scream. Michael frowned, as this was very uncharacteristic of her. He dived forward and dragged Steve back from the track.

"Steve, you alright?" he asked, concerned.

Steve nodded. "Yeah," he rasped, though it was clear to see he was in pain. "I'm good. Just rubber bullets. Nothing to worry about."

Michael stood up, pacing back and forward. "Alright. We go in pairs. I'll carry Steve. Teresa, go with Arthur. Alexandra, go with Joe. Hans go with Tim," he ordered. "Leave about five to ten seconds between goes."

Hans cleared his throat. "I appreciate your sacrifice Michael, but I think I should be the one to carry Steve. I am probably stronger," he said somewhat awkwardly.

Michael was about to protest, but nodded. Hans *was* stronger than him. "Alright," he agreed.

"Teresa and Arthur go first. Whatever happens, don't stop running," he impressed upon them. "Three … two … one … go!" he yelled, and Teresa and Arthur sprinted off. They were quickly under fire, but kept going, as Alexandra and Joe sprinted off after them.

Next were Steve and Hans. Steve insisted on running himself, but Hans still supported him as they ran. They sprinted off together, leaving just him and Tim.

"Are you ready?" he asked Tim.

Tim shook his head. "That's crazy!" he exclaimed stubbornly.

Michael glared at him. "Either start running or I'll drag you, how else will we get across?" he demanded.

"Now GO!" he yelled, and began sprinting off. Unfortunately, the runners in front had left a trail of mud behind them, making grip difficult.

For some reason, when he started running, all the guns seemed to turn to him. Suddenly, he was being poked with blunt objects as the bullets hit him. He kept going until he heard Tim cry out behind him as he fell.

He glanced back as he ran, and was about to stop when he heard a shout from ahead.

"Mike, keep going! I've got him!" came Joe's voice. Michael carried on, covering his head with his arms, only focusing on going forward.

He noticed Joe slide next to him along the floor towards Tim, but kept going.

Eventually, he reached the end on the track, and stood there, breathing heavily, exhausted. The adrenaline kept him going, but he knew he would soon feel as sore as hell.

Joe and Tim reached them, and the firing ceased. Joe was carrying Tim in a fireman's lift over one shoulder.

Michael faced Joe, incredibly grateful.

"Thank you," he said seriously, looking him in the eye.

Joe shrugged. "You're welcome," he said coolly.

He then went over to Steve, who was lying on the ground in pain as he had been shot twice more as he ran.

Michael helped Tim to his feet. "You alright?" he asked him.

Tim nodded. "I'm fine."

Michael gave him a small smile, and then went over to Steve. But Michael knew that they needed to finish this course quickly.

"Steve, Teresa is thinking you're a baby the way you're lying about," he taunted.

Steve opened his eyes and looked up, while Alexandra and Teresa laughed.

Steve gritted his teeth and got to his feet, and Michael grinned.

"Last one now," he said, looking out at the last stage of the course.

His heart plummeted as he saw what they were about to go up against.

"Erm ... g-guys," he stammered. They all followed his gaze.

Out in front of them was a huge lake. They could see Sergeant Raines waiting on the other side.

He looked left and right, but he reckoned it would take at least twenty minutes to run around it all.

He checked his watch to see how long they had taken so far: *43 minutes 12 seconds.*

However, if they swam, they could hypothetically make it within the hour Raines had given them. He looked at his squad.

Joe, sullen as usual, was standing by himself.

Steve, fighting back his pain.

Hans, confident as always.

Alexandra, looking determinedly at him.

Teresa, fired up to complete the course.

Arthur, fidgeting nervously.

Tim, shivering from the cold.

Michael made up his mind. "We're going to swim," he told them.

They looked at him. "Are you mad?" Steve asked.

Michael was adamant.

"We will have to go as fast as possible. Clothes will only slow us down. However bad this is, Raines will make us do worse if we don't make it in time," he stated.

Tim nodded. "M-mike's right. Let's go for it."

Teresa looked like she was about to protest, but Alex got there first.

"I am keeping my clothes on!" she said angrily.

Michael sighed. "Your choice. You can put your pride first if you want. Now let's get going. I'll go first," he said, and stripped down to his boxers.

Before he began to feel the cold air sink in, he dived into the lake and began swimming as fast as he could.

The ice cool water chilled his bones, and he thrashed his entire body just to retain the feeling in it. He hoped the others would follow his example and not hesitate.

He swam onwards, madly kicking his legs. He just needed to keep going, though the cold water seemed to sap his strength.

He desperately fought to keep his head above the surface. He couldn't go down now.

Random flashes of information came to mind, as he tried not to think about the effects of freezing water.

Hyperthermia. Frostbite.

Michael shook his head, and focused on positive thoughts. A nice warm shower. Sophie smiling at him.

He forged onwards, but he seemed to grow weaker. His head began to pound, but he kept going.

He had been taught how to swim when he was young in the village river, and had been quite good due to his natural fitness.

However, that was nothing compared to here. Michael's speed dropped dramatically, and soon, he could barely lift his arms above his head.

He switched to breaststroke, but his head began to drop as the cold seeped in.

Suddenly, he was reinvigorated as an arm wrapped itself around his torso and began to pull him along. He looked across to see Alexandra next to him. She could swim much better than he could. Fortunately, she was still wearing all of her clothes.

She gave him a reassuring smile. Michael blushed as he realised he was wearing very little, but he nodded and carried on, powering through the water with renewed strength. She withdrew her arm and carried on next to him.

As they neared the bank, they both became more invigorated, determined to finish. Michael used what strength he had left, but Alexandra gracefully glided past him and clambered out onto the bank. He glanced back, and saw Joe, Steve, Teresa and Tim approaching. Hans and Arthur were about half way.

Michael got out after her, and looked expectantly at Sergeant Raines.

Raines nodded. "Well done. There are showers and clean clothes in there," he said, pointing to nearby facility. As Michael's adrenaline faded and he began to shiver, he ran across towards it, not caring about the pain of his bare feet on the hard ground.

In all honestly, his feet were so numb he could hardly feel them. He found a shower, and stood there, letting the hot water run down his frozen body.

He exhaled, enjoying the pure bliss of hot water.

This satisfaction, however, was soon interrupted as he heard a shout.

"Michael!" Steve yelled. "It's Arthur! He's not strong enough! He won't make it!"

17 - **TOO OLD FOR THIS**

Michael quickly dried himself and put on his fresh clothes and shoes, then ran outside, carrying a towel with him for anyone who needed it.

Everyone was out of the lake except Hans and Arthur. Hans had obviously never swum before, but he seemed to be doing alright and was nearing the bank.

Arthur, on the other hand, seemed to be in the deepest part of the river and was thrashing madly.

Sergeant Raines swore under his breath.

"Right lads; don't even think about followin' me," the Scottish man ordered, taking off his khaki jacket.

Michael watched, his eyes wide as he realised what Raines was about to do. He wanted to go in himself, but he didn't dare disagree with his commanding officer.

He watched as Raines dived in and began swimming towards Arthur. He felt helpless, but his worries subsided slightly when he saw how powerfully Raines was swimming.

Arthur was in absolute terror, his eyes were wild and he was yelling as loud as he could. Michael felt sorry for him. As Arthur was usually an example of self-control, it was shocking to see him in such distress.

Raines grabbed Arthur, pulling him along as if he were weightless. He swam back to the shore, and hoisted Arthur onto the bank. Michael put a towel around Arthur.

Arthur looked freezing cold - Michael could see his teeth chattering.

"I'm too old for this," Raines muttered as he shook his head, and then looked at Michael sternly.

"Get him inside in a warm shower. I'll speak to him later about swimming lessons," he ordered.

Michael nodded and he and Steve practically carried Arthur in. They put him in one of the shower cubicles and left him to it.

"Wow, I never expected that," Steve remarked.

"Yeah, I just assumed everyone could swim," Michael agreed.

"No, I meant Raines going in. It was almost like he was being nice," Steve remarked with a grin.

Michael laughed. "Almost?"

"I don't think Raines feels actual emotion," Steve explained, chuckling slightly. "Anyway, I'm going to see the others. You coming?"

Michael shook his head. "I'll catch you guys later," he told Steve with a slight smile.

Steve nodded, and then left the building, leaving Michael alone.

Michael then sighed and sat down, head in his hands.

He had let his team down again. He should have been the one to rescue Arthur. As leader, it was his responsibility to make sure everyone was alright with his plan.

He should have at least asked if everyone could swim.

Michael stood up and began walking back to the common room. According to their schedules, they had a few hours of 'personal time' to recuperate and train privately.

So much for constant training

He wasn't complaining though, he needed the rest.

Michael wasn't sure what to do, so he decided to go and see if Jenny's ankle had improved.

As he was walking towards the Medical Centre, he heard someone call from behind him.

"Michael!" he looked back and saw Alexandra running towards him. He gave her a small sad smile as he waited for her to catch up.

"What's with all the gloom Mike? Why so dejected?" she asked him.

Michael sighed. "I ... I just can't help but feel responsible for Arthur ... I should have at least asked who could swim," he said quietly, looking down as they walked.

Alexandra bit her lip. "Michael ... you need to stop blaming yourself. We're a team. We should share the blame," she consoled him, placing a hand on his shoulder.

Michael flinched slightly at the contact.

"Yeah ... I know ... I just keep thinking that .... you know..," he said. "It's my fault."

"Michael," Alexandra said sternly. "Stop. There's nothing you can do about it now. It gets annoying if you keep feeling sorry for yourself. Move on."

She stopped him walking and stood in front of him. She then gently lifted up his chin, forcing Michael to look at her.

She smiled at him. "Hey," she whispered softly. "Be happy. We did complete the task in time. It's not all bad."

Michael returned the smile. He appreciated Alexandra's optimistic attitude. "Thanks."

He was suddenly aware of the close proximity between them and felt quite awkward. Alexandra noticed it too. His heartbeat sped up slightly, and he felt a slight surge of emotion although he couldn't quite identify it.

He blushed, stepping away.

His face was burning as he carried on walking.

Alexandra caught up with him. "Hey, don't leave me," she teased good naturedly, nudging him. "Anyway, where are you going now?"

"I was going to see how Jenny is doing," he told her.

Alexandra looked alarmed. "Oh no! I should be seeing her - I've forgot!" she exclaimed worriedly. "She'll think I'm not her friend."

"Alexandra, calm down, Jenny will be fine," Michael reassured her.

They entered the Medical Centre and went to Jenny's ward.

Michael knocked on the door.

"Come in," was the bored reply. Michael and Alexandra entered and they noticed Jenny brighten up, smiling at them.

"Hey Mike, Alexandra, how's training going? Thanks for coming by the way," she asked brightly.

Michael smirked. "Awful," he told her.

Alexandra shook her head. "Seriously Jenny, you should have seen what we had to do today! It was the Slog, it was horrible. We had to climb this huge wall then go on this zip wire where soldiers fired at us. Then there was this beam across this lake which we had to crawl across. Honestly, if Mike hadn't have saved my life, I might have died. He's such a hero," she told Jenny, exaggerating in Michael's opinion.

Michael blushed with embarrassment. "I didn't do that much. It was nothing compared to when you stopped me drowning at the end," he replied.

Alexandra nudged him. "Oh yeah, you were really weak at that swimming," she teased him. "But seriously, you didn't need to take your shirt off."

Michael's blush intensified. "Hey - it helped!" he protested. It was true - clothes would have slowed him down even more.

Alexandra winked at him, and then whispered to Jenny. "He was just showing off."

Michael groaned. Girls were infuriating.

He looked at Jenny and noticed she seemed muted in her excitement. He couldn't blame her. She had been alone all day, while Michael and Alexandra had been in their squad.

Michael cleared his throat. "You okay, Jenny? When do you think you'll be back?" he asked inquisitively. "We're really missing you."

She smiled sadly. "Not full strength yet, but I should be okay for the next competition - that's what the doctor told me," she said.

Michael placed his hand on hers. "Stay strong," he said.

She blushed and smiled. "If I had my way, I'd be out training with you. The stupid doctor claims I'll be better resting this damn ankle," she complained.

Alexandra nodded. "I know," she consoled, placing a hand on Michael's shoulder.

Michael slightly recoiled at the contact, having not been expected it. He glanced at Alexandra, who quickly withdrew her hand.

"Anyway, I'll head off now. I'm going to the fitness suite or something," he said and exited Jenny's room. As soon as he left, he began to hear Alexandra and Jenny arguing about something. He tried to ignore them but their voices carried.

He went out of the Medical Centre and sighed.

Girls were confusing.

18 - A SLIGHT HEADACHE

"Warfare has evolved. Throughout the last century, the scope of warfare has completely changed. Take the First World War, for example. The first time a tank was seen, the Germans had no way to combat it. Yet, in the Second World War, every nation had access to them.

Warfare is constantly changing, and it is our job to stay ahead of the enemy. Throughout history, we have developed new weapons and tactics with varying success," Raines informed them. They were in a tactics and strategy lesson. He pressed a button on his wristwatch and a projection of a tank appeared on the wall. The tank's turret was very wide yet low to the ground.

"1955 - the release of the Dragon Mark One. The world's first main battle tank. Instead of using rolled homogeneous armour, like we had done in World War Two, we opted for an advanced version of composite armour. In those days, the Russians still used shaped charges on their anti-tank guns.

This tank was designed to be a fear weapon, the very embodiment of Shock an' Awe tactics. Made with modern stealth technology to camouflage its heat signature, its purpose was to destroy enemy morale.

This was some of the last actual war footage captured, as the war became too violent to show the civilians for propaganda," Raines explained, and then pressed another button and the footage began playing.

There were about ten tanks rolling out on the battlefield, the camera was in a helicopter high above. The tanks were moving into a town.

As they rolled in, Michael could see bazookas and small arms fire coming from buildings, to which the tanks were completely impervious. He was surprised that they were using guns - he had thought they weren't that sophisticated.

The tanks opened fire on a building. They were armed with high explosive cannons as well as a short range flamethrower.

The Russian soldiers were massacred. Michael noticed Tim wince as they heard the soldiers' cries of pain.

The tanks advanced onto a large grassland.

The cameraman laughed. *"Now, that was easy. These tanks are the best weapon there is. As you can see, they have thermal cameras so they know exactly where the enemy is. No surprise attacks on these boys,"* he said in an American accent.

The tanks continued rolling onwards, untouched. Michael smirked, and then frowned. If these tanks were so good, then why weren't they being used nowadays? He found out soon enough.

The tanks carried on, when suddenly blurred shapes, fifty metres or so in front of them came rushing towards them.

The cameraman swore.

It was the Russians. Not the gun-using ones from earlier, but heavily armed stealth troops, covered in green foliage for camouflage.

The stealth troops opened fire, using odd shaped rocket launchers which fire strange disks at the undersides of the tanks.

The tanks aimed towards the stealth troops and prepared to fire, but the disks detonated, blasting the front tanks straight over onto their backs. Michael was amazed by the sheer power of the weapons.

The remaining tanks rolled around the upturned ones and began opening fire on the Russian stealth troops. Many were blasted apart but the remained stealth troops dived down into some sort of trench.

Michael wondered what they were doing. They seemed to be assembling some sort of mortar.

As the tanks rolled closer to the trench, the weapon fired some sort of shell up in the air. It flew a high arc before exploding over a tank. It exploded into some sort of goo which enveloped the tank.

"It's immobilised," the cameraman remarked. *"They've stopped it."*

The mortar fired again several times, covering the ground in a pool of the goo.

"What's happening?" the pilot shouted.

"I-I don't know," the cameraman admitted. *"It's not going well down there."*

Michael peered closer towards the projection and saw the tanks flamethrowers firing. They burnt through the goo in front of them, but could not rotate.

"The tank's motors are incredibly powerful, it can't stop them," the cameraman stated, though his voice wavered.

But apparently, 'it' could. The Russian soldiers emerged from the trenches and fired their bazookas at the remaining tanks, attaching magnetic projectiles to the undersides of the tanks.

The soldiers then turned and walked away, with the projectiles detonating after about twenty seconds, blasting a hole through the tank and leaving them as lifeless, empty shells.

The cameraman's breathing got faster.

"Let's just get out of here. No way would anyone use this for propaganda. Footage over," the cameraman said and the filming ceased.

"Brand new, expensive battle tanks, beaten by a bunch of stealth troops! Why? Because we were not prepared for them!" Raines impressed. "They were ready for us. Remember what Sun Tzu once said:

"All warfare is based on deception." We thought our tanks were the best there were and could detect any of their soldiers. Had the tanks seen them, they could have radioed in for a missile strike and none of that would have happened. The reason being that they were a step ahead of us, and could camouflage their thermal signature," Raines informed them.

"One might argue that there was no way of us knowing they could do that, but the problem was, they knew we could detect heat. They had accessed our information. In the early days of the war, there were countless spies and double agents: people switching sides. Russians who hated what they were doing, and Americans who were getting paid enough to join them. This is much harder today, but there are still spies in both camps."

Tim spoke up. "Surely someone would notice if there was a Russian in our base. I mean, they're like savages, right?" he questioned.

Raines snorted. "Laddie, ye really think that all Russians are savages? They're just the ones they use against us - who do you think creates the monsters? The Russians are masters of chemical weaponry. You saw that goo, no primitive caveman could create that. And there are plenty of Americans who would switch sides for enough money."

Michael was shocked. He had never really considered that possibility.

"S-Sir," he began. "Does that mean someone in The Institute could potentially be a spy?"

Raines looked at them, hard. "Yes. We've tested the backgrounds of everyone who has taken the tests, but people still slip through. And some people did not 'ave to take the tests," he impressed.

The group was silent, wondering who could be a traitor in The Institute. Raymon? Thomas? Sophie?

Michael sighed. It was useless thinking about that now. He would just have to continue with his training and hope for the best.

As he continued during that day, he felt increasingly drowsy. He found it difficult to concentrate during equipment training as they were being taught how to carry and assemble the H23 pistol.

He felt a throbbing in his head, as though there were something crawling inside his brain. He felt hot, despite the fact it was a cool afternoon.

He tried to focus on the pistol in front of him.

The magazine. It went somewhere.

It went in the ... Michael tried to think but the pain was too severe.

He shook his head almost lethargically and carried on trying to see how it fitted in, but the components in front of him floated around fuzzily.

Someone tapped him on the shoulder. He looked across to see Sergeant Raines looking at him expectantly.

"Having trouble, Bakerson?" he inquired.

Michael shook his head, not wanting to admit his weakness.

"N-no, sir," he said quickly.

Raines raised his eyebrows. "Well, if that's yer best performance, perhaps an evening session of physical training might help ye," he said.

Michael gulped, but didn't want to seem like he was making excuses.

"I'll do better, sir," he apologised.

Raines shook his head. "In war, laddie, there are no second chances. This stuff is important. Sergeant Veyon will see ye in Genghis 12 immediately after this session. I'm sorry laddie, but we gotta be tough here," he informed Michael.

"Five laps of ze hall, zen do sixty press ups!" Sergeant Vellon ordered in his French accent.

Michael and Tim, who had also been given this punishment, set off sprinting. Vellon was known for his uncanny ability to sense people not putting in one hundred percent effort in physical training.

If he caught any of them slacking he often threatened to 'whip you till your skin bleeds'.

Michael ignored his pounding headache. It was bearable as the running did not involve many sharp turns.

The problem came when he did the press-ups.

Everything blurred as he went down to the ground as he experienced a massive head rush.

He tried to focus. Down. Up. Down. Up.

He carried on, but his arms began shaking as the world spun around him. He found he was locked in position. He couldn't push himself up.

His arms ached with the effort, but they just would not obey his brain. He kept trying. His arms shook even more and he closed his eyes as the throbbing in his head grew more painful.

He breathed more rapidly as sweat began to pour down his forehead.

He cried out in agony as his arms finally gave way and he collapsed to the ground. He lost all of his senses as sweet, blissful darkness came and took his pain away.

19 - OUT AND ABOUT

Michael woke up in a bright room. It was all white, and must have been some sort of hospital. He was in a soft bed. Where was he?

He sat up but felt his head begin to pound and quickly lay back down again.

Right. The headache. He was in the Medical Centre. He sighed.

A nurse came in. "Oh good, you're awake. You have a fever, but it should clear up in a few days. It was most likely caused from overexertion. You just need to rest now," she told him.

"Where are my friends?" Michael asked her.

"In training. They will be allowed to visit you when they are finished. In the meantime you must rest," she said before exiting the room.

Michael groaned. Resting? For days? He would die of boredom before he had a chance to get back to training.

He lay back down on his bed and glanced around the room. Suddenly, something caught his eye.

A pile of clothes lay folded neatly in the corner of the room on top of a small table.

Michael frowned. The nurse must have forgotten to mention that she had brought his clothes down.

He laid down his bed once again. He realised that his life at The Institute had been so full of activities that he had had no time to think about it.

He wondered what his family were doing now.

As he thought this, a sickening wave of guilt washed over him.

His family.

He hadn't given them a thought while he was out training. They might be worried about him.

He clambered out of the soft hospital bed and went through the clothes in the corner, searching for the ones he had arrived at The Institute in.

There. He found the trousers his mother had made for him and began searching through the pockets until he found what he was looking for - the only souvenir he had from his village.

The pocket-watch his mother had given him. He sat down on the bed and opened it carefully.

There they were: his smiling, happy family in a black and white photograph that Grandpa Ted had taken.

His caring and protective mother, her arms wrapped around his fragile young sister.

Michael could see himself there, his own bright inquisitive eyes staring back at him. This picture must have been taken around six years ago, for he looked much different now.

He looked at the fourth person in the picture. Although when he first joined The Institute Michael may have felt mixed emotions towards him, now there was only fondness towards his proud, brave father.

Michael had completely forgiven his rant on the day he left the village. His father had always been there for him and it was his one regret he had not parted with him on happier terms.

Michael and his father had always been very close. They had similar personalities and his father had taught him many of the lessons he had needed when growing up such as good morals and strength of character. His father was tall, black haired and had blue eyes which all of his family shared.

His father had been very athletic when young, but had never been accepted into The Institute for a reason that Michael had never been told. He thought back to one of his early memories, being taught to swim in the river in the village. He had always had a fear of the water previously.

* * *

"Come on son, you'll be fine," Dad coaxed, standing waist deep in the water.

Michael shook his head stubbornly. "It's cold," he stated, crossing his arms. He was standing in his underwear at night time in at the edge of the river.

He had agreed to come out only because his father had presented it as an adventure. He hadn't realised he would be forced to swim in the river at night.

"Mikey, it is the only way you can learn. You have to face your fears. Be brave," Dad said.

Michael shivered, still hesitant.

"Michael Bakerson. I won't force you to come in, but you will have proved yourself braver if you do," Dad coaxed.

Even at a young age, Michael still had a sense of pride, so he stepped determinedly into the water. The river was very cold.

"Why can't I wear something?" Michael complained.

"You're doing great. I told you before; clothes will only weigh you down," Dad told him.

Michael then jumped in the rest of the way and shouted out.

"C-c-cold!" he stammered, thrashing about in the water.

Dad steadied him. "Let me tell you a story Michael. It's about courage. There were once a group of people called the Spartans. They were brave and proud warriors, and lived in Ancient Greece. But one day, the Persians wanted to invade Greece. At a place called Thermopylae was where they met.

The Persians had far more men than the Spartans, and a lot of people in Greece were afraid of them. They knew they were going to lose, but they had to fight," Dad told him

"But ... why?" Michael asked, confused.

"They had to show that the Persians could be fought. They were brave. They managed to hold off the Persians for a whole week by holding Thermopylae."

"Did they win?" Michael asked.

Dad shook his head. "No. They were surrounded and killed, but they never surrendered. They fought until they died."

"But then it was pointless!" Michael protested, laughing a little.

"No. It wasn't. Because in the long run, the Greeks won the war. That's what courage is about. You have to make sacrifices in the short term because you know, in the end, it will be worth it," Dad said with a smile.

"You don't have to learn to swim now. But if you can be brave, even though it might be hard, it will help you in the long run. Remember that, Michael."

* * *

Michael smiled fondly as he reminisced. Ever since, swimming hadn't been a problem for him. Whenever he had faced a tough decision, he thought of what the Spartans would have done.

It was a funny coincidence how he had been placed in this squad, but he would do it proud regardless. For his father if no one else.

He found paper and a pen lying on a table and set about writing a letter to his family.

Dear Mum, Dad and Jane,

I'm not really sure how to start this letter, but I wanted to let you know that I'm really enjoying training at the moment. It has been very busy and tough physically, but I'm improving and getting better at what I do.

So far, I've remembered to wash regularly AND cut my nails, so you don't have to worry about that. I'm doing well at The Institute and I have made plenty of new friends. The squad I'm in is really welcoming.

One thing that took me by surprise however is the number of girls at The Institute - I didn't really expect many. I always thought the army was more of a boys' thing. To be honest though, most of the girls here are smarter than the boys - with the exception of Arthur.

Arthur is my friend - he's very clever and amazing with technology. He's like the opposite of Hans, who is our other friend. He's Norwegian and he's incredibly strong.

We have nine people in our squad - me, Hans, Steve, Arthur, Joe, Tim, Teresa, Jenny and Alexandra.

Three girls and six boys - but the girls are friendly. I imagine they would get on well with Jane.

We have two squad leaders - Sergeant Raines, the guy who came to our village, and Sergeant Vellon, a French instructor. They are good leaders and teachers.

I'm really sorry I cannot write more often, but I just want to let you know that all is well here. The luxuries at The Institute are incredible - I have meat every day as well as a hot shower in my room!

I hope you are coping well in the village and that you have enough food - I wish I could send you some of my rations! I hope Jane is progressing well with her preparation for next year's test, and that Grandpa Ted is still alive and well.

Michael

P.S. - By the way, if Dad reads this, I would like him to know that I am grateful for everything he has done for me. I understand that he was angry, but I will try to make him proud. :)

Michael decided he felt well enough to walk, and slipped out of bed and put his shoes on. He then walked out of the building, sneaking past the nurses. He felt slightly nauseous, though he needed to send this letter.

He continued, trying to look like he had to deliver an important document to someone. He wasn't sure whereabouts his village was in relation to The Institute, so he would have to figure out how to get it there somehow. He just hoped that someone would pass it on the way north.

"BAKERSON!" Michael heard the familiar voice of Sergeant Raines roar. "What the hell do ye think yer doin' outside of the Medical Centre?" he demanded angrily.

Michael froze, terrified. "I-I was just trying to send this letter to my f-family," he stammered quietly, intimidated by his squad leader.

Raines softened, giving Michael a sympathetic look. "Alright. I'll take that letter. Next time a truck goes north I'll instruct the driver to drop it off there. But ye still need to rest, sonny. I hope ye didn't pass out for no reason," he said with a small smile.

Michael grinned in relief. "Thank you, sir," he said, handing the letter to him.

Raines nodded. "You better recover fast, Bakerson. The squad will be needing you," he said, then strode off.

Michael smiled, encouraged, then headed back to the Medical Centre. He did feel like he needed to rest a bit before going back to training, as the throbbing in his head had still not subsided.

As he was going back, he saw Steve also heading towards the Medical Centre. He caught him up.

"Hey, Steve, what's up?" he asked jovially.

Steve grinned. "Hey Mike, great to see you're up and about. I was just about to check on you. What the hell happened to you?" he said.

Michael shrugged. "I collapsed yesterday in the physical training. How's the squad?" he asked.

Steve smirked. "Quite a bit has happened since you've been out surprisingly," he remarked.

Michael frowned. "What is it?" he demanded.

"The Spartans have got two new members," Steve replied with a grin. "I think you're going to like them."

20 -   **THE NEW RECRUITS**

"What?" Michael asked, shocked.

"Jürgen and Nadia - German twins. Both dark haired, fairly tall. They seem alright," Steve informed him.

Michael processed this information. He had not expected this. "Right ... okay. H-how're the others taking it?" he asked cautiously.

Steve smirked. "The girls seem to love Jürgen for some reason. I don't get it,"

Michael felt a sense of annoyance, verging on jealousy. "I didn't mean like that," he lied.

Steve shrugged. "Well he seems to gel well with the whole squad. He'd be a great leader," he said, musing to himself.

Michael glared, making Steve realise what he'd said. Angry, he started to walk back into the Medical Centre.

"Crap, Mike, I'm sorry, I didn't mean it like that," Steve said, hurrying after him.

Michael, never one to stay too angry for long, forgave his friend. Steve *had* come to visit him after all.

Michael sighed. "It's alright. It's just ... I feel like everyone has forgotten me,"

Steve laughed. "We'd never forget you Michael," he promised, clapping him on the back.

However, when Michael returned to training three days later, it felt like they had. Jenny had already been released from the Medical Centre so Michael had not seen anyone until Steve's visits after training.

Now though, on a gloomy Monday, he would have his first glimpse of the newcomers. Not even Steve had visited him last night, most likely because there had been a competition the previous night. He hoped that his squad had done well.

He saw the Spartans making their way towards him together. He noticed they all seemed to be happy and talking to each other. He saw the new faces amongst them. Jürgen and Nadia.

Jürgen was taller than Michael, a similar height to Hans, but also very well built and muscular. He had short black hair and pale skin. His eyes were a dark brown.

Nadia was around the same height as Michael. She had flawless skin and black hair, but her hair reached down to the middle of her back. Her eyes were a dark brown and she was very pretty.

Michael noticed the way they carried themselves. Jürgen was very much the centre of the group, amiably chatting with Alexandra and Jenny, whilst Nadia seemed withdrawn and stood alone at the back, presumably shy.

When his squad noticed Michael, they carried on towards him. Steve smiled and stood next to him. "It's good to have you back. We won the competition as well," he informed him.

Alexandra, Jenny and Teresa all began vividly describing the competition.

"Hey Michael, you should have been there yesterday."

"Jürgen was great!"

"We beat the Legionnaires."

"You should have seen how angry Jones was."

"Jürgen punched Raymon in the face!"

Michael was pleased that they had won, but also annoyed that he had had no part in their first victory, especially as they had done so poorly in the first competition when he was leader.

As the girls stepped aside, Michael found himself face to face with Jürgen.

Jürgen smiled at him and extended at hand. "A pleasure to finally meet you, Michael, I've heard a lot about you," he said with a prominent German accent.

Michael shook it firmly. "Nice to meet you too," he said, smiling back, although he didn't feel happy inside.

They both looked at each other evenly, not wanting to break the gaze. Michael noticed Jürgen gripping his hand rather tightly, causing Michael to do the same.

After about twenty seconds, Steve broke them up.

"Come on guys, we can't have you staring at each other all day," he joked, clearly trying to defuse the tension.

Arthur then led Michael over to Nadia. Michael's assumption had been correct; she did seem to be very shy.

She looked down at the ground as he approached.

Michael didn't know what to say.

"Nadia, right?" he began.

She nodded.

He sighed. "Well, I'm Michael," he introduced.

"I know," she said simply. She also had a noticeable German accent.

Michael nodded. "Well, nice to meet you," he said, frustrated by her lack of social skills.

She bit her lip. "Sorry..," she trailed off.

Michael forgave her. "Hey," he said. She looked up. She was even more attractive up close.

He smiled, trying to reassure her. "Don't worry about it, it's fine," he said.

Her mouth twitched. "Thank you."

Michael nodded, and then faced Arthur. "What was the competition like?"

Arthur shrugged. "Alright. We won, but it was kind of all Jürgen. He took charge and planned this ambush. It worked, but ... "Arthur trailed off.

"But what?" Michael asked, concerned.

"I didn't feel like we were part of a team," he commented nervously.

Michael bit his lip. "Hey, well, at least we won."

"Is that all that matters?" Arthur questioned quietly.

Michael considered.

Arthur continued. "You really think they'll take the best squad to the Coliseum? They want the best people they can get, even if that means taking them out from their squads."

Michael shook his head. "I want us all to get through," he said, determined.

"Then we'll have to show that we're a team," Arthur said, before Sergeant Raines interrupted and gathered them around him.

"Alright, Spartans, I have few things to tell yer. Firs', well done with the competition last night. Ye did yerselves proud, and made up for las' weeks' abysmal performance," Raines announced with a smile.

The group exchanged glances, excited.

"And because of this, I've decided to give ye a reward. We're going to the moorlands of Wales for intensive survival training - Jones thinks the recruits aren't tough enough, and I agree. There's no use mollycoddling ye, as that won't 'appen in war," Raines said.

The Spartans groaned collectively. Typical Raines.

The journey to Wales was long, and the Spartans were sat uncomfortably in the back of a truck. Michael listened as Jürgen and Hans argued about which was the most deadly theatre of war - Scandinavia or Central Europe.

Michael sighed. "Guys, can we stop arguing? I was thinking this might be a good time to actually get to know about each other. We are a team after all," he said wearily.

His squad looked at him. Joe snorted, and folded his arms. Jürgen, however, seemed to understand.

"Ja. Michael is right. I'll begin, seeing as I'm the newest," he stated.

Jenny smiled at Jürgen. "Alright, let's hear your story," she said keenly.

"My name is Jürgen Bauer. My sister Nadia and I grew up in a country house owned by our father, a rich German weapons developer. We grew up with our mother and our butler, and had very little contact with the rest of the world. Our father kept us there to protect us from the war.

Our butler, a kind man named Karl, taught us most of what we know about the world. He educated us and taught us English, taught us how to shoot and ride, and made us as ready as we could possibly be for when our father enrolled us here.

We were originally going to be enrolled in *De Kazerne*, the Dutch training academy, but my father thought that the quality of training would be better here," he explained. "And here we are."

Nadia nodded. "Ve vere very lucky," she said.

Michael smiled. "Well, Steve and I grew up in the same village. It wasn't rich, but at least we were away from the war. Anyway, we spent a few weeks taking tests to get into The Institute, and we made it. Usually no one gets into The Institute from our village, but this year there were two.

I lived with my parents and my sister Jane. I hope that she makes it into The Institute next year," he told them.

Teresa cleared her throat. "I grew up in the city with my seven older brothers. They had all tried to get into The Institute, but I was the only one who made it. I never knew my parents, they died when I was a kid," she told them.

Michael felt sorry for her. He couldn't imagine living without his parents.

"We were fairly lucky," Alexandra began. "We had a house. I lived with my dad - he trained me as a child, determined to get me in. I went to school and had some friends there until I got accepted," she explained.

Michael grinned. His squad were actually getting to know each other.

"What is school like?" Teresa asked her.

Alexandra shrugged. "Like here but with boring subjects and none of the army stuff," she told them.

Michael chuckled. His school, if you could even call it that, had not been as bad. It had consisted of a single teacher telling students about various useful subjects, and reading out of extremely battered textbooks.

"What about you, Jenny?" Jürgen asked, glancing at Jenny, whom he was sitting next to.

She blushed. "Oh, you know nothing special. I lived in the country, went to a local school, life a normal life until I took the test. I have a baby brother called Al, and younger sister called Karen. I didn't expect to get in, I mean, there's nothing really special about me," she said.

"Jenny, of course there is. You deserve to be here just as much as anyone else." Jürgen consoled, before Michael had a chance to respond.

Steve spoke up. "What about you, Joe?" he asked, looking at the black boy.

Joe, who had his arms crossed, remained silent.

"Joe, please," Michael said. Joe glanced at him.

"Fine. I grew up in East London in a large family. We all hated the Americans, but I still tried to get in here. I thought it would be a better life than a scavenger. I passed the test, but some instructor didn't want to allow me in because of my colour. She thought I would not be loyal enough to the Western Alliance," Joe stated.

"However, Sergeant Raines convinced them to allow me in, and I made it," he finished, and then slumped back in the corner.

"Why do you hate the Americans?" Tim asked.

Joe glanced at him. "Because what they have done. The exiled my grandfather when all he wanted was equality. Because of them, we've been forced to live in poverty and be treated like second class citizens," he said coldly.

Arthur spoke up. "Your grandfather - I'm guessing he was part of the civil rights movement," he began. "What is your surname, Joe?"

"King," Joe said simply.

"So your grandfather was Martin Luther King," Tim said, impressed. Michael hadn't heard of him, but some of the others had.

Joe glared at him. "Why does that matter? Are you trying to mock me?" he demanded.

Steve interrupted. "Hang on, does that mean your name is Joe King?" he said with a grin. "Or are you *joking?*" he said, bursting out laughing.

The Spartans collectively rolled their eyes at Steve, and even Joe smirked.

"You don't know how many times I've heard that joke," Joe said wearily.

* * *

Eventually, Michael managed to get to sleep, and he found himself in some nightmare. He could see a light in the distance, and he ran towards it. He was being chased by some monstrous creatures.

He got closer to the light, and found himself in front of a large gate. He looked up and saw his squad at the top.

"Let me in!" he shouted up desperately, but they just laughed at him.

"Please!" he begged.

"We don't want you," Jenny said, but her voice was cold. *"We have Jürgen. He's our leader now," she said,* wrapping her arms around Jürgen.

Jürgen was standing up high, laughing cruelly. *"Leave him to die!"* he ordered, and the squad turned and left. *"Jürgen, Jürgen!"* they chanted as they left.

"No, please!" Michael shouted, but darkness consumed him.

* * *

He woke up in the back of the truck. Everyone asleep except for Arthur. He looked around at Jürgen, who was sitting next to Jenny.

Michael shook his head. It was stupid. They were a squad. They were a team.

Jürgen was just another person - there was nothing he needed to worry about. What was it about him Michael felt was so threatening?

His squad would still want him as leader, wouldn't they?

21 - **MOVING FORWARD**

Eastern United States of America

"Are you sure that this machine is viable for my department? Technological Integration is for quality items that can help the Western Alliance. I decide whether we fund inventions and technology so this better impress me," a pale, black haired man stated coolly. His name was Captain Blackburn, a tall man who managed to intimidate most men despite his slender frame. He was known for his lack of emotion and moral ambiguity, and that was why the military had placed him in this position. They needed Blackburn to be as ruthless as possible.

"Yes, quite sure. They're made to help rescue injured soldiers from dangerous situations. Incredibly durable, equipped with various tools to help access hard to reach areas," the young man explained keenly. His name was Alberto Morales, a Mexican scientist of twenty years of age.

"So you did not make them for combat?" Blackburn remarked with a smirk.

Morales shook his head. "No. They are designed to help people, not to harm them," he stated firmly.

Blackburn raised his eyebrows. "I see," he drawled. "Carry on."

"Now, as you can see, they are made with titanium frames, making them almost indestructible. They will be resistant to debris, gunfire, acids and most physical attacks. This means they will be able to move into combat zones and rescue injured humans," Morales explained.

"Next, we have the tools. Their 'hands', so to speak, can be equipped with pneumatic drills, carbon steel cutters, and various other items. Moving on-"

"Can they be armed with weapons?" Blackburn interrupted.

Morales hesitated. "They are designed to help people, Captain. Unless they are reprogrammed, their first priority is human survival," he informed Blackburn.

Blackburn waited. Morales did not say anything more.

In the end, Blackburn relented. "Carry on," he ordered.

Morales nodded. "They are controlled by a central computer which is currently located at my apartment. With a military investment, I can transfer the system to a much more secure location and improve its capabilities," he explained.

Blackburn held up a hand to stop him. "Does the computer control the robots?" he interrupted.

Morales shook his head. "No. They have their own artificial intelligence. The computer is only required to make updates to the programming."

Blackburn nodded. "Show me them. How many do you have?" he asked Morales.

"Just one prototype currently," Morales answered nervously.

"One? How long would it take to produce … say, twenty?" Blackburn asked.

"Well, a few months most likely," Morales admitted.

Blackburn sighed. "Would they be ready to be unveiled for the Coliseum?" he inquired.

Morales nodded. "Yes."

"Alright. Let's see it," Blackburn said.

Morales took him to where stood a humanoid robot, like a skeleton but much more powerful. It had cold, unblinking robotic eyes, and a dull metallic face without a nose and a small slit for a mouth.

Blackburn actually smiled. "Perfect," he commented. "Mr Morales, what will we need you for if we do decide to take these robots?" he asked.

Morales frowned. "Well, I know how to program them," he explained.

"But what if you were unavailable?" Blackburn questioned.

"Well, then you would need someone else to program to robots. Someone good with computers. Someone good with machines."

* * *

Michael trudged through the rain, gritting his teeth and rubbing his hands together. He was in the Welsh moorlands, along with the rest of his squad.

The Spartans currently had to do a twenty mile trek, carrying all their equipment with them, with a one night stop. All they had been given outside of food and equipment was a map and a six-figure grid reference of the location they had to reach.

He glanced across at Arthur, who seemed to be finding it especially difficult. He was shivering.

"Are you okay?" he asked his friend with concern

"I'm fine," Arthur said robotically, then glanced at Michael and sighed. "I just ... I mean, I expected the army to be physically demanding, but he had thought the Western Alliance would focus more on the technological aspect of training," he admitted.

Michael nodded. "I get what you mean," he agreed. It was cold, wet and muddy, and Michael hoped that they would make it to their destination soon.

He carried on going, but the uneven hilly ground made it hard to keep his footing. He forged onwards, but slipped, tumbling down the hill, his heavy bag dragging him down. After what seemed like ages of falling, he stopped, hitting the ground hard.

Michael lay there for a minute, sinking down into the muddy ground. The rain had sapped his energy. He glanced upwards at the enormous hill he had to climb and internally groaned.

Maybe he could just stay here.

"Michael," he heard a voice say. "Get up."

He recognised the voice as Arthur's but made no movement. He didn't have the energy.

"Michael, I know it's hard, but things will get better. You can make it," he heard Arthur's voice say. "It's a journey. You have to move on from where you are. Come on as my dad said: when the going gets tough, the tough get going."

Michael smiled slightly at his friend's attempts at motivation. He clambered to his feet and got him. He would keep going.

Arthur, was right, life was a journey. He just had to keep moving forward.

22 - SPONSORS AND PROSPECTS

Eastern United States of America

Blackburn paced up and down. "Are you telling me that *no one else* can understand those machines?" he demanded angrily.

It was one week after Morales had first showed his robots to him. His assistant, a young black man from Central Africa named Solomon, nodded. "Yes sir. We've tried military scientists and engineers. None of them seem to be able to fathom how Morales has made the robots work."

"What about Techno?" Blackburn asked.

'Techno' was the nickname given to a mysterious vigilante who operated in the impoverished areas on the outskirts of the city.

Techno apparently had once been an inventor who had pitched his ideas to the military but had been ridiculed. Following this, he had been committed to getting back at the military.

'Getting back' involved leaving bombs in military installations and sabotaging inventions which the military had decided to endorse. At the scene of each crime, there was usually a note left reminding the military to do more looking after the poorer people of the town.

Techno was infuriating for Blackburn, as they knew almost nothing about him. He seemed to be fond of hacking into the CCTV of military buildings, meaning that they did not even know what Techno looked like now.

"You believe that Techno may be able to understand the robots?" Solomon asked.

"Techno would be a powerful ally," Blackburn stated.

"We have been unable to locate him," Solomon informed him.

Blackburn nodded. "In which case, we keep looking. I will organise a sponsored trip to the various military academies around the world to evaluate potential prospects. While I'm there, I'll keep an eye out for anyone who might be able to understand these machines."

"What about Mr Morales?" Solomon asked.

"He's too stubborn. As soon as we find someone who can reprogram his robots to fight, we will send him off to Guantanamo Bay," Blackburn said.

Solomon nodded. "Very well. Arrangements will be made."

* * *

Raines cleared his throat as he faced the Spartans.

"Alright lads, this week in Wales has been a goodun. Ye've done well. If it were up to me, I'd keep you out here fer most of yer training. Unfortunately, I ain't in charge and Jones has recalled us back to The Institute," he explained.

"Why sir?" Jenny asked curiously. The Spartans had appreciated being away from Vellon's physical training and the monotonous equipment lessons for the past week.

Raines raised his eyebrows. "The Institute is being visited by sponsors. Personally I don't give a damn about them, but *apparently* they are very important to yer futures."

"What are sponsors for?" Tim asked.

Raines shrugged. "They are businessmen and military officers here to view promising recruits and have their name attached to them to gain publicity for their company. They're all rich bastards who just want more fame," he said casually as he got into the driver's seat of their truck.

Michael and the others got in the back.

"So what's in it for us?" Steve asked.

"Financial backing, and the fact ye can show the Yanks that we're going to smash them in the next Coliseum," Raines told them with a chuckle.

"But in all honesty lads, this is yer first real chance to prove yerselves. Lieutenant Jones'll be much more likely to pick recruits with sponsors for the Coliseum, as that will get us much better equipment to train with," Raines advised them.

* * *

When they arrived back at The Institute, they found the rest of the recruits lined up in their squads.

"Sergeant Raines. Good of you to finally join us," Jones drawled as the Spartans lined up.

The recruits all watched as a huge transport helicopter descended and finely dressed people began striding out.

"Welcome to The Institute," Jones announced as he walked forward to meet the sponsors. "It's a pleasure that you could join us."

Michael watched them. The sponsors all strutted around, as though parading themselves, as Jones spoke with them.

A large man with a pale face and a hooked nose interrupted Jones. "Who are the best prospects?" he demanded.

Jones gulped. "Erm, yes, Mr Collins, I'll read them out now," he said hurriedly.

Michael looked at the man. Mr Collins? This must be Raymon's father. They looked very similar. They both had cruel faces and large bodies, as well as an arrogant swagger when they walked.

"Please could the following people step forward," Jones read out from a sheet of paper.

"Raymon Collins," Michael noticed his father smirk. "Sophie Montague, Jürgen Bauer, Dan Fisher, Oliver Lee, Mark Thompson, Thomas Blackhurst, Alan McGregor, Darius Finch, Paul Adams, Thomas Butler, Dominic Butler, Elizabeth Walker and Carl O'Hara," he finished, and the recruits stepped forward.

Michael was annoyed he had not been chosen. He saw Sophie from the Jaegers, and obviously Jürgen from his own squad.

He noticed a pale man standing in the background. He watched as this pale man approached Lieutenant Jones and spoke to him.

Jones nodded.

"Might I speak to the technological instructor?" the pale man drawled. Sergeant Albrecht, the German instructor that oversaw zone Alexander, the equipment zone, stepped forward and went over to the pale man.

They spoke for several minutes before Sergeant Albrecht faced the recruits.

"Please could Darius Finch and Arthur Roebuck come here." Sergeant Albrecht stated, and Arthur went over to him nervously, alongside a boy from the 'prospects' group.

"Alright lads!" Raines announced to the rest of them. "There will be a wee competition for all ye recruits, to show what yer made of. As the sponsors have requested, there will be a specialised arena that we have prepared, as well as various weapons and equipment ye can use. If you'd like to follow me."

Raines began walking through The Institute, whilst all the recruits followed him, chatting nervously between them.

"Damn," Steve said. "We've been in Wales for a week, we'll be behind technology wise."

Michael sighed. "Yeah. We'll have to do our best though," he said. He wanted to impress the sponsors, but he wasn't sure if he would be chosen as squad leader.

When they reached the 'arena', the recruits were amazed. In the centre was a huge tower surrounded by small buildings. The buildings were dilapidated but seemed to be holding up. In the distance he noticed a large clock tower which Michael recognised.

Back at his village, Grandpa Ted had a room which was full of photos of places he had visited. When Michael had first seen it, he had been in awe. He could see pictures of the Hadrian's Wall, the Giant's Causeway, Loch Ness and Stonehenge.

Michael recognised the clock tower as Big Ben, formerly one of London's famous landmarks. However, now it was unkempt and empty. Ever since the Second Blitz of 1965 which decimated most of England, there had been very few people who had lived in the capital. Until the Americans arrived.

"This is our practice urban warzone," Raines explained. "It represents a typical town, however to test your skills of adaptation, we have placed various items of weaponry and technology inside buildings and around the arena. The central tower is of great strategic importance, however it is locked currently."

He let that sink in for a few seconds. "You will remain in yer existing squads. All the squads will be released at the same point. You will have five minutes to prepare before combat begins. It will be last squad remaining who wins. Any questions?"

Brooke raised a hand. "What level of force are we permitted to use?" he asked in his brutish voice.

Sergeant Raines looked at him. "You are not permitted to seriously injure your opponent. You can use hand to hand combat but you cannot use melee weapons. And the bullets are rubber. Once you've been shot you won't want to continue, unless you have body armour," he informed them. "The competition will begin soon."

The recruits descended into conversation once again as Raines approached the Spartans. Michael hadn't noticed but Arthur had arrived with the rest of them whilst Raines had been speaking.

"Alright, lads," he said to their squad in a low voice. "We haven't trained in weapons - I didn't think this would come so soon. For that, I apologise. But yer all smart lads. Ye can figure it out," he faced Arthur. "That tower is of great strategic importance. I hope you make the right decisions," he said cryptically.

"What was that about?" Steve questioned.

"He's obviously trying to tell us something," Jenny said.

Arthur nodded. "He's saying that we should capture the tower," he stated.

"But it's locked, he said that before," Steve pointed out.

"So we unlock it," Michael countered.

"How do we do that?" Hans asked.

Michael looked at Arthur, who nodded.

"I can get us in," Arthur stated determinedly.

23 - THE TOWER

Michael smiled. "Great. What will you need?" he asked.

"Access to the tower gate control panel," Arthur stated.

Jürgen arrived, having travelled in cars with the sponsors. "I'm sure ve can get you that," he said, immediately taking charge.

"The tower has two entrances. I suggest we enter the buildings in front of the tower during our preparation time and locate some veapons; vhilst Arthur breaks us in to the tower. From there ve close the door once we are all inside and achieve a dominant position vithin the arena."

"Who should go with Arthur?" Teresa asked Jürgen. Michael felt a little annoyed that he had not been consulted, but he didn't want to cause a fuss. Jürgen considered.

"Michael, Hans and Nadia should search the house on our right. Jenny and I vill accompany Arthur. Tim, Teresa, Alexandra and Steven shall search the building on our left. Try to find some body armour - that vill be critical," Jürgen told them.

"Thirty seconds remaining!" Raines announced through a megaphone. Michael looked around at his group.

"Alright," he said. "Let's give this a go."

The Spartans prepared to run. "Good luck," Nadia said to him.

Michael smiled. "You too."

A whistle was blown, and the recruits all sprinted off. The other squads seemed to underestimate the importance of the tower and ran towards other buildings. The only other notable structure was a factory about a mile away, which a lot of recruits began running towards.

Michael was the first one into his assigned house. It was a small bungalow, of only one floor and had a heavy machine gun on the table in the kitchen, along with some body armour.

"Hans, take that, quickly. You'll be strongest to carry that gun. Get to the tower and cover Arthur," he instructed, already checking for more equipment. In a cupboard he found several flash grenades and a pistol.

"Nadia, I've got you a gun!" Michael shouted back, glancing over his shoulder.

He saw her holding a large object. He turned and noticed that it was a sleek black sniper rifle.

"Well, you don't really need pistol then," he said with a smirk as Nadia admired the weapon.

"I will be able to cover you from a distance. Give me the pistol in case I run into trouble," she told him, and Michael obliged, handing it over to her.

"Do you know how to use it?" Michael asked, knowing she hadn't had much time learning how to assemble the weapons as she had recently arrived with Jürgen.

"Please," she said, raising an eyebrow. "I've been shooting since I was a child. I'm sure I can get the hang of this."

She then left the building, leaving Michael feeling a bit stupid. He hadn't ever fired a gun, rubber bullets or not. This was their first exercise where they were able to actually fire guns; previously they had only practised assembling them.

He was startled by the sound a large blaring honk of a horn. The five minutes of preparation time were up.

The contest had begun.

Michael made to leave the house when he tripped over a loose floorboard. He glanced at it and noticed a glint of light coming from underneath it. There was something down there. He wrenched up the floorboard and discovered a jet-black assault rifle.

He hastily grabbed it and sprinted out of the building. He could see the tower about one hundred metres away, but it was under heavy fire. He saw Jürgen, Jenny and Arthur there trying to get in.

Hans was outside the front of the tower drawing most of the fire, but he was protected by his body armour, and returning it with his heavy machine gun.

He noticed Steve was also with Hans, armed with a rifle. The pair seemed to be concentrating their fire on a tall house that was about two hundred metres away.

Michael weighed up his options. He could either try to sneak up on the tall house and take out whoever was firing at them, or stay with Hans and Arthur.

However, he glimpsed three figures heading off towards the house. Alexandra, Teresa and Tim. He wouldn't need to support them, so he ran over to where Arthur was and handed Jürgen the assault rifle. He now only had the flash grenades, whereas Arthur and Jenny were unarmed.

"You're a better shot," Michael explained in regards to Jürgen's confused look.

"Thank you," Jürgen replied, but Michael was looking at Arthur. "How's it going?" he asked.

Arthur ignored him, engrossed in his work. "Navigate the control panel. There's usually an emergency fuse somewhere," he muttered to himself.

Hans was still covering them whilst the four of them waited for Arthur to release the door.

"This is like the Battle of Endor," Jenny commented with a smirk. "With that door they have to break open to get into the base."

Jürgen and Michael both gave her blank looks.

"Did ve vin that battle?" Jürgen asked her.

Jenny looked shocked. "You mean you haven't seen -" she began, but was interrupted.

"Got it," Arthur said triumphantly, and the door slid upwards smoothly. The four of them quickly hurried in, relieved that they were out of the line of fire.

Michael studied the tower. It was dark on the inside, with smooth metallic walls. This building had clearly been built by the Western Alliance as it contrasted dramatically with the houses they had seen earlier. From the ground floor Michael could see some steep iron steps leading up to the next level.

"Nice work, Arthur," Jenny said, smiling at him.

Jürgen nodded. "Very well done. Steve and Hans should be able to use this door as a natural choke point. Can we close it?" he asked Arthur. "Michael, check for weapons."

117

Michael made his way towards the stairs, glancing back while Arthur and Jürgen discussed how best to defend the building.

"Guys, stop," Jenny said suddenly, looking at the other door at the other side of the tower, directly opposite. "I hear something."

They all froze, just as the opposite door slid open.

Everyone turned to face the other entrance, and saw Darius Finch, the boy who had been brought forward by Sergeant Albrecht with Arthur earlier, smiling cockily.

He was backed by his whole squad, the Praetorians, most of whom were armed with weapons. There were about ten of them in total.

Michael didn't hesitate. He unhooked the pin and chucked one of his flash grenades towards the group, causing them to scatter and take cover.

He then sprinted upstairs, hearing a loud bang as it exploded below. He heard many shouts and gunshots.

Michael reached the second level. Just like the ground one it was jet black and metallic. He quickly scanned around, looking for anything that might be of use as a weapon.

The floor was the same size as the one below, about ten metres long, and had many narrow windows which they could fire out of. He then glimpsed another set of stairs and sprinted up those too.

He needed weapons. Fast.

When he reached the third level, he found a whole rack full of them. Several assault rifles, pistols and sniper rifles were hung up against the walls, and in the centre of the room was a desk with several computer monitors.

He went over to the desk and noticed the monitors all had feeds of different locations on. He could see Teresa, Alexandra and Tim sneaking their way towards the building that had been firing on them.

He then noticed the feed for the lower floor of the tower he was in.

Jürgen, Jenny and Steve were all lying on the floor in pain. They must have been shot. Hans was slowly backing into a corner, constantly firing at the entrance from whence the Praetorians had come in. However, the Praetorians were hiding behind the outside of the tower, only appearing to fire several shots before ducking out of sight again.

Soon Hans would need to reload.

He looked at the floor of the tower. There were four Praetorians lying down, meaning Darius Finch and five others were still active.

He watched, horrified, as the Praetorians all ran through the entrance at once. Hans fired taking one of them down, but Darius fired some shots from his handgun, one of which hit Hans in the neck.

Hans was knocked back, and fell to the ground. One of the Praetorians seized his moment and dived on him, trying to wrestle the gun from his grip.

Hans carried on struggling until one of the Praetorians, a squat beady eyed girl with a red birthmark on her cheek, smashed Hans in the head with the butt of her gun.

Michael was shocked. That move was illegal, Raines had told them.

Darius glanced at the girl. "You shouldn't have done that, Daisy," he stated.

'Daisy' snorted. "No one will know," she wheezed. She sounded like her throat had been stepped on. Michael wondered what was wrong with her.

"That is incorrect," Darius said coolly. "There is a camera watching us. You will take full responsibility for your actions. Now, go upstairs and eliminate the remaining Spartan in this tower," he ordered.

Daisy looked worried. She snarled and went upstairs, muttering to herself.

Michael looked along the racks on the wall, searching for an appropriate weapon for close quarter combat.

A sniper? No. A pistol? Maybe. A shotgun? Definitely.

Michael lifted up the pump action weapon from its resting place. He had not had very much experience assembling these weapons but he knew how it worked.

He crouched at the side of the doorway.

Hopefully, she would be distracted by the monitor in the centre and advance towards that, giving him a clear shot.

He listened as Daisy advanced up the stairs.

"Alright, ya little Spartan, where are ya?" she called, and he heard her footsteps getting closer and closer.

He heard her stop in the doorway.

"Now what's this?" she muttered and she advanced towards the computer monitor.

Michael didn't hesitate. He pumped back his shotgun and fired it at her exposed back.

The recoil sent the shotgun thudding back into his shoulder, but that was nothing compared to the damage it did to Daisy. The bullets, fired from less than two metres away, were blasted straight into her back, sending her sprawling to the floor.

Michael was impressed with the power of his weapon. He stood up and went over to her body. The girl was lying on the ground, seemingly unconscious after having hit her head on the floor.

He regarded the girl with mixed feelings. He felt slightly guilty at causing this much pain to someone, but after what she had done to Hans, she definitely deserved it.

He glanced at the monitors. Darius had stood up, having heard the sound of the shotgun go off.

"Well, it is clear that Bakerson is more prepared than us. He has the higher ground and in a bottleneck such as this building, he can quite possibly beat us if we do not play our strategy right," Darius stated to his teammates as he paced back and forth. "We have already underestimated our opponents once, by not predicting that they would enter this building. It is critical to not do so again."

"But without the upper floor, this tower is useless," a robustly built recruit claimed. He was square jawed and had a very short brown hair.

"Actually Peter, that is not entirely true. We have enough weapons and ammunition here, as well as two sets of body armour. That is enough to hold the ground floor. Bakerson is effectively trapped here," Darius explained. "Now the doors are open, others will come in. So we stay on the ground floor watching the entrance. Bakerson

120

won't come down, so we won't need to watch him. Peter and I will go outside and hunt the opposition."

Michael smiled to himself. There would now only be two Praetorians he would have to beat. He watched as Darius disappeared out of the camera's field of view.

He looked around at the weapons rack. As there were two of them to deal with he would need something other than a shotgun.

Michael picked up two sub machine guns, strapping one around his chest and gripping the other in his hand. He would go downstairs, throw one of his flash grenades to disorientate the two Praetorians, and then open fire with his machine guns.

He hesitated, before putting some body armour on. He might need it in case they tried to return fire.

As he made his way downstairs, he could hear the Praetorians firing at people outside. Hopefully the rest of his squad were doing alright.

He reached the final set of stairs. He could see the back of someone - a girl. He cautiously unhooked the pin from his flash grenade, and rolled it through her legs.

He then quickly hid behind the doorway again.

"Two ... three ... four .... five ..," he counted, before the flash grenade exploded, and he heard a loud bang from within the room.

He sprinted in, letting loose with his submachine gun on girl he had seen earlier, who collapsed to the floor, her knees buckling.

Michael then looked around the room. The other person in the room, a short, squat boy was still reeling, shielding his eyes from the blast.

Michael didn't hesitate and let rip with his machine gun on the boy, who was immediately riddled and lying on the floor in pain.

He smiled in relief, and then knelt down next to Hans, setting his submachine gun on the floor next to an injured Jürgen. "Hans are you alright?" he asked him. Hans was unresponsive.

Michael sighed, and then went over to Steve.

121

"Steve? Are you alright?" he asked.

Steve groaned a little, but otherwise there was no response either.

Michael stood up, before being hit with a blow like a sledgehammer in his chest. His breath was knocked out of him as bullets thudded into his body armour. He was knocked onto the ground.

He tried to unstrap his other gun from his chest, but a foot stamped down on his arm. He looked up and saw the triumphant face of Darius Finch standing over him.

"Did you really think I didn't know that you could see through the cameras?" Darius gloated. "I knew you would fall for it. You thought you were so clever, coming down and taking out my friends. But you fell for the bait," he mocked Michael with a smirk.

Michael was about to reply, before something slammed into Darius and sent him reeling in pain.

He glanced across and saw Jürgen gripping Michael's other submachine gun whilst still lying on the floor.

Michael then threw himself at Darius' ankles, tackling him to the ground.

"Peter!" Darius yelled, and Michael was dimly aware of a figure appearing at the doorway of the building.

His stomach lurched as he leapt to his feet, wrenching Darius' limp body and intending to use it as a shield against Peter.

But as he stood up, he realised it wasn't Peter standing in the doorway.

24 -   TRICKED

It was Joe.

"Joe?" Michael said incredulously, letting Darius fall to the floor. He had completely forgotten about his squad mate.

Joe glared at him. "For your information I do exist and I am in your squad. Peter's down. Now let's hold this goddamn building," the coloured boy said, accessing a control panel on the wall, and making the door slide shut. Michael went and closed the other door.

"We keep both doors closed at all times," Joe said, taking charge.

Jürgen climbed to his feet. "No. We have to keep one open in case our other squad mates come," he said.

Joe shook his head. "No. There is a small screen on the control panel. Michael can use that to see who is coming in and let them in if they're one of us," he explained to Jürgen.

Michael felt indignant. "Why do I have to be the door monitor?" he protested, annoyed that he didn't have a say in it.

Joe shrugged, but Jürgen spoke. "We can shoot better," he explained diplomatically.

Michael was still angry, but nodded. He didn't want to argue with them. "Okay. The weapons stash is on the top floor," he told them.

"Thank you," Jürgen said gratefully, but Michael refused to meet his eye.

Joe and Jürgen then walked upstairs.

Michael sighed and began walking between the control panels, checking for activity. There was nothing.

The clouds in the distance seemed to grow steadily darker, floating towards the arena. The dull grey houses, once inhabited by families, were empty. The streets, once hubs of activity, were lifeless.

Thunder boomed in the sky, and rain began to trickle down.

After what seemed like hours, Michael noticed a figure making its way towards the tower through the downpour. Jürgen and Joe had been firing from upstairs, yet Michael had barely seen anyone.

"Hello?" he heard a voice call.

Michael squinted in at the small camera screen in the control panel.

When he saw who was standing out there in the rain he couldn't help smiling.

It was Sophie. She still looked nice, even when soaked.

"I'm not supposed to let you in," he replied cautiously, though felt pleased that she needed him for something.

"We're still allies, right?" she asked with a grin, though Michael could see her shivering slightly.

Michael bit his lip. "Only one squad can win," he said uncertainly. He couldn't just let her in too easily, she would suspect something.

"Please, it's just me. I'll help you, I promise," Sophie pleaded.

Michael sighed. He looked torn, as his fingers hovered over the control panel.

"Fine," he said, pressing a button as the door slid smoothly open. He tensed up in case she tried anything.

Sophie ran in, embracing Michael.

"Thank you," she whispered. He was shocked, but smiled slightly. She smelled nice.

Michael opened his mouth to speak, but he was suddenly thrown to the floor by Sophie. He hit the ground, hard, with the wind being knocked out of him.

Sophie placed a knee on his chest, grinning triumphantly.

"That was too easy, Michael," she gloated. "This is war; you can't show pity to the enemy."

"I thought we were friends," Michael seethed, furious. She had betrayed his trust, and humiliated him.

Sophie laughed. "Like I said, this is war," she said, before smashing her fist into Michael's temple, causing him to hit his head on the hard floor.

Michael didn't have time to cry out before a wave of darkness rushed up to him.

25 - TURNING THE TABLES

As Sophie walked to check the floor above them, Michael sprang into action.

Thank God for that body armour, otherwise the impact would have hurt a lot more. He would not have much time before Sophie's squad, the Jaegers, arrived through the open door.

He climbed to his feet, still not feeling great. He squinted out into the rain. It would take some time for the Jaegers to make it across to the tower so he calculated he had several minutes before the door had to be closed.

Michael took a deep breath, and then began making his way upstairs to find Sophie. She had taken his gun, but he would have the element of surprise.

He crept up stealthily, hoping she would not hear him. He would have to take her out quickly. Jürgen and Joe would most likely not be checking the monitors, as they would be too busy firing at the other squads from the top floor.

However, up in the top room, Joe *was* looking at the monitors. He was leaning back his chair and watching the screen that showed the Jaegers debating whether to rush for the building.

"You know, if Michael's plan works, it'll be pretty effective," Joe remarked. "Are you ready with the heavy machine gun?"

"Ja. Vhen they start moving I will set it up. Is that girl still here?" Jürgen asked.

Joe glanced at the monitors. "Yeah, she's surprise attacking us. Michael should have her though," he commented casually.

Jürgen narrowed his eyes at Joe. "You are very laid-back, Joe. You don't seem to be taking this seriously," he accused.

Joe shrugged. "We're not gonna lose," he said cockily.

Jürgen glared at him. "Ve might vith that attitude. Sort it out!" he ordered in his German accent.

"Piss off," Joe retorted, rolling his eyes and glancing at the screen. "The Jaegers are coming, get ready."

Michael stood at the top of the stairs and peeked a glance in. Fortunately, Sophie was entirely focused on the floor above.

He waited, taking deep breaths. What should he do? If she saw him coming, she would shoot him. He would need a distraction.

He glanced around the room. What could he use?

But before he could make up his mind, he heard Jürgen shout from upstairs.

"Michael, I'm coming down!"

Michael didn't hesitate. He knew Sophie would fire as soon as Jürgen appeared, so he charged at her.

Sophie, too intent on the stairs to the floor above, only had time to glance in his direction before he slammed into her.

Her body crashed into the wall making her drop the gun. This would be easy now.

Sophie reacted quickly however, kneeing him in the groin. Michael gritted his teeth as intense pain shot through him.

Maybe not.

He needed to get her on the floor where he would have the advantage due to his (hopefully) superior strength.

She threw a punch at his head and he was forced to step backwards to avoid it.

Adrenaline was pumping through Michael's body as he faced her. He needed to subdue her for the plan to work.

Sophie eyed the gun on the floor, but she knew she couldn't get it without Michael getting her first. She would have to take him down.

Michael lunged forward, hoping to take her to the ground, but she sidestepped away from him and the gun.

Michael considered. He had body armour, meaning he could take one of her punches.

He'd have to just go for it then. He sprinted at her, his arms out wide in case she tried to go around him.

Sophie scooted back, but he swiped at her, managing to get a grip of her shirt.

He didn't hesitate. He gripped tightly and pulled himself forward, taking her legs out and throwing his weight towards her, using the same move he had done on Teresa in training that time.

It worked.

Michael slammed her into the ground, his back on top of Sophie's chest. One of his legs was between hers so she couldn't wriggle away.

But for some reason, she didn't try to.

"You've got me now," she whispered coyly, moving a hand around his waist.

Michael couldn't deny it - he was tempted.

But he remembered what she had done earlier and hardened.

"Like you said Sophie, this is war," he said with a slight smirk, before raising his elbow and smashing it right into her nose.

Sophie's eyes rolled back in her head as her head lolled back, concussed.

Michael stood up, heart pounding, as Jürgen came down the stairs and passed him. Jürgen barely glanced at Michael and he carried on downstairs.

Oliver squinted out into the rain. He was a member of Sophie's squad, the Jaegers. Although small and weedy, he was a fast runner, and respected for his quick-thinking.

"The gate's open. Sophie did it," Oliver remarked.

Dan nodded. "She did. Let's go," he said, and then began sprinting through the rain towards the open tower door.

Oliver rolled his eyes as the Jaegers followed Dan. This was almost too easy.

Joe watched through the monitors lazily. Jürgen was downstairs, setting up a heavy machine gun. Visibility would be poor in the rain, but Joe could help with that.

Joe walked over to where the huge array of weapons was. He needed something that would catch Jürgen's attention.

He smirked as he saw something.

That would be perfect.

Jürgen, having set up the gun, waited downstairs for any glimpse of the Jaegers. They must have started running by now, but all he could see was pouring rain.

He thought to himself. If their strategy worked, he could really impress the sponsors and hopefully earn a better position for his future in the army.

That was the main reason why he was here, although he would never admit it to anyone. Jürgen knew that what he did would have very little impact on the war, but he wanted to secure a better future for himself and Nadia. He didn't care how he achieved that, as long as he did.

He watched outside, his hand resting on the trigger of the heavy machine gun. He pitied anyone who would be on the receiving end of the weapon.

Suddenly, he saw a bright red flare fly down from above him and land in the distance, and smiled.

Joe was a genius. Jürgen aimed his heavy machine gun towards the flare, and prepared to let loose the destructive power it contained.

The Jaegers were about to be annihilated.

"I think we've seen enough," Raines stated coolly, as many sponsors flinched upon seeing the damage Jürgen's heavy machine gun was causing. "We don't want to kill our recruits."

The instructors and sponsors were all sat in a lounge with many comfortable chairs and screens as footage of the competition played out before them.

Jones looked towards the sponsors, awaiting their opinion.

"Scottie's right, this thing has gotten boring," Alfred Collins drawled lazily.

Jones went bright red, before quickly speaking into the megaphone. "P-please could all recruits return to the starting point immediately," he stated, while Raines took charge.

"Alright, sponsors. Yeh've seen the recruits in action. On the screens will be the pictures of the recruits and what squad they're in. If yer interested, please speak to a squad leader," he said gruffly. He didn't like being called Scottie.

Alfred Collins stood up and went immediately to talk to Jones, presumably about Raymon, while the other sponsors talked amongst themselves.

Raines went to a chair in the corner of the room and leant back on it. He had been impressed by the Spartans' performance, and expected at least one sponsor to approach him.

Sure enough, one did.

Sheikh Bakir was a short fat Arabic man, who was obsessed with his own wealth. He had made his money by taking control of vast oil reserves in the Middle East and selling them to the Western Alliance. He tended to waddle around and would have been a laughing stock if it were not for his two tough-looking bodyguards that followed him at all times.

He bumbled forward and planted his large bottom on the seat opposite Raines. He wore excessive amounts of gold jewellery and wore long golden robes. He had a long black beard which covered up his lack of neck. He had a very flat and wide nose that seemed to cover most of his face.

"Sergeant Raines, it is a pleasure to meet you," he spoke in a deep throaty voice. "A pleasure," he repeated, nodding his head slowly.

Sergeant Raines nodded. "Alright, let's get to it. Which one are you interested in?" he asked.

Sheikh Bakir nodded his head very slowly. "Yes .... I am," he said slowly. "I would like ... to sponsor ..," he deliberated slowly, as though his fat clogged up his throat.

"Who?" Raines demanded, his patience wearing thin.

"Jür-gen Bau-er. Mich-ael Baker-son. Joe-seph King. Nad-ia Bau-er," the fat man said very slowly.

"Jürgen, Michael, Joe and Nadia? Alright. I'll give ye an audience with 'em." Sergeant Raines said, noting down the names. "Anything else?" he inquired briskly.

"Any-thing else ... I do not believe so ...." Sheikh Bakir deliberated very slowly.

"Alright, now go," Sergeant Raines told him, not having much respect for this man.

"It has been a pleasure," the Sheikh drawled as his bodyguards helped him to his feet. "A pleasure," he repeated before waddling back to the middle of the room.

Raines rolled his eyes. "Fat bastard," he muttered to himself as he scanned the room.

He noticed a tall, bony woman making her way towards him. He recognised her as Ellen Payne, one of the richest women in the world. She had run a vast shipping business as well as inheriting a large amount of wealth from her deceased husband. She had short grey hair and a small mouth, and was renowned for being very shrewd.

"Sergeant Raines," she said. Her voice was strained and high pitched.

Raines nodded. "Sit down."

"I prefer to stand," she said coldly. "I would like to sponsor Jürgen Bauer, Nadia Bauer and Michael Bakerson. See to it that I do."

Raines grunted. "I'll schedule yeh fer a meeting," he told her, shooing her away as he wrote down their names.

Payne's nostrils flared as she strode off.

Raines looked at the two sponsors' names he had written down.

Sheikh Bakir and Ellen Payne.

How wonderful, he thought sarcastically.

26 -   SPONSORED

"Sponsored? Me?" Michael asked incredulously.

"Michael, Nadia an' Jürgen by both Mrs Payne and Sheikh Bakir, Joe just by the Sheikh," Raines repeated.

Michael felt elated. He had been picked! He was going to get a sponsor! That meant getting much better equipment and a better chance of being picked to represent their Institute and Occupied Britain in the Coliseum tournament against the other military academies. His plan had worked.

"Why was the competition cut short?" Steve asked, having recovered by now.

"Sponsors got bored. Well done by the way, laddies, I reckon you might have won if it had continued," Raines complimented.

"What did Nadia do that was so good?" Tim whined.

Raines looked at Nadia. "I think the whole squad will be interested in knowing that," he said, motioning for her to speak.

Michael was curious too. He had only known what had happened around him, having had no idea about the rest of the arena.

One hour ago, Nadia had been in the hotel. She had been waiting for half an hour, alert, her gun trained on the factory building.

However, her patience was about to be rewarded. The main door of the factory burst open, as a column of recruits charged out. Nadia recognised Raymon Collins, from the Legionnaires squad, as one of them.

She did not hesitate.

Carefully selecting each shot, she sniped the recruits one by one, starting with the nearest. Every single time, she hit the target in the head, causing them to collapse on the floor.

Raymon was the last one. He seemed to look directly at her, before she fired at him, the rubber bullet hitting him right between the eyes.

"Woah," Steve said, summing up Michael's feelings too.

Tim had been silenced, yet Jenny and Teresa were quick to congratulate her.

Michael smiled at Nadia, meeting her gaze. She seemed embarrassed by the attention, but smiled back.

"So I believe that answers yer question," Raines said to Tim with a slight smirk.

Tim went red, abashed. "Sorry," he muttered to Nadia.

"So, while the rest of ye head back to the training room, could the four sponsored ones come with me," Raines said, turning away.

Michael looked at him sharply.

"Sir?" Michael questioned.

Raines glanced back at him. "Yes?"

"Has Arthur not been chosen to be sponsored?" Michael asked, feeling Arthur deserved to be selected.

Raines showed no emotion. "No, he hasn't," he said simply, before walking off.

Michael, Jürgen, Nadia and Joe all followed him, Michael feeling sorry for Arthur.

He was pleased to be here, but he felt it was more of a team effort than anyone in particular.

Raines took them to a long corridor, with several chairs laid out.

"When I tell ye, go into the room where yer required. Ye'll see one of yer sponsors there," Raines told them.

Michael bit his lip nervously as he waited.

"Joseph, please could ye enter the room on the left. There ye'll find Sheikh Bakir. Jürgen, please can you enter the room on the right. There ye'll speak with Mrs Payne," Raines told them.

Michael sat down next to Nadia on the chairs. He glanced at her.

"I never realised you were that good at shooting," he remarked, attempting to make conversation.

"I wouldn't expect you to. Jürgen told me about your plan by the way. Surprisingly, he was very complimentary of you," Nadia told Michael with a slight smile.

"Really?" Michael asked incredulously. That didn't sound like Jürgen.

"No," Nadia replied with a grin.

Michael laughed. It was the first time he had heard her make a joke.

Nadia grinned too, though seemed embarrassed slightly.

He glanced ahead, and felt her eyes on him. He turned to face her.

"What?" he asked.

Nadia blushed, opening her mouth to speak, but was interrupted as the door for Sheikh Bakir opened.

Joe strode out without a glance back, walking off to the training room. Michael assumed he had rejected the sponsorship as the interview had been very short.

"Bakerson, go in with the Sheikh," Raines ordered. Michael did so immediately, excited to see his sponsor.

Needless to say, when he went in, he was disappointed.

The incredibly fat Sheikh lay sat on a large sofa opposite a chair. Two burly bodyguards stood next to him, and they seemed quite angry.

Joe must have really annoyed them.

"Welcome, Michael!" the Sheikh boomed, as Michael closed the door behind him. "It is a pleasure to meet you. A pleasure," he repeated.

Michael stood there awkwardly. "Hello," he said to the man.

"Please, take a seat, my dear friend," sheikh Bakir said slowly.

Michael sat down opposite him nervously.

"Well, Mike-al. I am a very rich man. I can get you many things. Fine weaponry? Fine women? Fine food? I can provide for you. All I want is to help you," the Sheikh said.

Michael stared at him. The Sheikh seemed to have gone a bit overboard on the 'fine food' aspect.

He cleared his throat. "Well, thank you. W-what exactly can you offer that the other sponsors can't?" he asked the Sheikh.

Sheikh Bakir placed his hands together. "What can I offer? Well, many things, Michael. Many things," the Sheikh emphasised. "I can get you into high society, into good places. You will be a hero to the American people when you make it there, and I want to support you."

Michael raised his eyebrows.

To him, the Sheikh seemed to be a bit of a joke.

"Okay. Well, thank you for offering to sponsor me," Michael said quickly. "I'll think about it," he told the Sheikh, standing up.

The Sheikh nodded very slowly. "Good. It has been a pleasure, Michael. A pleasure," he repeated again.

Michael nodded awkwardly, and then left the room quickly. Sheikh Bakir seemed creepy if he was honest with himself.

He took a deep breath, before becoming aware that Raines was looking at him.

Michael looked up and noticed Raines had a smirk on his face.

"Were ye impressed?" Raines asked with a chuckle.

Michael shook his head. "No sir," he answered truthfully.

Raines chuckled. "Alrigh', ye can go into the other one," he told Michael.

Michael nodded, and entered the other room.

He saw a tall bony woman with short white hair and icy blue eyes. She regarded him with a piercing gaze, as though as she could see his thoughts. She was sitting alone on a chair.

"Michael Bakerson," Payne stated. "You are sixteen years old, with a bright future ahead of you. You should not waste it. I was impressed by your use of strategy in the competition. I would like to sponsor you."

Michael nodded, sitting down on a chair opposite her. "Okay."

"I did not tell you to sit," Payne said sharply, her nostrils flaring.

Michael stood up quickly. "Sorry," he said quietly.

"Furthermore, when you address me, you shall call me 'Miss'," she stated. "I am far more competent than Sheikh Bakir."

That didn't seem hard.

"I also am capable of ensuring the quality of the equipment you are trained with in the future is superior," Payne continued. "So, will you accept?" she asked suddenly.

Michael nodded. "I'll think about it," he told her.

Her nostrils flared. "There is nothing to think about," she said coldly. "Will you or won't you?" she demanded.

"I'll give you your answer later," Michael said nervously, before hurriedly leaving the room. Ellen Payne scared him.

"Yer dismissed. I'll expect yer decision by the end of today," Raines told him.

Michael sighed as he walked back towards his room. He had a lot to think about. Which sponsor should he choose?

27 - DECISION TIME

Michael knocked on Steve's door. He felt like he needed to see his friend after being chosen.

"Yeah?" Steve called from inside.

"It's me, Mike. Can I come in?"

"Of course," Steve replied, and Michael entered cautiously.

Steve was lying back on his bed, looking at some magazine full of topless women. He put it down as soon as Michael entered and looked at him expectantly.

"Yeah?" Steve asked coolly. Michael guessed there was some bitterness about Steve not being picked.

Michael cleared his throat. "I ... I need some advice," he admitted.

His friend sat up immediately.

"Sure," Steve said with a slight smile. "Take a seat, laddie," he said, mimicking Sergeant Raines' voice.

Michael grinned, sitting in the chair in Steve's room.

"I'm not sure which sponsor to go for," he admitted.

Steve indicated for him to carry on.

"The first one I saw was Sheikh Bakir, who was this obese Arabic guy. He seemed a joke, obsessed with money and stuff. He seemed friendly, but a bit creepy. Then Ellen Payne was the other one, she was the opposite. She seemed to promise more but seemed very cold and not very nice," Michael told Steve.

Steve nodded. "Well, laddie, ye 'ave to think about what will benefit ye the most in the long run. What do ye think will give ye a better future?" he asked in a perfect imitation of Sergeant Raines.

Michael considered. Sheikh Bakir could give him money, but what could he do with that? Sure, 'high places' seemed somewhat promising, but would it really help him as a soldier?

Ellen Payne, on the other hand, claimed to increase the quality of his military equipment and technological training. She seemed a more serious opportunity, despite her lack of patience. Michael thought that she could probably help him more than Bakir could.

Michael nodded.

"Thanks Steve," he told his friend. He glanced at the magazine. "Where did you get that?" he asked.

"Found it left in the common room. Do you want it?" Steve asked Michael.

Michael shook his head quickly. "No," he said firmly. He didn't want anything to do with that sort of stuff.

Steve shrugged, scrunching it up and chucking it in the bin. Michael glanced around awkwardly.

"How're things with you and Jenny?" Steve asked with smirk.

Michael glanced at him quickly. "What do you mean?" he asked carefully, though he suspected what Steve meant.

"Have you made a move yet?" Steve asked in a dumbed down voice.

Michael raised his eyebrows, not wanting to admit anything.

"Have you made a move on Tim yet?" he teased with a smirk.

Steve chuckled. "Nice one, mate. That was really funny, you know," he replied sarcastically.

Michael shrugged. "You didn't deny it," he remarked.

Steve gave him a deadpan look. "I'm not gay," he told his friend.

Michael laughed. "I know, don't worry," he told Steve. "But is there anyone you like in our squad?" he added curiously.

Steve raised his eyebrows and looked at Michael. "If there was, you'd be the last person to know."

Michael clutched his chest in mock hurt. "Ow, that really stung," he exclaimed, then remembered something.

"Steve," he said tentatively. "What do you think we should do about Raymon and Lieutenant Jones?"

Ever since they had followed Raymon out of bounds and witnessed his secretive meeting with Jones a few weeks ago, Michael had been telling himself that he would do something about it.

Steve looked thoughtful. "I don't know that there's much we can do, as of now. Jones clearly loves Raymon's dad - that sponsor Alfred Collins, and we have no proof he's corrupt," he reasoned.

"Well, yeah, but we have to do something. We should tell Raines or something," Michael suggested.

Steve shook his head. "He wouldn't believe us. He'd just think we were trying to spite Raymon," he stated.

Michael sighed. "Yeah … I guess you're right," he admitted, looking down. "I better head off, and tell the sponsors my decision."

He left Steve's room and went off to find the sponsors' room. He walked down some stairs, thinking to himself, when he noticed a familiar face also heading to the sponsors room.

Jürgen.

"Michael," the boy said with a nod. "I assume you've chosen your sponsor."

Michael nodded back coolly.

"I cannot imagine who in their right mind vould choose Sheikh Bakir; Ellen Payne is by far the superior option," Jürgen stated confidently.

Michael remained silent. He felt suddenly that choosing Ellen Payne was a much less appealing option.

"So I'm guessing you and Nadia are going with her then?" Michael asked.

Jürgen hesitated. "Nadia has … difficulties. Her interview with Mrs Payne did not go particularly well," he explained. "I vos hoping you could convince her."

Michael felt a selfish pleasure at Jürgen's discomfort. He knew that it was probably wrong to feel pleased at this, but he didn't like Jürgen much anyway.

"Actually Jürgen, I'm choosing Sheikh Bakir too," Michael remarked. It was all he could do to keep himself from smirking.

Up until now he had been leaning towards choosing Ellen Payne, but having Jürgen there had swayed him towards the Sheikh.

Jürgen looked at him incredulously. "Vhat?" he questioned, in apparent disbelief.

"You heard," Michael replied with a small smile, feeling spiteful yet triumphant.

Jürgen looked down at the floor, sighing. "I alvays thought that you valued your future, Michael. We're not so different, you know."

Michael was disappointed by Jürgen's lack of reaction.

"Well, maybe we're more different than you thought," Michael remarked unsympathetically, before walking off to see Ellen Payne.

The sponsors' room contained a set of chairs and tables, with the various sponsors sat down behind them.

Michael noticed that Ellen Payne and Sheikh Bakir were sitting next to one another and smirked. All the better for his announcement.

He strode in confidently, and took a seat across from Ellen Payne.

"I didn't say you could sit," Payne said sharply.

Michael grinned. "I'm *very* sorry, Mrs Payne, but I've decided to go with Sheikh Bakir," he stated clearly.

Ellen Payne's nostrils flared and she sat up a little straighter. Michael notice the Sheikh rubbed his hands with glee.

"Are you joking, Bakerson?" Payne asked coldly. "I do not take well to *jokers*."

"No, I'm being fully serious. I believe Sheikh Bakir will benefit my future more," Michael replied calmly, giving Ellen Payne a false smile.

"*This* is a serious mistake!" Payne seethed, glaring at Michael. "You overestimate your own importance."

Sheikh Bakir clapped. "Michael, you have made a very wise choice. We shall do very well together," he exclaimed, beaming.

Michael grinned, standing up. He felt himself rather enjoying the two sponsors competing for him.

"You've made an unnecessary enemy today," Payne stated coldly, looking at Michael.

Michael shrugged. "I'm sorry you feel that way," he commented, realising having Payne as an enemy was probably not a good idea.

His satisfaction quickly faded.

Payne's expression did not change.

Michael looked down, unable to hold her piercing gaze. She unnerved him. He hesitated, before walking off.

"I shall catch up with you later, Michael! We have much to talk about!" the Sheikh boomed as Michael left the room.

Michael smirked slightly. The Sheikh looked too fat to catch up to anyone.

He wasn't sure what to think as he walked back to the common room. He had the sensation of having made a mistake, yet he felt that he couldn't work with Ellen Payne and Jürgen.

He sighed, pushing open the door and entering the large common room. It was fairly crowded with recruits. He scanned around for any members of his squad. They were sitting on the sofas near the fire.

As he walked past groups of people, he caught snatches of conversation.

"-there's a new instructor here apparently-"

"-did you hear Raymon got an offer from almost every sponsor-"

"-I've been sponsored by three people-"

Michael tried to block out the constant talk of sponsors, his feeling of unease deepening.

He reached his friends and was pleased to see Nadia there, along with Tim, Hans and Alexandra.

"Hi," he said, sitting on the spare sofa next to the fire.

Hans nodded at him and Alexandra smiled at him.

140

"Hey," she replied brightly. "We were just discussing where our first assignment will be. Hans reckons Norway, Tim thinks the Middle East and I think Germany."

Michael nodded. "What does Nadia think?" he asked curiously, glancing at Nadia.

"I have no opinion on this matter," Nadia informed him.

Michael nodded. "I can't say I know much either. Back in the village, we barely knew anything about the war," he admitted.

The others resumed their discussion and Michael zoned out, focusing on Nadia.

Had he made the right choice, going with the Sheikh?

"Nadia," he said eventually. "Which sponsor did you pick?"

Nadia looked up and gave him a small smile. "The same as you," she told him.

Michael breathed out, relieved. "Oh, that's good. I thought you might go with Jürgen," he admitted.

Nadia frowned. "Jürgen went for Ellen Payne as well, you know," she stated slowly.

Michael blinked, panic beginning to rise in him.

"Y-you went for Payne?" he asked uncertainly. He was dimly aware that the others had stopped their conversation.

Nadia nodded slowly. "You ... didn't?" she questioned, frowning slightly.

Michael shook his head, leaning back on the sofa. He didn't want to lose face in front of his teammates.

"I went for the Sheikh," he informed them. "I didn't like Payne much."

Tim, Alexandra and Hans resumed their discussion about the war, whilst Nadia looked at him searchingly, as though she knew he hadn't told the whole truth about his reasoning to choose Bakir.

He found he couldn't relax, even with the warm glow of the fire and walked off to get some sleep.

Michael fumed as he lay down on his bed that night.

Jürgen had lied to him.

He was stuck with Sheikh Bakir as his sponsor.

He had definitely made a mistake.

28 -   BRIBERY

Darius Finch, the leader of the Praetorian squad, walked through the corridors in a good mood. He had had several sponsor offers, yet had not pledged his allegiance to any of them.

He was in the Recruit Centre, heading back to his room, when he glimpsed a figure in front of him, lurking in the shadows.

The figure stepped forward, and Darius recognised him as the pale officer that had arrived with the sponsors - Lieutenant Blackburn.

"Good evening, Master Finch," Blackburn greeted him coolly.

Darius nodded. "I assume you have something to say to me," he replied, halting.

Blackburn nodded. "I was impressed with your performance at hacking the tower control panel. I have come to inform you that you will be selected by the military to compete at the Coliseum. Provided you keep up your technological skills, I will be able to find you an employment option within my department," he explained.

"Your department?" Darius questioned.

"Technological Integration. If you can help me, then I can set you up for life," Blackburn replied.

"You're not the only person who has told me that today," Darius stated. "And if I'm going to enhance my skills, I'm going to need to be able to access military technology."

Blackburn raised his eyebrows. "Meaning?" he queried.

"I want to you give The Institute the latest weaponry and technology. How do you think we can improve if we don't have access to it?" Darius told Blackburn.

The Lieutenant nodded. "Very well. This Institute will be given a shipment of neural integrators and various technological developments which should enhance your training," he stated.

"Not just me," Darius stated. "I want everyone to have access."

"Why?" Blackburn questioned.

"So we will do better in the Coliseum," Darius replied simply. "I want The Institute to have a chance of winning."

Blackburn smirked slightly, seeing this as an unlikely prospect.

"As you wish. My budget isn't exactly limited. You'll have your tech, Master Finch, but when you arrive in America, you are going to offer me your services," he stated.

Darius nodded. "That seems reasonable," he stated. "Is there anything else you wish to discuss?"

"No. I won't expect any contact from you until you reach the United States. This meeting never happened," Blackburn told Darius before striding off.

Darius frowned, wondering what Lieutenant Blackburn could possibly want with him.

* * *

"Morning, everyone! I'm pleased to tell you that out of everyone at The Institute, over fifteen have received sponsors! Even more surprising, not all of them were Prospects - Raines obviously should have selected them better!" Jones announced with a chuckle.

The recruits were lined up outside in front of The Institute stage, the biting morning cold chilling them to the bone.

"But, anyway, here they are!" Jones called, pulling out a list.

"With Sheikh Bakir, the recruits sponsored were Michael Bakerson and Dan Fisher.

With Ellen Payne, the recruits sponsored were Jürgen Bauer, Nadia Bauer, Darius Finch, Elizabeth Walker and Oliver Lee.

With Alfred Collins, we have Raymon Collins, William Brooke, Gregory Gilmore and Mark Thompson.

With Julian Quinn, we have Sophie Montague, Thomas Blackhurst, Alan McGregor and Carl O'Hara.

And with Count von Richter, we have Dominic Butler and Thomas Butler." Jones finished, and put his paper away.

Michael felt his heart clench. Only one other person had chosen Sheikh Bakir?

And he didn't mean to be offensive to Dan Fisher, but he didn't seem to be the brightest person around.

Not to mention the fact that Sophie and Nadia were both in other groups and that Sheikh Bakir seemed to be the weakest sponsor possible.

He took a shaky breath, trying to think positive.

At least he wasn't with Jürgen.

He looked up again when Jones continued.

"The sponsors are leaving at midday, I suggest any recruit who wishes to speak to their sponsor do so this morning," the American stated. "Please could everyone meet here at one o'clock for the arrival of our new instructor."

Jones and the instructors then walked off, leaving the recruits chatting excitedly.

"A new instructor? I hope he's not like Vellon," Tim remarked, shuddering at the mere thought of the physical training instructor.

"Sergeant Vellon seems a most reasonable man," Hans interjected slowly. "He merely values physical perfection."

Michael wasn't too sure how to react about a new instructor. He didn't really care if he was honest with himself.

He zoned out from the conversation.

"Michael? May I have a word?" a familiar German voice spoke.

Michael turned and saw Jürgen. He gritted his teeth as he remembered how the boy had lied to him.

"Jürgen," he replied coolly. "Sure you can."

Jürgen looked awkwardly at the ground. "Privately?" he added.

Michael nodded. "Lead the way," he told Jürgen emotionlessly.

Jürgen looked grateful, and walked away from their squad. Michael followed, trying to contain his anger.

Did Jürgen want to gloat?

When they were far enough away from their squad, Jürgen cleared his throat and looked at him.

"Michael," he began. "I would like to apologise."

Michael was surprised, but didn't show it.

144

"I unintentionally misled you. I vos not avare that Nadia had changed her mind. It vos ... most dishonourable of me. I ask for your forgiveness," he stated, looking at Michael intently.

Michael watched him coolly. He saw himself as a forgiving person, but he didn't like Jürgen very much. He was still annoyed from what had happened and suspected Jürgen of doing it intentionally.

He wondered if this was another trick.

However, he knew he couldn't allow a rift to form in their squad and thought it would look better if he accepted Jürgen's apology.

"I accept your apology, Jürgen," Michael told him, looking him in the eye.

Jürgen nodded, holding his gaze. "Thank you," he said carefully.

Michael held his gaze until a figure stepped between them.

He was relieved to see it was Jenny.

"Jenny, how's your ankle?" he asked casually.

Jenny raised her eyebrows. "Why were you guys looking like you wanted to fight each other?"

Michael laughed slightly. "We were just talking," he told Jenny.

Jenny seemed sceptical, and looked at Jürgen for confirmation.

"Ja," Jürgen said quickly, nodding. "Just talking."

Jenny narrowed her eyes at them. "Well ... fine," she said suspiciously. "I'm assuming you're seeing your sponsors today?"

Michael sighed. "Yeah ... I told the Sheikh I would," he admitted.

Jürgen shook his head. "Ellen Payne and I have already discussed everything ve need. She is a very efficient sponsor," he stated.

Michael's jaw clenched, feeling annoyed. He felt like that comment seemed to be directed at him.

Jenny nodded. "So, do you want to do some training with me?" she asked Jürgen.

Jürgen smiled. "I'd love to," he said brightly.

Michael turned away, feeling jealous. He turned and stalked away, heading back inside to speak to Sheikh Bakir.

"Michael!" he heard a voice call. He turned his head, wondering who could want him now.

He looked wearily at the direction the voice came from as saw Dan Fisher, the other recruit that had been sponsored by Sheikh Bakir.

Dan was a tall muscular boy with broad shoulders and dirty blond hair. He was a member of the Jaegers, Sophie's squad. Michael recalled that they were the squad that Jürgen had decimated with his machine gun fire.

"Dan," he said with a friendly smile. Michael didn't mind Dan as he seemed a decent person.

"Are you going to see the Sheikh?" Dan asked, catching up to him.

Michael nodded. "Yeah, he said he'd catch up to me," he told Dan.

"Same," the boy nodded.

"Did you get any other sponsor offers?" Michael asked, hoping Dan had chosen the Sheikh voluntarily as well.

Dan snorted. "I wish!" he exclaimed, leaving Michael feel even worse.

Dan seemed to notice this, and cleared his throat.

"Well, at least we got sponsors!" he said brightly. "Very few people in my squad did."

Michael considered. He hadn't thought of it that way before.

Whilst he was feeling annoyed that he got Bakir, there were people like Steve and Jenny that would do anything to get one.

He nodded slowly. "True," he commented, as they entered the Recruit Centre.

Michael heard a familiar voice coming from one of the corridors nearby.

Raymon.

"You go on ahead," he told Dan. "I left something outside."

Dan looked unconvinced, but carried on walking.

Michael took a deep breath and then doubled back, following the sound of the voices. It seemed to be coming from one of the sponsor interview rooms.

He stood outside the closed door and listened intently. He could hear Lieutenant Jones' American accent.

"Mr Collins, I understand your concern for your son, but he will have to earn his place in the Coliseum. Although having a sponsor increases his likelihood of getting in, no one can say for certain," Jones was saying.

"Bah! That's nonsense! You'll ensure my son gets in. How much do you want?" spat the voice of Alfred Collins, Raymon's wealthy father.

"I don't take *bribes*, Mr Collins," Jones drawled. "But I'm sure a donation will be looked upon kindly by my colleagues."

"Don't *you* pick the squad that's going?" Michael heard Raymon's voice ask.

Michael heard Lieutenant Jones sigh. "Unfortunately not ... due to the fact I have not been an instructor for very long, there are three instructors needed to make a collective decision on who is going. That will be myself, Sergeant Raines and Sergeant Vellon," Jones explained wearily.

"You know of Prometheus, I gather?" Alfred Collins asked sharply.

"Prometheus?" Jones replied, sounding confused.

"The mole in The Institute, amongst the recruits," Alfred stated, as though it were obvious. "Have you caught him yet?"

Michael breathed in sharply.

There was a spy in The Institute?

He listened in again.

"Sir?" he heard Raymon's voice say.

"Silence, Raymon!" Alfred snapped. "Have you caught him yet Jones?"

Jones cleared his throat. "Well, we're looking into-"

"I think there's someone outside!" Raymon blurted out.

Michael's eyes widened in fear.

He was going to be caught.

THE INSTITUTE

29 -   **MIND GAMES**

Michael turned and ran away from the door as he heard it open behind him.

He pelted around the corner and crashed into a very large, soft object.

He stepped back, and realised he had ran into the huge form of Sheikh Bakir.

Fortunately, the Sheikh seemed to be unharmed, as his fat must have absorbed the impact.

"Michael, I'm so glad I caught up with you!" the Sheikh boomed, taking his arm and beginning to walk down the corridors.

Michael glanced to the corridor where he had come from.

Raymon was standing there, glaring at Michael with narrowed eyes.

"Sheik Bakir, how long have you been talking with Michael?" Raymon seethed.

Sheikh Bakir slowly ambled around to face Raymon.

"Master Collins! Have you decided to join me?" Sheikh Bakir asked very slowly.

Raymon rolled his eyes. "No. Now answer the question, you fat oaf," he spat at the Sheikh.

Sheikh Bakir blinked.

"Michael has been with me for at least ten minutes," he explained slowly. Michael inwardly breathed a sigh of relief.

Raymon gritted his teeth, glaring at Michael, before stalking off back to where he had come from.

Michael felt immensely grateful to the Sheikh for covering for him.

He looked at the Sheikh. "Thank you," he said quietly.

Sheikh seemed not to know what Michael was talking about. But Michael suspected for all his feigned stupidity, the Sheikh knew a lot more than he let on.

"I told you, you would not regret choosing me," the Sheikh replied with a wide smile.

Michael smiled back slightly. "Yeah," he said, still regretting it somewhat, although he was beginning to believe it might not be a bad decision after all.

The Sheikh nodded. "Well, Michael is there anything you'd like me to get you?" he asked.

Michael considered. Was there anything he needed?

Not especially. There were people who needed things much more than him.

He nodded. "You said you could get me food, correct?" he asked the Sheikh carefully.

Sheikh Bakir nodded a gleam in his eye.

"I can!" he exclaimed.

"Is there a limit to how much you can get me?"

The Sheikh shook his head, his chins wobbling.

"Not at all!" he exclaimed. "Food is my speciality."

Michael smiled. He wasn't surprised.

"Well, in that case, Sheikh Bakir, I'd like weekly food shipments to be delivered to my village. Enough food for ... five hundred meals?" he asked the Sheikh boldly.

"I see," the Sheikh said, in a much less friendly tone. "And what would you do in return for me?"

Michael bit his lip, thinking. What could someone like him do for Sheikh Bakir?

"I can get other people to join you?" he asked hopefully.

The Sheikh snorted. "Michael, it is I who chooses whom to sponsor, not the recruits who choose me. I chose you very carefully," he stated.

"Well ... then I'd be in your debt," Michael told the Sheikh with a sigh.

The Sheikh would never grant his request.

Sheikh Bakir seemed to consider the offer. "Your services? That is interesting ... do I have your word?" he asked slowly.

"Yes," Michael replied immediately. "As long as my village receives food, I'll be in your debt."

The Sheikh nodded slowly. "Very well, Michael. We have ... a deal," he told him seriously.

Michael smiled. "Thank you, Sheikh," he told the man gratefully.

The Sheikh patted Michael on the back. "I told you, you would not regret this," he stated with a smile.

Michael grinned. He couldn't imagine Ellen Payne donating anything to help someone else.

* * *

"You pledged him your services?" Alexandra asked, as Michael sat in the common room in the seats by the fire.

He was sitting with Alexandra and Tim. Joe was sitting by himself in the corner, whilst Arthur was in the Strategy Building somewhere.

He wasn't sure where Teresa and Steve were, but assumed they were together somewhere. Michael wasn't blind, and guessed there might be something going on between them.

Hans would most likely be in the gym, and he knew that Jürgen and Jenny were somewhere together.

He didn't know where Nadia was.

"Yeah," he said to Alexandra. "I couldn't exactly offer him much."

Alexandra bit her lip concernedly. "But that means he's got power over you. Your village might become dependent on his food!" she exclaimed.

Michael considered. "Better that than starving," he reasoned.

Tim seemed to agree with Alexandra. "Do you trust the Sheikh?" he asked Michael.

Michael hesitated. "Yes," he said eventually. He did believe that the Sheikh would keep his word.

Tim shrugged. "Fair enough then. It's your life, not mine," he remarked, leaning back on his chair.

Alexandra shot him a scolding look. "Tim!" she chastised. "That's no way to treat your friends!"

"Alexandra, it's okay," Michael insisted. "Tim's right, it's not his problem."

Tim looked a bit guilty, and looked down.

Alexandra, however, refused to drop the subject. "You think Elizabeth will like you if you act like that?" she questioned Tim.

Tim went bright red and looked at Alexandra angrily. "I thought that was a secret!" he protested, clearly annoyed.

Alexandra rolled her eyes. "Michael's a friend - he can keep a secret," she told Tim.

"Unlike you," Tim retorted, standing up and storming out of the common room.

Michael raised his eyebrows. That seemed an overreaction.

"Who's Elizabeth?" he asked Alexandra quietly.

Alexandra seemed upset. "Oh, no one," she told him, and then sighed. "Elizabeth Walker. She's Tim's crush."

Michael nodded. That made sense. "Hang on, Elizabeth Walker? From the Jaguars?" he asked, referring to the squad.

Alexandra nodded, biting her lip. "I know," she said quietly.

Michael raised his eyebrows. Elizabeth Walker was one of the best recruits, having been chosen as a Prospect earlier as well as being sponsored. She was very good-looking, having a nice figure as well as long black hair that had streaks of purple in it. A lot of the boys at The Institute seemed to like her, and she was always surrounded by a group of them.

If Michael was honest with himself, she seemed very much out of Tim's league. Nothing against Tim, but he didn't seem to have anything special about himself.

"And Tim wanted you to help him with her?" Michael asked Alexandra.

Alexandra nodded. "I said I'd try," she admitted meekly.

Michael nodded, glancing across the room. Elizabeth was chatting to Thomas, the tall muscular leader of the Jaguar squad.

Poor Tim.

He scanned around the room, and noticed Sophie chatting to Darius. He thought it might be nice to go over and make friends with them.

At least, that was what he told himself. He suspected that his real motive was to talk to Sophie.

"Michael?"

Michael looked at Alexandra. "Sorry, what did you say?" he asked, going slightly red at having being caught.

Alexandra smiled. "I was asking you if there was anyone you like," she told him.

Michael bit his lip, considering.

He found a few girls attractive, but that didn't mean he *liked* them. In all honesty, he was confused as to how he'd know if he liked them in that way.

He did feel jealous when he saw Jürgen with Jenny, but he wasn't sure if that was just friendship or protectiveness.

And then there was Sophie. He felt butterflies in his stomach whenever she was around. It was as though he had something to prove to her, but he couldn't understand what.

He sighed.

"I don't know," he admitted to Alexandra honestly. "I guess I've got bigger things to concentrate on."

That was certainly true. With the emergence of this mysterious Prometheus, concentrating on his training, trying to qualify for the Coliseum and figuring out what to do about Alfred Collins bribing Lieutenant Jones.

Alexandra laughed. "That's okay - we all do, really," she reassured him.

"What about you though?" Michael asked her curiously.

Alexandra blushed slightly, glancing away.

Michael followed her gaze and smiled when he saw Darius and Sophie.

"Darius?" Michael asked with a smirk.

Alexandra blushed further, telling Michael all he needed to know.

He grinned. "Come on, let's go over," he told Alexandra, having wanted to go there anyway.

Alexandra blushed, shaking her head. "No," she said stubbornly.

Michael shrugged. "Well, I'm going. Catch you later?" he told Alexandra with a smile.

Alexandra nodded. "See you," she told him, as she left the room.

Michael, slightly nervously, went over to where Darius and Sophie were talking.

Darius looked pleased when he saw Michael.

"Here's the cunning fox!" he exclaimed with a chuckle.

Sophie turned and smiled at him. "Hey," she said to Michael. "We were just talking about you."

Michael smiled, feeling much better.

"You were?" he questioned, sitting down next to them.

"Yes. We were discussing your good use of strategy in the competition," Darius told him with a smile.

Sophie rolled her eyes. "We were wondering what made you choose *Sheikh Bakir* over Ellen Payne," she said bluntly, leaving Michael feeling annoyed.

"I, er, didn't really like Payne," Michael told them coolly.

Darius nodded. "Understandable. But surely you feel that she could benefit your future more?" he questioned.

"Well, it's not just my future I'm worried about. And I feel that Ellen Payne would be far less generous," he told Darius.

Darius nodded respectfully. "A noble choice. I'm interested to know how that works out for you," he told Michael with a slight smile.

Michael smiled, nodding back. "Thank you. I will do," he told Darius.

Sophie rolled her eyes. "Yeah, how *noble*," she commented.

Michael frowned, and then slowly smirked. She was still bitter about him tricking her in the tower.

He had beaten her.

"Thank you," he told Sophie, as though he had taken her sarcastic compliment as sincere. "You did well in the competition too."

Sophie chuckled as she glanced at him. "You got me there," she admitted, to Michael's surprise. "You're a lot more ruthless than I took you for."

Michael detected a hint of grudging respect in her voice.

"Thanks?" he told Sophie uncertainly, although he was not sure whether it was a compliment.

Darius looked at Michael suddenly. "Michael? Do you know where Arthur is?" he asked intently.

Michael shook his head. "I'm guessing the Strategy Building, knowing Arthur. Napoleon, maybe?" he suggested.

Darius nodded. "Alright. I shall pay him a visit now," he informed them, standing up.

He offered Michael his hand to shake. "Very well done, Michael. I would rather be defeated by you than anyone else," Darius told him.

Michael smiled a little, standing up and shaking Darius' hand. He had a lot of respect for the boy. It took a lot of courage to say that.

"Thank you. But you would have beaten me if it weren't for Jürgen and Joe," Michael reminded Darius.

"But I did not. There is no use thinking of what could have been, for the past cannot be rewritten. However, the future can," Darius replied with a smile, breaking the handshake.

"Good day to you as well, Sophie," he told her, before striding off.

Michael nodded at the boy, then realised he was alone with Sophie.

Sophie stood up and faced him, a twinkle in her eye.

"Now that he's gone, we can enjoy ourselves," she remarked with a mischievous grin.

Michael felt butterflies rise in his stomach. Her brown eyes looked alluring as he held her gaze. "What did you have in mind?" he asked with a slight smile.

Sophie smirked, stepping closer to him. He could feel his heart rate quickening.

"*Well*," she said slowly. "You do kind of owe me after elbowing me in the nose. You could have damaged my looks."

Michael blushed slightly. "Sorry about that ... my bad," he said nervously, biting his lip.

"I might forgive you," Sophie whispered, stepping closer to him. She had a playful look on her face.

Michael could feel his heart pounding, his mouth growing dry.

"But not today," Sophie told him with a wink, as she turned and left the common room.

Michael stood there for several seconds, trying to figure out what she had meant.

He realised she had played him for a fool.

Damn.

He quickly grew angry. She thought she could manipulate him? Well, next competition she would have another thing coming.

Michael glanced around. There were a few people from the other squads there but they paid him no attention.

He walked outside of the common room, heading towards floor Genghis - Physical Training.

His father had always taught him: 'If you're angry, use your anger. Do something useful.' In his village, that had meant helping out with the physically demanding farm labouring.

Here, that would mean striving to achieve physical perfection and hopefully impressing the instructors.

Which would be hard work, but he was angry.

* * *

Arthur was in the Strategy Building, using a basic simulation. He was attempting to achieve victory in the Battle of Waterloo controlling Napoleon's forces.

He enjoyed simulations like this. They allowed him to ignore real life for the time being. It reminded him of video games back home, where he had been able to immerse himself for hours at a time in the aftermath of his mother's death.

"You know, your cannons are far too close to the enemy cavalry," came Darius' voice from behind Arthur.

Arthur didn't look up. "That's intentional. I've got fusiliers in wait," he told him, pausing the game and looking up at Darius.

Darius smiled. "I came to speak to you. Firstly, I wished to congratulate you on breaking open the tower. I believe you managed to do so before I did," he told Arthur.

Arthur looked pleased. "Well, that's only because you chose to enter on the far side of the tower," he reasoned modestly.

Darius chuckled. "No, I still believe you were faster than me. Anyhow, I wanted to inform you that The Institute should be getting a shipment of new tech, courtesy of Lieutenant Blackburn," he remarked with a cheerful smile.

Arthur looked up hopefully. "You were selected?" he asked Darius eagerly.

Darius nodded. "I believe so. He gave me a guarantee that I will reach the Coliseum," he stated calmly.

Arthur smiled. "Well done," he told Darius.

Darius looked at Arthur with respect. "Thank you. It is admirable how your first reaction is to compliment me. Without offending you, I would have expected you vied for the offer yourself," he commented.

Arthur smiled slightly, shrugging. "I didn't expect to get it," he admitted.

Darius nodded. "But it is interesting, is it not, that the only two people who had the confidence to attempt entering were us," he remarked.

Arthur considered. "I suppose it's how we think. We can use tech better than most," he admitted.

Darius looked at Arthur intently. "Indeed. But I advise you against becoming reliant on technology. You're more than just good with machines. Always remember, the mind is the best weapon," he told him seriously.

Arthur smiled slightly. "Thank you, Darius. I'll remember that."

30 -   A NEW INSTRUCTOR

"I'd like to officially introduce our new Instructor, Sergeant Wallace!" Lieutenant Jones announced.

The recruits all applauded as a red haired youthful man stepped up to the microphone. They were lined up outside, the sponsors having departed three days ago.

"Good moo-erning everybody. My name is Sergeant Wallace, and I am teh be yer new instructor," the man spoke loudly. "I have jus' returned from Norway, and I have firs' hand experience of the Russian threat. My regiment was massacred by Hunters, so I can provide ye with some pretty vivid details on what teh expect when ye get there," Wallace announced.

Sergeant Wallace waited to let that sink in, before continuing.

"As I'm sure yer all aware, Scandinavia is a critical area for the Western Alliance, due to oil reserves found there. Unfortunately, it is also the area where the Russian general, nicknamed Fenrir, has made his base.

Once ye've become soldiers, that is most likely the area where ye'll be sent. Fenrir is a dangerous foe, and I'm here to help ye know what yer up against," he explained confidently.

Michael felt alarmed. Until he'd met Hans, he had never even known the Western Alliance fought in Norway. And if Fenrir was such a dangerous enemy, shouldn't they be sending more experienced soldiers to fight him?

There was a muttering amongst the recruits which told Michael that he was not the only one with concerns.

Lieutenant Jones stepped to the front, looking like he had swallowed something unpleasant.

"Alright, settle down, I'm sure you can cope with a bit o' cold," Jones called in his prominent American accent, signalling them to settle down.

The recruits carried on muttering until Sergeant Raines roared, "SILENCE!" They then quietened down quickly.

Jones cleared his throat. "Yeah ... you're going to prepare to go to Norway. This means that you will be relocating to a new area and your training will be tailored to the Scandinavian environment. Thanks to the generous American military, we have also had a shipment of advanced technological equipment, including neural integrators. These devices will be vital to your training, and will prepare you for combat. Training will begin immediately," he announced.

Michael was shocked. This had come too fast. He felt like he was still at the beginning of training; he wasn't ready for war yet.

Despite this, he couldn't deny that he had changed since he had left his village. He realised it must have been at least a few months since he had arrived at The Institute, but time had flown by.

He had grown in more ways than one. When he had left his village, he had been fairly skinny, but the daily physical training had helped him gain a lot of muscle. Although he wouldn't class himself as strong as Raymon, he reckoned he would be able to hold his own against a lot of the other recruits.

His confidence had also increased. He now felt much more capable of leading the Spartans, and knew he had the support of his squad behind him.

He glanced around. He could see fear in other people's faces.

Lieutenant Jones glanced nervously back at Raines. "Let's begin," he muttered. Raines nodded, and the instructors left the stage and approached their various squads individually.

For Michael's squad, the Spartans, that meant Sergeant Raines, however to his surprise, Sergeant Vellon approached them. The physical training instructor rarely led the Spartans' team exercises, but Michael guessed he would have something painful planned for them on this occasion.

"Garcons! Listen!" Sergeant Vellon barked in his French accent. "The task you have ees simple, so you useless recruits better get eet right. Your 'ave to locate your new reseedense. You 'ave one map. I am not going to 'elp you, so eet will be a chance for you to use your tiny brains," Vellon spat, handing the map to Jürgen.

Jürgen held it up. It was a map showing the buildings of The Institute and the surrounding area. There was a red 'X' where Michael assumed their destination was.

"So ... where are we on this map?" Steve asked.

"Here," Jürgen told them, pointing to the area near the Recruit Centre.

Michael nodded. "So, we go ... south west?" he suggested, looking around. "Which way is that?"

"This way," Arthur spoke up, pointing. "May I ... have the map?" he asked Jürgen.

Jürgen gave it to him. "Vhat are you planning?" he asked curiously.

"Well ... our watches are designed to be able to send and receive signals. So, whatever sends the signals would have to know where to send them to, right? That means these watches have some sort of built in tracking device," Arthur explained.

"I ... don't get it," Hans stated.

But Michael did. "You want to use the location on the watch so we know where we are at any point," he said slowly.

Arthur nodded. "And I use the built in camera on our watches to scan the map, and use that. From there, I'll be able to figure out a route, and we'll know exactly where we are," he told them.

Michael was impressed by Arthur's ingenuity. "That's ... a really good idea, Arthur," he admitted, surprised.

"Arthur, you're a genius!" Steve exclaimed.

"I-is it allowed, though?" Tim asked worriedly. "I mean, we're meant to be using our map skills, right?"

Arthur bit his lip, shrinking back slightly.

"I say ve do it," Jürgen stated firmly.

Jenny nodded. "I agree with Jürgen. They didn't give us any set of rules to follow. And Western Alliance all about being adaptable," she stated.

Michael felt a bit annoyed that Jenny had made out as if Jürgen had been the one advocating Arthur's plan, but passed no comment.

"Then it's settled," Michael told them. "Arthur's going to scan the map to his watch, whilst we begin navigating the old fashioned way."

Jürgen looked like he wanted to disagree, but nodded.

"Ja. Good plan, Michael," he muttered, looking down. Michael was surprised, but then saw Jenny looking at Jürgen expectantly.

She had clearly told Jürgen to be nice to him.

Michael nodded. "Well, lead the way," he told Jürgen, who began leading the group off in the direction they were meant to be going. Arthur hung at the back, whilst Michael fell into step with Steve.

Steve glanced at him. "You really don't like Jürgen," he remarked with a grin.

Michael frowned. It wasn't *that* obvious, was it?

"W-what makes you think that?" he asked carefully.

Steve chuckled. "You always scowl whenever he speaks," he commented.

Michael scowled. "No, I don't," he protested.

Steve laughed. "You're doing it now," he insisted.

Michael felt annoyed, but tried to hide it. "I don't hate him," he stated, keeping his voice level.

"But you don't like him," Steve pressed.

"You're right, I don't, now shut up," Michael snapped, irritated. He wished people would stop going on about Jürgen.

Steve held his hands up defensively. "Woah, calm down," he impressed. "No need to get mad at me."

Michael sighed, feeling slightly guilty. "Sorry ... it's just everyone seems to be going on about him," he admitted.

Steve looked about to respond, when Arthur spoke up. "I've got it!" he exclaimed excitedly.

Michael glanced up, having not really been paying attention to where they were. They had reached the edge of the buildings, reaching a small wooded area. The trees were mainly deciduous, with the cold weather having causing their once golden leaves to have fallen to the ground, now crunching under their feet. The breeze was much stronger here and an unpleasant smell of smoke wafted through the air towards them.

"We're about thirteen degrees off course," Arthur told them worriedly, checking his watch which had the map uploaded.

Jürgen nodded. "Thank you Arthur. Let us change course," he told the group.

"But ... we have to go through this forest," Arthur told them.

"What is wrong vith that?" Jürgen asked him.

"Oh ... n-nothing," Arthur said quickly.

Jürgen frowned, and then carried on walking, Jenny immediately following him.

Hans looked at Arthur. "What is wrong?" he asked quietly.

Arthur sighed. "This just seems too easy. Even with just a map we would be bound to make it there eventually," he commented.

Hans looked thoughtful. "Perhaps the real exercise begins when we get there?" he questioned.

"That doesn't seem like Vellon's style," Michael interjected. "He wouldn't ever want us to have it easy."

Hans nodded. "Good point," he told Michael.

Michael scanned around the forest. Apart from the sound of their footsteps on the frosty leaves, it was silent.

"Stop," Joe said suddenly. The group stopped and looked at him.

"What?" Jenny asked, concerned.

"I saw something moving in the trees," the dark-skinned boy replied coolly.

Jürgen looked alert. "Proceed vith caution. Arthur, remain in the centre of the group. Joe and I vill go up front. Michael and Steven, guard our right flank. Teresa, Alexandra guard our left. Hans and Jenny vill be the rear-guard," he instructed them quickly.

"What about me?" Nadia demanded to Jürgen.

Jürgen glanced at her. "You and Tim stay out of harm's way," he said dismissively, then faced the group. "Are we ready?"

"Joe only thinks he saw something, why are we getting so worked up?" Tim asked them.

"Expect the worst, hope for the best," Jürgen replied, as they got into positions and resumed their trek through the forest.

Michael kept his eyes peeled as he carried on walking. He heard a rustling to his right, and glanced sharply over his shoulder.

He opened his mouth to shout as a figure stepped out from behind a tree, but felt a sharp prick in his right arm.

Immediately feeling woozy, he looked down and saw a long silver dart embedded in his arm.

He sank to his knees as the world spun around him. He heard a shout before darkness came up and enveloped him.

31 - BROKEN

Michael woke with a start, breathing heavily. He had had a nightmare of being captured and tortured by a man named Fenrir. He was glad to be awake.

He opened his eyes, but he couldn't see anything. Everything was dark, like the light had been sucked out of the place. He didn't even know what the place was.

Michael tried to move his arms, but they were tied down to whatever he was lying on. It was hard and rough, like the wooden table in his hut at the village. He struggled, and realised his ankles and chest were tied down as well with thick, coarse rope that rubbed against him.

He turned his head left and right, but only darkness stared back at him.

Michael sighed, tried to remember how he had got here. The last thing he remembered was a long, silver dart sticking out of his arm as they had been ambushed in the forest.

He took a deep breath.

Okay. First of all, where was he?

He had seen a dark figure before he had got shot, but that was all. The dart was very effective, and was most likely military, meaning this was probably part of an elaborate training exercise.

That fitted. Sergeant Vellon must have planned this.

He was most likely indoor, as he couldn't feel any breeze. It was probably a small room, and fairly well designed as it felt very hot and humid, which was rare for this cold time of year.

That reinforced his view that this was a training exercise.

That helped. Secondly, where were his friends?

"Steve?" he called out tentatively. "Hans? Arthur? Jenny?"

There was no response.

Michael sighed, but then heard muffled footsteps approaching. He looked up hopefully, waiting.

He heard the twist of a doorknob and heard the sound of a door opening.

A switch was flicked, and Michael was suddenly blinded as a glaring white light shined directly at him.

He clamped his eyes shut, the brightness of the room too much for him. He groaned. "Who are you?" he asked groggily.

A voice laughed, a deep throaty chuckle which felt oddly familiar to Michael.

Michael opened his eyes and saw a man in an old khaki uniform. He was bald, and had a large bulbous nose. He was wearing dark sunglasses that covered his eyes, and had a devious smirk on his face.

Michael stared at him. He had seen this man before, he was sure of it.

"I've seen you before," he commented.

The man looked annoyed, bringing his head close to Michael's. His rancid breath smelt disgusting, reminding Michael of some old cheese that a brigand had once acquired for his village.

"No, you haven't," the man snarled, his spit flying out. "And you're gonna wish you'd never met me."

Michael was unnerved, but tried not to show it.

"Wh-what do you want?" he asked the man.

The man smirked. "Call me ... Boss," he told Michael. "And I'm the one who asks the questions."

Boss ... he had heard that name before. His father had once mentioned him, but he wasn't sure where.

Michael racked his brains, thinking back to his village. The man definitely wasn't a farmer, Michael would have seen him if he had worked on the farm. There was a possibility of him being a miner, but he doubted that.

He could be brigand. That would make sense.

But what was Boss doing here? Was this really a training exercise, or had Michael been captured for real?

The thought scared him. The brigands hated the military for not helping the villages, and he didn't imagine they would show him any mercy. They would most likely view him as a traitor for joining The Institute.

Boss looked at him. "So what's ya name?" he asked him.

"H-Harvey," he lied.

"Is that so?" Boss replied with a smirk. "Cos, that's not what your friend said."

Michael breathed in sharply, shocked. His friends had talked?

"My friend?" he asked carefully, trying not to show any emotion.

Boss laughed, and then turned on a TV screen on the wall.

It showed a girl tied to a wooden table, with cables running from straps on her wrists.

She turned to look at the camera, and Michael winced when he saw it was Nadia tied there. Her long dark hair fell loosely around her face. One of her eyes was black and her face was badly bruised.

Boss turned to Michael. "You speak, or that bitch gets electrocuted," he snarled.

Michael's eyes widened. He was faced with an impossible choice.

"What's your name?" Boss spat.

Michael took a deep breath. "Harvey Gold," he told the man.

Boss smirked, glancing at the screen. Michael could hear, through the tinny audio, the sound of a generator rumbling.

He watched a man pull a lever and saw Nadia writhing in pain. She was gritting her teeth, her face twitching. He could see the pain in her eyes, but knew she wouldn't give in.

Michael struggled against his bonds, wishing he could help her.

"What do you owe the military? Boss asked him. "Why won't you tell us what we want to know?"

It hurt Michael to see someone suffering because of him, but he knew he couldn't give into Boss.

"Just tell us, boy. The longer you wait, the closer to death your girl gets," Boss told Michael.

Michael looked away, not being able to bear watching Nadia's torture.

"Fine. Then we do it on you," Boss whispered Michael sadistically, tightening his straps.

Michael took a deep breath. If Nadia could endure so much pain, then so could he.

Boss placed on a pair of headphones. Michael frowned. He wasn't going to be listening to music while he tortured Michael, was he?

Boss then adjusted turned a dial on the wall, and the light intensity increased, becoming so blinding Michael had to clamp his eyes shut again.

He heard Boss moving some more, and suddenly a high pitched ringing sound filled the air. It blared out loudly, hurting his ears.

He opened on eye to find that Boss had left the room.

Michael was alone, without food or water, in a torture room full of glaring light and deafening sound.

And he didn't know how long for.

* * *

One day - twenty four hours. That was how long it took for Michael to be completely and utterly broken.

Nothing was worth the pain he had gone through. It had felt like years. Every second he was in pain. And that lasted for minutes, which lasted hours, which lasted forever.

His mouth was dry, his ears were constantly ringing, and he had not slept at all. He couldn't take it anymore.

Nothing he had ever felt had compared to this torture.

"I'll tell you everything," Michael croaked. "Just make it stop."

He waited, and eventually, the door opened.

Boss returned with a cruel smirk on his face. The headphones were still in place, and he turned off the machine emitting the sound.

However, it made no difference to Michael. The ringing had been going on for so long it now reverberated in his mind.

Boss dimmed the lights back to normal.

"What's your name?" Boss asked him.

"W-water," he muttered hoarsely.

Boss sighed, and picked up a small water bottle. He held it up agonisingly over Michael's face.

Michael tried to move his head up to reach it, but Boss just laughed. He then tipped some onto Michael's face, who drank it greedily.

Then Boss stopped tipping it and smirked. "Now, what's your name?" he asked.

Michael sighed. "Michael Bakerson," he told the man.

Boss grinned. "Tell me about the layout of The Institute. Where are the weapons kept?" he asked Michael.

Michael racked his brain, trying to remember Arthur's maps, but he found it hard to focus. "The ... the weapons are kept ... in the armoury, which is east .... no, south of the main complex," he told Boss.

Boss nodded. "And where are the food supplies kept?" he asked Michael.

Michael hesitated, making Boss look at him sharply.

"E-east. The food store is kept on the east side. There's also a secondary supply at the north west," he told Boss quickly, fearing torture.

Boss nodded, and asked Michael more questions. He answered them the best he could, but he didn't know very much about the layout of The Institute. He told Boss practically everything he knew.

After what seemed like hours of grilling, Boss stood up.

"You know, you won't be able to beat the military," Michael warned Boss.

Boss glanced at him. "We don't need to. It will be enough to turn the villages against them. They can't fight a war on two fronts," he remarked.

Michael looked at Boss with pity. "They already do. There have been countless rebellions crushed, why would yours be any different? It's suicide," he told him.

"Better to live one day as a lion, than a hundred years as a sheep," Boss pronounced with a smirk.

Michael frowned. That sounded too poetic for Boss.

Boss chuckled. "Michael, you really think I'm still a brigand?" he asked, opening the door. "The military gave us a lot of supplies for doing them this little favour."

Michael stared, as Sergeant Raines walked in. The Scottish man looked disappointed with Michael.

"Y-you're with them?" Michael asked Raines incredulously.

"Laddie, ye really think the brigands could nab our recruits so easily?" Raines snapped, raising his voice. "This was a training exercise, Bakerson, and ye've failed."

32 - WAKING UP

It had been two weeks since Michael's torture, and he still didn't think he had fully recovered. His squad had all been tortured, and had broken at various different stages.

The first to break, surprisingly, was Jürgen. As soon as they had tortured Nadia, he had given in. The next was Tim, who had given in when they had started electrocuting him.

The brigands had used different techniques on the Spartans to test what stage they would reach. Michael, Steve, Alexandria and Arthur had all broken down after about a day without sleep.

Teresa had also been subjected to sleep deprivation. It took them longer time to break her resolve, but after two days, they did.

Nadia, Joe and Hans had lasted the longest. The torturers had initially subjected them to the sleep deprivation, but they proved resilient. They then began beating them, using old fashioned methods of torture. They lasted for three days, until Sergeant Raines entered and demanded the brigands stopped.

Joe and Hans were the only ones to pass the test.

Nadia had been continually shocked with electricity until they accidentally set the voltage too high. The shock knocked her unconscious, and, fearing that she had been killed, she was rushed off to hospital. It was deemed that her exercise was neither a pass nor a fail.

As Michael had quickly discovered, Raines was disappointed with them for giving in. However, he softened upon seeing their injuries, and gave them time to recover. He spoke to Lieutenant Jones, and they decided that the brigands were too brutal to be used for recruits' training again.

After one week, Michael, Steve, Jürgen, Tim, Alexandria, Joe and Jenny returned to normal training. They had been the least affected by the torture. Hans joined them a day later, and Teresa joined them a day after that.

Arthur and Nadia remained in the hospital. Michael had visited them every day after his training. They said Arthur had experienced 'psychological damage' and they did not know how long it would take him to recover.

Michael had tried talking to him, but the boy had not responded.

Nadia was in a coma. Michael and Jürgen had both visited her together, their rivalry forgotten when confronted with their comatose squad mate.

It turned out that some brigands had been hired by the military to test how well the recruits could hold up under torture. Raines was annoyed with them for supposedly going 'too far'; however Sergeant Vellon believed that the recruits were too soft and needed toughening up.

Michael hadn't seen much of the other squads, seeing as he hadn't really visited the common room; however Steve had informed him that everyone had gone through at least some form of torture.

He and Jürgen were currently sitting in the Medical Centre, watching Nadia. Arthur lay in a bed next to her.

Michael had been there ever since training earlier that day.

Jürgen yawned and stood up. "I think I shall get some sleep now Michael. I shall see you tomorrow," he told Michael.

Michael simply nodded.

Jürgen cast one sad glance back at his sister, then left the room.

Michael stayed there, watching Nadia.

Guilt had been gnawing at him ever since that day. Maybe if he had given in, this wouldn't have happened to her.

He hadn't known Nadia long, but he had a lot of respect for her. She always put her best effort into every activity, and was a credit to the Spartans.

"Pining, are we?"

Michael glanced behind him to see Darius Finch standing in the doorway.

"Wh-what?" Michael asked.

Darius sighed. "Michael, do you realise how sensitive you are? You blame yourself for everything that happens to anyone in your squad. I understand that, but as a leader you need to show more backbone," he told Michael.

Michael clenched his jaw, looking at Darius coolly. "Why are you here?" he asked.

Darius held up a small multi-coloured cube. "This is a Rubik's cube. A puzzle," he explained.

Michael frowned. "What's it for?" he asked.

Darius looked towards Arthur. "I was hoping he wouldn't be able to resist solving it," he admitted, walking over and placing the Rubik's cube in Arthur's hand.

"He likes puzzles, you know," Darius said thoughtfully. Michael felt slightly guilty. He had been thinking about Nadia far more than Arthur.

Michael glanced up to see Darius watching him intently. "Why are you here?" he repeated, thinking Darius wasn't finished.

"I am here to hopefully talk some sense into you," Darius admitted. "You are training to be a soldier. If you can't bear someone close to you getting hurt, then this is not the right place for you. We are going to war. Every day, thousands of soldiers go to battle. A lot of them die. You have no understanding of the scale of this conflict, Michael," Darius told him sternly.

Michael looked at him with a frown.

"You are training to fight. You're willing to sacrifice your life for the Western Alliance, I know that. But that doesn't mean you're the only one. Everyone has made their own decision to come here, Michael. Do not blame yourself," Darius finished.

Michael sighed. Darius was probably right.

"Think of life like a car journey. You have to keep moving forward," he heard a familiar voice say.

Michael looked up sharply. Arthur was sitting on his bed with a rueful smile. The Rubik's cube was in his hand, solved.

"I suppose you're not the only one who needs to wake up," Arthur admitted.

Michael felt annoyed. He was perfectly fine. Was it wrong to care for his friends?

Darius was grinning. "I knew you would not be able to resist solving it," he remarked.

Arthur shrugged. "You were right," he confessed, standing up.

Michael stood up as well. "I'm going to bed," he told them briskly, then stalked out quickly. He breathed heavily, looking down at the ground. The bright lights of the Medial Centre were an annoyance, reminding him of the lights in the torture room.

He walked outside, and sat down on the floor by the Recruit Centre. It was a dark and crisp evening. In the distance, thunder boomed and lightning crackled. Michael closed his eyes.

He didn't see what he had done wrong. He was only caring for his friends, wasn't he? If being a soldier meant he couldn't do that, then maybe he was too sensitive.

Michael felt guilty. He should be happy that Arthur was back, but for some reason felt annoyed. He just wasn't sure why.

"Mike?"

Michael looked up to see Steve standing there, looking at him with concern.

"Jürgen said you were still there ... are you okay?" Steve asked him. Michael could hear the worry in his voice.

He sighed. "Yeah ... I'm fine. I've just not been feeling myself. Ever since ...," he trailed off, knowing full well that Steve had experienced the torture too.

Steve nodded sympathetically. "None of us have," he agreed, sitting down next to him. "How's Arthur?"

Michael smiled slightly. "He's back," he told Steve.

Steve grinned. "That's brilliant!" he exclaimed. "Now our squad is pretty much full again!"

Michael couldn't help but smile at his friend's enthusiasm. "Except Nadia," he reminded him.

Steve shrugged. "There's not much we can do about that. I doubt she'd want us to stop training because of her," he said casually. He spoke lightly, though Michael suspected he was trying to tell him something.

Michael bit his lip, looking out at the dark silhouettes of the buildings which stood out against the lightning.

"You're right," he admitted quietly.

Steve grinned again. "I know," he remarked with a cocky smirk.

Michael rolled his eyes, making Steve chuckle.

"Hey, at least you and Jürgen don't hate each other anymore," Steve commented, trying to lighten the mood.

Michael shrugged. "I never hated him," he replied.

This time it was Steve who rolled his eyes. "Come on, let's go back. You'll need to sleep, Raines said he has a surprise planned for us tomorrow," he told him.

Michael stood up and entered the Recruit Centre. "I wonder what it'll be," he commented, heading through the dimly lit reception area into the elevator.

Steve followed him. "Knowing Raines, it'll be something to help us 'bond as a team'," he said, mimicking Raines' Scottish accent.

Michael laughed, pressing the button for the male floor, 'Wellington'.

"What do you think of that new instructor, Sergeant Wallace?" Steve asked him curiously.

Michael considered. He hadn't really thought about him.

"I don't know," he admitted. "He seems okay, I guess."

Steve was about to reply when the elevator door opened. Michael looked up and was surprised to see Jenny leaving a room.

"Jenny?" he asked, smiling a little. "Wrong floor?"

Jenny laughed. "No, I was only saying goodnight," she reassured him with a smile.

Michael smiled. "Goodnight," he told Jenny. He always felt better around her.

Jenny chuckled. "How's Arthur?" she asked him.

Michael grinned. "Back to normal. Darius managed to wake him up," he informed her, feeling more relaxed than he had previously been.

It was good that Arthur was back. He didn't know why he had been annoyed earlier.

Jenny brightened up, making Michael feel proud to be the bearer of good news.

"That's brilliant!" Jenny exclaimed. "I'll have to thank him. Darius Finch, right?"

Steve nodded. "That's him. The mighty Praetorian," he remarked sarcastically.

Michael laughed. "We still beat him," he reminded them.

"Well, *you* did," Jenny observed with a grin.

Michael felt slightly embarrassed at the praise. He felt his face flush slightly. He shrugged, not sure what to say.

Steve seemed to sense this. "Goodnight Jenny," he told her with a friendly nod.

Jenny nodded, giving Steve a small hug. "Goodnight," she replied quietly.

Michael glanced at the room that Jenny had come out of.

It was *Jürgen's*.

He scowled, his jaw clenching slightly. Jenny had never visited *his* room to say goodnight.

"Goodnight Michael," he heard Jenny's voice say and turned as she gave him a small hug.

Michael stiffly hugged her back. He wasn't really one for physical contact.

"Goodnight," he replied quietly, with little warmth in his voice.

Jenny frowned slightly, then turned and walked towards the lift.

Steve smirked, clearly assuming Michael's coldness to be due to awkwardness. "You're clueless around girls," he teased him.

Michael rolled his eyes again. "Better than you," he retorted, carrying on towards his room.

Steve chuckled. "Mate, you have no idea," he replied cockily.

Michael looked at him curiously. "Teresa?" he questioned.

Steve's blush told Michael all he needed to know. He winked at Michael, and then entered his room.

Michael sighed and went in. He got changed into his grey pyjamas and laid down in his bed. He tried to shut off his emotions, and fell into a deep, dreamless sleep.

33 - FROZEN

BOOM! The grenade exploded, blasting the Russian into pieces.

"Good work, Bakerson! Now keep going!" Sergeant Wallace ordered.

The Spartans had been placed in a simulation of a typical Norwegian environment. They were using the new neural integrators that had been shipped from the US. These provided a detailed simulation of various battlegrounds that the Western Alliance soldiers would have to face. Although the recruits' bodies were not physically moving, they would experience the battle around them as if they were actually in Norway.

Sergeant Wallace was overseeing the exercise. Just the mere thought of Norway caused him to remember his own regiment's tragedy, and he felt it was his duty to ensure that these recruits did not go down the same way.

Within the simulation, the Spartans were all equipped with standard military winter uniform, which consisted of a thick skin-tight black bodysuit to keep heat in and protect them from impacts. On top of that, they wore plated body armour, which increased protection at the cost of mobility.

They were equipped with standard M16 rifles, the usual type of weaponry for the Western Alliance soldiers. The Spartans also wore helmets with various filters to help them navigate the cold Artic weather: infrared, thermal, radar and sonar.

"Alright lads, what do ya see?" Sergeant Wallace asked the Spartans through his communications link.

"Nothing! It's a blizzard!" Steven Green protested.

"The blizzard is interfering with radar and sonar, but on thermal I'm picking up heat signatures to the North West," Michael Bakerson told him.

"Good. Remember, the Russian army is split into two main types. There are the shock troops, heavy men with heavy weapons. They're nicknamed the Hammers. Then there are the Sickles, the lighter units who use mainly ranged weaponry, speed and stealth," Wallace informed them, reeling off his standard briefing like he had done before he left Norway.

"What about the Hunters?" Hans Sigurd asked. Sergeant Wallace didn't trust Hans. He was Norwegian, and his file stated he had had an experience with Fenrir when he was younger.

"The Hunters are a branch of the Sickles. They are Fenrir's personal elites," Wallace explained. "Fenrir is a ruthless and cunning general. He's one of the Big Three-"

"The what?" Jenny Mercer interrupted. Wallace hadn't yet figured out what Jenny was like.

"The Big Three: Fenrir, Attila and Saladin. They're the nicknames of the three most powerful Russian land generals. Fenrir commands Northern Europe, Attila fights fer Central and Southern Europe, and Saladin controls the Middle East and Northern Africa," Wallace explained, surprised at the lack of knowledge the recruits had about the wider war.

"What about the rest of Africa?" Tim asked.

Sergeant Wallace sighed. Tim's whiny voice annoyed him.

"The rest of Africa is a confederation of tribes and warlords within which Russian influence varies. There isn't much infrastructure there, so it's not worth fighting over. It's a very different kind of war there. But ye need to focus on Norway. That's yer priority fer now," he told them. "Focus on the mission at hand."

Sergeant Wallace checked the mission log. It read:

ASSIGNMENT 13B – TYPICAL RECONNAISSANCE MISSION

BRIEFING: There has been intelligence of a Russian division in the area you are located. Your task is to confirm or deny this by searching for any hostile forces, and report back to base with your findings.

THREAT LEVEL: Low

Currently, the Spartans had only discovered two Russian soldiers. They were mostly likely a patrol and Steve had quickly dealt with them with a grenade.

The Spartans pressed onwards. Sergeant Wallace noticed that Michael Bakerson and Jürgen Bauer seemed to be taking the lead and making the decisions, although there did seem to be some tension between them.

"Remember lads, Norway is not a forgiving environment. If yer teh be a soldier, ye must *always* be on yer guard," Wallace warned.

He watched as the Spartans proceeded cautiously.

"Remember lads, as Sun Tzu said, you have to know yerself and know yer enemy. Timothy! What are the strengths of a foot soldier?" he barked at Tim.

"Short ranged combat, sir. The M16 is proficient at close to medium range," Tim explained.

Sergeant Wallace nodded. According to his map, the Spartans were very close to the Russian encampment. It was located in a U-shaped valley, and well concealed by the snow.

The Spartans carried on, before the lead one stumbled at the edge of the valley, losing his footing.

He was poised to topple down, but one of his squad mates yanked him back. Wallace recognised that it was Jürgen who had lost his footing and Michael who had pulled him back.

"I don't see anything down there," Steve remarked.

"No heat signature," affirmed Arthur.

"Don't rely on tech. Remember that footage we watched? The Russians might be able to camouflage their heat signatures," Michael commented, squatting at the edge of the valley.

Wallace smiled slightly. The boy was a natural soldier.

"Should ve fire a flare?" Jürgen suggested.

"Negative, that'll give away our position," Michael stated. "Check radar and sonar."

"But the blizzard will interfere with them," Tim protested.

"But at this range we might be able to get a rough picture," Michael explained.

Arthur flicked the filter on his helmet. "Tim's right ... it's very unclear," he stated uncertainly. "But there is definitely uneven ground."

"There's either a lot of large boulders, or we've found them," Steve stated, sounding pleased.

Michael squinted down the valley, into the blizzard. There didn't look much there.

"Guys, we've got two heat signatures approaching from the north-east. A hundred metres out," Jenny broke in quickly.

Wallace watched intently, interested to see how the Spartans would respond.

Hans Sigurd quickly aimed his rifle, preparing to fire silenced rounds at them.

"Hans hold fire," Michael warned him. "They could be friendly. Everyone, stay low."

Hans reluctantly got down to the ground, as the figures approached.

Wallace watched them. The figures were Norwegian ski troops, mercenaries hired by both sides for their knowledge of the terrain.

They were discussing something in Norwegian. Wallace knew Hans would be able to understand them.

The two Norwegians moved closer to the Spartans, but were unaware of their presence. One of them was tall and stocky, with a long black beard. He was smoking a cigar, whilst the other, a young woman with pale skin, walked alongside him. They both wore white fur coats and ski goggles.

Michael breathed a sigh of relief, pleased to see that they were human. The Russians would look far more barbaric.

When they were less than five metres away, Michael thought it might be a good idea to ask them what they knew.

He stood up, and approached them. "Hello?" he began tentatively.

The large man turned to face them, and alarm registered in his eyes before the click of a silenced shot sounded. Michael stared as a large patch of red staining the white fur coat.

The woman opened her mouth to scream, but a rough hand clamped over it. Hans was grabbing her, his gun placed at the side of her face.

Jürgen stormed towards Hans and the woman. "Vhat are you doing?" he whispered to Hans.

Hans told the woman something in Norwegian, and her eyes widened in fear.

"Drop her," Michael ordered Hans sternly.

"She's a Russian, I heard them talking. She should die!" Hans told Michael.

"She's not Russian, she's human!" Steve scoffed, clearly having some preconceived idea that the Russians were not human. Michael also seemed surprised that a seemingly ordinary person would join the Russian Army.

"She's a prisoner," Michael replied firmly. "Let go."

Hans looked reluctant, but let go. The woman fell to the floor.

"I'm no Russian ... we're ... oh my God, Gunhild!" she exclaimed, staring at her friend's now lifeless body.

Michael could feel his heart hammering as he stepped back, a tight knot in his stomach. For a simulation, this was very realistic.

The woman looked up desperately. "Just ... go ... I'm a civilian," she pleaded.

Michael felt horrified at the fact that they may have killed an innocent person. The woman couldn't be Russian, could she? If there were any around, they would have come out by now.

Hans could easily have been mistaken.

"Let's go," Jürgen told the squad.

Hans frowned. "I tell you, they mentioned Fenrir!" he protested, seemingly angry.

"Hans, that is enough. Everyone knows who Fenrir is. This is a simulation; of course they would know who he is. They were probably just trying to bait you into overreacting – which you did!" Michael scolded Hans.

Hans snorted, then stalked ahead, annoyed.

Wallace was disappointed. The squad did not work together well.

The blizzard subsided, and Michael realised the landscape was quite bare. He glanced back to make sure there were no heat signatures. There didn't seem to be much around at all.

Except...

Michael spun around, looking at the valley they had come from. The woman had vanished, as had the body of the man.

"Halt," he told his squad. However, there didn't seem to be anything there.

He opened his sonar and what he saw surprised him. There was a huge amount of movement on the valley floor.

"We've got movement in the valley," he told his squad, as he saw some figures emerge from the side of valley, about one hundred metres away. He could see they were armed with weapons.

"Open fire! Radio in for an air strike!" Michael yelled out, as his squad leapt into action.

Wallace watched. The Spartans seemed to be responding well to the threat.

Michael let off some shots off his gun, taking calculated shots like he had been taught.

It was important that he did not panic. He fired at one of the shapes, and it disappeared, presumably into the valley. He took another deep breath.

'*Aim for the torso*,' he told himself.

More figures appeared, and the Spartans found themselves under fire.

Michael's breathing quickened as bullets whizzed by him. He could see the figures getting closer.

Suddenly, a cry of pain sounded out from near him. Michael ignored it, focusing on his foe. Adrenalin pumped through his body as the threat got closer.

He began to recognise that the Russians were the Hammers that Wallace had mentioned.

"Incoming!" he heard someone shout, and glanced up to see small grenades shot up into the air from the valley.

Michael froze. How was he meant to counter mortar fire?

He watched, helpless, as the grenades soared up high into air then began to dip down, instinctively taking a step backwards.

"I'm firing an EMP at them," Arthur informed them, causing Michael to glance back. As he did so, he became aware of a slight whistling sound coming from somewhere.

THUNK!

A searing pain shot through him. He looked down to see a long, silver arrow sticking out of his neck.

Michael tried to breathe, but could not. He coughed blood; his body shaking as he sank to his knees.

His entire body shook, writhing in pain.

The world span around him; everything was a blur.

A wave of darkness hit him as the simulation ended.

34 -   BLAME

Michael was brought back to consciousness with a start. He was covered in a cold sweat. He pulled off the neural integrator which had been attached to his head.

Breathing quickly, Michael glanced around at his surroundings. He was sitting in a chair, in a dimly-lit room. The neural integrators were unusually shaped helmets which simulated all the senses he would experience.

Even pain.

Michael placed a hand to his throat. Even though he knew there was no wound in real life, he could still feel the ghost of the pain he had felt.

It would be a horrible way to die.

He looked at the rest of his squad, who were all sitting in chairs in a row. Steve was awake, having removed his helmet, but his eyes were closed and he leaned back on his chair.

"Are you okay?" Michael asked him concernedly, standing up.

Steve opened his eyes and glanced at him wearily. "Yeah ... I just ...."

Steve sighed. "I never expected it to be like this. The Institute was always like a dream, meant to be something good. Now we're here, there just training, torture and death," he muttered.

Michael bit his lip, feeling sympathy for Steve. "I know what you mean. It's what war will be like," he remarked.

Steve closed his eyes again, nodding slightly.

Michael opened his mouth to speak again when Jenny let out a gasp, her eyes snapping open. She looked around wildly, breathing very heavily. She must have also been killed in the simulation.

Michael hurried over to her. "Jenny, it's okay, we're out," he reassured her.

Jenny met his eyes and breathed a sigh of relief, placing a hand to her own throat.

"Sometimes ..." she whispered. "You forget it's a simulation."

Michael smiled ruefully. "Yeah," he remarked, right before the rest of the squad woke up simultaneously.

The room was suddenly was full of noise as people adjusted back to reality. Jenny held his gaze, jumping a little at the sudden onslaught of sound.

"After you got shot, Arthur was able to set up the EMP to stop the grenades. But that didn't stop the arrows. I got shot in the neck," Jenny explained.

Michael winced slightly. He didn't like the thought of his squad mates in pain.

"Are you okay now?" he asked Jenny with concern.

Jenny smiled at him. "I'm fine, don't worry," she reassured him.

Michael looked relieved. He glanced across as Jürgen made his way towards them.

"Michael," Jürgen began. "Thank you for saving me earlier."

Michael was surprised. He hadn't expected an apology for stopping Jürgen from falling into the valley.

"I ... you're welcome," he told Jürgen awkwardly.

He noticed Jenny looking at Jürgen with admiration, presumably at his "gallant" apology.

"Well, see you later," he said quietly, a slight frown on his face as he moved away.

"Bye," Jenny called after him softly.

Michael was annoyed. She clearly liked Jürgen. What was so good about him?

He walked onwards, and then suddenly stopped.

Why was he annoyed? Why was he jealous of Jürgen?

Michael sighed inwardly. He knew the answer, just struggled to admit it, even to himself.

He was interrupted from his thoughts by Sergeant Raines striding into the room, accompanied by Sergeant Wallace.

"Alright lads!" Raines announced. "I think ye know that that exercise wasn't yer best. Let's go through it, what went wrong?" he asked them.

"Hans shot an innocent man," Tim said quickly.

"Or so you think," Wallace interrupted. "Hans is the only member of your team to speak Norwegian. Why didn't you trust him? What you should have done was apprehend those two Norwegians. In actual fact, they were locals, working for the

Russians. As soon as you left, they alerted the main base, which, by the way, *was* at the base of the valley," Wallace explained.

Michael sighed. "I take responsibility for that ... it was my decision to leave the area," he admitted quietly. He had a lump in his throat. He looked down, too embarrassed to meet anyone else's eyes.

How could he have messed up so badly?

Michael could feel Sergeant Raines' gaze upon him, and could feel himself going red.

"Well," he heard Raines say. "It's needless to say I'm disappointed, but -"

"Vith respect, sir, Michael led us vell," Jürgen spoke boldly, shocking Michael at his confession.

He looked up sharply at Jürgen. Raines also seemed surprised at the admission.

"Thank you, Jürgen," Raines said with a slight frown. "Though I don't take kindly to being interrupted."

Jürgen was looking at Raines resolutely. Michael was surprised, suddenly feeling guilty for his earlier resentment.

Raines held his gaze for a second, before continuing.

"As I was saying, I am disappointed, but that's not too bad a performance. When ye first arrived here, ye wouldn't even know how ta react to that patrool," Raines explained. "Ye've come a long way, Spartans. But I've got news. In eight weeks, yer being sent to Nurway fer real. Training will be amped, until in combat, knowing how to react is second nature. Eight weeks might seem like a way off, but it'll come faster than ye think."

Raines was silent for a few seconds while he let that sink in.

"Sergeant Vellon will be doin physical training every morning still, but we'll be focusing on these combat simulations instead of the outdoor stuff. Basically, any equipment that we use at The Institute, we can replicate with these," he motioned to the neural integrators.

"Now, let's start by repeating this exercise," Raines told them, making the whole squad groan at the prospect of another simulation.

* * *

Fifty three .... fifty four ...

Michael gritted his teeth as he pressed onwards with his press-ups in room Genghis 3. He was alone, still trying to come to terms with the events of the day.

The second time they attempted the exercise, it was changed slightly, but they were suspicious of everyone. They shot the two Norwegian mercenaries before they even got close.

Wallace remarked that this strategy could lead to innocent casualties, but it was unlikely that they would see many civilians in Norway.

Michael had taken a back seat in that exercise, and it was mainly Jürgen that had led them. He was still feeling guilty for letting the exercise fail so badly the first time.

Sixty ... sixty one ...

Michael forced himself onwards, even though his arms were aching. He grunted as he pushed up for another press up, using his emotion to help drive himself physically.

Sixty two .... Come one, just one more!

But he couldn't. Michael collapsed on the gym floor, his arms exhausted. He lay there, breathing heavily.

"Michael?" he heard Steve's voice call.

Michael quickly got up. Was something wrong?

"Yeah?" he asked, turning to face the entrance.

Steve ran in, looking around urgently. "Mike - Nadia's awake!"

* * *

"You can see her now," the medical orderly told them, stepping aside. All of the Spartans were there except for Joe.

Jürgen was first to enter the room, followed by Hans. Michael entered last.

Nadia was lying on her white bed, just as she had been. She was sitting up and looking around, seeming slightly embarrassed by the attention.

"Welcome back, Nadia," Steve told her with a grin.

Jürgen took Nadia's hand, and said something in German to her. Nadia smiled and nodded, before scanning around the room.

Michael met her eye and nodded to her, unable to stop himself from grinning. Nadia smiled back, before looking around.

"Thank you for coming to see me," Nadia told them quietly.

Teresa smiled, which was a rare thing for her.

"What happened?" Jenny asked Nadia.

"I don't really remember," Nadia said evasively. Michael sensed she didn't want to talk about it. He still partly blamed himself for not giving in when she was given electric shocks.

"Let's give Nadia some space," Michael suggested. "She'll need to rest, we've got some tough training ahead."

The squad nodded reluctantly and left the room one by one, with the exception of Jürgen. Michael guessed that they would want to catch up, so he followed his squad.

Michael felt much better as he lay down in bed that night. Although training was hard, his mind was elsewhere. He slept deeply, his exhaustion finally catching up with him.

35 - LOCKED

Stay light on your feet. Be ready for anything.

Michael circled around his opponent, looking for any opportunity. He was currently sparring against Hans, with the rest of his squad watching. They were in Genghis 3, fighting on the hard gym floor. He was wearing standard clothes so any impact on the ground would be painful. He had also had to remove his watch to prevent unnecessary injury.

It had been eight weeks since Nadia had woken up from her coma, and training had been very intense ever since. Firing a gun was now second nature to Michael. He was now able to effectively utilise the radar transmitters and as well as the combat gear they would be given in Norway.

"Watch out!" Steve called, but Michael had already seen the punch that Hans was throwing.

He ducked under it and aimed a hook at Hans' side.

To his surprise, Hans took it and aimed a kick at Michael's head. It was only his fast reactions that saved him as he leapt back. The kick however, still caught him slightly and he was knocked off balance.

Hans pressed his advantage with a flurry of punches, leaving only Michael's instincts stopping him from a quick defeat.

Michael knew that if Hans landed a punch, he would not be able to continue much longer. He just needed to stay out of range.

He stepped back a few times, Hans pressing him still. Michael knew he would have to make a move soon.

He decided, and lunged forward with a right hook to Hans' face. Hans seemed taken by surprise, but was able to catch the punch.

Michael tried to pull away, but Hans wrenched his arm backwards, further than it could ever normally go.

He gritted his teeth in pain, but was unable to fight back. Hans twisted his hand further, and Michael was pulled off balance and fell onto the floor, hanging with his hand still in Hans' iron grip.

"Do you submit?" Hans asked him.

Michael nodded. "Yes," he admitted, wincing.

Hans let go, then offered Michael a hand up. "No hard feelings?" he asked, with a small smile on his face.

Michael still felt embarrassed at being humiliated but accepted the gesture. "None," he reassured Hans as his friend pulled him up.

"You'll have to show me that move some day," he told Hans.

Hans chuckled. "There's not much to it. You just have to twist it. Grip the wrist firmly and twist," he told Michael. "My father, that is, my adopted father, taught me it," he explained to Michael.

"And it vos very effective," Jürgen interrupted, clapping Hans on the back.

Michael smiled, thinking to himself. Over the course of the last eight weeks the squad had become much more unified. Maybe it was the tough simulations, but his squad had definitely bonded. He could swear he had even seen Joe crack a smile once.

His squad burst into chatter, with Jenny, Jürgen and Tim all interested for Hans to show them how to perform that move. Michael naturally found himself going over to Steve, and found him in conversation with Arthur.

"It's time," Arthur was saying. "Raines said we leave to Norway today."

"Are you sure?" Steve asked him. "They might have changed their minds."

"Why would they? Fenrir hasn't been neutralised," Arthur reasoned.

"Actually, ye'd be surprised," Michael heard the now familiar voice of Sergeant Wallace state loudly.

The Spartans immediately turned their attention to him. Sergeant Wallace had entered with Sergeant Vellon.

"What?" Tim asked him.

"We have news, laddies. Me friend Jack has given intelligence that Fenrir's location has been pinpointed!" Wallace exclaimed to them brightly.

Michael noticed the squad all react to this in different ways.

Joe merely raised his eyebrows, whilst Hans stood up straight, a flash of pride in his eyes.

Michael noticed Jürgen seemed shocked by the news as he breathed in sharply.

Sergeant Vellon glanced at Sergeant Wallace with a frown.

"Ees this source reliable?" Vellon asked him.

"Very. In fact, very few people know about this, but ah thought the lads deserved to know," Wallace explained.

"So ... will we catch him?" Tim asked him.

"Ah hope so. We attack tomorrow, supposedly," Wallace told them.

Michael breathed a sigh of relief. "Are we still going to Norway?" he asked them.

Wallace nodded. "Yeah. It'll be good experience for yus," he told them. "Ye leave tomorrow. So pack yer things .... the time has come."

Michael felt a pit of nervousness begin to form in his stomach.

All they had been training for was about to become a reality.

"Who vill be coming with us?" Nadia asked him.

Wallace looked at Nadia with pity. "Lass ... yer not going. On account of yer medical condition, ye can't go. The instructors will all be remaining at The Institute, except Vellon and me," he explained apologetically.

Nadia looked stunned. "Who said I can't go?!" she demanded.

Sergeant Wallace grimaced. "Sergeant Raines did," he told her. "If ye have a problem, speak te him. The rest of ye are dismissed!" he announced, and the squad went inside.

Michael thought he would wait behind to ask Hans if he could have a go at the wrist lock he had used.

Hans went and approached Sergeant Wallace and Sergeant Vellon. "Sir, are you sure Fenrir will be caught tomorrow?" he asked him. "I mean, what if someone was able to notify Fenrir and he moved location?"

Wallace looked at Hans very intently. "Do you think someone here is a traitor, Hans?" he asked slowly.

Hans shook his head. "No, sir," he told the sergeant.

"I see ... well, rest assured, even if anyone in The Institute is a spy, it'd be very unlikely they would be able to get a message out by tomorrow," Wallace reassured him, clapping Hans on the back.

Michael, however, saw a glint of worry in the man's eyes.

"Joseph!" Sergeant Vellon barked suddenly. "Why are you not going to pack?"

Michael looked back to see Joe standing with his hands in his pockets, watching Vellon coolly.

"I'm interested to hear what Wallace has to say," he spoke slowly, holding Vellon's gaze.

Michael felt awkward and glancing towards the room's exit. It was slightly ajar. "Let's go," he told Hans and Joe, and walked towards it quickly.

The door swung shut before he reached it, and he quickly pushed it open to see who had been listening in. The corridor was empty.

He looked around and saw the elevator door closing.

"Hey, wait up!" he called, but the doors closed.

Not, however, before Michael had glimpsed the person standing inside.

It was Jürgen.

Michael stood there, as Hans caught him up. "Why were you running?" he asked him.

Michael shook his head. "Just trying to catch the lift," he said, not untruthfully.

Hans nodded. "I do hope they catch Fenrir," he remarked. "It will be good to see my father avenged."

"Of course," Michael said quietly. "Why ... why were you asking about a spy?"

Hans grimaced. "There aren't many who I trust, Michael. Remember Raines said someone in The Institute could be a spy? Well, I just don't want to take any chances," he explained.

"Basically, he thinks that any one of us could be a spy," Joe interrupted, approaching and pressing the button on the lift.

Michael looked at him.

"What makes you think that?" he asked Joe as they entered the lift.

"My brain," Joe replied sarcastically.

Michael took a deep breath. Joe could be infuriating to deal with sometimes.

"I mean, have you heard anything?" he asked.

Joe shook his head. "Nope," he remarked. "Nothing special."

Michael sighed, then went back up to floor Wellington to pack his things.

He was faced with Sergeant Raines and Nadia talking in the corridor.

"Ah, Michael, I was just lookin' for ye," Raines told Michael. "Nadia wants to go to Norway."

Michael nodded. "Okay ..,'' he said, having already knew that.

"And I've decided to let you make the decision," Raines told him with an amused grin.

Michael started, his eyes widening. "What?" he asked, not sure if Raines was joking.

"I want you to decide whether Nadia goes to Nurway," Raines told Michael, folding his arms. "Yes or no?" he asked Michael.

Michael paled. He knew he would blame himself if anything happened to Nadia in Norway. But if he didn't let her go, she might not forgive him.

"Being a leader is about making tough choices," Raines informed him. "Yer call."

Michael bit his lip. He couldn't do this. His shoulders sagged.

"H-Jürgen can make the decision," he told Raines.

Raines looked mildly disappointed, whereas Nadia looked furious. "Michael, you know he won't let me!" she exclaimed.

"He's your brother, Nadia. He should have more say than I do," Michael said quietly, looking at the floor.

"Very well," Raines remarked. "Let's find yer brother."

Michael looked down at the floor as they walked off, looking for Jürgen. He glanced at his wrist, but then realised he had left his watch downstairs.

"I'll catch you later," he told Hans and Joe, as he stepped back into the lift which took him down to floor Genghis.

He stepped out into the corridor and walked towards room three. Unfortunately, the door was closed and he needed an instructor to open it.

Michael scanned around, looking for someone. There was a door slightly ajar at the end of the corridor.

He approached it, and peered his head in.

What he saw very much surprised him.

Michael entered the room. There were screens, so many different monitors on the wall. The room was small and dark, with a dim light up ahead. There was a lone figure sitting on a wheeled office chair, studying the screens.

Michael watched, transfixed. Although he had become used to seeing technology around the place, the sheer quantity of displays intrigued him.

He peered closer. They seemed to show footage of the various rooms. In the centre was a map, with several small lights occasionally flashing.

Whilst looking at the figure on the chair, Michael cleared his throat.

"Sir?" he asked hesitantly.

The figure spun around, standing up quickly and causing the wheeled chair to shoot backwards.

"Who are ye? Oh ... Michael," the man said.

As the man stood under the dim light, Michael recognised the bright red hair of Sergeant Wallace. He breathed a sigh of relief.

"Sir ... what are you doing?" he asked, his curiosity getting the better of him.

Wallace sighed. "I suppose it'd do no 'arm to tell ye. Just ... don't tell anyone about this, eh?" he instructed Michael as he walked back to the wheeled chair and sat himself down on it heavily.

Michael closed the door and walked forward, looking at the screens.

"Ye know earlier, ah mentioned that Fenrir 'ad been located," Wallace told Michael wearily. "Well, it ain't true."

Michael's eyes widened. "So ... why did you say it?"

"Ain't it simple? I want te bait out the spy. I'm monitoring the screens 'ere to see who goes where, and what transmissions are sent out," Wallace explained.

"So ... if Prometheus does send out a message, we can see that?" Michael questioned, seeing what Wallace was doing.

Wallace looked at him sharply. "Who gave ye that name, Michael?" he asked coldly. "Because I never mentioned any Prometheus."

Michael gulped, realising his mistake. "I ... I heard Raymon's dad mention it to Jones," he admitted, looking down.

Wallace didn't say anything so Michael continued. "I heard them talking as I passed a corridor. Mr Collins was trying to bribe Jones to get Raymon in the Coliseum, and he then asked him if he knew anything of Prometheus. Jones didn't seem to know anything," he explained.

Wallace frowned. "That's a bold claim ye make, Michael. Bribery?" he questioned, then nodded thoughtfully as he thought to himself. "I reckon Jones suspects me. A few of folks back in Norway suspected I leaked information to Fenrir that destroyed my regiment. As if!"

Michael watched, biting his lip. Who could be the spy? Raymon? Joe? Jürgen? Hans?

Wallace sighed. "But I trust ye, Michael. Is there anyone you suspect?" he enquired curiously.

Michael shook his head. He couldn't give any names until he was sure. It wouldn't be fair.

Wallace nodded. "Ya know Michael, something I've learnt is to always trust your instincts. Yer gut can sometimes tell you more about a person than any file," he advised him.

Suddenly, there was a flash of red on the screen and a small beep. Wallace immediately turned to it.

"Ah'm monitoring the radio waves for any possible transmission. A red one means it 'as been sent to Norway," Wallace explained as he rapidly typed on the computer.

Michael nodded. "Can you see who sent it?" he asked, feeling excited at the prospect of catching the spy.

"I can see where it was sent from. I'm just sending the contents to me friend Jack," Wallace explained.

Just then, there was another red flash from the screen, but from a different location. "There's two spies?" Michael exclaimed in surprise.

"No... At least, I don't think so," Wallace said thoughtfully. "There might be official communications going to Norway."

Michael bit his lip again. "But how do we know which ones which?" he wondered.

"We don't," Wallace said simply, then was struck with an idea.

"Why don't you take the first and I take the second?" Wallace suggested, typing on a keyboard. "I'm inputting the location into yer watch."

"But ... what do I do when I get there?" Michael asked nervously. "And I, er, don't have my watch. It's still in Genghis Three," he explained apologetically. "That's why I came."

"Find out who it is," Wallace instructed as he walked out of the room and opened the door to Genghis Three. "Now be quick or they might get away!"

Michael rushed in and grabbed his watch, before nodding to Sergeant Wallace.

"I'll do my best," he told him, going down the stairs. He couldn't afford waiting for the lift.

Once they were out, Michael turned left, following the directions on his watch. The transmission came from the east side of The Institute.

He sprinted along the darkened road. It was early evening, the sky a cloudy grey.

The street was mainly empty, and although he got a few funny looks from the occasional officer, no one paid him any particular attention.

He pelted through the street, going as fast as he could. His heart was hammering in his chest, and not just because of the exertion.

Eventually, Michael reached the location that his watch showed. He was in front of a tall yet modern building. It seemed entirely composed of tinted glass. He had not been to this part of The Institute before, and the ominous looking structure made him feel apprehensive.

He wandered up to the sliding glass door. It was dusty, and didn't look like it had been used for a long time.

Michael scanned around, looking for anything of interest. There was an abandoned subway station nearby, as well as an old computer shop.

He sighed, walking around the side of the glass building, looking for a way in.

There wasn't much around.

Michael was about to give up when he saw a lone figure hurrying along at the far end of the street.

The figure was a very familiar one.

37 - HIDDEN

Sergeant Wallace hurried along. The signal was coming from the communications centre.

His watch beeped, signalling another message from Jack.

He opened it, and the call came through.

"Hey Wally!" Jack exclaimed brightly. "I got your message!"

"What did it say?" Wallace demanded, not in the mood for a chat.

"Well ... yeah, about that. One of the messages has official military encryptions so ... I can't access that," Jack said apologetically.

"Can't ye hack it?" Wallace asked irritably.

"I could, but that's not the point. It's the other message that's interesting. Once decrypted, it simply reads 'Ragnarok, Prometheus, Now'," Jack told him.

Wallace frowned. "Do we know where it was sent to?" he asked.

He heard a chuckle come through his watch.

"I was hoping you'd ask that!" Jack exclaimed. "Yes, we do! It's a town named Auli near the base at Oslo. I've told Captain O'Reilly, and he's agreed it would do no harm to send in your recruits to scout it out."

"What?" Wallace exclaimed. "Yer sending in the recruits to fight Fenrir?!"

"No, no, calm down Wally. The town is a peaceful one in our territory. It's only a few miles away from Oslo. It's unlikely that anything serious will be there, and it'll be good experience for your recruits to do a recon mission and could even produce some results. Fenrir won't be there, it'll just be another outpost. There won't be any threat to your recruits, except maybe a few nasty locals," Jack reasoned. "If it were anything to worry about, we'd have noticed."

Wallace sighed. "Alright," he muttered, as he entered the communications centre.

"The agent might have already gone by now, so don't worry," Jack reassured Wallace.

It was empty, except for a Polish technician working overtime and a cleaner hovering around the building.

Wallace approached the technician. "May I have access to the latest message sent overseas from here?" he asked him.

The technician, looked up sharply. "I'm sorry sir, that's classified," he said nervously.

Wallace had had enough of not getting information on Prometheus.

"It bloody well shouldn't be!" Wallace roared, grabbing the technician by the scruff of his neck and throwing him towards the computer.

"Get it open, or I'll call in Sergeant Albrecht," Wallace threatened. Sergeant Albrecht was the head of technology for the recruits.

The technician paled, opening the message.

Wallace leaned forward, expecting to see it read 'Ragnarok'.

The message read:

Ruth, I accept that going to norway was a grave risk, I object to killing innocents. Privately, if rescuing hostages overcomes guilt, must you endanger yourself trying to help innocents. Even though u are safe Now. Your Second brother André.

Wallace fumed. The message was pointless, just gibberish.

"Who sent this?" he demanded.

"A man gave it to me to send. I didn't recognise him," the man said quickly.

Wallace sighed. "If he ever tries again, tell me. But this is useless," he muttered.

Now all of his hopes rested on Michael.

38 -   CAUGHT

Michael was about to give up when he saw a lone figure hurrying at the end of the street.

The figure was a very familiar one.

It was Jürgen.

Michael breathed in sharply, shocked. Jürgen was Prometheus? Could that be possible?

He watched as Jürgen turned a corner, and then pelted after him, fuelled by anger.

Jürgen was a traitor.

Michael couldn't help but feel a sense of triumph. He had been right all along not to trust Jürgen.

He skidded around the corner, and saw Jürgen walking down the street away from him. He was probably trying to get away from the area where the transmission had been sent.

Michael followed him quickly, and saw Jürgen glance around, as though he was waiting for someone.

As he ran, Jürgen turned and looked at him. "Michael?" he asked, looking confused.

Ha, Michael thought. *He's pretending like he doesn't know anything.*

Michael slowed down as he reached him. "Hello Jürgen," he said coldly, glaring at him.

Jürgen frowned. "Ja ... vhy are you here?" he asked him.

"I could ask you the same question," Michael replied. "Prometheus."

Jürgen raised his eyebrows. "Vhat?" he asked, still frowning.

"You know what I mean!" Michael seethed, tackling Jürgen to the ground. Jürgen was taken by surprise and didn't have a chance to react.

As they hit the ground, Jürgen grunted. "Michael, I don't know vhat you - URGH!" He was stopped by Michael punching him in the face.

"Shut up!" Michael told him. "I know you're the spy, Jürgen!"

Jürgen's eyes widened. "I'm not the spy!" he exclaimed, chuckling.

Michael hit Jürgen's temple with his fist, hard. "Then why are you here?" he demanded, letting his anger take over. He couldn't deny it, he got a kick from having power over his rival.

Jürgen groaned. "I came to see Jenny," he muttered.

Michael faltered slightly, his heart pounding in his chest. "Wh-what?" he asked.

"We ... we're meeting nearby," Jürgen explained.

Michael felt jealousy rise up within him. He let it boil over and punched Jürgen in the face again. "I don't believe you," he told him. "I have proof you sent the transmission!"

Suddenly, Michael was wrenched up, an iron vice around his throat. He was dragged away from Jürgen, struggling to breathe.

"Fool!" he heard a voice spit down his ear.

He was thrown the ground. He groaned, looking up at Sergeant Vellon.

"What transmission?" Vellon demanded.

Michael coughed. "S-sir, you have to believe me ... Jürgen is the spy!" he protested.

"What spy?" Vellon demanded, anger flashing in his eyes as he lifted Michael up by the scruff of the neck.

"Prometheus," Michael said quickly.

He noticed Vellon's eyes widen slightly, fear flash in them. "Who told you of Prometheus? And what transmission?"

"It was on the screen in Genghis, I saw it!" Michael babbled, frightened.

"How did you get in?" Vellon demanded.

For some reason, Michael thought he shouldn't include Wallace.

"Err ... It was left open," Michael said weakly.

Vellon snorted, dropping him. "You will enquire no more into zis matter. Prometheus is not your problem!" he barked.

"Jürgen?" Michael heard a voice call, making his heart sink.

It was Jenny. Jürgen had been telling the truth.

He looked at the ground, listening to what they were saying.

"Jürgen … what happened to you?" he heard Jenny say.

Vellon smirked. "Usually I would punish you for zis, but I think you will be in enough trouble anyway," he remarked in his thick French accent.

"All of you, back to ze Recruit Centre!" he barked, before walking away.

"Ja … nothing … I fell over," Michael heard Jürgen say.

"Why is Michael here?" Jenny asked.

"He was with Sergeant Vellon," Jürgen told Jenny.

"Is that true?" Jenny asked Michael.

Michael looked up. He saw Jürgen's bleeding nose, and locked eyes with him. The boy nodded.

Grateful for his cover up, Michael nodded to Jenny. He didn't want her to be mad at him.

"Yeah," he told her, swallowing. "Vellon and I were doing extra training."

Jenny looked between them, before placing a hand on Jürgen's arm. "Are you sure you're okay?" she asked him.

Jürgen nodded. "Ja, we should probably go back," he remarked, glancing in Michael's direction.

Michael sighed, walking back alone. He could only hope that Wallace had fared better than him.

He walked quickly, ahead of Jenny and Jürgen, as the guilt of what he had done settled in.

He had got the wrong person. Jürgen was most likely innocent, unless Jenny was in on it too.

No. She couldn't be. Michael was certain of that. He trusted Jenny.

But why? he asked himself. Why did he trust Jenny?

He sighed, knowing the answer.

He could deny as much as he wanted, but he knew he was attracted to Jenny.

Prometheus was his enemy, and he was jealous of Jürgen. That was why he wanted them to be the same person.

He sighed again as rain began to fall.

They had run out of time. They were leaving for Norway tomorrow, and Prometheus hadn't been caught.

He still didn't know who he could trust.

And he had attacked Jürgen for no reason.

It had been a long day.

39 - PROGRESS

Eastern USA

"Sir?" Solomon, Blackburn's assistant, asked him. "I have news from The Institute."

Lieutenant Blackburn was inspecting the progress of the inventor Morales' robots. Technological Integration, Blackburn's department, had so far made twelve prototypes out of their target of twenty, and were testing the durability of the robots. They had not managed to override Morales' programming yet, so they were still functioning as search and rescue robots.

Blackburn remained silent, so Solomon continued.

"The recruits, including the one you made a deal with, Darius Finch, are being shipped to Norway tomorrow. They probably won't be fighting, but I thought it would be a good opportunity to test the prototype in a combat situation if one arises there," Solomon explained.

"I don't want to risk anything happening to our chances of hacking these robots. Darius Finch must remain alive until he has broken into the code for us," Blackburn stated.

"Exactly. These robots will be the best chance he's got of surviving. Also, it would get him used to how they operate in the field," Solomon suggested.

Blackburn slowly nodded. "A field test. That would give us a much better indication of their performance than laboratory testing," he remarked, then looked towards one of the scientists examining the joints of the robot.

"Malcolm," Blackburn said quietly. A large, square jawed man approached. He had a shaved head with a tattoo of a dragon down the side of his face.

"I would like you to go to Norway with one of these robots immediately, and activate it there. Go with the recruits and analyse its performance. Also, allow Darius Finch to analyse its source code," Blackburn said very quietly.

The man gave a single nod.

"We will be monitoring through robot's eyepiece lens. I expect the robot to be returned to us once it has been sufficiently tested. Do you understand?" Blackburn asked in a low voice.

Malcolm gave another nod.

"Very well, you may go. I shall hire a military jet for you to use," Blackburn stated.

Malcolm nodded again.

"Sir, may I interrupt?" Solomon asked.

Blackburn glanced at him, waiting for him to speak.

"The machine needs to be licensed to be allowed into Oslo. That means its name and purpose," Solomon explained.

"Sort that out," Blackburn ordered.

"I will ... I just thought you'd like to select the name," Solomon pointed out.

Blackburn remained silent for several minutes. Eventually, he spoke.

"Trojan."

Solomon smiled. "I will add that, sir," he told Blackburn.

Blackburn motioned to Malcolm, who then picked up one of the robot prototypes and left with it.

"Has there been any update on Techno?" Blackburn asked Solomon, referring to the former inventor whose ideas had been rejected by the military. He was now officially a terrorist, known for planting explosive devices at military establishments.

"No, sir," Solomon told him. "Though we suspect he may try something around the time of the next Coliseum Games. The protests are getting worse," he informed Blackburn.

Blackburn nodded slowly. "Alright. Let's hope these robots are ready to be unveiled soon."

40 -   GOODBYE

'BEEP! BEEP! BEEP!' sounded the screen on the wall.

Michael shook his head, not wanting to get up. He was too tired.

'ALERT! SUBJECT IS DESIGNATED AS HAVING DEPARTURE TO NORWAY SCHEDULED IN FIFTEEN MINUTES!' it said aloud in a robotic voice.

Michael sat bolt upright, remembering what day it was. The day they left for Norway. He climbed out of bed, doing his normal routine of washing his face before putting on his standard grey clothes, before heading over and looking at the screen.

ACTIVITY: MILITARY DEPARTURE

OVERSEER: LT. JONES

FLOOR: GROUND

ROOM: JULIUS 1

TIME: 05:00

ADDITIONAL INFO: Recruits, be ready to leave. Take only your standard clothes, all equipment and uniform will be provided. Norway is a four hour boat trip, so we are leaving at 05:30. Eat the provided energy bar and drink before you leave. - Sergeant Raines

Michael felt his heart hammering. It was finally happening. He was going to war. To fight.

He hadn't been particularly looking forward to fighting, but he knew it was necessary. It had just come so fast.

He ate his energy bar quickly, washing it down with the foul-tasting drink before taking a last look around his room.

He wasn't sure when he'd be back. He went over to the wardrobe, pulling out the worn out clothes he had arrived to The Institute in. He picked up his father's pocket watch, and held it to his chest.

He would do his family proud.

Michael pocketed it, before heading outside into the lift. Several other people were there. Michael recognised Thomas, the leader of the Jaguars, and Dan, the other recruit who had chosen Sheikh Bakir. Thomas was tall and muscular, with short brown hair similar to Michael's.

Dan gave him a nod, and Michael returned it.

"Nervous?" Thomas asked them.

"Yeah," Michael admitted. "I don't feel like we've trained much."

Thomas shrugged. "They won't send us into actual combat," he reasoned, and the lift re-opened on floor Julius.

"Line up in yer squads!" Raines roared, and Michael hurried over to the Spartans. He noticed Nadia was not there.

"Today ... is an important day for ye lads," Wallace announced. "It may be the last of yer lives, or the beginning of a promising career. It is a chance to make history, to do yer duty. I would say to do it for yer country, but there is no country any more. There's just the Western Alliance. So, yer not doing it for patriotism, for your king, for your nation. Yer doing it for freedom! For a chance that yer families won't live in threat, so that the world can rebuild, and the Russians won't take over.

Yer doing this for the people standing at yer side. Ye can look them in the eye, and tell them yer willing to die for them. And they'll do the same for you. Because when ye go to the battlefield, yer no longer boys. Yer men. Yer comrades. Yer brothers in arms, and nothing is stronger than a bond forged in battle between friends. Yer not fighting for yerselves. Yer fighting for each other."

When he was finished, the recruits stood silent as they took it in. Michael felt inspired. He looked to the side and locked eyes with Jürgen. Michael still owed Jürgen for covering for him.

He held the boy's gaze, not with hostility, but with respect.

No words were spoken, but Michael knew that he and Jürgen were no longer rivals. They were friends.

"Yeah, yeah, great speech Raines," Jones called, clapping slowly. "We're all inspired."

A few of the Legionnaires laughed, but no one else did. They had far more respect for Raines than Jones.

Jones cleared his throat. "Basically, don't die. It'll look bad on me if you do. As much as I hate to admit it, I need you guys for the Coliseum. I don't want to finish last next year," he told them.

Michael felt a bit annoyed at Jones. He only cared about his job, not whether they were hurt.

"Is there anything else I need to tell them?" Jones asked the other instructors.

"The briefing," Raines said pointedly.

"Oh ... yeah. Erm, Sergeant Wallace will now brief you," Jones announced, quickly stepping off the stage.

Wallace looked surprised to be asked, but stepped up anyway.

"Right, yeah, the briefing, which Jones definitely wasn't meant te make," he remarked, causing a laugh from the recruits.

Jones went bright red as he gritted his teeth and pointed his finger at Wallace menacingly, except that it wasn't very menacing.

"Yer going to Norway, lads. You'll be shipped in to the port of Oslo, where ye'll meet a regiment commander. Ye will then be sent to scout out the town of Auli for any hostile activity," he explained.

"Auli is a medium sized town situated along the River Glåma, about twenty miles from where the wall around Oslo begins. It is one of the three main crossing points over the River Glåma, which gives it important strategic advantage. It is manned by a twenty four hour guard, and explosives are planted on the underside of the bridge in case the Russians somehow arrive. However, ye shouldn't have te worry, as it's quite far from the front lines," Wallace reassured them.

"Anyway lads, make yer way to the docks, we're leaving!" Wallace told them, and the recruits began moving, led by Jones, who hurried off at the front.

Sergeant Raines approached the Spartans, as did the relevant squad leaders, all keen to give their squads some last minute advice. With the exception of Sergeant Vellon, the instructors wouldn't be joining them to Norway.

This was goodbye.

"Lads, lasses," Raines said, looking around. "This isn't the first time I've had te part with a squad. But I can say that ye've been the best one I've ever had the privilege of training."

Coming from Raines, this was quite a statement.

"What ye've been taught will save yer life. Trust yer instincts. Always be ready. Remember, all warfare is based on deception," Raines told them seriously, looking at each group member in turn.

Michael. Jürgen. Steve. Jenny. Teresa. Alexandra. Hans. Joe. Arthur. Tim.

"Thank you, sir," Michael told him.

Raines smiled ruefully. "Laddie, remember. A good leader can see the bigger picture," he told Michael.

Michael nodded, grateful for all the support Raines had ever given him.

"Anyway lads, good luck," Raines told them, before striding off.

Michael breathed deeply, not sure what to say. The rest of his squad were equally speechless.

"It's time to make them pay," Hans muttered, looking around as he started walking. "Let's show them!"

Michael nodded mutely as he walked, alone. When they reached the large docks, which were full of all sorts of ships, he glanced back at the place that had been his home for the last six months.

He would miss it. It had become somewhat of a second home to him.

He realised, that this might be the last time he would ever see England.

He might never see his family again.

Michael swallowed as the emotion threatened to overwhelm him.

"Goodbye," he whispered, before turning away, ready to leave for Norway.

41 - COLD

"Michael, wake up! We're almost there!"

Michael woke with a start, looking around, Steve was sitting next to him. He had fallen asleep whilst reading the brief. He was surprised he had been able to do so in the hard, uncomfortable seats of the ship.

He glanced down at the page he had been reading. No wonder he had fallen asleep.

The Order of a Russian Army - by A.G. Phelps

Although the format of a Russian Army varies each battle, there are several patterns of behaviour and strategy which can be identified and prepared for. We must first look at how the Russian army is structured. They can be split into two main groups:

The 'Hammers' and the 'Sickles'.

These names were inspired by the symbol for the USSR, and describe the two types of soldiers in the Russian Army.

The first group of the Russian Army is frequently a division of the Sickles, known as the Scouts. These are scouts for the main force, usually fast moving. Examples of these are Norwegian Ski Troops, Saladin's 'Riders' and Cossacks. They possess light vehicles and are usually very similar to a typical Western Alliance division, as they possess standard weapons and equipment.

Michael sighed as he closed the projector on his wrist watch. The order of a Russian Army probably wouldn't be important.

"Thanks, Steve," he told his friend, who nodded.

"Nervous?" Steve asked him.

Michael let out a breath. "Yeah," he admitted. "Are you?"

Steve shrugged. "*Well,* you know me. I'm never nervous," he said cockily.

Michael laughed. "You're bricking it," he teased him.

Steve smirked. "As if," he remarked.

"Michael? Can I have word?"

Michael instantly brightened up upon hearing Jenny's voice. "Sure," he told her, looking up to see Jenny in the doorway. He quickly stood up and went over to her, smiling, as he quickly tried to straighten his hair.

Jenny smiled back, then lead him outside, to the deck of the ship. The huge landmass that was Norway was coming into view. The weather was bleak, as the grey sky boomed with thunder. However, that did not dampen Michael's mood.

"What is it?" he asked Jenny.

"I've been thinking," Jenny commented. "I was probably a bit harsh on you when you ... saw Jürgen. And, I owe you an explanation."

Michael smiled. "It's fine, don't worry about it."

Jenny let out a small laugh. "No, seriously. Jürgen and I ... well, it's nothing official, but I like him. A lot," she admitted.

Michael stayed very still, trying not to let any emotion show as he felt a pang of jealousy in his chest.

"And ... I think he likes me," Jenny admitted, biting her lip.

"Great," Michael said quietly.

"I was just wondering ... Do you think you could see whether he does?" Jenny asked Michael hesitantly.

"Sure," Michael said simply, not trusting himself to say anything more.

Jenny hugged him. Michael placed a hand on her back, feeling awkward.

"Thank you, Michael," she told him.

"You're welcome," Michael replied stiffly, trying to keep the emotion out of his voice.

"Are you okay?" Jenny asked him. He could hear her concern.

"Just nervous," Michael said dismissively, pulling away.

Jenny looked sympathetic. "Same," she admitted. "But I'm sure we'll be fine. I doubt it will be dangerous."

Michael nodded, looking out to the mainland which was coming ever closer.

"I hope so," he said quietly, shivering a little. "It's cold here."

Jenny nodded. "We should probably head inside," she agreed.

Michael turned and walked back into the cabin. Just then, an announcement sounded on the speakers throughout the transport ship.

"PLEASE COULD ALL RECRUITS MAKE THEIR WAY TO THE CENTRAL BAY."

Michael, glad for the excuse not to have to talk to Jenny, went to the Central Bay quickly. It was a large hanger with room for all the recruits.

"Line up in squads!" Vellon ordered.

Michael did so, for once wishing he was in a different squad. Being around Jenny, although nice, hurt.

"You are arriving. Your uniform will be given. You are expected to behave as soldiers," Vellon stated curtly, as the ship slowed down.

Eventually, the back of the room opened up, the bright light cascading in.

Vellon called the squads up one by one to walk onto the pier.

When the Spartans were called up, Michael followed, taking a deep breath as he stepped outside.

The first thing that struck him was the cold.

Icy, bitter cold.

He could see he was not the only one feeling it. Arthur and Tim were both shivering as well.

It was only Hans that seemed unaffected. He had bright smile on his face as he walked.

"Home, sweet home," Hans muttered with a grin.

Michael laughed. "I prefer Britain," he informed Hans.

Hans just shrugged. "Some aren't tough enough to take the cold," he said with a grin.

Michael shrugged. "You're right," he admitted. "It's too cold."

Hans laughed, clapping Michael on the back. "Just think, soon we'll be able to take this fight to Fenrir," he enthused.

Michael smiled briefly to hide his nerves, but deep down he was worrying a lot.

He suddenly felt his training had been far from adequate for preparing them to fight Fenrir.

"Laddie, that's nonsense," Wallace assured Hans. "There's no chance ye'll meet Fenrir."

Michael felt slightly relieved, but was still worried. He wasn't a soldier yet.

He noticed Wallace hurrying to the front, and looked around at the head military base in Norway.

Oslo.

The capital of Norway.

He had read that it was one of the most important ports in the Western Alliance, as it was the only major link from Scandinavia to the rest of the world.

They had arrived.

Michael looked around at the huge port. There were a large amount of transport ships, and there were two huge battleships pulling into the docks.

"Today is the day those battleships are refuelled," Arthur commented quickly, fiddling with something in his hands. "Usually they're patrolling the North Sea. They have artillery guns with a range of over one hundred miles."

"So today would be the perfect day to attack?" Tim asked worriedly.

Arthur frowned. "Well, how would they know? The day that the ships come in is random," he pointed out.

"A spy?" Michael suggested, knowing full well of Prometheus.

Arthur paled. "W-well, if they did happen to know the exact day they came in then they'd have to get a message out quickly. I mean the day is only finalised a few hours beforehand," he explained.

Michael was relieved. Prometheus could not have known that early.

No. He was just worrying too much, as per usual. He was being paranoid.

The recruits were led through the city towards a central plaza.

Michael looked around. This was the first ever large civilian city he had seen. Ordinary, non-military people walking, shopping and living normal lives.

He looked at two children running up and down the street. They looked poor, wearing worn brown jackets and battered shoes.

Michael gave one of them a respectful nod as he made eye contact. However, the Norwegian boy spat on the ground, giving Michael a resentful look.

Michael was surprised, but could see why the locals would dislike the military.

The Western Alliance had moved into the capital and made it just another one of their bases. Just like they had done with Occupied Britain.

"What, er, security is there around this city?" he asked Arthur, as he couldn't remember what it had said in the handbook.

Arthur nodded. "A lot. Around the edge, there is a large wall with three main gates. These have two watchtowers one with a Bofors Mark V anti-aircraft gun.

"How are the gates opened?" Michael asked Arthur.

"There's an officer in each watchtower. The gates need a full handprint scan from each one to open. They can only be opened from the inside," Arthur explained.

"What if someone attacks the base?" Michael asked him.

"Every section of the wall, there's a fully rotatable turret which can target both ground vehicles and aircraft. The Russians would have to destroy everyone to take the city," Arthur told him. "They're all powered by a central grid, which needs someone of at least lieutenant rank to get in."

"What about artillery?" Hans asked.

Arthur nodded. "The Bofors Mark V AA guns fire out small explosive rounds, which can destroy any artillery shells in mid-air," he said.

Michael nodded, feeling the city was secure enough. "So if the Russians did want to get in, they'd need to take two watchtowers over one gate from the inside whilst also disabling all the turrets from the main power grid," he said. "With a lieutenant's rank."

Arthur nodded as they reached the main plaza. "The city's secure."

"Recruits, line up!" Vellon barked, and Michael stood at the front of the line of the Spartans.

"Captain O'Reilly will speak with you now," Vellon told them.

There was a man walking up and down the ranks of the recruits, looking them up and down. He had light grey hair, but did not look too old. He had very bright green eyes that were slightly eerie.

"Wallace?" he asked, his Irish accent prominent.

Sergeant Wallace saluted, but the man walked up and clapped him on the shoulder.

"Welcome back, my friend," Captain O'Reilly said warmly.

The pair had evidently met before.

"Thank ye, sir," Wallace said, a grin on his face. "I 'ope these recruits are up to scratch."

"Let's hope they're better than the Royal Scots, at any rate," O'Reilly joked with a booming laugh, before seeing the flash of pain across Wallace's pain and apologising.

"Too soon, I know," O'Reilly told Wallace, clapping him on the back.

"But in all seriousness, we need them," O'Reilly said in a low voice, before addressing the recruits as a whole.

"Members of The Institute, you've come just in time," O'Reilly announced. "Today, there's been reports of a huge attack on the oil rigs to the North, and we've dispatched the emergency garrison to help deal with them. This is the largest offensive we've seen in a long time. In fact, some intel says this is the Russians' push to take all of the oil in the country. They're calling this offensive 'Ragnarok'."

Michael stiffened, realising what had happened. The spy had called the invasion with the signal sent out. That mean he was partly responsible for the invasion as he had failed to stop Prometheus.

"We're taking no chances. All forces have been dispatched from here to help protect the oil fields. You're all we've kept behind," O'Reilly explained.

"How do we know all the Russians are up North?" Wallace asked him.

"The reports we've seen are conclusive. Elements from every Russian division have been seen, with the exception of the Hunters," O'Reilly told them.

"Are the recruits still being sent to Auli?" Wallace asked O'Reilly.

"Not all. I want three of your squads here in Oslo, manning the gates. The Brown Coats have been increasingly active recently, and we don't want any trouble," O'Reilly informed them.

"Brown Coats?" Sergeant Vellon enquired.

"Local supporters of the Russians. They're Norwegians who dislike the Western Alliance's presence in their country. Rumour has it, some of them have been leaking information to the Russians," O'Reilly told him.

Vellon nodded, and O'Reilly clapped his hands together. "Alright! Tell them whose going where, and then you can be off!" O'Reilly exclaimed, walking away from them. "I've got more important things to do, so good day, and good luck!"

Vellon cleared his throat.

"The squads which will be going to Auli are the Legionnaires, Jaguars, Jaegers, Spartans and Companions," Vellon announced. "The Praetorians, Varangians and Immortals will remain to guard the gates."

Michael took a deep breath. It was finally happening.

"Vellon will remain, whereas I will be going to Auli," Wallace announced. "Ye'll have to manage yerselves. There's no one telling ye what te do anymore. This is it. The real thing."

Michael glanced across to see how the rest of his squad were taking it. They all seemed to be remaining fairly calm, except for Hans, who was grinning enthusiastically.

"Hans?" Michael asked, surprised.

Hans chuckled.

"This is it, Michael!" he said quickly. "Payback time. Auli, here we come!"

43 - TROJAN

"Please put on yer uniforms!" Wallace announced, pulling a cover off a truck which contained a rack of sleek, black combat suits.

The group of recruits all went over to them. Michael climbed aboard one of the trucks and took one of the suits.

They were almost foamy in texture, made to provide good insulation. Although similar to the material of a wetsuit, they had several plates of what looked like glass. The plates covered the chest, arms and thighs, however the joints were only covered with the insulating material. The suits came with several jet-black helmets, similar to the ones Michael had once seen a motorcyclist wear.

Michael guessed that the glass-like material was probably something high-tech like -

"A structured polymer composite?"

Michael heard the familiar voice of Darius Finch.

"This is *very* impressive. I wonder how Wallace's regiment were destroyed wearing these," Darius commented as he put one on.

"Because, laddie, these don't do much to stop a razor sharp arrow through the neck," Wallace pointed out. "The polymer's too inflexible, so it will work well protecting something immobile like yer chest, but fer yer joints an' neck, it won't work."

Darius nodded. "They must have been very accurate," he remarked.

Wallace had a pained look in his eyes. "They were," he muttered.

Michael put on his combat suit over his normal gear, the uniform fitting him quite snugly. He stretched his muscles, finding he retained a lot of mobility.

"Darius Finch?" he heard Sergeant Vellon call in his thick French accent.

"Yes, sir?" Darius asked.

"Zis man wants to see you," Vellon told him, indicating a large bald man with the tattoo of a dragon down the side of his face.

Darius studied him for a few seconds before glancing at Michael. "Accompany me, Michael," he instructed.

Michael was surprised, but he didn't mind. He respected Darius, and counted him as a friend. "Er, sure," he told Darius.

Darius looked back at the man, who gave a single nod before turning and walking away.

Michael and Darius followed side by side.

"Any idea what this is about?" Michael whispered.

Darius nodded. "I assume you'll see soon enough. My guess is some form of advanced piece of technology that the military have acquired, but have yet to reprogram," he commented.

"How do you know that?" Michael asked, impressed he knew so much.

"They wouldn't need me otherwise. If you recall, several weeks ago we performed a competition before the sponsors. That tower was a test to see who was able to break into it," Darius explained.

"Then why isn't Arthur here?" Michael asked.

Darius frowned slightly. "That, I cannot answer. My assumption is that they deemed my personality better suited to the task," he remarked.

Michael bit his lip, as the man led them towards a nondescript wooden warehouse.

The man opened a barn door, revealing the large space inside to be seemingly empty.

Well, almost. Michael could see a metallic figure in the centre of the warehouse.

He approached it, brimming with curiosity.

It was a robot, in the shape of a human. It had thin metal arms and legs, and a blank, emotionless face. Its frame looked slender but robust.

Darius also approached, circling the robot.

"*My, my,*" he commented, staring in rapture. "This *is* impressive."

A small beep sounded, and a green light blinked on where one of the robot's eyes should have been.

"Good morning, Master Finch," a voice said. Michael didn't like the sound of that voice. It was too cold, even for a robot.

He looked into the camera in the robot's eye wondering what was behind it.

Little did he know the Lieutenant Blackburn was on the other side, thousands of miles away in the USA.

"I hope Malcolm has treated you well. I brought this robot here so you analyse how it functions and try to understand how it works," the voice continued.

Darius nodded. "I thought so."

"You will- who are *you?*" the voice asked sharply, making Michael recoil a little from the camera. It had probably just noticed him.

Michael cleared his throat. "Michael Bakerson, sir," he told him.

He thought he heard a small laugh. "I was impressed by your ingenuity in the tower," the voice remarked.

"Thank you ... sir," he said, feeling a little uneasy saying it to a robot.

"Mister Finch, the Trojan will remain with you throughout your time at Norway. I expect you to be fully familiar with how it operates by the time of the Coliseum games," the voice told him.

"The Trojan, sir?" Darius questioned.

"The name of the robot," the voice clarified.

Darius frowned. "Why Trojan?" he enquired sharply.

"Because these robots are going to destroy the enemy from the inside," the voice stated. "Anyhow, is there any important information you need to know? I have no time for idle conversation."

"Nor do I," Darius replied sharply. "What is the purpose of these robots?"

The voice sighed. "Currently, just for helping the wounded," he informed.

Darius remained silent for several seconds, before speaking. "And that's why you need me," he deduced eventually.

The voice also remained silent. "You're very intelligent, Mister Finch. Let's hope you don't perish here," he commented.

Darius didn't say anything. He was still examining the Trojan.

"Goodbye, Mister Finch. This conversation never happened," the voice said, before cutting out as the camera lens blinked shut.

"Who was that?" Michael asked Darius incredulously.

"No one," Darius said slowly, his gaze flickering to Malcolm and then back to Michael.

Michael understood. "We better go," he told Darius.

"But not straight away," Darius told him. "The Trojan is now mine to command."

Michael looked at the emotionless robot. "I thought that man controlled it?" he asked Darius.

"No, it possesses artificial intelligence. It is driven by its programming. A remote control is too unreliable," Darius commented, placing his hand on the back of the Trojan's spherical head and feeling around.

"Ah," he remarked, as he pressed a button, and a blue light in the Trojan's other eye turned on. The robot was activating, meaning only the camera and the voice could be controlled remotely. The rest of the robot had to be enabled using the button which Darius had just pressed.

"Trojan, identify yourself," Darius spoke.

"Unit zero-zero-four. Medical assistance unit," the robot replied in a mechanical voice.

Darius nodded. "They've not made many then," he informed Michael.

"Correct," the robot confirmed. *"I am Unit zero-zero-four of twelve active databases."*

"So it sees itself as a database," Darius mused. "Trojan, what are your current orders?"

"Current orders: Search for Western Alliance wounded and rescue. If no wounded in two-hundred metre radius, then stand by until activated."

Darius nodded. "I see. Well, continue with your current orders," he told the robot, before turning to Michael and nodding.

"We may leave now," he told Michael.

Malcolm opened the door to the barn, and Michael and Darius walked out.

After about a minute of walking, Darius spoke.

"That was Lieutenant Blackburn, do you remember him?" Darius asked him.

Michael shook his head. "Not really."

"Well, he's in charge of the Technological Integration Wing at the United States Military. I believe this will help me acquire a job there in the future," Darius told Michael.

"And you'd want that?" Michael asked him.

"Of course. The technology that is there is exceptional. The Trojan itself has potential to be revolutionary," Darius enthused.

Michael formed a smile at his enthusiasm, a rare thing for Darius.

"That's great," Michael told his friend, as they re-joined the rest of the recruits. They were in trucks, leaving behind the three squads which would be manning the gates.

This would mean separation for Michael and Darius. Darius was a member of the Praetorians, who would be guarding the gates, whereas Michael was a member of the Spartans, who would be going to Auli.

Darius faced Michael, a rueful smile on his face. He offered Michael his hand to shake.

"Goodbye, my friend," Darius told him.

Michael shook it firmly. "Bye, Darius. Good luck," he told him.

Darius nodded, before letting go and heading to his squad.

Michael breathed deeply, filled with foreboding.

He wondered if he would ever see him again.

44 -   ODIN HAS FOUND US!

Michael sat down in the truck nervously. He nodded at Jürgen, who nodded back. They were about to go to Auli.

Sergeant Wallace was talking to his friend Jack, making Michael wonder if anything new had been found out about Prometheus.

He shuddered at the thought of the spy that might be with them now.

"It's finally time."

Michael looked up, surprised to hear Joe speak. The dark-skinned boy usually was very sullen, barely looking at anyone.

"Yeah," Steve said, but Joe wasn't finished.

"This is it," Joe said quietly. "The bit where we show whether we're ready to kill for the Yanks. This is what they want. To let us do their fighting for them, while Lieutenant Jones and them sponsors just sit back and live the high life. We're just tools to them, machines made to do their dirty work."

"It's not like that, Joe," Alexandra protested.

"Yes, it is. It's what the Americans always do. They sit back, let other countries fight for them. Look who's here. We've got Norwegians, Irish, Germans, English and Scottish all fighting. But no bloody Americans!" Joe said passionately. He wasn't looking at anyone, just venting out his anger.

Michael felt a bit uncomfortable. Was Joe right?

"It's like Raines said, Joe," Arthur spoke up. "We're not fighting for a country, or an ideal. We're fighting for our families. We can't say that the world will be a better place if we win, but we know it will be a worse one if we lose."

"I still think America should have stayed a colony," Steve joked with a grin, trying to lighten the mood.

Michael smiled. "Yeah. You know, I read a book once," he began.

"Really?" Steve asked sarcastically, his jaw dropping in mock surprise. "By God, it's a miracle! He can read!"

Michael rolled his eyes. "Yeah, but it was set in America, and it said they say things differently over there, even though it's the same language," he commented, trying to change the topic.

Tim laughed. "That's stupid! I hear they call crisps 'chips'!" he exclaimed, always the immature one.

"What are crisps?" Michael and Steve asked Tim at the same time. Michael had never tasted them before.

"They also call racism 'border control'," Joe said savagely. "They deport anyone who looks different to them."

Michael almost facepalmed. He hadn't meant to feed Joe's hatred of America.

"Isn't it ironic that you're accusing them of being racist? I mean, you're the one slating off a whole country," Steve pointed out.

Joe glared at him. "When you've lived your whole life in poverty because of what the Americans have done to your family, then come back and say I don't have a right to hate them," he told Steve.

Steve held his gaze. "Joe, we've all had it hard. Our village was almost wiped out by the war," he told Joe. "We've suffered just as much as you."

"Exactly. They've done nothing for us, why should we fight for them?" Joe argued.

"Both of you, shut up!" Teresa told them, folding her arms. "We're going to fight the Russians, so stop arguing."

"I agree," Sergeant Wallace said firmly. Michael hadn't noticed him come over. "The one to way te victory, is through unity."

Michael raised his eyebrows, surprised.

"Now lads, let's make the Russians pay for they've done!" Sergeant Wallace roared as he climbed into the truck, flooring the accelerator.

The Spartans were silent for most of the journey, which lasted about twenty minutes.

Michael felt very nervous, and was sure the rest of his squad did as well.

Eventually, they arrived, as the truck drove up to a bridge with a watchtower on either side.

"This bridge is very important, lads. The watchtowers both contain explosives te blow it if necessary," Wallace explained.

He went and spoke with an elderly security guard, who nodded, raising the barrier in front of the bridge.

Wallace climbed back in and drove into Auli. It was a medium sized urban town, full of people walking around. Michael guessed it was around midday.

"Alright lads, ye've read yer briefings," Wallace told them. "Off ye go."

As the rest of the squad left, Michael breathed deeply. He couldn't remember reading the briefing.

"Sir?" he asked Wallace.

Wallace nodded. "I want ye to come with me," he told Michael.

Michael was surprised. "What for?" he asked Wallace.

"Jack's pinpointed the signal location to a building by the outskirts," Wallace explained. "We're going te check it out."

Michael nodded. "Alright," he agreed, as Wallace continued driving the truck. He was relieved he hadn't been exposed for not knowing what to do, and could only assume this was about Prometheus.

Wallace parked the car by a nondescript bungalow. It seemed fairly old fashioned, and Michael would never assume anything of it.

He took a deep breath as he climbed off the truck. It was just starting to snow, but Michael was too nervous to feel the cold.

"Alright," Wallace said, pulling out his rifle. "Get yer gun."

Michael placed his hand to his waist, where his M16 assault rifle hung in a large holster. He had barely noticed it before now.

"We believe that Prometheus' contact is here," Wallace told him, breathing quickly. "I'm still new to this, but we're going in and finding him."

Michael nodded. "Yes, sir," he told Wallace.

Sergeant Wallace took a deep breath, then approached the building, rapping on the thin wooden door.

The door seemed to do very little to keep out the cold, Michael thought.

Michael gripped his gun tightly, hearing movement from within.

"Who is it?" a voice called out. It sounded elderly.

"Military," Sergeant Wallace replied gruffly. "Open the door."

"Oh ... alright," the elderly voice mumbled. "Let me just find the key."

Michael stepped back, gripping his gun even more tightly now.

"Ah," the man replied. "Got it."

The door was shattered as gunfire ripped through the flimsy wooden structure. The sound of a machine gun being fired erupted loudly from within the house. Sergeant Wallace took the brunt of the hits, as bullet holes covered the door.

Michael started, pulling up his gun and returning fire at the door. The recoil of his own rifle shocked him, the gun flying back into his shoulder.

However, he steeled himself, his training taking over. It was just like a simulation.

He fired until his magazine was empty, before standing to the side of the doorway and reloading. He tried not to look at the body of Wallace lying on the floor.

He heard someone frantically rummaging around inside, and kicked down the remains of the door. The person was in another room, speaking quickly.

"H-hello?" the person was saying. "Fenrir, this is Ruth. Mission compromised. Odin has found us, I repeat, Odin has-"

Michael burst into the room, opening fire at the figure, who fell back to the floor, the phone line receiver in his hand.

It was an elderly man with wispy grey hair. He had a glazed look in his eyes, and his baggy shirt was covered in blood. He wore a brown leather waistcoat, and had silver ring on his left hand.

He was dead.

Michael had killed him.

Michael's hands shook as he leant over the body, taking the phone receiver out of the man's hand and holding it up to his ear. Was it Fenrir?

"H-hello?" he asked down it, his heart pounding in his chest.

There was breathing on the other side.

"Did you kill my agent?" a powerful, deep voice asked. It had a Russian accent.

Michael gulped. He was speaking to one of the most powerful commanders in the world. He took a deep breath.

"Yes," he told Fenrir, trying to keep the emotion out of his voice.

"Thank you. He was inept. I will reward you with a quick death," Fenrir's voice told him, chilling him to the bone.

Michael couldn't hide his fear. "I know what you're planning. We all do. Ragnarok? Prometheus? You played into our hands," he bluffed. "When you come, we'll be ready."

Fenrir laughed, a harsh, cold laugh. "You know nothing. Already, you are helpless. I can hear the fear in your voice. You're no more than a child! The Western Alliance will fail you, and you will die for nothing! You are nothing! What is coming will-"

Michael cut the link, dead. He was terrified. He heart was beating like a jackhammer.

Had that actually been Fenrir, or just someone masquerading as him?

He staggered out of the room, looking for Wallace. Was he alright?

Michael's breath shook as he looked down at the figure lying in the doorway.

Sergeant Wallace was there, his combat gear stained with blood.

Michael felt sick as he squatted down next to him.

He wasn't moving.

45 -   **BLOODSTAINED**

"Sir? Sergeant Wallace!?" Michael pleaded, shaking him. There was no response.

They had been taught first aid at The Institute. First, he needed to assess the injury. He frantically checked Wallace's pulse, and it was still there, albeit faint.

He pressed the alarm button on his wristwatch, sending a message to everyone who was in Auli. He took a deep breath.

"This is Michael Bakerson. Sergeant Wallace has been critically injured. We were attacked by a Russian agent, and Wallace is currently bleeding out. I really need assistance in transporting him back to Oslo. Send a truck over to my current location immediately. Please." He ended the message.

The Jaguars were the first on the scene. Widely acknowledged as the best squad, Michael was incredibly relieved to see them and desperately hoped they could take Wallace to safety in time.

Thomas, their leader, instructed two people to carry Wallace's body to the truck parked nearby.

"Michael, what happened?" Thomas demanded.

Michael looked up at him fearfully. "A Russian agent was in there. He fired through the door. I killed him. He was contacting Fenrir," he explained, recalling the details.

Hang on. The agent had been contacting Fenrir.

Michael activated his wristwatch, sending a message to Arthur.

"Arthur? Come to my current location immediately, I need you."

Michael ended the message, watching as Wallace was gingerly placed the back of the truck.

"What is that for?" Thomas asked him.

"Arthur can track Fenrir's location. We had a link open with him," Michael reasoned.

Thomas nodded. "What did Fenrir say?" he urged.

"That we knew nothing. That the Western Alliance would fail," Michael told Thomas. "He sounded crazy."

"Maybe he is," Thomas remarked. "Anyhow, I'm going to call in the squad leaders. You can represent the Spartans."

Michael nodded.

Thomas walked off, speaking into his wristwatch.

Michael leant against the wall, the sheer intensity of what had just happened hitting him.

He had killed someone.

Sure, the man had shot Wallace, but the Russians were still human beings.

He stood there, motionless as he waited for the squad leaders to arrive. He was dimly aware of the snowfall getting heavier, but didn't care. Eventually, he heard a voice.

"Michael? What happened?"

Michael looked up to see Sophie, the leader of the Jaegers. Michael hadn't trusted her since the incident in the tower.

"We're having a squad leader meeting," he told her, wanting to appear confident. "I'll tell everyone then."

Sophie nodded, as Michael turned as walked over to where Thomas, representing the Jaguars, and someone from the Companions whom Michael did not recognise.

"Dominic," the boy said, offering his hand to Michael. He had ginger hair and a freckly face, with very dark brown eyes. "I'm the leader of the Companions."

Michael shook it firmly. "Alright, let's get to it," he told them.

Raymon was also there, representing the Legionnaires, but he paid no attention to Michael.

Thomas cleared his throat, taking charge. "This place is dangerous. There was a Russian agent here, which means there may be more," he stated firmly.

Michael agreed. "The spy was speaking to Fenrir, saying that the mission was compromised. That was when he knew we were here. I'm assuming that this has something to do with Auli," he suggested.

Sophie looked worried. "Are you sure?" she asked him.

"No, but -"

She was cut off by the sound of gunfire for the edge of the town. Suddenly, all of their watches erupted in sound.

"We're under attack! East side of the village, we've got Russians coming in. They've got silenced weapons, so put your helmets on! I think they're heading for the bridge. There's at least forty of them! They're Norwegian Ski Troops, so watch out!" a panicked voice said, before the message ended.

Thomas immediately took command. "Michael, you take the Spartans and head to the east side of the town. Evacuate civilians and take out the Russians. Sophie, take your Jaegers with him.

Dominic, the Companions will come with my squad to the bridge," Thomas instructed.

"What about me?" Raymon asked. "And who put you in charge?"

Thomas glanced at him. "We do not have time for a debate. Please could you take your squad to the main road, where you will ambush the Norwegians."

Raymon grunted.

Thomas gestured. "Let's go!" he exclaimed, before sprinting off towards.

Michael ran breathlessly in the other direction, towards the east side of the town. Auli was a large place, so he would need to find his squad.

He sent a message to the Spartans.

"Spartans, this is Michael. Regroup at the church," he urged them, spotting a church not too far away.

He was glad the Jaguars were here - Thomas was a natural leader.

Michael sprinted over to the church, luckily finding Jenny, Steve, Arthur and Hans waiting there.

"Is this it?" he asked them.

"Jürgen led the others away; a fire has been started in the North and he wanted to help civilians," Hans told him.

Michael nodded. "Have any of you seen the Russians?" he asked them.

"No, but I can guess," Arthur spoke up. "They'll be fast, so we've got about two minutes before they come. They'll have skis and snowmobiles. This is the main road, they'll probably come along here."

"Okay," Michael said, stepping outside. "We'll meet up with the Jaegers."

He looked around. Sophie's squad, around eight of them, were in a group at other the side of the road further ahead, going towards the outskirts of the town.

"Helmets on," Jenny reminded them, as Michael began walking quickly towards the Jaegers, who were about twenty metres in front of the Spartans.

This had all happened far too fast. He looked around as his boots crunched through the carpet of snow.

The gunfire ceased in the distance, leaving only a curious low humming sound.

Michael looked back at his squad. Hans was there, looking determined.

Steve, loyal as always. Arthur, probably thinking through some plan.

And Jenny.

Michael's helmet obscured his face, but he smiled at her. He turned and looked towards the Jaegers up the road.

The humming was getting louder; it sounded like an engine.

Suddenly, several white shapes emerged from around the corner, fast.

Norwegian Ski Troops.

They were dressed all in white, and were mostly on snowmobiles, with others on skis.

Before Michael could react, they opened fire on the Jaegers with silenced rounds. The recruits were taken by surprise, were soon lying on the ground, the snow stained with their blood.

Michael stared, dumbstruck. This wasn't happening.

"No!" Hans yelled out, firing at the white mass of Russians.

Michael dived behind a wall, snapped out of his stupor. He readied his gun, then fired at the Norwegian Ski troops. A spurt of red amongst the white told him he had hit his target.

He heard the low roar of the snowmobiles as they rushed past him, skiers going with them. He fired at them as they came past, sending a man tumbling as blood erupted from his wounds. The snowmobile spun around in the snow, skidding to a halt.

As the Russian Scouts carried on towards the bridge.

Michael made his way over to the man he had shot, only to find that he wasn't a man.

It was a pale blond boy, around Michael's age. He had blue eyes, and his face was splattered with blood.

The boy muttered something in Norwegian. His eyes locked on Michael, pleading.

Michael gripped his gun tightly, his throat constricted. He had seriously hurt this boy. Michael had no hate for him, only guilt. They were just unlucky enough to be on opposite sides of the war. It was a good thing he was wearing a helmet, for he could bear to look the boy in the eye.

"I'm sorry," Michael said quietly.

"Please...," the boy whispered in English. "Don't let me die..."

Michael breathed heavily, as he noticed the bulky figure of Hans walk up to him. Hans took one look at the boy, then mercilessly shot him again.

Michael recoiled, shocked. "Wh-what? What the hell, Hans?" he demanded, checking the boy's pulse vainly, but he was clearly dead. His eyes had a glazed look in them.

Hans turned to look at him. Michael couldn't see through the boy's helmet. "What?" Hans asked. "He's an enemy. I put him out of his misery."

Michael was horrified at how Hans could so easily kill someone their age.

He remember Grandpa Ted's words.

The military doesn't turn boys into men. It turns men into machines.

Michael looked at the corpse of the boy, closing the boy's eyes. He then stood up and looked towards the Jaegers. Had anyone been shot?

He ran over, and saw Sophie kneeling in the snow, holding a girl's head in her hands.

"Jane, no," she was whispering. Jane was a girl in Sophie's squad.

"Sophie?" Michael asked her. "Are you okay?"

"I'm fine," Sophie snapped. "What are you waiting for, go after them!"

Michael was taken aback. He looked towards the corpse of the Norwegian boy, with his long white ski uniform and sniper rifle, and then to the unmanned snowmobile sitting in the snow.

Time to take this fight to the enemy.

46 -   A BRIDGE TOO FAR

I'm sorry, Michael thought as he pulled the uniform off the Norwegian boy. It was a white coat, lined on the inside with fur and designed to insulate the wearer as much as possible. The inside reminded Michael of the fur on one of Grandpa Ted's jackets, and it seemed to be stitched together only roughly. It was a stark contrast to the high tech combat gear of the Western Alliance, and led Michael to believe that these Norwegian mercenaries were not very well equipped.

The boy was a similar build to Michael, so it was a tight squeeze to fit the coat over his combat gear. Underneath the coat, the boy wore brown leather clothes, but Michael didn't want to disrespect his corpse further by removing anything more.

Back in his village, they had always been taught to honour the dead. The deceased were cremated in a field which was a short walk from the village. Michael hoped Grandpa Ted was still alive and well.

His mind snapped back to the present as he zipped up the white coat over him. He had no idea if the disguise would work. He reckoned he shouldn't wear his Western Alliance helmet as it would give him away too easily. Instead, he pulled on the boy's ski goggles and pulled the hood of the coat up tightly. He could feel the biting cold on his face, but at least the rest of his body was warm.

He then knelt down again and inspected the boy's weapon. It was a long, brown hunting rifle. Bolt action, with a sniper scope. It would have good power and accuracy, but took time to reload. He would need to make his shots count.

He exchanged it for his M16 assault rifle, but kept his sidearm stashed inside the coat.

Michael now headed towards the snowmobile as he slung the rifle onto his back. He was incredibly lucky that it was undamaged. However, they had only ever practiced one snowmobile simulation with the neural integrators, and Michael had struggled to drive it.

He took a deep breath, thinking about his teammates. He had to do this; for all the recruits that had died so far. He had to at least try.

Michael climbed onto the snowmobile, gripping it tightly. It was heavier than the ones he had practiced with, but the concept was the same.

He pressed down on the accelerator, the power of the vehicle shocking him. A loud roar filled his ears as the snowmobile thundered forward, like wild animal waiting to be unleashed. He gripped it tightly, doing his best to steer it up the road as he pressed down further on the pedal.

Michael's heart thumped in his chest quickly, as the air resistance almost blew off his hood. The icy wind seemed to cut against his face as he rode down the road, trying to remember the layout of Auli. He passed the ominous church as he headed for the bridge.

He wondered what had become of the other squad leaders.

Michael pressed onwards until he saw a number of dead Norwegian bodies. This must have been where Raymon's squad had ambushed the ski troops. As Michael glanced to the side, he saw the corpses of recruits. The Norwegians clearly had not gone down without a fight.

CRACK!

A bullet whizzed over Michael's shoulder, thudding into a building behind him. He was under fire. He revved up the snowmobile, driving onwards.

CRACK! CRACK! The steady fire of bullets continued, the shots getting closer and closer as he powered forward. Luckily, the shots seemed to be quite inaccurate.

He realised the shots were probably from his own side, as he was dressed like a Norwegian. Damn.

Michael surged on until he reached the long stretch of road before the bridge. There were bodies littered all around the bridge. Michael squinted, looking to see which side controlled it.

There were several white-coated people, standing sentry at the end. He wished he had his helmet so he could see how many there were. Thermal vision would be very useful right now.

Michael drove up slowly. The Norwegians hopefully wouldn't see through his disguise. However, he wouldn't be able to accomplish anything alone.

He activated his wristwatch, ringing the rest of the squad leaders.

"Guys? It's Michael, I'm going in, disguised as a Norwegian. They have control of the bridge. What is the sit rep?" Michael asked them.

"Michael? Thomas here. Our forces have been depleted massively, the Norwegians took us by surprise. I'd say there's at least twenty of them guarding the bridge. Approach them with caution. We've got a few recruits scattered in nearby buildings, so as you get close, we'll open fire. When we do, you run for the watchtower. They've got explosives in there. Use them to destroy the bridge. Notify Oslo about what has happened from the watchtower radio."

"Destroy the bridge? Thomas, the villagers would be trapped on your side. So would all of you. There would be no way for you to get back to Western Alliance territory. You'd be trapped on the Russian side of the river."

"Michael, this is a much bigger invasion than Auli. The Norwegians are just the first part of the Russian army. We must sacrifice this village in order to protect the route to Oslo. That's an order, Michael."

"We can't do that, Thomas. We can keep the bridge open."

"Michael, I'm ordering you to blow the bridge."

"Thomas, you're not my commanding officer. The bridge stays. Squad leaders, I need a status report," Michael instructed.

"Sophie here. Jaegers are depleted. Proceed without us."

"Dominic here. Companions have seven fighting recruits still active. We're in a courtyard not too far from your position."

"Raymon here. The Legionnaires are ready to fight. We're marching towards the bridge now, ETA two minutes."

Michael heard Thomas sigh. *"Thomas here. Jaguars are in buildings near the bridge, spread out. We can cover the Legionnaires. I want the Spartans to continue helping civilians with the fire that the Russians started up north. Any able Jaegers will help them. Dominic, bring the Companions to the bridge. We're taking it back."*

Michael took a deep breath as he reached the far side of the bridge, but his heart was hammering in his chest.

A few of the white coated men glanced in his direction. They were in a group, talking. One of them called something in Norwegian loudly, followed by a chuckle. The rest of the Norwegians around him all laughed too.

Michael brought the snowmobile to a stop near the right-hand side watchtower.

Michael lowered his head as though embarrassed, as he headed up towards the watchtower. He walked up the steps, though he shuddered slightly as he saw the elderly security guard lying down in a pool of blood.

The door was closed, though it had glass windows. There were two Norwegians inside, chatting. One of them was gripping his gun tightly, whilst the other looking out across the bridge.

Michael looked at his watch. As well as all of its additional features, it still told the time.

The Legionnaires were predicted to arrive in about thirty seconds.

Michael took a deep breath, then knocked on the door. Inside, on the table, was a radio, with an emergency button. He just needed to press it to contact Oslo.

The man holding the gun turned around. He was a red faced bearded man, and had a very large, broad build. Michael was filled with trepidation, realising that his life could soon be over.

Michael tried to steady his breathing as the man wrenched the door open, letting the cold in.

He barked something in Norwegian.

Michael was about to reply (although he wasn't sure what with), when shots erupted from the far side of the bridge. The bearded man muttered something, then pushed past Michael and ran down the steps from the watchtower. Michael entered quickly, closing the door behind him.

Through the misty panes, he could see the muzzle flashes of gunfire at the far side of the bridge. The Norwegians were well organised, and returned fire quickly. Michael immediately turned his attention to the other Norwegian in the room.

He was surprised to see it was a female. She had brown hair, pale skin and dark brown eyes. She looked to be in her thirties. She had a look of experience in her eyes, though Michael could also see concern in them. Was she fearful for her fellow soldiers?

It made Michael consider his own situation. People he knew had died. Killed by these Norwegians.

Michael had no hatred to the woman here. No anger. She hadn't caused the war. Soldiers were just pawns, no more than tools to both sides.

Maybe Joe was right. The Russian soldiers weren't to blame. It was the commanders that were. The leaders. The ones who wouldn't try to negotiate for peace.

Michael pulled the hunting rifle from his back nervously. The Norwegian woman glanced at him, but returned her attention to the battle.

She clearly thought he was just nervous.

Michael gulped. He wasn't a monster. He wasn't a machine.

But he couldn't let his friends die. It was them, or the Russians.

He raised the hunting rifle and quickly fired at the woman. The recoil shocked him, but he had not missed.

The bullet entered her chest at point blank range, blasting her back and ripping through her. She was killed instantly.

Michael had no time to think about what he had done. He pressed the emergency alarm button.

"Please state your emergency," the alarm said robotically. *"We have connected you to Oslo Gate One."*

"This is Michael Bakerson. Auli is under attack, from Norwegian Ski Troops. They had taken over the bridge, and the recruits are severely depleted. Oslo may be threatened. This is an emergency," he spoke urgently.

There was no response from Oslo Gate One, only the faint trickle of static.

Eventually, there was a cough.

"M-Michael?" The weak voice belonged to Darius Finch. "We've been compromised .... Oslo's defences are down. You're on your own ... Oh God, I have to go. They're coming. Michael, you're our only hope! I hav-"

The line cut, dead.

Michael paled, looking out across Auli. What should he do?

47 - COMPROMISED

Darius Finch stood, in the darkened watchtower at the Eastern gate of Oslo. His squad, the Praetorians, had been tasked to guard it.

Peter, the tall blond boy, was manning the manual Bofors Mark V, which was rotatable anti-air cannon with several gun barrels. It required someone to sit in it at all times, but Peter was more than happy to be in charge of such a large weapon. The Bofors cannons were placed at the three main gates to protect from air attack, whereas on other sections of the wall, there were automated guns controlled by the main power grid. These guns were designed to shoot down incoming artillery shells using motion and heat sensors.

It was a cold, snowy night, as Darius stood inside, thinking. They had access to thermal cameras which monitored every section of the wall, both inside the city and out. The recruits felt like it was a lot of responsibility for them, but there wasn't much of a choice due to the Ragnarok Offensive.

The watchtower was made of reinforced glass, supported by metal girders. It was supposedly impervious to bullet fire, or, at least that was what Sergeant Vellon had told them before he'd left.

Darius watched the cameras. There was a small boy inside the city, throwing a ball against the wall. He looked impoverished, and wore a tattered brown coat.

For the average guard, that would be nothing to worry about. But Darius wasn't taking any chances.

"Daisy, check out that boy. I want him away from the walls," Darius ordered coolly.

Daisy, a short, pudgy-faced girl, snorted. "He's just a kid," she remarked.

"Nevertheless, you will ask him to leave this area. I don't want anyone near the walls. A child may be an agent," Darius told her, holding her gaze.

Daisy raised her eyebrows, then went outside.

Darius tracked her movements on the camera as he saw her go over to the boy. When the boy saw her, he turned and ran away.

Darius was about to turn away from the camera when a glint, coming from the shadows behind Daisy, caught his attention.

It was the barrel of a gun.

"Daisy, get out of there!" he called, but it was too late.

Darius heard the bang from within the tower as he saw the flash of light through the screen. Daisy collapsed to the ground.

He immediately made for the alarm, but the electricity in the room flickered and died.

"Christ," one of the Praetorians muttered, looking out of the window. All across the city, the dim electric lights had shut off.

The central power grid was down.

Which meant...?

Darius looked towards the automated AA guns which were positioned along the city walls. They had stopped moving. Now there were only a few Bofors cannons defending Oslo. The warships were still undergoing maintenance in the docks, which meant Oslo had no way to defend against enemy artillery until the ships were deployed to sea.

BANG!

A grenade exploded outside the gate, as gunfire pounded the glass. "Don't open the door!" Darius told his squad mates. He glanced outside.

Peter had rotated the Bofors cannon to face inside the city.

There were people, armed with weapons, charging towards the gate. They intended to capture it. Peter opened fire with the Bofors, the high-powered gun ripping into them. Darius wanted to help, but couldn't risk opening the door. He squinted, looking to see who the attackers were.

They looked like ordinary civilians, though were actually members of the resistance group known as the Brown Coats. They hated the Western Alliance's presence in Norway and wanted to liberate it, by crippling the capital and letting the Russians take over.

They were led by a man named Ingolf Sørensen, a deviously intelligent man in his mid-thirties. He had been planning this operation for a while, and had been assisted by certain traitors within The Institute.

Ingolf had never met Prometheus, but his information had been valuable.

Having already disabled the power to the city, all they needed was to take the gate for the Russians to get in.

Ingolf was a well-built man. He was watching the battle, and was frustrated by the lack of progress against the Bofors.

Peter continued firing, the devastating power of the Bofors clear to see. He didn't see Ingolf sneaking up at the base of the wall, a Molotov cocktail in his hand.

Ingolf ran, lit the bottle and threw it at the Bofors. It exploded over, showering Peter and the turret with fire.

However, it wasn't ordinary fire. The bottle had contained a special chemical mixture which had been smuggled in by the Russians. It burned through metal, melting the Bofors' cannon's barrel. When Peter tried to shoot again, the gun misfired, exploding and blasting Peter back. Peter was killed instantly, and silence filled the night once again.

Darius stood inside, picking up the emergency flare as the snowstorm was interfering with signals. He remembered how Joe had used this during the Tower competition and knew he needed to warn the Western Alliance somehow. They had to get those warships out of the docks, as Oslo was vulnerable to a Russian attack.

But he would need to get outside to fire the flare.

Darius walked towards the door, and saw a person on the other side of the glass.

Ingolf faced him, knocking on the door. "Open up," he stated in heavily accented English. "Or we kill you."

Darius stared him out. "Then we shall die."

Ingolf's eyes flashed with anger, as he kicked the door. He yelled something in Norwegian, as two men began working on planted explosives at the door.

Darius gripped the gun in his hand, pointing it towards the doorway. He would die fighting.

There was silence as his squad mates all waited in nervous anticipation.

Darius cleared his throat. "It has been an honour to fight by your side. Let us live through this battle," he told them, taking a deep breath, then speaking boldly.

"For the Western Alliance."

The door blasted open. One of the Praetorians fired out of fear, but there was no one in the doorway.

The Brown Coats waited outside for Ingolf's order.

Ingolf smirked. "Roll a grenade in," he told them in Norwegian.

One of his men complied, slowly rolling a grenade into the watchtower.

Darius reacted instantly, taking off his helmet and clamping it over the grenade, intending to reduce the impact. It exploded, sending him flying back as darkness rushed up to him.

* * *

Eventually, he woke up. The watchtower was in ruins. The radio lay on the ground in front of Darius. He could barely move his arms, and couldn't feel his legs at all.

He coughed, reaching for the radio, and got a small hold on the receiver, dragging the rest towards him.

It suddenly burst into life.

"This is Michael Bakerson. Auli is under attack, from Norwegian Ski Troops. They were holding the bridge open. Oslo may be threatened. This is an emergency," the voice spoke urgently.

Darius coughed.

"M-Michael?" he muttered. "We've been compromised ... Oslo's defences are down. You're on your own."

He heard movement outside the watchtower.

"Oh God, I have to go. They're coming. Michael, you're our only hope! I hav-"

He cut the line as he saw a shadow of a person in the doorway. Darius looked around frantically for a weapon, but there was none in sight.

The figure marched in, and Darius was shocked.

It wasn't a person.

It was the Trojan.

The robot pulled away the rubble near Darius' legs, then picked him up effortlessly, slinging him over one shoulder. The blue light was on in its eye, which meant it was running on autopilot.

It effortlessly walked through the rubble, making its way down the street.

The boy who had been throwing the ball earlier was outside, and he turned and ran in fear of the humanoid robot.

Darius, though wounded, twisted his head back to look at the gate.

It was as he had feared. Ingolf Sørensen stood in the centre of the open gate, looking out towards the East.

The only thing which stood in between Oslo and the Russian Army was Auli.

Darius prayed that Michael had got his message. Everything depended on what the recruits chose to do next.

48 - GOING BACK

Gunfire raged around the bridge at Auli. The Norwegian Ski Troops struggled to fight off the relentless attack from the recruits.

The recruits were able to use buildings to their advantage within Auli, but there was no cover for the Ski Troopers were picked off from a distance, one by one.

When there were fewer than five Norwegians left, the recruits charged over the bridge towards the Western side, led by Raymon Collins.

The Norwegians' bolt actions rifles were not suited to this kind of attack. Although they could shoot accurately, their long reload time meant there was only time for one volley before the recruits were over the bridge.

The remaining Norwegians surrendered, dropping their weapons and raising their hands. There were only four of them. Several recruits stood and guarded them.

Michael had watched all of this from the watchtower, which was located on the Western side of the bridge. He activated his wristwatch to speak to the other squad leaders.

"Squad Leaders, this is Michael. We've beaten the Norwegians, but I have bad news. Oslo has been compromised, their defences are down. We're on our own," Michael told them.

There was silence for a few seconds.

"Who told you this?" Sophie asked.

"Darius, before the line was cut," Michael told her. "If Oslo' defences are down ..."

"Then they're vulnerable," Thomas cut in. "We will have to destroy the bridge to stop the Russians from advancing. We can't afford the Russians to capture Oslo whilst the warships are still docked."

"But, Thomas," Michael interjected. "Without defences, Oslo could still be hit by artillery even if we blow the bridge. If the Russians start firing at them, without the warships Oslo has no way to fight back. They've sent most of the army up north to protect the oil fields."

"That isn't our problem," Raymon stated coldly. "The commanders can figure out how to save Oslo. We just have to blow this bridge before the Russians send in Wave Two."

"But the civilians - " Michael began.

"The civilians aren't a priority, Michael!" Thomas stated, before changing the channel so all recruits could hear. "All recruits head towards the bridge, we're evacuating. Spartans and Jaegers, you stay and warn us when to blow the bridge."

Michael was outraged. Thomas was going to leave the rest of the Spartans and Jaegers on the Russian side of the bridge! He knew he couldn't allow that. He was going to join them.

He calmed himself, as he glanced towards the small bag of explosives in the corner of the watchtower. "There are explosives in both watchtowers, right?" he asked them.

"Yes ... why?" Thomas asked suspiciously.

Michael didn't reply, picking up the explosives as he hurried down the steps towards the snowmobile.

Raymon saw him, and hurried over. "What are you planning?" he asked him.

Michael climbed aboard the snowmobile, praying Raymon wouldn't notice the explosives. "You heard Thomas. The Spartans have to go and warn you guys when the Russians are coming. I'm a Spartan," he told Raymon.

Raymon narrowed his eyes. "Then go," he said coldly. "You're gonna die out there."

Michael gave him a false smile. "Isn't that great?" he said sarcastically, before driving off on the snowmobile, heading over the bridge.

"Wait!" he heard Raymon shout from behind him, but ignored it, grinning at the adrenalin rush.

They could still blow the bridge without his explosives. He would need them for something more important.

He then called his squad on his wristwatch. "Jürgen, is the fire out yet?" he asked them, referring to the chemical fire the Russians had started in the outskirts of the city.

"Ja, but there is a large group of civilians who are now homeless," Jürgen replied.

Michael sighed as he carried on driving. "Direct them to the bridge, quickly. But it won't be open much longer."

"Affirmative," Jürgen stated.

"Spartans, what is your location?" Michael asked his squad.

"We're all by the east of the village, near where the fire was," Michael heard Alexandra's voice say.

"I'm on my way," Michael told them, speeding up through the town. The snowstorm was even thicker now, making visibility difficult. He drove through the town, which was deserted except for the occasional group of villagers making their way towards the bridge. He prayed Thomas would keep it open long enough for them to make it.

He then contacted Sophie's squad, the Jaegers, who had also been ordered to stay.

"This is Michael from the Spartans, how many Jaegers are alive?" he asked them.

"Michael?" Sophie's voice asked. "Jane's been killed. So have three others. Oliver's wounded, with me, Dan, Marcus and Lucy."

Michael didn't know who Lucy or Marcus were. "Okay. Will Oliver survive if you leave him?" he asked her.

"Probably not," Michael heard an unfamiliar female voice say. "I'll remain with him."

"Can the rest of you come to the east side of the village? We're supposed to be keeping a look out for the Russians," Michael explained as he drove.

"Aren't you on a snowmobile?" Sophie asked him.

"Yeah?" Michael replied slowly, not sure what she was getting at.

"Can you give me a lift? Dan and Marcus already have one, and I don't want to be the only one walking," Sophie told him.

Michael couldn't help but smile. "Sure, where are you?" he asked Sophie.

"Near where we were last time, by the church," she told him.

Michael sped there, quickly, coming to a stop in front of a group of about nine black-clad recruits. Some were lying on the ground, dead. They were all wearing helmets, so Michael couldn't tell who was who until Sophie took off hers and gave him a warm smile.

Michael smiled back, feeling hot. He held her gaze for a second until he realised he was staring.

"You ready?" he asked, glancing around.

There was another snowmobile nearby, which two Jaegers climbed on. Sophie went over to Michael and sat behind him, placing her hands on his sides.

Michael started off, feeling very hot inside the ski suit. He felt a rush as he sped through the city, and didn't think it was just the adrenalin.

The snowstorm grew heavier, and Michael had to be careful not to take any bends too fast so he didn't slip.

Eventually, they reached the Spartans.

Michael climbed off the snowmobile, looking around at the group. They were all gathered in a semicircle, waiting for him.

Steve clapped him on the shoulder. "Welcome back, laddie," he said in his impression of Raines.

Michael nodded, feeling overwhelmed with the emotion. This might be the last time he would ever see them. His squad. The Spartans.

He looked at his friend. Steve held his gaze, nothing but a fiery bond of friendship there. If there was one person who he would rather die at the side of, it was his childhood companion.

He cleared his throat. The fire had burnt out.

"How did that fire start?" he asked. Jürgen shrugged, but Alexandra spoke.

"The Russian's threw a chemical firebomb as they drove," she explained. "It just wouldn't go out, it was something different to normal."

Michael nodded. "Okay, have you all heard the news?" he asked them.

"No?" Jenny said, looking confused.

Michael looked at her. "I'm probably the one with the most knowledge, so I'll tell you. Basically, this whole attack is part of a much wider invasion. Ragnarok. Oslo's been compromised from the inside, and these Norwegians were sent here to keep the bridge open," he told the group.

"For who?" Tim asked.

"Fenrir."

It was Hans who spoke. "It has to be Fenrir. This is his masterstroke. He's been planning this, and now he strikes!" he enthused, a mad glint in his eyes.

"No," Tim said firmly, the skinny boy decisive for once. "We know nothing for certain. We're just guessing. We should follow our orders. It's our first mission, we're just recruits! Stop pretending we can be heroes and do what Thomas is telling us!"

"How did you know we weren't going to do what Thomas tells us?" Michael asked Tim.

"I can see it in your eyes. In Hans. You're all crazy," Tim told them. "We're soldiers. We follow orders. When these Russians come, I'm radioing Thomas to blow the bridge."

"But the civilians-" Alexandra began.

"Can die. So can we. Let's face it, the only reason we want the bridge to stay open is so that we're not trapped on the Russian side," Tim told them seriously.

There was silence as they absorbed what Tim was telling them.

Michael was beginning to doubt himself. What if Tim was right?

"Actually," Arthur said, very tentatively. "We do know something."

Michael looked at him sharply. "What?"

"I looked at the communications device that the old man was using to talk to Fenrir with. The one you killed."

Michael closed his eyes, wishing Arthur wouldn't remind him he was a killer.

"Anyway, I found where it was being sent to. The signal was moving, and it was about ten kilometres north of here last time I checked. Which means...?"

"Fenrir's coming here?" Steve guessed.

"Maybe. Fenrir will want to either capture Oslo, or destroy it, right? If the bridge is open, he can capture it, but if Thomas blows it ... " Arthur trailed off again.

"He'll destroy it," Michael realised. "We have to stop him."

Arthur nodded. "I'm gonna guess most of you read the briefing, so I assume you know about the artillery-"

"Just go over it again for everyone," Michael interrupted. He hadn't read the briefing himself.

"Oh ... okay. The Russians have heavy artillery batteries which, if they get in range, could shell Oslo. Usually this is ineffective due to Oslo's defences, but since they're down, Fenrir will use them as his insurance policy. They'll be what he uses to destroy Oslo," Arthur told the group.

"How do you know that?" Hans asked.

"Well, A.G. Phelps wrote about it in the briefing. It would be an expected military strategy. That was why the defences were vital," Arthur said. "Did no one read the briefing?"

"But where would Fenrir fire from?" Michael asked him.

"Well, whilst you were fighting the Norwegians, I searched the old man's house. He wasn't a very good spy, as he left a map in one of the drawers. It showed Auli and Oslo, as well as the distance the artillery would be effective from. Fenrir doesn't actually need to cross the bridge to fire at Oslo. There's a nearby hill which would be the most effective location for him to bombard Oslo from. Once Thomas has blown the bridge, that's where he'll be," Arthur explained, unfolding a map and pointing to a hill.

"It's about three kilometres from here," Arthur explained. "So if they start firing, we'll know about it."

"Hold on. This is Fenrir we're talking about," Tim stated. "We can't just go in there and destroy his artillery. He's one of the Big Three! He's got the Hunters guarding him! What exactly, do you think we can do?"

"Hans," Michael said suddenly. "You can speak Norwegian, right?"

Hans nodded. "I can."

Michael thought for several seconds, then looked up at the recruits.

"I have a plan."

49 - HUNTED

"The Hunters are used to choosing the home ground. They are best suited to open terrain and poor visibility, where Western Alliance technology doesn't work as well. They rely on mobility, and fear. Fear of the unknown," Arthur explained over the communications link. "But we know that they will come."

The Spartans and remaining Jaegers had taken up defensive positions around the main road of Auli. They knew they would have to hold off the hunters for as long as possible.

Michael, Hans and Jürgen were in the church, which was the tallest building in the town. Using their Western Alliance helmets, they would effectively be able to see everything that was going on if the Hunters attacked.

"Now, those Hunters will be expecting Auli to be controlled by the Norwegian Ski Troops. They'll come in, quickly, and expect to have a clear route to Oslo," Michael reckoned. "But we're going to stop them."

He had put the recruits in different buildings, hoping that they could ambush the Hunters when they came.

Marcus, the Jaeger, and Jenny were placed in the building closest to the outskirts of the town. They would lie low until the ambush began, and then prevent the Hunters from retreating.

Joe and Arthur were in one house, whereas Steve and Sophie were in another. Situated on either side of the road, Michael hoped they could get the Russians in crossfire.

"Our main advantage will be surprise. We've got to make the most of that," Michael told them, as he placed his helmet on his head, switching the display to thermal.

"This is suicide," Tim interrupted. "We're facing the elite of the Russian army. They're the Hunters! They've got hounds, and have never been beaten!"

"The only reason that the Hunters haven't been beaten is because of fear. The Mark of Fenrir? The Hounds? They all affect morale," Arthur said quietly. "Their weapons are not suited to urban combat. They have no choice but to take us head on. We have the strategic advantage."

Michael then changed the channel, speaking on a direct line to Thomas.

"Thomas? This is Michael. Don't blow the bridge. As soon as you do, Oslo will be shelled. We need to hold the town ... Thomas, we need you," Michael said.

There was no reply.

Michael sighed, then changed back to the Spartans and Jaegers.

Arthur was speaking. "The force won't be large, most of the Russian forces will be been diverted to the oil field. So ... I'd expect a force no larger than two hundred Hunters, with about one third of that remaining with the artillery," he stated.

"Wait, what?" Michael asked Arthur. "We'll have to fend off a hundred and twenty Hunters?"

"Yes. Have you ever seen Zulu?" Arthur asked Michael

"Is that relevant?" Michael asked him.

"Never mind. But, with superior technology, a smaller force can beat a much larger one. They are armed with bows -"

"And chemical weapons," Tim interrupted.

"But we still have a chance. This town is a bottleneck. They have to go through us to get to Oslo," Arthur stated.

"But why don't we blow the bridge?" Tim protested.

"Because that vould show ve're afraid," Jürgen spoke for the first time in a while. "And that vould show them, that ve are villing to let Oslo be destroyed to save ourselves."

"I hate that accent," Steve muttered.

"Jürgen's right," Michael stated. "We're going to fight. We're going to show Fenrir that we're not afraid. We're going to defend this town ... until we die. Blowing the bridge is a last resort."

There was silence on the communications link.

A wolf howled in the distance.

"The Cry of the Wolf!" Tim told them, panicking. "They're coming!"

Michael steeled himself. "Let them come," he stated, determined. "Do not fire until I give the order," he warned his fellow recruits.

"Good luck," Sophie told them through her wristwatch.

Michael didn't reply. He stared out of the tower at the top of the church, over the town. He could see thermal signatures emerging from the snowstorm. They were running, with dogs at their sides.

"Hostiles incoming," Michael spoke down his wristwatch. "Jürgen, prepare to fire."

Jürgen aimed his assault rifle towards the street from the church tower.

The Hunters advanced. They were masked soldiers, carrying bows and quivers of arrows. Dressed all in white, they would be very difficult to see without them thermal scanners on the Western helmets. Michael was glad he had retrieved his.

He could hear the hounds howling, even from his vantage point.

The front of the group of Hunters passed Jenny and Marcus' house, but they remained undetected.

Michael guessed there were about forty of them now running, with about half of them accompanied by dogs.

"Ready..," he stated, as the front passed Joe's and Arthur's location.

Michael was impressed with their speed, and knew they would not have much time.

"Fire!" he shouted, and gunfire erupted from the houses, taking the Hunters completely by surprise.

He could see the flashes of shots as the recruits let loose with their fully automatic weapons. Jürgen and Hans both began firing down at the Russians.

Michael was relieved to see many Hunters collapse to the ground, but the Hunters soon reacted, returning fire.

However, there was no cover for the Hunters as they were being hit from both sides, so the outcome was inevitable.

"Make sure you hit the arsonist," Michael told Jürgen, noticing a Hunter unhook a small explosive from his waist.

"Ja," Jürgen said, and fired a precise burst towards him.

It hit its mark, a bullet catching the explosive and blasting the Hunter to pieces with a green explosion.

Michael wasn't surprised - Jürgen, along with his sister Nadia, were some of the best marksmen in The Institute.

The Hunters didn't go down without a fight, as one of them took aim and fired, the high powered bow launching an arrow which struck Hans in the shoulder.

Hans let out a cry of pain, and Jürgen quickly fired at the Hunter. The Hounds were sent into frenzy at the conflict, one of them leaping through the window into Arthur and Joe's house. Several of them ran wildly off down the street.

Michael, relieved the skirmish seemed to be going in their favour, turned his attention to Jenny and Marcus' house, the one closest to the enemy positions. There were still muzzle flashes coming from it, although Michael sensed more heat signatures coming from the Russian territory.

More Hunters were coming.

Now they had lost the element of surprise, this fight would be much tougher.

A whole lot tougher.

"Michael, do you hear that?" Hans asked him.

Michael frowned, listening. A low humming sound. He switched his visor to sonar, trying to make out what was coming.

His eyes widened as he saw what it was.

They had a tank.

It was nothing like the Western tanks, very different to the Dragon Mark One they had watched in the video. It had huge tracks, with a small turret on top. It was designed for high explosive attack instead of armour penetration. The vehicle was made to be able to move fast in the Norwegian terrain.

"Alert, we've got a tank rolling in from the East. Do not engage, lay low," he told the recruits.

"But Michael, we're sitting ducks!" Jenny replied. With her position nearest the Soviets, they were most vulnerable.

"Hit the dirt," he told them, as he saw the tank's turret rotate to face Jenny's house. It fired, blasting the house's door off. Michael flicked his helmet to normal, and could see it in the distance fire another shell, exploding someone inside. He could see their blood splatter the tank.

It rolled on, as Hunters behind cleared the house, sending the hounds in. Michael heard a female scream, causing his heart to lurch.

Jenny! That meant Marcus had been killed.

He saw her get dragged out by two Hunters. Jürgen tightened his finger on the trigger, as though he was wishing he could fire but not wanting to hurt her.

Michael clenched his fists, furious. If he could not do something soon, the rest of his squad might be blown to bits, just like Marcus had been.

But without any weapons powerful enough to pierce the tank's armour, what could he do? They needed to hang onto the explosives in case the Russians fired their artillery. The explosives were currently with them in the church tower.

Michael looked at Hans and Jürgen, hoping one of them would have an idea. They were desperate.

He breathed heavily as the tank rolled on towards the next house, blasting it to pieces. Luckily there was no one in there, but the tank was systematically destroying the town.

"Michael?" his wristwatch crackled into life. "It's Thomas here. We're coming to help."

"Thomas?" Michael asked, surprised.

"Yes. You are right. They will not expect us to attack. Better to die on our feet than live on our knees," Thomas stated through the communications link.

"They have a tank," Michael told him quickly.

"Watch us deal with it," Thomas replied calmly.

Michael looked outside the church tower, seeing the tank rolling on, nearing Arthur and Joe's building.

The hum of snowmobiles filled the air, as Michael saw about five recruits driving them towards the tank. The tank turret rotated and fired, blasting the first snowmobile along with its rider.

The Hunters also reacted, launching a volley of arrows over the tank.

The shots, deadly accurate, struck three of the recruits in the neck. Now there was just one recruit on a snowmobile left. Michael squinted, unable to see who it was through their helmet, but could see a bundle of explosives strapped to them.

He watched the recruit unhook the explosives as the snowmobile swerved around the tank.

The recruit threw them and they landed on the back of the tank.

The recruit then dived from the snowmobile, crashing through the glass window of a house as the explosives detonated.

The blast ripped the tank to pieces and shattered the walls of nearby buildings, killing the Hunters that were too close to the explosion. The Hunters fell back, taking cover behind the wooden structures.

Michael hoped that the remaining recruits were okay.

"Well done, Raymon," he heard Thomas say over the communications link. "Jaguars and Companions, move in!"

That was Raymon who had thrown the explosives? Michael couldn't help but be impressed by his skill, though found it hard to believe anyone could have survived that blast.

Had Raymon been killed?

Michael watched as the recruits pressed up the streets, keeping constant fire on the Hunters to prevent them from advancing.

Not even the elite of the Russian army were immune to getting shot.

Michael's stomach suddenly lurched as he remembered what had happened to Jenny. She had been captured. He had to do something.

"Jürgen, Hans?"

He looked at them both. "Jenny," he stated, his voice wavering. "We'll head to their base on the hill, we're going to get her back and blow the artillery."

Hans and Jürgen both looked eager, and they nodded. Michael could guess why.

For Hans, this was a chance to get back at Fenrir and avenge his adopted father.

For Jürgen, this would be a chance to save Jenny.

Michael realised his motives were the same as Jürgen's. But he wasn't just doing it for Jenny. It was also for all the recruits that had been killed today. It was for Sergeant Wallace and the Royal Scots.

"Jürgen, you still have the explosives?" he asked him.

"Ja."

"Alright, here's what we're going to do. We will take the snowmobiles and exit the north of the town, then loop round to reach the hill. Jürgen, you will sneak up and plant the explosives on the artillery pieces. Or the ammunition, whichever is easiest. Also, you might want to wear a Norwegian uniform so you don't get caught. Hans will come with me, where we'll find Jenny and try to break her out," Michael explained.

Jürgen nodded. "Ja."

Hans grinned. "Time to take this fight to Fenrir," he said with a maniacal glint in his eyes.

Michael nodded. "Yeah," he agreed, though he was he knew it was a longshot.

***

Ten minutes later, the three recruits were ready to leave. Michael still wore the Norwegian's coat, though kept his Western Alliance helmet. He climbed aboard the snowmobile for the third time, and tried to steady his breathing.

He was going to the camp of the Hunters. The base of Fenrir.

Hans was on his right, in full Norwegian uniform. He had his assault rifle on his back, as he gripped the handles tightly. Michael couldn't comprehend what he must be feeling at the moment, being so close to facing the man who killed his father.

Jürgen, on the other hand, showed little emotion. His face was a mask, and he did not reveal anything to Michael. He was also wearing a full white Norwegian uniform, and carried one of their rifles on his back.

Michael gritted his teeth as he faced straight ahead, setting his helmet to sonar.

"Let's do this," he told them, as he floored the accelerator. It was a different experience to previously, as his helmet protected his face from the wind. The blizzard was thick, so he was glad for his helmet. He focused and tried to prepare himself for what was about to happen.

Was he really ready to go to Fenrir's base? Was he leading his friends to their deaths? Michael powered on, noticing the incline become more prominent. Checking his sonar, he could see that they were nearing the top of the hill. They were almost there.

He braked, looking at them both. "Jürgen … remember, be confident. Your mission is the most important," he told him.

Jürgen barely glanced at him. "Just get Jenny out," he told Michael, before driving on.

Michael and Hans looked at each other before climbing off their snowmobiles and sneaking up the hill.

As they reached the top, Michael switched to normal vision, where he was amazed by what he saw.

On the top of the hill, there was a large camp with many white tents, which perfectly camouflaged with the snow.

Michael caught a glimpse of one tent larger than the others. That must be Fenrir's.

But what was most eye-catching were the huge artillery batteries that were being wheeled into position. They were about five metres high, with a huge barrel that looked at least a foot wide.

Next to each battery, there was a large crate which was firmly bolted down. Michael guessed it contained the ammunition for the artillery.

He then switched to thermal vision, checking to see where Jenny was. There were about forty Hunters there, many of them armed with bows. He looked towards Auli, and saw two people dragging another towards the main tent.

That must be Jenny.

Michael told Hans what he had seen, and the pair walked forward, praying the blizzard would prevent anyone seeing them.

"There are some crates there, I'll go hide behind them. You're dressed as a Norwegian and you can speak it, so you shouldn't have a problem," he whispered to Hans.

He hurried over, crouching down among several large boxes which were probably storing supplies. He was actually feeling quite hungry, although that was the least of his priorities now.

He looked through his thermal visor as Jenny was dragged into the largest tent: Fenrir's.

Inside there was a huge man, at least two metres tall. He was broad and muscular, and covered in hair. He was exactly like Michael had imagined the general to be.

There were about eight Hunters either side of him, with a diminutive man standing next to him. The small man looked nothing special. He had a mousy face and a slight build, and was probably an advisor to Fenrir.

Jenny was dragged in by the Hunters, and thrown to the feet of the huge man.

'Fenrir' spat something in Russian to the Hunters. They replied, and then the general smirked, squatting down so he was at eye level with Jenny.

"You think you can stop me?" the general asked. Michael could just hear them. The voice didn't sound like the one Michael had heard on the radio, but it must have just been distorted by the device.

"We ... will," Jenny muttered.

Fenrir laughed, a harsh cold laugh. "What is your plan? To beat my hunters? I know your recruits, how many of them are there? Fifty? Fifty untrained children, already having fought my mercenaries-"

"Fought and *beat* your mercenaries," Jenny stated. "We're more capable than you know."

"On the contrary. I know exactly how capable you are. This is why you will all be killed. What is your plan?" he demanded to Jenny.

Jenny remained silent.

Fenrir snorted, pulling out a knife and grabbing Jenny's hand.

"Every time you refuse to talk, you reduce your chance of living!" he seethed.

Michael breathed shakily, feeling his heart thump in his chest.

"What is your plan?!" Fenrir roared.

Jenny remained silent, though her body was shaking.

Fenrir didn't hesitate. He struck her across the face, then kicked her to the ground.

"What is your plan?" Fenrir asked, holding the knife to her throat.

"We ... we intend to ... destroy the artillery," Jenny muttered, clearly in pain as the knife began causing her neck to bleed.

"Good. Now we kill you," Fenrir stated with a smirk.

"NO!!!" Hans roared, charging out of nowhere. He opened fire on Fenrir with his assault rifle, taking the Hunters by surprise.

The huge man was riddled with bullets and knocked to the ground.

"For my father!" Hans declared, before the Hunters fired at him.

Silver arrows whistled through the air before embedding themselves in Hans' body. One arrow went straight through his throat.

Hans coughed, sinking to his knees, before falling forward into the snow.

Michael watched, shocked. Hans was dead. He had killed Fenrir.

But the Hunters barely reacted to the loss of their leader.

The small man stepped forward. He had brown hair and an average looking face, with nothing to mark him out except his icy blue eyes. Jenny was sobbing uncontrollably.

"That man was not Fenrir," the small man gloated with a slight smirk. "Your friend died for nothing. He was a mere tool, designed to be my face."

Michael was shocked. This small man was Fenrir?

The huge man had just been a decoy?

The real Fenrir looked at Jenny emotionlessly. "One might argue that Fenrir does not exist. It is a name. It creates fear. No one has seen Fenrir, but no one has to. They only see his mark. But I am the general of these forces. I am Fenrir. And no one will know, for you will die. Just like your friend," the small man stated coldly.

"You can kill a man, but you cannot kill an idea. A mark of fear. War is all about soldiers, about morale. I have created a monster. It has no face but my Hunters. Tell me girl, did you ever guess where Fenrir comes from?" he asked Jenny, looking at her.

She didn't answer.

"It came from the wolf that killed the king of the gods. And I will destroy your gods. The Western Alliance will crumble. My artillery will fire on Oslo." Fenrir then looked at the Hunters and barked something in Russian.

Several of them sprinted out of the tent. They must be heading for the artillery.

Fenrir looked at Jenny coldly. "You will die now. You are nothing but a child of a regime that enslaves you. Only when you have conquered fear you become truly free. And the only way to conquer fear ... is to become it."

Fenrir pulled a pistol from a holster. Michael was paralysed with terror.

"Your gods have failed you," Fenrir stated, before pointing the gun at Jenny's head, and firing.

51 - **DESTROYED**

"Your gods have failed you," Fenrir stated, *before pointing the gun at Jenny's head, and firing.*

Jenny limply fell to the side, dead.

Michael watched, in disbelief, then horror.

No.

No! Jenny!

She couldn't be dead!

Michael felt anger, a passionate hatred building up inside of him, and he pulled the bolt action rifle off his back. He didn't care that he would only have one shot before he would be detected.

Fenrir had killed Jenny.

Michael only now realised how much she meant to him.

He held his gun tightly, his hands shaking. Fenrir carried on, as if nothing had happened and began talking in Russian to his men.

"Michael?" he heard Jürgen's voice crackle through his wristwatch.

"Yes," he answered, with no emotion in his voice.

"I've planted the explosives ... is Jenny okay?" Jürgen asked him.

"Detonate them, Jürgen," Michael told him.

"Michael, vhat's wrong?" Jürgen asked him.

"Jenny and Hans are dead. Fenrir killed them. Detonate the explosives before they are disarmed. They're coming for you," Michael told Jürgen, looking around at the white tents.

"Vhat? They're dead?! Jenny? Michael, vhat happened!? Tell me now!" Jürgen demanded, sounding horrified.

"Just detonate them!" Michael ordered, before cutting the link and looking up towards Fenrir.

Fenrir looked alarmed, like he had heard something.

Damn. Michael had probably been too loud.

Michael gripped his gun, and aimed it at Fenrir.

Fenrir's eyes scanned around, until they locked with Michael's. A slow smile curled on the man's face, as though victorious.

Michael pulled the trigger, the rifle impacting back into his shoulder as he fired.

The shot hit Fenrir in the chest. The small man looked down, then looked back up at Michael, with what looked like a triumphant smile. Maybe he thought he'd won, that Ragnarok would succeed in defeating the Western Alliance.

Fenrir fell to his knees. The Hunters for once seemed unsure what to do.

There was silence for a second then -

BOOM!

* * *

Ringing.

That was what Michael heard when he awoke. A loud ringing sound in his ears. It reminded of him of that time he had been tortured by Boss, the brigand. Loud ringing.

Where was he?

He opened his eyes and looked around. It was all white. White with scattered fragments of other colours.

There were pieces of rubble lying around, some of them on fire. There had been an explosion.

Michael looked towards where the large tent had been. The tent was gone now, probably having been destroyed. In fact, a large number of tents had gone. Michael wondered where.

He blinked a few times. His head felt heavy. He couldn't think very well.

Where had the Hunters gone? There were a few figures running off in the distance, but he couldn't make out who they were.

Michael saw some figures lying where the ruins of the large tent had been. Were they Hunters?

Michael groggily climbed to his feet, using a crate to push himself up. One of the crates must have landed on his head and knocked him out.

He looked inside the crate, as there was a small hole in it. It was full of grain. That reminded Michael of his village. There was grain there.

He hoped his village was alright. Maybe he would go back there, just to make sure Grandpa Ted was alive and well.

He stood up straight, looking towards one of the figures. It was wearing a Norwegian uniform, and had many arrows sticking out of it.

Michael walked towards it, a name sticking out in his mind.

Hans. Hans. Hans was dead, full of arrows. What had happened?

Michael knelt down next to his friend's body, trying to recall what had just happened.

They had arrived at Norway earlier today. They had come to Auli. Sergeant Wallace had been shot. The Norwegians had arrived. They had been fought off. The Hunters had attacked, with the tank. Maybe the Hunters had won and conquered Oslo.

Then Michael, Hans and Jürgen had come here. They had seen Fenrir, who turned out to be an imposter. Hans had shot him, then been killed with arrows. Then the real Fenrir came, and fired at …

Jenny.

Fenrir had killed Jenny.

Michael looked up at the other bodies sharply, running over to them. There Jenny was, lying in the snow. She looked almost peaceful.

There was a small bullet hole in her forehead, with dried blood running down her face. Her eyes were open, looking almost pleadingly at Michael.

Michael looked down at Jenny. She was dead! Jenny had been killed! He had done nothing!

Emotion welled up inside him, and he began sobbing.

It was only now he realised how much she meant to him. She was his friend. Hans was his friend. They had both been killed in front of his eyes.

"I'm so sorry, Jenny," he whispered, cradling her. "I'm so sorry."

Guilt, anger and sadness overwhelmed him. He could have done more to stop it. He should have fired.

It was his fault. He had failed her. Jürgen had told him to get her back, and Michael had failed. Two of his teammates had been killed because of him. Two of his friends. He wished he had died and they had lived.

Michael cried, until there was nothing left in him. Just a pit of emotion, and hurt. He didn't care when he fell down on the snow and lay there.

He didn't care when the blizzard restarted.

He just wanted the pain to end.

Michael closed his eyes.

"I'm sorry," he whispered.

52 - ACCEPTANCE

Michael woke up slowly. He was in a bed. A warm, soft bed. He opened his eyes. The room was plain, a standard grey Institute room.

It was his room from The Institute. He recognised the pile of clothes in the corner he had left. He climbed out of bed tentatively and went over to them, searching through the pockets.

In Norway, Michael had been found lying in the snow by Jürgen. Apparently, the recruits had been able to hold Auli long enough for the warships to be deployed. The Hunters had retreated, and their whereabouts were now unknown.

The regular army had fought off the invasion in the North, protecting the oilfields, and when they returned they quickly dealt with the Brown Coats in Oslo. Ingolf Sørensen, their leader, had been arrested, and was now inside a prison, sentenced for life.

The power grid had been repaired, and now strengthened, with each turret acting independently so there would be no way in future for them all to be disabled at once.

The soldiers who had died were buried in Auli, under a single cross. A tribute to those who had given their lives to protect the Western Alliance.

All of the surviving recruits had been shipped back to Occupied Britain. About sixty had survived out of the hundred recruits that had been dispatched. Michael had been asleep for most of the journey, so hadn't spoken to anyone. He hadn't wanted to.

He felt ... empty. He had lost friends. He knew it would take a long time to get over that. But it was war. He was a soldier. He wasn't the boy who had left his village anymore. He was something else.

He just didn't know what that something else was.

Michael found what he was looking for. A small pocket watch, given to him by his mother on the day he had left. He opened it.

The small hands of the watch were steadily ticking on, showing the unyielding passage of time. Michael knew that whatever he did, time would keep on ticking. He looked at the picture.

It showed his mother, smiling happily at the camera. His father, a slight grin on his face as though he was slightly embarrassed. His sister, Jane, was also there, beaming. She was always a happy child, who could always cheer Michael up.

And then there was him. Smiling at the camera. He remembered the moment well. His mother had insisted on having a photo taken, so they could all remember what they used to look like.

Michael smiled fondly. He missed his family.

"Michael?" he heard a voice call from outside the door.

"Come in," Michael said, looking up.

He grinned when he saw Darius there, though his eyes widened when he saw what he was sitting on. Darius was in a wheelchair.

He stared, shocked. "Darius, what happened?" he asked him.

"Falling rubble, I assume," Darius commented, looking regretful. "I am currently paralysed from the waist down."

"Oh dear God, I'm so sorry," Michael told Darius, horrified, his sympathy immediately going out to his friend.

"No need, it was not your fault. In fact, you are somewhat of a hero. It was your plan that saved Oslo," Darius commented with a smile as he pressed forward a joystick which wheeled him over.

"I don't think of myself as a hero," Michael commented, surprised.

"I did not imagine you did. After a loss, it is sometimes hard to see the positive things in life," Darius stated.

"You know how it feels?" Michael asked.

Darius raised his eyebrows. "You are not the only one who has lost teammates, Michael. An estimated fifty recruits have been either killed or injured. My friend Peter among them," he recalled seriously, holding Michael's gaze.

Michael looked down, ashamed.

"We all lose people, Michael. It is how we deal with it that defines us," Darius told him.

Michael looked up at him. "How do you deal with it?"

Darius looked thoughtful. "How do I?" he mused. "I suppose I try to see what will benefit me most. And mourning, although it helps deal with emotion initially, will not help me move on."

"That seems ... kind of cold," Michael remarked.

"Cold? Perhaps. I can't say I am ruled by my emotions. Does that make me cold? Or just sensible?" Darius said with a slight twitch of his mouth, seemingly amused.

Michael smiled. "I better see the others. I've not been looking forward to it," he admitted, thinking they might blame him for what happened.

"A wise choice," Darius agreed. "Friends are very useful. They can give us hope, strength and support."

"Seriously?"

"Yes, they do. They also can help with managing emotions," Darius continued.

"No, I meant is that all you see friends as? Tools to help manage you?" Michael asked him.

"On the contrary. I only choose friends that I have great respect for. Yourself and Arthur included," Darius stated.

"Have you seen Arthur recently?" Michael asked him.

"Yes. He was affected by the loss of his friend Hans greatly. I believe that currently, the majority of the recruits are either in their rooms, as you are, or in the common room," Darius told Michael. "It is interesting how some humans seek solace by being alone, yet others have relied on human company to console them."

Michael let out a deep breath. "Do you always speak like that?" he asked Darius.

"Like what?" Darius questioned, raising an eyebrow.

"As if you're not human," Michael said with a slight grin.

Darius tilted his head to one side. "I honestly do not know. I try to contribute to a conversation with my opinion as impartially as I can, regardless of my own emotional feelings."

"Sometimes, people want to hear your feelings," Michael pointed out.

"Is this one of those times?"

"Yes," Michael told him.

"Then I think you should see your squad. They need a strong leader," Darius stated as he turned and wheeled out of his room. "But first, I think you would want to visit an old friend."

"Who?" Michael asked him as he followed.

"Oh, you'll see," Darius stated, going in the lift. Michael thought that it was a good thing they had lifts in the Recruit Centre, as stairs would be very difficult for anyone in a wheelchair.

The pair went towards the Medical Centre, as Darius led Michael to a room.

"Open it," Darius told him.

Michael did so, looking to see what was inside.

The room was plain enough, with a white bed and some pieces of equipment located around. Lying in the bed was a young, red haired man in his early twenties. When Michael saw him, he broke into a smile.

"Sergeant Wallace!" he exclaimed happily, glad to see he was alive.

"Aye, laddie," the man said with a chuckle. "Ah'm alright, thanks to you."

Michael just smiled. "What happened?" he asked him.

"Well, it was actually quite a funny story. I was on me way back, injured, as two recruits drove me in one of the trucks. As we were getting close to Oslo, they slowed down, cos the gate was open. Now, I heard 'em discussing what to do. The gates weren't normally open. So, we tried to radio in, and there was no answer. So instead, we fired a flare. That got some attention, because we heard gunfire inside Oslo. Something to do with Brown Coats or whatever," Sergeant Wallace commented.

"So, eventually we drove in, and I met up with me friend Jack, who was able to get the power back online. Apparently, as Captain O'Reilly was performing his routine check-up, he was attacked by the Norwegians as they stormed into the power grid."

Michael nodded. "How did the Brown Coats get so much support?" he wondered.

"Well, the Western Alliance are seen as foreign invaders. There were rumours of Fenrir promising independence. Speaking of Fenrir, what happened to him? Up here in the medical wing, I don't get told nothing," Wallace stated, folding his arms.

Darius smirked slightly, as Michael shrugged modestly.

"He's dead," Michael told Wallace.

"What?" Wallace asked eagerly. "Dead? How?"

"He was shot," Michael told him quietly.

"By who?" Wallace asked. "Whoever killed Fenrir, I'll have to buy 'em a drink. They deserve a medal, that's fer sure!"

Michael sighed. "By me," he muttered.

"Laddie, what was that?" Wallace asked him.

"I killed Fenrir," Michael said firmly, looking at Wallace. "I saw Fenrir kill Jenny, and his men kill Hans. So I shot him."

Wallace's jaw dropped, as he stared at Michael.

"Ye've got to be taking the mick, right?" he asked, sounding unsure.

Michael didn't say anything.

"Yer not? Jesus Christ ... ye shot Fenrir?" he questioned. "Bloody hell."

Michael dwelled on this. He had shot Fenrir. He had killed Fenrir. Fenrir was only a man. A tactical genius, but one who had underestimated his opponents. No one was invincible. Every great general died at some point.

In Norway, the Western Alliance were lucky. Fenrir had outwitted them. It was only the fact that the recruits from The Institute were there that they stood a chance.

"Michael ... I'm proud of ye," Wallace told him. "And grateful. I lost a lot of friends in the Royal Scots. I miss them all, even Old Greg. Now they can rest in peace, because of you."

"No," Michael said quietly. "It wasn't just me. It was all of us. We all played a part."

Sergeant Wallace nodded. "I know, laddie. And I'm grateful to all of ye," he said, meeting Michael's gaze. There was a fiery passion in his gaze.

Michael smiled slowly.

"I think, perhaps Michael should go back to his squad now," Darius said, looking at Wallace.

Sergeant Wallace looked disappointed. "Of course. I'll, er, get back to me reading," he commented, picking up a book and looking at it.

"Off ye go!" he told them. "I'll just be all alone here, on my hospital bed. At least until that pretty nurse comes along."

Michael grinned, shaking his head as he walked out of the room. He liked Sergeant Wallace, and was relieved he was alive. His loud and talkative nature was a stark contrast with the other instructors.

Michael walked outside, looking up. It was a bright day, although a little cold. It was winter now, the start of December. Luckily, the weather here wasn't as extreme as in Norway. He could see why Hans thought it was warm here. Hans *had* thought. Michael had to remind himself that his friend wasn't there anymore.

He walked inside the Recruit Centre again, and noticed Darius wasn't following him.

"Darius?" Michael questioned.

Darius looked up. "You go ahead. I'll join you later," he said dismissively, driving his motorised wheelchair away.

Michael opened his mouth, then closed it, a little disheartened. Darius seemed to have more important things to do.

He walked up the stairs and entered the common room.

It had a lot of people in, though the atmosphere was a little subdued. People were talking, but there was no enthusiasm in their conversations. Some people were crying, some were hugging, some were doing both.

As people noticed Michael, they looked at him. He could feel their glares upon him. Michael ignored them, not meeting their gaze.

272

He noticed Raymon there, seemingly intact from the explosion of the tank. Michael was surprised, and a little relieved he had survived, but didn't say anything. They met each other's eyes for a second, before Michael carried on.

Michael saw Thomas there, talking with Sophie. Both of them looked at him, and Thomas nodded at Michael, a small smile of his face.

Michael nodded back, respecting Thomas a lot. He avoided looking at Sophie, thinking she might blame him for Marcus' death.

He walked towards the fire, and saw his squad sitting down on the various seats there.

Steve. Arthur. Jürgen. Nadia. Teresa. Joe. Alexandra. Tim.

But no Jenny or Hans.

Michael faced them, and they all turned to look at him.

Jürgen stood up, facing him and looking him in the eye.

Michael tensed up, expecting him to be angry about Jenny. He saw hurt in Jürgen's eyes.

"I trusted you," Jürgen accused, straightening up.

"I know," Michael said quietly, holding his gaze. "I'm sorry."

Jürgen clenched his jaw, then slumped down into a chair, closing his eyes.

Michael scanned around the group. Steve looked up at him.

"Michael," Steve said. "Don't blame yourself. You saved us. You're a true leader."

Michael felt Steve was only saying that because he was his friend.

"Steve is right," Alexandra told him. "We're not angry at you ... we're grateful."

Michael sighed, sitting down. "I don't know what to say," he told his squad.

"You don't have to say anything," Joe said, speaking up for once. "You made a call, and we supported you. There's nothing to feel guilty about."

Michael looked at him, surprised.

"You blame yourself too much, Michael. You always do," Tim said.

"So, we're just gonna carry on as normal?" Michael asked them.

"I don't think we can call it normal anymore," Steve said. "But we'll carry on. We'll make it through. We're a good team. We've got each other."

Michael appreciated what Steve had said.

There was silence as they all thought about the ordeal. Michael closed his eyes and leaned back, being dimly aware of the others descending back into conversation.

He could feel the warmth of the fire against him. It helped with the empty void that was in his chest. He wondered if Jenny would be proud of him, of what he had done.

Michael felt a soft hand on top of his own, and opened his eyes.

Nadia was sitting next to him, a gentle smile on her face.

"Michael ... I know I wasn't there," she told him. "I know you cared about Jenny. And Hans. They were your friends. And I am sorry to see you in pain like this."

Michael sighed. "Jenny ... she was more than a friend to me. I liked her a lot, but I never told her how I felt."

"She knew," Nadia told Michael quietly. "I know she did."

Michael looked up at her. "She knew?"

Nadia nodded, giving Michael a small smile.

Michael felt better. "But ... she liked Jürgen, right?"

"That ... I do not know. But Michael, thinking about her will only hurt. You have to move on. You are a soldier now," Nadia told him quietly.

Michael nodded. "I know, that is what Darius said. But it's not as easy as that," he told her.

Nadia bit her lip. "Just ... try. Ah, also, vhile you were gone, I spoke to Sergeant Raines," she began. "I was thinking that, for the Coliseum games, ve are going to give it a shot at winning."

Michael felt that was a poor choice of words.

Nadia sighed, trying again. "I think you should lead The Institute team for the Coliseum. Raines agrees, and I think you can do it," she told him.

Michael looked startled. He had forgotten about the Coliseum. It seemed so insignificant in light of what had happened. He couldn't think about it now. "What about Thomas? What about Jürgen?" he asked her, alarmed.

"Sorry, this is a bad time, I know. I'll ... discuss it when you get back," Nadia said with a sigh.

"Get back? From where?" Michael asked.

Nadia looked up to a tall figure that was approaching them.

Michael looked up, and smiled. It was Sergeant Raines.

"Lads, lasses, I think ye need a break from war," their instructor told them. "Which is why, yer going home."

"Going home?" Steve asked him.

"Yes. Fer the next three days, I've gotten permission for yous to be sent back to yer homes. Ye can go to yer village," Raines told him.

Michael felt warm inside.

He would see his family again.

53 - HOME AGAIN

Michael walked forward, with Steve by his side.

He was walking back to his village. The sky was a light grey, and the air was cold. Birds flew in the sky ahead. The frosty ground crunched under his feet as the cold wind rushed against his face, blowing back his hair slightly.

Ahead of him, he could see the river at the edge of the village.

Sergeant Raines had dropped off Michael and Steve, before driving on to take the others.

Michael glanced back at his friend, giving him an apprehensive smile. This was almost as nerve-racking as going to The Institute.

It was winter, on the run up to Christmas. Christmas had always been a happy time for Michael. Although there were no huge meals, it was when families from the village bonded together in front of the large outdoor fire, enjoying each other's company and dancing.

It was common for people to ask each other to the Christmas dance, and although Michael had never been asked, it was usually a key conversation topic for the young people of the village.

Michael walked up to the bridge and looked down. The river was still flowing, just as it always had been. Life would have continued on for his village. He hoped everything was the same.

"What will we tell them?" Steve asked Michael.

"The truth," Michael stated. "Jane has to know what The Institute is like for when she goes there."

"Do you think they'll remember us?" Steve blurted out quickly.

Michael looked at him, and was surprised to see him looking worried. Steve was usually the confident one. "Steve, of course they'll remember us. We'll be like heroes," he tried to reassure his friend.

Steve nodded, though his eyebrows were still furrowed.

Michael continued walking into the village. He passed the houses on the outskirts, and saw the Cuttings, one of the families Michael had known, working in their garden.

"Dear God, is that Michael Bakerson?" Mr Cutting muttered as they passed.

Michael gave them a friendly smile and nod, but they just stared at him. He looked across the street towards Grandpa Ted's house, and walked towards it.

A horrible sense of foreboding filled him. Was Ted alright? Michael knew he had been ill, but he had always seemed so full of life.

The air seemed much colder now.

He went towards the open door, and stepped inside. The house hadn't been lived in for some time. The familiar smell of old leather greeted him, and the pictures on the walls had been taken down.

Michael walked back outside, breathing heavily.

Steve looked at him sympathetically.

"He's gone," Mr Cutting called to Michael, a grave look in his eyes. He was a round shaped man with a receding hairline. He was usually very sarcastic, though had taken a liking to Michael when he was young.

"Gone?" Michael was horrified.

No. Grandpa Ted couldn't be dead.

"Long gone," Mr Cutting said, shaking his head regretfully. "He's living with your parents now, they wouldn't let him stay on his own. But he insisted on taking with him those damn pictures. I can't say I'm surprised, Ted was a bit of a hoarder. But he's back at your place now. This house is empty."

Relief washed over Michael, and he felt a huge weight lift off his chest. He was alive. Thank God.

"Where 'ave you been, Michael, eh?" Mr Cutting called. "I thought you'd come back! Visit us once or twice, eh?"

"I'm sorry sir ... I've been busy," Michael apologised.

"Hmm. Well, I suppose I've no right to be angry. Though I can't say the same for your family, they have been harshly treated. The new leader seems to have a grudge against any military," Mr Cutting said, as he attacked a weed viciously with his hoe.

"The new leader?" Steve asked, frowning.

"You don't know him? My, my, things have changed an awful lot since you left. I better let your family tell the story though, it's not my place to tell. Aha! Gotcha!" Mr Cutting said, bending down and picking up the weed. He ignored Michael and Steve from then on, going back to tending his garden.

The pair shared an uneasy glance, before they carried on.

"I better check on my family," Steve said, before hurrying off.

Michael could guess why. His friend must be worried for his family, after what Mr Cutting had said.

He neared the centre of the village, and began noticing some subtle changes about it. The huts looked more flimsy. The people looked wary, and angry.

As Michael walked, a few people began to recognise him. Whispers followed him.

"Is that Michael?"

"He's changed so much..."

"All this is his fault..."

Michael tried to block them out as he went on. He was just going home to visit his family, there was nothing wrong with that.

He walked towards their hut, and entered. It looked the same as it always had. It was not too large, and had a main area with a small woven rug on the ground. There were three small sleeping areas, and the kitchen lay in the middle.

In the area Michael used to inhabit, Grandpa Ted now lay, with Michael's mother kneeling next to him and giving him a container of water.

"Mikey-boy?" Grandpa Ted whispered.

His mother looked up sharply, shock in her eyes.

"M-Michael?" she asked, her eyes widening as she turned to look at him. He could see lines of stress on her face, and she looked older than she had done.

"Hi Mum," Michael told her with a smile. He could tell something was wrong.

His mother gave him a small smile. "You've ... grown," she said, biting her lip.

Michael raised his eyebrows. Why was his mother acting so strangely?

"Is something wrong?" he asked her.

"Michael ... why are you here?" his mother asked him quietly. He could see concern in her eyes.

"To visit you?" Michael said, confused. "What happened?"

"I'll tell you what has happened," a female voice said from behind him.

Michael turned with a smile to see his fifteen year old sister, Jane. Her blonde hair seemed darker now, and was tied back in a ponytail. He immediately noticed a change in her. Her expression, which Michael remembered as being always happy, was serious.

"Food. That's what happened. For some reason, the military began sending us trucks of food. No one knows why. It was courtesy of some Sheikh guy?" Jane questioned, raising an eyebrow.

Michael smiled. Sheikh Bakir had kept his word.

"It was more of a curse than a blessing. Word began spreading that our village was receiving extra food, and people began arriving. Brigands. Previously, they were on our side, but now they've taken over the village. They're just taking all the food for themselves," Jane said, folding her arms.

"What? So, you don't get the food?" Michael asked, growing alarmed.

"No. We still have to farm our own, but now the brigands run the village. They used to be bearable, but now their leader has taken things too far. He's treating us like slaves," Jane replied, sighing.

Michael grew angry.

"Listen, Michael, I'm glad to see you, but there's nothing we can do. People are scared of the brigands. Too scared to act," Jane said, placing a hand on his shoulder.

"You've changed. And so have I," Michael said.

Jane smiled at him slightly. "I can tell."

"We got your letter," his mother said quickly. "But the brigands wouldn't let us send a reply. We did miss you, you know."

Michael smiled at his mother, then hugged her. "I missed you too. And I'm going to have to tell you all about it, so much has happened," he told them both.

"Mikey-boy?" he heard a whisper.

Michael knelt down next to Grandpa Ted. He looked so much older and more frail.

"I'm here, Grandpa," Michael told him, taking his hand.

"You're still my boy, Michael. You're still you, aren't you? Not a monster? Not a machine?" he croaked.

"I'm still me," Michael told him softly, squeezing his hand. It felt very fragile. "I'm still me, don't worry."

"Good..." Grandpa Ted whispered, coughing again.

"Grandpa's gotten a bit of an illness," his mother stated. "Nothing to worry about, I'm sure it will pass."

Michael closed his eyes. He knew it wouldn't pass. He could hear the fear in her voice.

"Where's dad?" Michael asked his mother.

She remained silent, and Jane spoke up.

"He's joined the brigands."

"What?" Michael asked, stunned. He blinked. "Dad was a farmer?"

"Not anymore. When you left, he really began hating the military for taking you away from him. He joined the brigands to get back at them. When they came here, he made sure we had enough food, but this new leader has some special hatred," she explained, looking tired. "It's been all Dad can do to stop them from taking me."

Michael clenched his fists. The brigands were trying to take his sister? Well, he would show them.

"Where are the brigands?" Michael asked them.

"Don't go there," Jane pleaded.

"Where are they?" Michael demanded, angry. He had come back, just to find his village being ruled by brigands?

"In one of the old houses up north," Jane told him. "If you're going, I'm coming with you."

Michael looked at her. His protective instincts were making him want to leave her behind, but he could see a fiery anger and stubbornness in her eyes that mirrored his own.

"Alright. Let's go," Michael said, before striding out of the hut.

He knew his way around the village instinctively, but couldn't help but notice the changes. Some huts were gone, and there were dark areas of the ground.

"There was a fire a few weeks ago," Jane said quietly.

Michael didn't say anything. He strode on, quickly and purposefully.

Eventually, Jane pointed it out to him.

"There it is."

It was a large building, quite old. It looked like some sort of mansion or country house. Usually, there would be no point living in one of these as they were so far from the farms, but the brigands must have a large supply of food somewhere.

There were two guards standing in front of the large doors.

Michael approached the door, not looking at them.

One of them, a large man with a square jaw, stood in his way.

"Why are you here? Only brigands can enter," the man said, folding his arms.

"I want to speak to him. My name is Michael Bakerson, and I'm a member of the Western Alliance," he told the brigand.

"Bakerson? Yeah, I think yer dad's in here," the man said, opening the door.

Michael strode in, followed by Jane. They were in a hall, with a long dining table inside, with many people sitting there and eating. The brigand who had opened the door went up to the head of the table to speak to this leader.

"Michael Bakerson?" he heard a voice call, surprised. "Michael Bakerson!?"

The people at the table fell silent as the man at the end stood up. Michael realised with horror who this new village leader was.

He was a man in an old khaki uniform. He was bald, and had a large bulbous nose. He was wearing dark sunglasses that covered his eyes, and had a devious smirk on his face.

It was Boss.

The man who had tortured him.

54 -   FAMILY

"Boss," Michael seethed, furious. He clenched his fists, glaring at the man at the head of the table.

Boss laughed. "Don't tell me this is your village?" he asked mockingly.

"It is," Michael said, looking at the people at the table. He recognised some of them. There was a brigand there named Jarod. He had dark skin and brown eyes, renowned among the brigands for being an excellent tracker. Michael remembered him as a kindly man. The brigands had used to help the village get hold of meat from time to time. But now it seemed like they had taken over completely.

Sitting next to Boss was a tall, hook-nosed man. He was pale and had small, calculating eyes. He was named Henderson, and was the founder of this group of brigands. Michael didn't know much about him, but knew he had a deep hatred for the Western Alliance.

Michael then saw a man sitting down, next to Jarod. He had brown hair and blue eyes, just like Michael. He looked at the table, not meeting Michael's eye. Michael's jaw dropped.

"Dad?" he asked.

His father looked up at him, alarm in his eyes. He didn't say anything.

Boss looked between them. "John? That brat is your son?" he asked incredulously.

He began guffawing, and many other brigands on the table joined in.

"Oh, this must be heart-breaking for you, eh, Michael? To see your father with us?" Boss taunted.

Michael watched his father, shocked. His father was a brigand, on Boss' table?

"You see Michael, you seem to have gotten the wrong impression of us," Boss told him. "We just want for the people of Independent Britain to be truly independent. We want freedom. Look what the military have done! There are a lot of villages, just like this one, which are destitute because of the Western Alliance. You've just come from The Institute, eh? I bet they had food there. I bet you never had to go hungry. Well, people here are going hungry."

Michael looked down. What was Boss saying? That the Western Alliance were to blame?

"Michael, I know you want to help your village. And you have, you've given us this food. But you can do so much more. Join us, and you can make sure that your family doesn't go hungry again. Your father understands. We just want to be free. It's in your blood, Michael," Boss told him.

What Boss was saying wasn't untrue. The Western Alliance should help the villages more.

"What, exactly, do you want here?" Michael asked Boss, looking up. He was unsure. He wanted to help his village, but he owed so much to the military.

"Just be our man inside. Give us information. Tell us where the military food convoys go, for example. Let us give the people of Independent Britain what they deserve. There are a lot of people that need our help," Boss said, opening a hand out to Michael.

Michael thought. Was it really in his blood? He remembered feeling that the Western Alliance were not helping people enough. Would working with Boss help?

He looked at his father. His father nodded, his eyes pleading.

But Michael realised it would meant choosing between his village and The Institute. Choosing between his old home and his new one. It wasn't easy.

It would mean keeping secrets from his friends. Working against his superiors. Michael wouldn't have a problem with going against Lieutenant Jones, but he knew he couldn't betray Sergeant Raines or Sergeant Wallace.

Michael was contemplating this when Jane spoke up from his side.

"You don't help people, though, do you?" Jane asked them. "You say you'll help our village, but you're not. We've got extra food, but you're keeping it for yourselves, not sharing it with the villages. You're making yourselves the elite. We won't gain independence, we'll just be ruled by brigands. Like we are now."

Michael saw Boss falter. Boss then gave Jane a sad smile.

"I know we have our flaws, but we will improve. You could help us be better leaders," Boss told Jane with surprising softness.

Jane looked down, shifting slightly. Michael looked at Boss, suspicious, and saw a victorious smirk on his face. He thought he had won. He wanted Jane to join him too.

Michael's anger flared up again, his protective brotherly instinct taking over.

"You know, Boss, you're not a leader," he remarked. "No one here respects you. You're not one of the people. You tortured me, and you enjoyed it. It's true that the Western Alliance should be doing more to help, but I'd rather be ruled by them than be slave to you."

He looked around at the other brigands. "This man is in charge of you? Why do you do what he says? You're all afraid of him. He rules by fear. And no one has the bottle to stand up to him."

Boss smirked. "You think you can turn them against me with your poetic little speech. No. They're loyal. And you will be made an example of. No one speaks to me like that," he said, looking furious.

"Get them!" he commanded, and the two brigands from outside stepped in. "Take these-"

"Stop!"

Michael's father had stood up. "You will not take my children," he said, his voice low, but filled with anger.

Boss looked at him. "John? You're challenging me?" he asked.

"My son is right," his father said, walking round the table towards Boss. "You rule with fear and for yourself. What the people need a leader who believes in fairness and justice. It's time for you to go. You will no longer lead this village."

"And you will?" Boss asked, raising his eyebrows.

"No. But I will not serve you any longer," his father said coolly.

"Nor will I," Jarod said, standing up.

"Nor will I!" a short brigand roared, standing up.

285

"Then you will be punished as well," Boss sneered. "Get them!"

One of the brigands from the door lunged towards the table, but Michael kicked his legs out from underneath him, taking him by surprise.

He then faced the other, who threw a punch at him. Michael blocked it, and wrenched the man's hand back, using the wrist lock Hans had taught him.

Jane then kicked the man savagely, sending him to the ground.

Michael looked up at the table. Jarod had drawn a knife and was pointing it towards Boss' throat. Henderson was backing away. Several of the other brigands stood behind Michael's father. He clearly had their support.

"You have dishonoured us, Boss," Jarod said. "You made us blind to the suffering of the people. We have followed you too long. This boy is right."

"He's not a boy," Michael's father said, looking at him with respect. "He's a man."

Michael smiled slightly. He had made his father proud.

Jarod looked at the other brigands. "This clan of brigands shall disperse. Our purpose was to gain food from the military to help feed the villagers. We have gone astray from our promise. But we will fulfil it now. We will give the village people the food that was promised to them," he vowed.

Michael's father walked over to him and Jane.

"I'm sorry," he told them both.

Michael shook his head. "I don't blame you. Sometimes we all do the wrong things but for the right reasons," he commented, knowing he had also been considering joining the brigands a few minutes ago.

Jane folded her arms. "How could you side with that man?" she asked him, looking unimpressed.

Their father looked down. "I was afraid," he admitted.

"Dad, you've made up for it. We'll get the food, and bring it back to the village," Michael reassured him.

Michael's father looked at him. "You've changed a lot, Michael," he told him.

Michael let out a shaky breath. "I have. And I'll tell you all about it."

* * *

That evening, the villagers ate outside. It was the largest meal they had ever had, with the food supplies that Sheikh Bakir had sent shared out between them.

Michael sat with his mother and his father. They watched as Jane danced with some of her friends. Even Grandpa Ted's bed had been brought out for him.

Michael smiled as he ate his bowl of rice. He had been telling his parents all about his time at The Institute. Jane still wanted to go there.

His mother had been put off by the possible danger of her being hurt, but his father believed she could take it. Michael still hadn't mentioned he had been to Norway.

"So, do you get fed enough?" his mother asked Michael.

"Yes. More than enough," Michael said.

"And is this Sergeant Raines person a reasonable man?" his mother asked.

"Yes ... why?" Michael asked.

"Then I want you to take Jane with you and look after her," his mother decided.

"Woah, woah, what?" Michael asked his mother. His father just shrugged.

"She'll be happy there. She's grown restless lately," his mother said.

Michael considered, then thought it could do no harm. "I'll ask Raines if she can take the tests early," he decided.

His mother seemed pleased, for she stood up to go and speak to one of her friends, leaving Michael alone with his father. She was probably telling them about Michael's achievements or something.

"Michael ... " his father said. "I have to apologise."

"It's fine," Michael reassured him.

"No. I do. When you left for The Institute ... I never said goodbye," he admitted.

Michael smiled. "I know ... and that hurt," he told his father quietly. "But I've forgiven you. It must have been so hard for you to lose your son."

His father shook his head. "I just thought you wouldn't be the same after going," he said.

"I'm not the same."

"No ... I mean - you're still the kind, brave, determined son I knew. The military can change you if you let it. But you're stronger than that," his father said proudly.

Michael couldn't help but grin at his father's words as he looked at the fire. Despite all that had happened, he still wanted to make his father proud.

"What will happen to the brigands?" Michael asked him.

His father looked thoughtful. "I do not know. They will disperse, go back to being farmers or miners. Some might go and help other villages," he commented.

"What will we do about the villages and the food?" Michael asked him.

"We'll share it with them. It's not our resources, it is the military's. That's where we went wrong before. I think we can really start something with this food," his father said, a glint in his eyes.

"What do you mean?" Michael questioned.

"Imagine, if the villages began working together. We could become a network, and trade with each other. Now that we finally control the surplus of food, we can make things better here. We could get hold of some timber - rebuild houses!" he enthused.

Michael was pleased. His father was a visionary at heart.

"And who will lead them?"

His father smiled. "The people will decide. I think Jarod will be the favourite."

"We'll have a democracy?"

"We'll have a lot of things, Michael. I've got ideas. And it's coming because of your sponsor. Make sure you thank him," his father told Michael.

"I will," Michael reassured him, looking up at the people dancing. He recognised a few, and was glad to see that Steve was there.

"How long will you be staying with us?" his father asked him.

"Just a few days. We've got an important competition coming up," Michael said.

"Competition, eh? And here's me thinking you'd actually be fighting," his father remarked.

Michael smiled ruefully, his throat feeling dry. Tears welled up as he remembered the friends he had lost fighting.

"Yeah," he whispered quietly.

His father sensed his pain. "Hey, lighten up, Michael. Enjoy the dance. I bet there are some girls here you might like. What was that girl you used to like? Laura?"

Michael blushed. "I'm not dancing, Dad, and that was four years ago!" he exclaimed.

His father grinned. "Alright son, I'll leave you alone. But if they have a dance at The Institute, you better join in," he said as he stood up and walked over to speak with Jarod.

Michael sat there, watching the fire flicker, as the music slowed down. It was played by a group of older people, all with homemade instruments.

"Hey."

Michael looked up, to see his sister Jane sit next to him. Michael found that she looked more like him. There was something about the expression in the eyes.

"Hey," he replied. "Enjoy the dancing?"

"More than you," she said with a smirk.

Michael laughed. "I like watching," he said, though his excuse sounded pathetic even to him.

The real reason was that he had never danced before.

"So, what is The Institute like? I'm guessing it's a lot more dangerous that you told Mum and Dad," Jane said curiously.

Michael shrugged. "Yeah," he said, trying to keep the emotion out of his voice.

"So, do you think I'll be okay there?" Jane asked him. "Is it fun?"

Michael shrugged again. "Fun isn't the word I would use," he said, "But it's a big decision though, and you could die. I've lost friends. They train you, but it's all down to luck who lives and who dies. I know you want to get out of the village, Jane, but you've gotta be absolutely sure you've considered what it could mean."

Jane nodded slowly, then glanced at him and blurted out, "Do you have a girlfriend yet?"

"No!" Michael exclaimed, blushing. "Why does everyone ask that! I'm training to be a soldier, not a - romancer or something!"

Jane laughed. "It's fine if you want to hide it, but when I go there, I'll find out," she teased him. "And then I'll tell them your secrets. Remember that time you tried to push me in the river and fell in yourself?"

Michael rolled his eyes, shaking his head. "You're unbelievable," he muttered.

"Now that's true," Jane said smugly.

"Now I know why I left!" Michael grinned at her. "It was you, all along!"

Jane laughed again. "Now come on, enjoy yourself. I'll dance with you," Jane told him.

"I, er, don't know," Michael protested, as she dragged him to his feet.

"Exactly. I can't let you go back as clueless as you are," Jane insisted, pulling him towards where people were dancing. "Just go with it."

Michael had no choice.

Michael really enjoyed himself that night. He loved his family. He felt closer to his family than he had ever been. In the past, he had taken them for granted, but now he appreciated his time with them much more.

He would miss them when he went back.

55 - CODENAME

"First of all, I'd like to welcome you back to The Institute. Some of you survived. Second, I'd like a goddamn mission report on why so many of you died out there!" Lieutenant Jones yelled, shaking a fist.

He was speaking on the stage at The Institute, where the squads were lined up facing him. The numbers of recruits were noticeably smaller now. Michael had been taken back here after spending one week at his village. While he was there, he had lived as he used to, and spent time with his family. Grandpa Ted had brightened up before he left, and seemed to be slightly recovering.

Michael recoiled at the mention of death. Jones wasn't even there, how could he talk about it?

"I'm meant to be taking the best of you to the Coliseum, and a bunch of you get yourselves killed! I mean, you lot survived, but a ton of you are injured. How can I work with that?" he demanded, looking around as though expecting an answer.

Sergeant Raines coughed.

"Er, yeah, anyway, back to business. In Norway, according to some crackpot there, you performed admirably," Jones said with a frown. "So, you will be given the official Western Alliance ceremony for initiation into the army. You'll graduate to become actual soldiers now. You'll be awarded with the Gallantry Medal, for outstanding bravery. You will then be required to attend the traditional military ball, which apparently is a custom over here. Furthermore, Sergeant Raines, Sergeant Vellon and I will be choosing the Coliseum team soon. Not that we have many left to choose from."

Michael smiled slightly. A medal? That would be nice. He wondered what the ceremony would be like. And the ball.

His stomach lurched. A ball? With girls? Would he have to ask someone?

Damn. Should he fake being ill or something?

"Michael?"

It was Alexandra. Jones had stopped speaking, and the recruits had descended into chatter.

He looked up. Was this about the dance? Did she want to go with him?

"You know, this ball?" Alexandra began.

Oh God. How should he turn her down? He didn't like her in that way!

"Yeah?" Michael asked.

"Do you think ... you could speak to Elizabeth? About whether she would go with Tim? I promised him I'd try," Alexandra began, biting her lip.

"Elizabeth?" Michael questioned, dimly remembering a conversation with Alexandra on the subject. "I've never spoke to her?"

"I know, but no one knows who I am. She'll respect you after what has happened," Alexandra admitted. "And, Tim would never be able to ask her himself."

Michael laughed. He wasn't the only one nervous about this dance. "Who are you going with?" he asked her.

Alexandra shrugged. "Whoever asks me," she admitted, glancing over at Darius, who was wheeling himself over.

"Greetings, Michael, Alexandra!" Darius said cheerfully. "How was your trip to your homes?"

Michael raised an eyebrow. Darius didn't usually make small talk.

"Erm, it was ... eventful," Michael said, considering.

"Oh, mine was amazing," Alexandra gushed. "It was so nice to see everyone. How was yours?"

"Excellent, thank you," Darius said, seeming a little nervous.

Michael broke in. "Are you going to go to this ball, Darius?"

Darius looked pained. "I don't think it would be fair for me to ask anybody, in my condition. I doubt anyone would want to go with me," he said.

"You could go with Alexandra?" Michael suggested.

Darius blinked, glancing across at Alexandra, who was blushing crimson.

There was silence. "Anyway, I better go. I need to talk to someone," Michael told them, slipping away and leaving them together.

He scanned around, remembering Nadia had wanted to speak to him. He saw her talking to Jürgen, and went over.

"Nadia?" he asked.

She looked up and smiled. Jürgen frowned.

"Ja?" Nadia said.

"You wanted to speak with me?"

"Oh, of course. Come vith me," Nadia said with a smile, leading him inside.

Michael glanced at Jürgen, who narrowed his eyes, before following her.

"What do you need?" he asked Nadia, as she walked into the elevator, pressing the button for the girls' floor, Boudicca.

"I was thinking of discussing something vith you," Nadia began.

"I gathered that," Michael said, raising his eyebrows. "Why are we going to the girls floor?"

Nadia sighed. "You are so impatient!" she said. "Vill you let me explain when we get there?"

Michael blinked, surprised. "Sorry," he told her, as the elevator opened as she walked forward, opening one of the doors.

Michael entered, looking around curiously. He had never been in a girl's rooms before. It turned out they were exactly the same as the boys' ones.

"Alright. I apologise," Nadia said. "I have been studying the remaining candidates for leadership to the Coliseum. If the Institute team vins, it vill be incredible for The Institute, and ve vill have much better opportunities in the future."

"But don't the Americans always win?" Michael asked her.

"Ja. But this year, ve have something the Americans don't," Nadia said.

"A good sense of humour?"

"Ha, no. Experience. Ve've fought in Norway, and they haven't. That gives us an edge over them," Nadia explained.

"Nadia, you weren't in Norway. We literally only just survived. It didn't help us, it just weakened us," Michael told her.

"But the other teams won't know that. Ve can paint The Institute as heroes, as experienced fighters," Nadia explained.

"Why? We're not," Michael pointed out. "We'd by lying."

"Not lying ... just making the other teams scared. If they're afraid of us, they won't be as effective," Nadia explained.

"But surely if they underestimate us, we can surprise them," Michael countered. "The sponsors will love an underdog."

"Ve'll always be an underdog. But if there's a chance the Americans vill lose their own Coliseum games, they'll be scared," Nadia said.

"And what does this have to do with me?" Michael asked her.

"Vell ... as I said, I was looking through the potential leaders and, vell, you were the one who shot Fenrir. That vill carry weight," Nadia explained.

"You've thought a lot about this," Michael remarked.

"I didn't go back to my family. I've had time to think," Nadia said with shrug.

Michael realised how lucky he was. At least he knew his family were safe. Nadia's family was in Germany, where there was fighting.

"What do want me to do?" Michael asked her.

"Vell, I just needed to see if you vere up for it. Because, I've called in your sponsor," Nadia explained.

"What? Sheikh Bakir?" Michael asked incredulously. "Why?"

"I contacted him and put forward my idea. He said he was visiting anyvay to make sure his recruits were okay from Norway," Nadia explained.

"What if I say no?" Michael asked her.

"Then, hopefully the Sheikh can convince you," Nadia said with a smile.

* * *

"Mike-al!" the Sheikh announced slowly, waddling towards him.

294

Michael couldn't help but smile at the sight of the enormous man. They were waiting outside, as a large helicopter, with gold logo on the side, had just landed. The Sheikh had clambered out, with his burly bodyguards either side of him. He wore golden robes.

"Good afternoon, sir," Michael told him with a nod.

Dan Fisher, the other recruit sponsored by the Sheikh, was waiting with him, and Nadia was nearby.

"Greetings, my dear recruits," the Sheikh said slowly, beaming. "We have *much* to discuss!"

The Sheikh then began slowly making his way towards a building. This would probably take a while, so Michael decided to speed things up.

"We can discuss while we walk," he suggested to the Sheikh.

"Yes, yes," the Sheikh said. "Now, were any of my recruits injured in Norway?"

Dan raised his eyebrows.

"Erm, sir, there's only two of us. We're both right here," Michael told him.

The Sheikh slowly looked to one side, then beamed. "Dan!" he announced slowly, just noticing the tall boy.

Dan nodded, not saying anything.

"Sheikh?" Michael said. "I want to thank you for providing food to my village. Things are much better there now."

The Sheikh beamed. "Good, good! You are most welcome. Remember, you promised me your services."

"Anyway Michael, I understand you want my backing for the Coliseum," the Sheikh said, looking at him.

"Well, er, yes, I do," Michael said, glancing at Nadia to clarify. She nodded.

"Good, good. Now, Miss Bauer, you are not one of mine, are you?" Sheikh Bakir asked her.

Nadia shook her head. "No, sir. But, I have a proposition that I think you will find beneficial," she stated.

"Good, good. Tell me," the Sheikh told Nadia.

"Vell, for the upcoming Coliseum games, I vas thinking you could use your influence to portray Michael as someone to be feared. This vould enhance The Institute's chance in the games, and also give you a chance to be known as his sponsor," Nadia stated.

Michael guessed Nadia was trying to show the Sheikh how the offer could benefit his profile. He frowned, slightly. Didn't he get a say in this?

"What do you want me to do?" the Sheikh asked.

"Vell, ideally, present our Institute team as experienced fighters. Show Michael as a hero, create an identity for him," Nadia said.

"Woah, woah, don't I get a say in this?" Michael asked them.

Nadia looked surprised. "I thought you vanted to do this."

"Well, you thought wrong. I'm not being made out to be some merciless killer! I'm not! I'm just me! I did it for my friends, not for anything else!" Michael exclaimed, angrily.

"Michael, you'll have a reputation vhether you like it or not. Ve just want to harness that," Nadia told him.

Michael furrowed his brows, annoyed. "I thought we were friends. You've just done this behind my back."

Hurt flashed in Nadia's eyes. "I'm doing this for everyone here," she said defensively.

Sheikh Bakir looked at Michael with sympathy. "Mike-al, Miss Bauer is right. A large part of the Coliseum is appealing to the fans. That will get me more investments in my companies because I sponsor you, and you and The Institute will gain more recognition. You'll be famous, and if you win, some of the prize money will be donated to The Institute," he said.

"And, who needs to think this idea will end at the Coliseum," the Sheik continued. "If we play it right, the Russians will fear you too. My recruit will become famous, and you'll be able to get back at your enemies."

"Isn't that what Fenrir did? Use fear to intimidate his opponents?" Michael questioned.

"Fenrir did it effectively. You can now use it *against* the Russians. You've killed Fenrir," Nadia encouraged him. "He was ruthless, and cruel, and you defeated him. You are a hero to the Western Alliance. The people need that."

"I don't want to lead with fear! I don't want to change!"

"You von't have to! You're a hero, Michael, just let them see that," Nadia insisted. "Please, think about it!"

Michael sighed, looking down. Should he really be doing it? Letting them portray him as a war hero? Did he deserve it?

He remembered Fenrir. How fear could be effective. Fenrir was a monster.

But the fear he instilled in the Western Alliance had undermined the Western Alliance. Should he now use that against the Russians?

The only way to conquer fear ... is to become it.

The memory came out of nowhere. Fenrir shooting Jenny.

Would taking this role make him change? Would it make it more like Fenrir?

No. Michael was his own person. He had become a soldier, but that hadn't corrupted him. He was strong enough to remain himself. He would be able to use the death of Fenrir for the benefit of The Institute, and the whole of the Western Alliance.

He looked up at the Sheikh. "I'll do it."

Nadia smiled. "It is the best choice," she told him.

Michael looked at the Sheikh. "What is the next step?" he asked the large man.

"Well, here's the thing. You have to do very little. I will hire people to promote what you've done for the Western Alliance. I think, there is only one thing we need to work out," the Sheikh said as he bumbled along.

"What is that?"

"You will need a name," the Sheikh said.

Michael blinked. "A name?"

"Ja," Nadia said. "I mean, Michael Bakerson is not very intimidating," she said with a slight shrug.

Michael raised his eyebrows. "Alright. Alright. What sort of name does it have to be?"

"Vell, you choose. Something that shows you," Nadia suggested.

"Like, what?"

"Some hero, perhaps?"

"What, like Panther, or Tiger? That doesn't seem very original," Michael commented.

"Perhaps, Hawk?" Nadia suggested.

"What about Leonidas?" Dan said, speaking up.

"Leonidas?" Michael questioned. "Who is that?"

"He vas the leader of the Spartans in Ancient Greece," Nadia said. "He made a famous stand against a force much larger than his."

"Didn't he die?" Michael questioned.

"Vell, ja, but it's just a name. It suits you," Nadia encouraged.

Michael considered.

"Leonidas it is."

56 -   COMPLICATED

This was it. The day of the ceremony. Also, the day of the ball.

Michael still hadn't asked anybody to the ball. He just didn't know who, and time had gone by quickly. A lot of people had already planned to go with others, although a lot were just going to go there on their own. Michael had decided that he would do that as well. Steve was going with Teresa, from the Spartans.

He was currently walking into the common room, looking around. He had promised to help someone, and he intended to keep that promise.

He found who he was looking for, chatting to a group of boys Michael didn't know the name of.

Elizabeth Walker, Tim's crush, was known as one of the best recruits. She was very good-looking, having a nice figure as well as long black hair that had streaks of purple in it. Alexandra had asked Michael to see if she would dance with Tim.

Michael was feeling that it might be very difficult to get her to go with Tim. She was probably already going with someone. If he had known her better, Michael might have even wanted to go with her himself.

He walked over to her nervously.

A few of the boys gave him dirty looks, but he ignored them as he cleared his throat. "Elizabeth?"

She turned to look at him. "Michael?" she asked, surprised.

"Can I talk to you for a second?" he asked her.

She smiled slightly. "Yeah, sure," she said, leading him over to an unoccupied couch by the fire and sitting down, crossing one leg over her other.

Michael stood in front of her. He wasn't sure how to start.

"Erm ... you know, the ball?" he asked her.

Elizabeth raised her eyebrows, her eyes widening. "Michael, I didn't think you'd be asking me that," she commented.

"No, no, it's not what you think. Are you going with anyone?" Michael asked her, blushing in embarrassment. The fire seemed a lot warmer now.

"No ... I'm not. But Michael, are you asking me?" Elizabeth commented, a slight grin on her face. "My, this is flattering."

Michael inwardly cursed himself. He didn't want to offend her, but he had to tell the truth.

"Er, actually, it's for a friend. You see, he's gonna go there, and I was wondering if maybe, when you are there, you could dance with him, if you fancy?" Michael asked awkwardly.

Elizabeth considered. "So you're not asking me yourself?"

"Well, I mean, that wasn't my intention. I mean, I thought, well, if you wanted to, you know, you could," he said, now feeling very hot. "It's Tim, from my squad."

Elizabeth leaned back on the couch, crossing her legs over the other way. "Alright, when I go there, I'll dance with Tim. He seems alright. Nothing official though, mind. A few people have asked me, so I thought I'd go there on my own and see when I get there," she told him with a slight smile.

Michael smiled in relief. "Thanks, Elizabeth. That means a lot," he said gratefully.

"But, on one condition," Elizabeth added, a mischievous glint in her eyes.

Michael raised an eyebrow quizzically. "Go on," he told her.

"When we're there, you'll dance with me," Elizabeth said, grinning.

Michael raised both his eyebrows. "What?"

"You heard."

"You mean, just like, one dance?" he asked, unsure.

"Yeah, don't worry. I'll still dance with your friend."

"Why?"

"I have my reasons," Elizabeth said, playing with her long hair. "So, is it a deal?" she asked him.

Michael considered. He didn't really know Elizabeth at all. But then again, he didn't want to have no one to dance with the whole night, and she was very good looking. It could do no harm, and if it meant getting Tim a dance, he would do it.

He nodded. "Deal," he told her.

Elizabeth smiled. "Well then, see you at the ball," she said, standing up and winking at him before striding back to her friends.

Michael stood there for a second, pleased with the outcome. His heart was still beating quickly.

Maybe he should invite someone to the dance. How bad could it be?

He looked around. There was only really one person he could think of.

He went to the area where the remainder of the Jaegers were talking. There were pitifully few.

Sophie was there, along with Oliver, Dan and Lucy. They looked sad.

Michael approached them, steeling his nerves. "Sophie? Can I talk to you for a second?" he asked her.

Sophie looked up with a smirk. "Sure," she said, not moving.

"Privately?" Michael asked, giving her a pointed look.

Sophie sighed. "Alright," she said, holding out a hand for him. "Hand up?" she asked him.

Michael clasped her hand, pulling her up. She tugged a little too hard, as though she was trying to pull him down.

However, he held firm, and Sophie ended up falling into him.

Oliver raised his eyebrows. Sophie just grinned.

Michael, feeling awkward, let go and walked away, expecting her to follow.

She did. "What's up, then?" Sophie asked him, folding her arms.

Michael took a deep breath. She was attractive. It was hard to keep himself from panicking.

"Would you like to go to the ball with me?" he asked, tensing up.

Sophie raised her eyebrows in surprise. She smiled at Michael sweetly.

"I'd love to," she whispered, hugging him. Michael hugged back, feeling very warm.

"But ... I've already said I'll go with someone else," she added. "Sorry."

Michael's hand dropped to his sides. Why did she do that? She made him feel special, then just ruined it!

"Who?" Michael asked her coolly.

"Thomas," she said. "Don't feel bad, I've rejected a lot of guys," she reassured him.

Michael didn't feel reassured at all. He felt hurt.

"Alright," he said, not looking at her as he pulled away. "Have fun."

"Michael, don't be like that. It's nothing personal," Sophie said, though she sounded like she was enjoying it.

Michael looked up to see she had a slight grin on her face, amused at the scenario.

He looked at her. Any good feeling he had felt at being in her presence had gone.

"It's fine," he lied, then walked off, feeling awful.

Urgh. Girls were so complicated!

He walked over the where the Spartans were. Steve and Teresa were sitting next to each other, whilst Jürgen and Arthur were playing chess. Joe sat by himself, whilst Nadia watched the chess game.

"That is an awful move, Jürgen," she commented critically. "Now Arthur can take your piece."

Arthur did indeed take Jürgen's piece.

Michael went over and sat by himself. He wasn't in the mood for talking.

Nadia noticed this. "Are you okay?" she asked him.

"Not really," Michael admitted. "I ask Sophie to go to the ball with me and she just laughed."

Nadia frowned. "I see. That is unfortunate," she said quietly.

"Yeah," Michael agreed.

"Do you vant to go with me?" Nadia asked him.

Michael looked up. "Sure," he told her. He didn't have anyone else to go with, and he didn't mind Nadia.

He wondered whether to tell Tim that Elizabeth would be dancing with him. He decided to leave it a surprise.

"Checkmate," Arthur said quietly.

Jürgen looked dumbfounded. "Vhat, how!? I can still - argh, no I can't. Vell done, Arthur. You outvitted me."

"Ja, very vell done, Arthur," Steve imitated in a German accent.

Michael smiled slightly. He looked up at his squad, a question springing to mind.

"Guys," he said. "Do you think I should be leader at the Coliseum?"

Jürgen looked surprised, whereas Nadia smiled slightly.

Arthur nodded. "Yeah, you should. If you can handle it, then I think you'll be a good leader. Although, if you are, you'll have to know the strengths and weaknesses of each person going to the Coliseum. Research as much as you can. And be confident. If you lead by example and trust yourself, others will too," he said.

Michael was surprised by Arthur's blitz of advice. He would struggle to remember it all. "Oh ... okay, thanks," he told him.

"Yeah, you'll be fine," Steve reassured him.

"Ja. But, you must not let personal disagreements get in the vay of picking the most effective teams," Jürgen warned.

Michael nodded, feeling a little overwhelmed. "Thanks guys," he said gratefully.

"Michael!" he heard Alexandra's voice call as she ran over to him from the common room entrance.

"Hi..," he said uncertainly as she leant down and hugged him.

Steve wolf whistled and Michael blushed in embarrassment.

"Thank you so much for telling Darius to go with me. I owe you one," Alexandra said as she pulled away, sitting down.

Michael smiled, a warm feeling spreading through his chest. "No, you don't. It's what friends do. We're a team, we look out for each other."

Steve laughed. "You know what, Michael, you're already a good leader. Just keep doing what you already do."

57 - THE CEREMONY

The ceremony was not at all what Michael had expected.

He had imagined a band playing on a warm day, while people cheered and Michael walked up to collect his Gallantry Medal from the General of the Army.

In reality, it was much less exciting. Michael and the other recruits were standing for what felt like hours in the cold, whilst Lieutenant Jones read out a long, boring speech about the merits of bravery and the history of the Gallantry Medal and its significance to The Institute.

By the time they had actually got around to handing out the medals, Michael was frozen stiff. There was a crowd of military personnel and other civilians watching, as apparently there were not many ceremonies at The Institute. Michael felt like that anyone watching would be disappointed.

"Alright, now for the medals. The names will be read out in alphabetical order," Jones said, stifling a yawn. "Paul Adams, Michael Bakerson, Thomas Blackhurst..."

Michael walked up onto the stage. Sergeant Raines was presenting the medals. They were a dull bronze colour, with an inscription on the bottom, reading 'Superbia In Praelia'.

Michael couldn't help but smile as Sergeant Raines had a fiery look of pride in his eyes.

"Well done, laddie," Raines said as he attached the medal. "Ye deserve it."

Michael beamed. "Thank you, sir."

Raines nodded, and Michael walked onwards. He walked off down the stage, to where Paul, the first recruit called, waited. Michael looked up as Thomas joined him.

Thomas nodded. "You deserve this more than all of us, Michael. You saved Oslo," he told him.

"I got people killed," Michael said.

"But saved countless more," Thomas reminded him.

Michael looked up at him. "Thanks, Thomas."

The ceremony continued, as Michael waited for all the recruits to receive their awards. They had submitted their mission reports, and Michael had been as honest as he could, recounting everything, including Prometheus and Ragnarok.

When everyone had received a Gallantry Medal, they lined up again.

"There you go," Jones announced. "Well done, everyone. Now, I will announce the Coliseum squad that Sergeant Raines, Sergeant Vellon and myself have selected, along with input from the other squad leaders."

There was a hum of excitement in the air. Michael hoped he would make it.

"From the Legionnaires, we have Raymon Collins and Henry Blake.

From the Praetorians, no selections.

From the Jaguars, we have Thomas Blackhurst, Elizabeth Walker.

From the Spartans, we have Michael Bakerson, Jürgen Bauer, Nadia Bauer, Arthur Roebuck and Joseph King.

From the Jaegers, we have Sophie Montague.

From the Companions, we have Dominic Butler and Amelia Leigh.

From the Immortals, we have Emily Wilson and Paul Adams.

And from the Varangians, we have Carl O'Hara," Jones finished, folding up a piece a paper. "The rest of you will be going to the Coliseum to watch. We leave in two weeks."

Fifteen recruits. Most of them had been prospects, but not all. Michael hadn't spoken to half of them.

"Oh, I almost forgot," Jones added. "The leader for this team will be Michael Bakerson, of the Spartans."

Michael froze.

What?

He was the leader? Had Sheikh Bakir interfered?

Everyone was looking at him, including Jones and Raines.

Michael composed himself, nodding at Jones respectfully. He had to appear confident.

Jones seemed satisfied, for he looked back at the other instructors. "Anything else?"

Vellon cleared his throat. "On certain mission reports, there has been a mention of a spy in The Institute. Any information you hear relating to this spy will now be handled by myself. Thank you," he stated in his French accent then retreated.

Michael raised his eyebrows. Why was Vellon handling Prometheus and not Wallace?

Vellon's eyes locked with Michael's. *He* had mentioned Prometheus in his mission report. Was Vellon trying to tell him something?

Michael looked down, worried.

"Yeah, yeah, all that stuff," Jones dismissed. "Now, the military ball will commence in one hour. You will find a selection of clothes in your rooms. I don't know how it works over here, but apparently the ball is a part of the ceremony, so please don't break any rules."

Michael noticed Raymon smirk.

"Alright, now go away and have fun," Jones muttered, though he sounded reluctant. "I'll see you all when this is over."

Michael felt a pit of nerves open in his stomach.

The ball was finally here.

* * *

Fifty five minutes later, Michael stepped out of his room, nervous. He was wearing a light grey buttoned shirt with a black tie, with dark trousers. All the boys had been given the same clothes, but they were well made. Tradition clearly meant a lot to the people at The Institute.

When getting ready, Michael had showered for at least half an hour, thinking over what might happen. Would he embarrass himself? What if everyone danced differently to how he did?

"You alright?"

Steve's voice snapped Michael out of his worries. He nodded.

"Yeah, I'm fine," he reassured his friend. "You ready to go?"

Steve nodded. "Yeah. The ball shouldn't be too bad," he said, though his voice lacked enthusiasm.

Michael prayed he was right. The ball was supposedly taking place in a building not too far from the Recruit Centre. There were a few other recruits milling about getting ready, but Michael thought it wouldn't do any harm to arrive early.

He just nodded and began walking down the stairs. He was too nervous to take the lift, and he wasn't really in the mood to talk.

As Michael continued, he saw a huge building with a small dome on the roof. There were bright white lights shining, crisply illuminating the streets.

There were a few people standing near the entrance. Surprisingly, Michael noticed several suits and khaki uniforms there, and he realised that it must not just be recruits that were invited to the ball. It was a big ceremony for the whole Institute.

Michael was glad that he was with Steve as he walked forward. There was a sign above the canopy, reading 'THE PALACE' in luminous lights.

"Evening, gentlemen," a tall officer with a wispy moustache greeted as they approached. "I suppose you are two of the recruits who fought so excellently in Norway?"

"Yes, sir," Michael responded, looking down.

"Bravo, bravo! I'm sure you fully deserved your award!" the man enthused, tipping his head towards them as he took out a small electronic tablet. "Anyhow, I'm afraid I will have to take your names."

Michael and Steve gave their names.

"Michael .... Bakerson," the man muttered as he typed it into his device. "Blasted thing! Back in my day, the pen and paper was the way we had to do it all. Now all these technological gizmos have taken over, it all gets all complicated."

Michael smiled politely.

"Hang on, Bakerson, eh? Aren't you the fellow who shot that blasted Fenrir?" he asked, peering towards Michael.

Michael was about to deny it, as he didn't want any attention, but Steve nudged him.

Michael nodded. "Yes, sir."

The man raised his eyebrows in surprise. "Wow! Well, I must say, you did a spiffing job! The whole Norwegian theatre is very grateful to you. He was quite a foe. Ah, forgive me! I have not introduced myself! My name is Major Cunningham, it is pleasure to meet you," he said, offering Michael a hand to shake.

Michael shook it, surprised. A major was quite a high rank in the army. Why was he just manning the door?

"Not much of a talker, eh? Ah well, enjoy the ball. I remember my first one ... but don't let me keep you here. In you go! Break a leg!" the Major told them, waving them inside.

Michael hurried in, going into a foyer where he saw more recruits there, waiting.

"Break a leg?" Steve asked, frowning.

"It means good luck," Michael clarified. "He seems a nice guy."

"Cunningham? He's trying too hard. Trying to get all pally with us. Majors shouldn't do that with soldiers, no one likes officers anyway," Steve decided.

"You think?" Michael questioned.

"Well, yeah. Who actually likes Jones?" Steve reasoned.

"Good point. Hey, there's Teresa," Michael pointed out to his friend. Teresa was there in a pale dress, chatting to Alexandra.

"Let's go over," Steve said with a grin, running a hand through his hair as he strode over confidently.

Michael followed with a smile.

"Hello girls," Steve said, putting on a deep voice. "You look fabulous."

Michael laughed, and Teresa raised an eyebrow.

"You don't look too shabby either," she commented.

"Hey Alexandra," Michael said with a smile, nodding at her.

Alexandra grinned. "Isn't this exciting?"

Michael laughed. "Yeah it's not bad," he said.

Alexandra smiled at him. "Thanks again for telling Darius to come," she said, then her eyes widened as she stared at something behind Michael.

"Is that ... Jürgen and Nadia?"

Michael looked behind him. Jürgen was striding in, filling out his grey clothes. He had his hair combed back and walked confidently.

Nadia was next to him. She had her hair down long, and wore a simple dark grey dress. She possessed a gracefulness which enhanced her beauty.

In Michael's opinion, she looked amazing. He found himself suddenly very glad she had asked him to take her to the ball. Although she wasn't as alluring as Sophie, she had an elegance and dignity about her that Michael had never noticed before.

The pair stopped in front of Michael, and he realised he was staring.

He smiled, blushing a little. What was he supposed to say now?

"Hi..," he said awkwardly, his mouth dry as he looked at them. He looked at Nadia, who had a slight smile on her face.

"You look ... amazing," he admitted. Nadia turned a slight shade of pink.

"Thank you," she said quietly.

Jürgen cleared his throat. "Hello, Michael. I hope you enjoy this evening. Congratulations on becoming leader. That is a lot of responsibility. I hope you can handle it," he said, offering Michael his hand to shake.

Michael shook it firmly, holding his gaze. "I'm sure I will. I'll be glad to have your support," he told Jürgen, glad their rivalry had been overcome.

However, Jürgen was not pleased, and Michael felt his hand being squeezed very tightly.

"Ja. I hope you can dance. Nadia only deserves the best," he said pointedly.

Was that a threat? Michael could guess he was being protective, but surely it was a little much for a dance.

Michael decided to lighten the mood. He grinned. "I hope I can too," he told Jürgen, pulling his hand away.

"Who are you with?" Michael asked him.

"Amelia," Jürgen replied, turning on his heel and striding off. "I must see her now."

Michael raised his eyebrows. He didn't know who Amelia was, but recognised her name from the ones going to the Coliseum.

"Is Jürgen alright?" Michael asked Nadia, unsure why Jürgen was acting differently.

Steve looked at him, surprised. "Can't you guess?"

"Guess what?"

"He's annoyed because you were picked to lead the Coliseum, even though he was the one who destroyed the artillery," Steve commented.

Michael's eyes widened. He had never thought of it in that way. He had just thought they had all played a part in the team.

"He is also annoyed because ... " Nadia took a breath, looking at the floor. "He is angry at me for recommending you to Sheikh Bakir to become Leonidas."

"Woah, woah, slow down," Steve interrupted, holding his hands up. "Who the hell is Leonidas? What sort of name is that?"

Michael sighed. "It's a long story," he said, then heard a loud voice call, "LET THE BALL BEGIN!"

Steve grinned. "Finally! This place is huge, I can't wait to go in," he enthused.

"Let's head through," Michael said, walking towards a corridor into which several other people were going.

"I'll wait for Darius," Alexandra said, as Steve, Teresa and Nadia followed Michael.

They walked through a set of double doors, into a view that was absolutely breathtaking. There was a large stage at the front, surrounded by bright spotlights with loud music playing. The sound reverberated around, spreading around the huge dance floor. At the back, there were tables, full of food and bars selling drinks and cocktails.

"This is brilliant," Steve muttered, awestruck.

Michael looked around. He had never seen such a huge room before. There was a band on the stage, and there were crowds of people moving towards the dance floor.

Michael didn't even know there were so many people at The Institute. The lead man on the stage cleared his throat, and people quieted down. He had long sandy hair, and had a guitar strapped to him.

"Alright," he announced, his voice radiating around the room through the microphone. "Welcome to another post ceremony ball! We're gonna go with a mix of songs here, you know, but they're all gonna be great. Remember, everyone, just enjoy yourself!" he roared, and the crowd cheered.

"Alright, this first one is a classic, so get your dancing partners ready," the man said, looking back at another band member.

Michael looked at Nadia with a sheepish grin. "Do you want to dance?" he asked nervously.

Nadia smiled slightly. "I'd like that very much," she replied.

Michael took a deep breath and led her to the dance floor. Hopefully, this would go well.

58 -   THE BALL

"Is that ... Tim?" Steve asked.

"Sure is," Michael told him with a grin, looking up to see Tim dancing with Elizabeth. He hadn't spoken to him or Elizabeth at all, so was pleased to see that they had ended up dancing several songs together

Michael had spent most of the evening dancing with Nadia, and had loved it. It had been much more enjoyable than he had expected. He was sitting down, taking a drink of water, talking with Steve and Teresa. The sheer amount of people there still amazed him.

Michael looked across at Nadia. He had seen a different side to her tonight. She was a lot more open than usual, and kept smiling. Michael was surprised, but he liked that she was feeling more comfortable with him. Luckily, they had avoided Jürgen most of the night, so their spirits had not been dampened.

The music had started off lively and fast, but was now slowing down as the evening was drawing to a close.

As one of the songs ended, Elizabeth and Tim wandered over to join them.

"Hi, guys," Tim said with a wide smile, as he sat down.

Michael was surprised to see him so friendly. "Hi," he told Tim. "How's it going?"

"Great," Tim said. "I never expected to be asked by anyone."

Michael shared a conspiratorial grin with Elizabeth.

"Would you like to dance with me, Michael?" Elizabeth asked him with a slight smile.

Michael looked over at Nadia, wanting her permission.

She just shrugged. "I don't mind," she said quietly.

Michael felt a bit bad for leaving her, but thought it wouldn't do much harm. Anyway, he did owe Elizabeth for dancing with Tim.

He stood up and went towards the dance floor, with Elizabeth by his side.

She smirked. "Follow me," she told Michael. She wore a nice purple dress, which showed her slender figure well. She must have been wearing makeup, as Michael could not imagine how anyone's skin could be so smooth.

He wondered why she had wanted to dance with him.

"We'll dance here," she decided, stopping near the centre of the dance floor.

"Why here?" There was nothing remarkable about the area they had stopped.

"You'll see."

"I sure hope so," Michael said with a laugh.

He couldn't deny, he felt a little nervous, but he was much more confident after dancing with Nadia.

"So, how did you get on with Tim?" Michael asked her, as he moved towards her and began slowly dancing with her. She was very graceful, but her dancing seemed a little too forced, as though she was focusing on something else.

He noticed a slight hint of red tinge her cheeks. "Not bad," she said dismissively.

"Not bad? That all?" Michael pressed with a slight smile.

She raised her eyebrows. "Yes," she said firmly.

Michael shrugged. "I won't press it," he said, as the tune became slightly faster.

Elizabeth didn't say anything. "Here they are," she muttered.

"Who?" Michael asked, turning his head to look behind him.

"Don't look behind. Just keep dancing - hold me close," Elizabeth ordered.

Michael did so, but was very confused. They carried on dancing. Elizabeth was making eye contact with someone behind him.

As they slowly turned, Michael was surprised to see who it was.

Sophie and Thomas were dancing with each other, but Thomas seemed to be paying more attention to Elizabeth.

"Explain," Michael said quietly.

"I asked Thomas to dance with me. He refused. He decided to go with that Sophie instead. So, I'm letting him know what he's missing out on," Elizabeth said with a slight grin.

Michael frowned. "You're just trying to make him jealous?"

"Partly. Also to spite Sophie," Elizabeth admitted.

Michael stopped dancing. "So you're using me?"

"No! I like you!" Elizabeth protested.

"You like me? We've barely even met."

"I didn't mean in that way," Elizabeth snapped. "Just, you seem like a decent friend to have. I don't have many."

"You don't? But you're always with people," Michael commented, dubious. Elizabeth was one of the most liked people in The Institute, at least among the boys.

"They're just guys that want to hit on me. You're the first that hasn't," Elizabeth said.

Michael doubted that. "Just because people are being nice to you, doesn't mean they're hitting on you," he said coolly.

"How do you know?"

Michael didn't have a comeback to that. "Alright, fair enough. But honestly, why did you pick me to make them jealous?" he asked her. "You could have picked anyone."

"Because you're now leader of the Coliseum squad, so Thomas will feel threatened. And because I think Sophie might like you."

"That's - wait, what? Sophie might like me? That's not true," Michael protested.

Elizabeth smirked a little.

"And you ... you're just trying to use me," Michael declared, pulling away.

Elizabeth raised an eyebrow, "Excuse me? Aren't you overacting? Now, keep dancing."

Michael narrowed his eyes. "Just stay away from me."

"Can't we just have a dance?" Elizabeth pleaded. "I'm not trying to mislead or anything, I promise."

"No, we can't. Sorry, Elizabeth, but no," Michael said firmly. "I don't want to get involved. If you have any problems with Thomas, then you sort it out with him. Don't bring me into this."

Someone cleared their throat. "Is something wrong?"

It was Thomas.

Michael looked at him. "Nothing's wrong, Thomas. I was just leaving," he retorted, storming off the dance floor. He wished he was still dancing with Nadia, but he couldn't see her or any of his friends around.

He walked over to one of the bars. "I'll have something strong," he told the barman.

"You a recruit?" the barman asked. He had a large walrus moustache and beady eyes.

"Yeah," Michael said, looking up at him. "That a problem?"

"Well, you don't have any cash at the moment, so I'll take it out of your allowance," the barman told him.

"Whatever, just do it," Michael told him.

The barman looked sympathetic. "Rough night?" he asked him. "Girl trouble, I'm guessing?"

"You have no idea," Michael muttered, as the barman put down a whiskey.

"This stuff's pretty fiery, so take small sips," the barman advised, taking Michael's wristwatch and scanning it with a small machine.

"You've not spent any money so far, so you've still got plenty of allowance to use up."

Michael just nodded, taking a large gulp of his drink as the barman moved away to deal with another customer.

Ouch. The whiskey burnt his throat as it went down. Michael's eyes watered, but he managed to keep himself from retching.

"I'll have the same," a voice said from the side of him.

Michael glanced across. It was Steve. He looked annoyed.

Michael betted his problems were worse than whatever Steve had.

"What're you looking at?" Steve said defensively.

"Calm down," Michael replied, frowning. "Don't take it out on me."

"Oh, sorry, of course, you're the almighty leader of the Coliseum squad," Steve mocked, his lip curling up.

"What? No, that's nothing to do with it!"

315

"Of course not. You don't even think about it for others. You just get the Sheikh to ensure you have a place in the squad, but don't even think about getting anyone else in. Not even me, your best friend?"

Michael opened his mouth to reply, but Steve continued, venting out all his thoughts.

"I don't wanna hear it. You might be a big hero for killing Fenrir, but your still one of us. You're acting all high and mighty, now, calling yourself Leonidas, going behind everyone's backs to make secret deals with your sponsor. You're just as bad as Raymon with his dad!" Steve spat, snatching a drink from the barman.

"Go to hell," Michael retorted, glaring at him.

Steve narrowed his eyes. "What's wrong? Can't you take the truth?" he pressed.

"Steve, I'm not in the mood for this," Michael said. "Just go."

Steve kept looking at him. Michael clenched his fist tightly.

Idiot.

"Go," Michael repeated quietly.

"Or what? You'll make me?" Steve sneered.

"Or I'll do something I'll regret," Michael said. His nails dug into his palm.

"OY!" the barman shouted. "You, kid, go! You're not helping with my business!"

Steve started, looking at the barman defiantly. He realised he couldn't win and rolled his eyes, walking away, holding the drink.

Michael took another gulp of the fiery drink. It didn't even taste nice.

He tried to relax, trying to block out what Steve had said.

He was still Michael.

Was he wrong to speak with Sheikh Bakir?

No. Steve was just being selfish. It was for the good of The Institute.

But was it? Had he been fairly selected? Could Michael actually lead a team of all the best recruits? It was one thing leading the Spartans, who were all his friends, but these were the best recruits in The Institute.

He took another drink. He needed to clear his head. There were too many complications at the moment.

Michael stood up and walked away. Stupid ball.

Why were any good things that happened always ruined?

"Michael."

He looked to his right. Darius was standing there, his expression disapproving.

It took Michael a second to realise what was different.

"How can you stand?" he asked him, looking down at his legs.

"An exoskeleton. A necessity in case of combat injuries, Lieutenant Blackburn had one sent to me. Luckily it is able to fit underneath my trousers. I'm currently reprogramming it to replicate my usual gait," he replied sharply. "I certainly hope you are not feeling sorry for yourself."

"Of course I'm not," Michael defended.

"Good. In which case, why are you drinking so much?" Darius asked him.

"I ... why do you care?" he shot back, not having a valid answer.

"Because I expect that any leader of The Institute team should be fully alert at all times. Your task has already started, Michael. You're being watched. Major Cunningham is watching you. You are expected to behave as an exemplary representative of The Institute from now on," Darius told him.

Michael frowned. "What if I'm not cut out for leader?" he questioned. "Has it ever occurred to you, maybe, that I don't want this? That I don't like the spotlight?"

Darius held his gaze. "You feel pressure on you. That is natural. What is not natural, is that you are drowning your sorrows in whiskey," he snapped.

"Not you as well. I've already had Steve rip into me."

"I am merely stating a fact. Your friend Steve acts purely on emotion. It is critical as a leader that you are able to think clearly," Darius replied.

"Why don't you lead then?"

"Steve may be at one end of the spectrum, but I am at the other. Pursuing the logical cause of action may not always be the wisest choice. Therefore, I am at risk of being predictable. You, however, are capable of both inspiring others, and being a sound planner. That is why you were selected to be our leader."

Michael blinked. He had never thought of himself in that way.

"And Thomas?" he wondered. "What about him?"

"In Norway, you took a calculated risk," Darius stated.

"Not sure about that."

"Well, whatever the case, it paid off. If we had stuck to Thomas' plan, the artillery would have devastated Oslo," Darius reasoned. "You are not perfect, you know that. You are not invincible, your friends will make sure you know that. But it is up to you to have the confidence in yourself to be able to lead The Institute."

Michael looked at him. "You're right," he said eventually.

"I know," Darius replied, a slight hint of a smile on his face.

Michael looked at the glass of whiskey in his hand, then handed it over to Darius. "Thank you, Darius. I needed that."

"I know you did. I'm your friend, Michael. I have immense respect for you. I wish you every success in the Coliseum," he said sincerely.

Michael nodded, lowering his head. "I'll try my best."

"I know you will," Darius replied.

59 -   **TEAMBUILDING**

"We leave in three weeks. During that time, ye have to know yer squad. Yer in charge now, so I'll accept any input you might 'ave," Sergeant Raines explained.

He and Michael were walking towards Genghis 7, the room where anyone competing in the Coliseum had been told to go. It was the day after the ball, and Michael had not slept well at all.

"Thank you, sir," he told Sergeant Raines.

Raines nodded, pushing it open. All of the instructors were there, along with fourteen recruits.

"Last but not least, eh?" Lieutenant Jones joked. "Go and join them."

Michael obeyed, making brief eye contact with Arthur before facing Lieutenant Jones.

"Alright, let me give you a bit of information about this Coliseum. It happens every four years. The five countries competing are Occupied Britain, The Netherlands, Australia, Canada and the United States," Jones began, indicating to a screen on the wall which showed the last Coliseum's points table.

Four years ago, the USA had finished top, with Occupied Britain a miserable fourth.

"The Institute usually comes a solid fourth. The USA always win, Canada and Australia usually go for second place, and the Dutch are always last."

"There are three rounds in the Coliseum, each with a maximum score of five points. The first round is physical. Last time, it was an aerial duel. The combatants were each given a choice of weaponry, and they fought on a beam a hundred metres in the air. Naturally, the Americans won. They always choose tasks well suited to their recruits. They knew exactly what to train for. We don't. Whoever hosts the Coliseum sets the task, and the United States has been the safest place to hold the tournament," Jones explained.

"The second challenge is a mental one, for strategy. Last time, it was actually Canada who won the second round, but that was more luck than anything else. It involved a series of obstacles. The teams, had to plan their route and get through, whilst trying to hinder the other teams. The American team made it through the most obstacles,

319

but were ambushed by the Australians. The Canadians just walked it. You can be sure they'll make it more difficult this year," Jones said, taking a look around, then proceeding.

"The final challenge is a surprise, but it usually involves adapting and using technology. Last time, the recruits were attacked by a pack of robotic dogs, and they had to use available technology to beat them. The Americans knew exactly what to do; they set up an electromagnetic field then disarmed the dogs."

Jones looked around. The recruits were all silent, watching the screen in fascination as they listened. "The point is, you've got no chance. If you play by their rules, you'll lose. The Americans have been training their whole lives for this. They'll know exactly what's coming."

Michael looked at him. "What if we don't play by their rules?"

Jones smirked. "I thought someone would ask that. Twelve years ago, the Canadian team hacked into the simulation they had been placed in. Were they adapting to their simulation or just cheating? There was a large debate about whether it should be allowed. Sponsors of the American team complained, so the Canadian team were disqualified. That was the only year that The Institute team managed to finish third."

Michael was shocked. He had always assumed it would be a fair competition.

Jones looked at the other instructors. Raines stepped forward and cleared his throat.

"For the next few weeks, ye will be preparing in several physical and mental tests. You can expect the Coliseum to be very tough, and anyone who does not give their all will be replaced. There are plenty of recruits who would like very much a place here, so ye better prove that yer as good as we think you are."

He let that sink in, looking at Michael.

"Now, ye'll have access to all the training facilities and equipment The Institute have. Practice whatever you need to. Familiarise yourselves with the other members of yer team. We've got tapes of all the other Coliseum games. Let's hope we'll finally have a team we can be proud of," Raines said.

There was silence.

Then the instructors walked out of the room, leaving the fifteen recruits that had been selected together.

Michael looked up, keen to meet his new teammates. He wondered if anyone would say anything.

His eyes widened as he realised that most of them were looking at him.

Of course. He was the leader.

"Alright. You heard what the instructors said. We're going to train hard, and try our best to win," he said quietly.

Someone at the back snorted. "Why the hell are you leader?"

Michael inhaled sharply as he saw Raymon Collins step forward. He looked a lot bigger than Michael remembered.

"I didn't choose to be in charge," Michael defended. "If you have a problem, take it up with the instructors."

"You know what this means, right?" Raymon pressed. "If we mess up, you get the blame."

"Well, let's hope no one messes up then," Michael replied. "So, does everyone know each other?"

There was silence. Was he doing something wrong?

"No," Thomas said eventually. "I don't know everyone here. So, my name is Thomas Blackhurst. I'm leader of the Jaguars, and I like to think I'm pretty good at giving orders."

There was a laugh. Michael was grateful for him to speaking up.

Michael smiled. "I'm Michael Bakerson. I'm leader of the Spartans," he told them with a slight shrug.

"Where do your strengths lie?" a girl asked him. She had light brown hair, with a freckly face and brown eyes.

Michael furrowed his brow. "I'd say, I work hard. I don't give up," he decided.

She raised her eyebrows, then walked forward and offered her hand to him. "Emily Wilson, Immortals. I'm fast, and I'm good at hiding."

Michael shook it. "Nice to meet you. I want to see what everyone's good at," he told the group, letting out a nervous breath as he tried to appear confident. "Let's get to know each other."

He walked to the front, picking up a tablet and bringing up the profiles of everyone.

"Hello. Dominic Butler, here, Companions," a ginger-haired boy told him. Michael recognised him from Norway.

According to his file, he was strong, logical, and intelligent.

"Thanks," Michael told him.

More people came up to introduce themselves.

Amelia Leigh. Small, blond, with a permanent scowl on her face. Skilled at hand-to-hand combat, and a decent shot.

Paul Adams. Also fairly small, he fidgeted as he told Michael he was good at planning, and skilled with explosives.

Henry Blake. Tall, dark, muscular, and looking a bit thuggish. Good at fighting.

Sophie Montague. Blond hair-

"Sophie, why are you here? I already know you," Michael said, looking up from his tablet.

"You don't know what I'm good at, though," Sophie replied with a coy grin. She twirled her hair around her finger.

"I know exactly what you're good at," Michael replied coolly.

"You do?" Sophie questioned, stepping close to him as she raised an eyebrow.

"Yes. I do. You're manipulative. You can use people to get what you want. You're sly, and also ruthless," Michael said, holding her gaze.

Sophie let out a guilty laugh, glancing down. "You're not still bitter after the ball, are you?"

"No. There's nothing wrong with that. I'm sure that your talents will be useful at the Coliseum," Michael replied, smiling slightly.

Sophie bit her lip, looking at him. "For what it's worth, I'm sorry if I hurt your feelings," she said, brushing her hair out of her face.

"I ... I accept your apology," Michael said firmly.

Sophie raised an eyebrow. "Isn't that a bit formal?"

"I'm trying to be a good leader here."

Sophie laughed. "You take it too seriously, Michael."

"I don't think you take it seriously enough," Michael shot back.

He folded his arms. "Please, Sophie, don't ruin our chances of winning by playing mind games with the squad members. Not Thomas, not Elizabeth, not me."

Sophie tilted her head to one side. He could see she was calculating something. Was she surprised by his coolness?

"Okay," she said simply.

Michael blinked. "Okay?"

"Yeah, okay. I'll consider it," Sophie said, before walking off.

Michael sighed.

This would be more difficult than he anticipated.

"Yo, dumbass."

It was Raymon Collins. By his side was Henry Blake.

"Are you talking to me?" Michael returned, putting down his tablet. He instinctively tensed up.

"You think you're a leader now, right? Well, you're not. Whatever the instructors say, I'm in charge. You don't have a clue what to do," Raymon said coldly.

Michael looked at him. He would have to be very careful what he said next.

"I'm sure we can compromise," he remarked casually, trying to stay relaxed.

Raymon stepped closer to him, standing over him. He held Michael's gaze, and Michael could see his jaw clenching.

Michael knew he could get into a fight. Hopefully, it wouldn't resort to that.

"Thomas?" Michael called, looking over.

The brown-haired boy glanced over, then walked towards them. "Something wrong?" he asked them.

Michael gave him a friendly nod. "I know they've made me leader, but I really want your backup. Raymon here's offered to help too, so do you reckon you'd be up for helping?" he queried, desperately praying his gamble paid off.

Thomas looked at Raymon, then back at Michael. His face was neutral, but his eyes were narrowed slightly.

Michael silently pleaded with him. He needed Thomas' support.

"Of course," Thomas replied. "I'm your friend. If our team does not cooperate, how can we hope to win?"

He looked at Raymon.

Raymon grunted, then he and Henry walked away.

Michael grinned in relief. "Thank you, Thomas," he told him honestly. "I'm going to need all the help I can get."

Thomas shrugged. "Listen, Michael, we're a team. All of us. We have to work together. And we're going to do ourselves proud in the Coliseum. No matter what they throw at us. We survived Norway. If we can do that, then the Coliseum should be easy."

Michael, for the first time, felt inspired.

They *had* survived Norway. All the recruits here must have at least something special. Michael didn't know about the American team, but he knew no other team would have their determination.

His big problem would be how to get the team to work together.

60 -   THE TESTING

Strength, endurance and speed," Michael told the squad, pacing up and down. "That's what the first task in the Coliseum is designed to test."

Michael was addressing the recruits going to the Coliseum. It was the day following his introduction. He had spent time researching and watching videos of past Coliseum games. Currently, he had some draft units where he thought people's skills would complement each other.

"So, that's what we'll train for first," he told them.

There wasn't much reaction.

"Great," Raymon said sarcastically. "Thanks, *leader*."

"You're welcome," Michael told them. "The instructors have prepared some intense tests for us, and we'll use that to see who the best in each category are."

Several recruits straightened, and Michael could see them sizing each other up.

Michael knew that they would want to win, and he had decided a competition would be the best way to motivate them to put effort in.

"So, let's go," he said, walking out. Thomas was the first to follow, hurrying after Michael.

"You sure this is a good idea? We don't want anyone getting injured," he commented worriedly.

Michael smiled slightly. "I think getting injured is the least of our worries. We're going to the Coliseum, it'll be a lot tougher there."

Thomas still looked concerned. "But we want to maximise our chances."

"We won't be able to do that if we can't push ourselves in training," Michael reasoned.

Thomas tilted his head to one side. "I suppose so ... will you be competing?"

Michael nodded. As much as he was nervous about going up against the best people in the Institute, he knew he had to be seen as one of them.

* * *

One hour later, Michael was waiting outside nervously for the speed test. The physical tests so far had been the hardest he'd ever done.

The first exercise had been a test of strength. The recruits had had to climb across a steel beam which hung in the air, and get as far as they could, whilst only using their arms. Michael had volunteered to go first, as he felt he had to lead by example.

Michael had always been fairly light, so he was able to lift his body weight easily. Unfortunately, he had struggled with moving himself along the beam. After two minutes of slow progress, however, his arms were aching and he was struggling.

He wanted to do well, but he just didn't have the strength to continue.

"Go on, Michael!" Nadia had shouted, and some others had joined in. They could see how tough the exercise was, and were just willing each other on.

Somehow, he had found reserves of energy. He had carried on, made over halfway on the beam before his lost his grip and fell onto the netting below.

One by one, everyone had a go. Jürgen made it to just before halfway, Thomas got to around the same area as Michael, but Raymon had got further than anyone, almost reaching the end before he dropped.

Michael had cheered everyone on, rooting for his team to bond together.

The next task was simple. Everyone had to simply hold a position, which Sergeant Vellon called 'the plank', for as long as they could. Nobody wanted to be the first to fail, but Arthur collapsed after about a minute.

It was actually Nadia who was able to last the longest, which surprised Michael. He chastised himself for being surprised, but he had expected one of the physically stronger members of the group to win.

The speed challenge had been set by Sergeant Albrecht, the instructor involved with technology. He had placed them in a simulation where they simply had to walk from one point to another. The distance was about two hundred metres, and each recruit had been sent into the sim on their own.

When Michael had entered, he had been surprised. The simulation he had been placed in was that of a ruined city. There was rubble all around, but he could see the end point - a glowing red circle on the ground.

Michael looked around. This didn't seem too hard.

"Welcome, Michael Bakerson. This simulation represents the city of Kronstadt, a place ravaged by Western Alliance biological weapons, before the historic Rome Treaty of 1970 which banned such weapons. Please look to your right, to see the main port."

Michael did so. It was a tall, ominous building. However, he noticed a movement out of the corner of his eye on his left.

"This port was the main base of the Russian Navy, a critical factor in ..."

But Michael zoned out. He scanned around. Something wasn't right. The simulation was a test of speed, why were they giving him this information? It was either relevant to his survival or ...

A distraction.

Michael, instinctively, dived to the ground behind a piece of rubble.

Gunfire erupted from a building, a heavy machine gun tearing into the block Michael hid behind.

He had no weapons, and was pinned by a heavy machine gun. He would have to wait for it to reload.

After ten seconds, the gunfire stopped. Michael sprinted out from behind the block and pelted towards the red circle.

He heard shouting from his left, and was dimly aware of an object being thrown towards him. He dived to the ground, rolling out of the way, as it exploded, sending him flying back, his ears ringing.

He clambered to his feet, and pelted onwards. He now saw why this was a test for speed. The longer the task went on, the harder the task would become.

He looked on. One hundred metres left. The ground ahead had cracks in it, so he changed course, arcing his run around the ruins of a small building.

Fifty metres.

He could hear dogs barking.

Twenty five metres.

There was a glint of metal just before the red circle.

Ten metres.

It was a tripwire. He sprinted towards it and jumped, diving over the wire and rolling into the safety of the circle.

He had made it.

"Congratulations, Michael Bakerson. Your time was one minute and five seconds."

The simulation ended.

* * *

It turned out Michael had got the third fastest time. The top one was set by Joe, who had simply sprinted there from the start, getting there in thirty one seconds. The second was a girl named Emily Wilson, who managed forty eight seconds.

Several recruits had not been able to finish the test, including Raymon.

Michael sat down on the ground, as he let his heart rate slow down. The simulation had been horrifyingly realistic.

He stood up, realising he needed to appear strong for his squad. He looked over at Nadia, who gave him a small smile.

"Alright, I've got the rankings here," Michael announced to everyone, picking up his electronic tablet. It contained the results of each activity and overall scores for each recruit.

They recruits gathered around him.

"Go on, then," Elizabeth told him.

Michael looked at it, then read out the rankings.

"First - Raymon Collins,

Second - Thomas Blackhurst,

Third - Nadia Bauer,

Fourth - Michael Bakerson,

Fifth - Jürgen Bauer,

Sixth - Joseph King,

Seventh - Emily Wilson,

Eighth - Henry Blake,

Ninth - Elizabeth Walker,

Tenth - Sophie Montague,

Eleventh - Dominic Butler,

Twelfth - Amelia Leigh,

Thirteenth - Carl O'Hara,

Fourteenth - Paul Adams,

And fifteenth Arthur Roebuck."

Michael finished and looked up at them. He was pleased with his position, though felt sorry for Arthur.

"The rest of the day, we'll practise using technology. We'll keep training every day until we leave. Try to work on what your weakest at, and hone your strengths," Michael explained.

"Cool," Carl O'Hara said. He had an Irish accent.

Michael nodded, then walked away, as people began talking about the activity. He headed outside, leaving the Recruit Centre and going into the crisp winter air.

Something didn't seem right.

The planning for the Coliseum was alright, but he just wasn't sure how he was doing as a leader. If he was doing exceptionally well or badly, it would be easier to pin on what was wrong, but he just found himself doing average.

His team weren't as driven as he hoped they would be.

Michael walked to Zone Alexander, hoping to improve his focus by firing a few weapons. There wasn't much time until the Coliseum, and he just feared they wouldn't be prepared enough.

He typed in the code to access the equipment store, and picked out the M16 rifle, his favourite weapon. It was an assault rifle, not too specialised, but a good all-rounder. A bit like him, now he thought of it.

He walked towards the shooting range, setting the weapon mode to semi-automatic. He needed control here, not power.

He lined up the far target. Deep breaths.

The slight breeze would have to be accounted for.

A steady arm. He placed the gun against his shoulder, squinting down the iron sights.

He gave the trigger a small squeeze, the gun recoiling against his shoulder as it fired.

Miss.

"Not bad."

Michael looked to his side. Nadia was standing there, eyeing him critically.

"Am I doing something wrong?" Michael queried, raising an eyebrow. How long had she been there?

"Ja. Your posture is all wrong. You're far too stiff," Nadia replied.

Well, she certainly didn't sugar-coat it.

"Alright, thanks," he retorted, lining it up again. He could easily do this.

He aimed, and fired.

Miss.

He rolled his eyes, waiting for a criticism.

Nadia looked at him. "Try again. That wasn't bad, just a little rushed."

Michael nodded, lining up the target again. He took his time, resting it against his shoulder. He relaxed a little, but not too much.

He saw the target, aiming his gun again.

Michael took a breath, then squeezed the trigger a third time.

"You got it."

She sounded impressed.

Michael couldn't help but smile. "I usually can, just I was having trouble focusing today."

"You do take a lot of the veight of leadership on your shoulders," she remarked, as Michael lowered his gun and walked back towards the store room.

It was a fair point. She was probably right, but what choice did he have?

He glanced at Nadia curiously. "Did you follow me here?" he inquired.

"Ja," she replied, her eyes flickering towards him then back down.

"Why?"

Nadia hesitated. "I ... I was going to congratulate you on coming fourth."

Michael smiled slightly. "Thanks, but you did amazing, coming third. And you won the endurance task."

Nadia bit her lip, letting out a breath. "I guess that means people vill be watching out for me now."

"What do you mean?"

Nadia shrugged. "I prefer being under the radar."

Michael smiled. "Same, but I don't really have a choice, do I?"

Nadia looked down. "Was I wrong?" she muttered.

"Wrong doing what?" Michael inquired.

"Leonidas. I mean, you clearly don't vant to be leader, and it's because of me that you had that fight vith Steve," Nadia replied, clenching her jaw and shaking her head.

"Hey, Nadia, it's not your fault," Michael reassured her. "Trust me, I chose this. I could have said no if I wanted to."

Nadia raised an eyebrow. "Are you telling me you felt no pressure to accept?"

Michael considered. "No. I didn't. I think this is the best decision for the Institute."

"You're a poor liar," Nadia said with a despondent laugh.

"I am? I mean - I wasn't lying!" Michael protested.

"Honestly?" Nadia pressed.

"Yes. Honestly," Michael told her, looking her in the eye. They were standing in front of the equipment store.

Nadia smiled a little. "Thank you, Michael," she whispered. "I have faith in you."

Michael felt himself go red. "That's good to know," he said with a nervous laugh. Her eyes were really dark. He opened the door to the equipment storage and returned his gun.

"Michael?"

He looked back. "Yeah?"

"You're a good shot," she told him with a respectful nod.

Michael nodded back, then headed back towards the Recruit Centre.

He couldn't help but smile.

61 - PREPARED

Knock, knock, knock...

Michael rolled over in bed, hoping it would stop. It couldn't be morning yet, could it?

"Michael, open up! This is the day we leave!" a male voice called.

What did he mean, the day they leave?

The day they leave?!

Michael flung his covers off him, lunging for his watch on his bedside locker.

05:00 - 21st December

Damn it! It was the day they left to the USA for the Coliseum! Where on earth had the last few weeks gone? Their training had flown by!

Michael leapt out of bed and stumbled over to the door in his grey pyjamas. He opened it, out of breath.

"Yes?" he asked, stifling a yawn.

It was Dan Fisher.

"Sheikh Bakir wants to see you. Also, I'm now in your squad," he informed Michael.

"What?"

"Yeah, basically, Carl O'Hara got in a fight so the instructors kicked him out and replaced him with me," Dan mumbled. "Is that alright?"

"Yeah, Dan, sure. Listen, when does the Sheikh want to see me?" Michael asked him, not knowing about this meeting. He thought he had another two hours before they had to gather on the ground floor.

Dan glanced at his watch. "In twelve minutes. I thought I'd wake you up early to give you time to shower."

"Who showers in *twelve minutes?*" Michael demanded.

Dan shrugged. "I don't shower at all."

"What?!" Michael's jaw dropped.

Dan gave a throaty laugh. "Ha, just kidding. But seriously, you have ... eleven minutes left," he told Michael.

Michael shook his head in disbelief and closed the door.

* * *

Eleven minutes later, Michael hurried out of his room. He had been so preoccupied with training, he hadn't realised how close it was. He wondered why Sheikh Bakir wanted to see him today of all days, though suspected it was something to do with his role as Leonidas.

Luckily, his role hadn't distracted his training much, although he still hadn't spoken to Steve since the Ball. In fact, he had barely spoken to any of the Spartans, apart from the ones that had made it into the Coliseum team.

"Took your time," Dan remarked as he walked down the stairs. "I take it you don't normally get up at this time?"

"You *do*?" Michael asked, aghast.

Dan shrugged. "Yeah. My dad always said you only need five hours of sleep."

"Are you not, like, always tired?" Michael wondered.

"Well, yeah, but, I've gotten used to it."

Michael laughed, thinking it probably wasn't possible. As they reached the ground floor, Michael grinned upon seeing the large figure of the Sheikh, standing with his two burly bodyguards. Also there was a woman, her face so full of makeup that it was hard to tell what natural ethnicity she was. To Michael, she looked kind of an orange colour.

"Good morning, Sheikh," Michael announced as he walked into the room.

The Sheikh slowly looked up. "Good morning ... Leonidas!" he announced slowly. "Hello ... Dan!"

Michael nodded. "You wanted to see me?"

The Sheikh nodded slowly. "Yes ... I did. I shall be journeying to the Coliseum with you as your sponsor. And, ah yes, I would like you to meet my associate, Miss Edna Sanders."

The orange woman stepped forward. "Leonidas, it is an absolute pleasure to finally meet you in person," she squeaked.

"What do you mean, in person?" Michael inquired.

"Edna has been in charge of drumming up support for you in the United States. You've been the figure point of our propaganda," the Sheikh said, clapping his hands together as he began waddling towards the door. "I'm sure you and Edna have much to discuss."

Michael felt uncomfortable. *He* was the figurehead of the campaign. Surely the Sheikh was exaggerating? His role as Leonidas could not be that big, right? He was only leading the squad?

"You look quite different in person," Edna remarked, a frown on her face which made it seem like a criticism.

"Erm, sorry?" Michael replied uncertainly.

"Am I still needed here?" Dan spoke suddenly.

"You? Ah, no," Edna dismissed, waving him away. She placed a hand on Michael's shoulder, leading him towards a room.

Michael panicked, shooting a pleading glance at Dan as this strange woman dragged him in.

The room was fairly large, with several benches and cameras. There was a green wall at the back. In front of Michael were three people.

On his left was a young-looking girl who couldn't have been older than eighteen. She had green eyes and blond hair with streaks of brown in. She gave Michael a nervous smile.

In the middle was a young man with clear, fair skin and pearly white teeth. He had short blond hair , combed back into a quiff. He gave Michael a wide grin.

To his right stood a tall, stocky, black man. He gave Michael a single cold nod.

Edna indicated to them. "This is your team. I'd like you to meet Mabel, Carter and Winston. Us four will be in charge of how the people in the USA see you!"

Michael held his hand up. "Woah, woah, what? What does that involve?"

Carter, the man in the middle, laughed. "Oh, silly, we're gonna get you prepped for your big trip today!"

Michael's eyes widened in fear. "What are you going to do to me?" he asked worriedly.

"Well, get you all dressed up," Carter said. "Haven't you been told anything? Honestly, we do this to the American teams all the time, they don't complain."

"Dressed up? I think I'll wear what everyone else is wearing," Michael retorted, his face burning red.

Edna frowned. "Nonsense. You're Leonidas, and so you must fit to your role. Now, we've got a few designs for a 'Spartan', so let us know which you'd prefer," she said, handing him a screen that showed a group of warriors armed with spear and helmets.

Michael breathed in sharply. "Why aren't they wearing shirts?" he demanded.

"Well, that's what Spartans wore, don't you know?" Carter asked.

Michael sighed. "Listen, I know the Sheikh has paid you for this, but I really don't want to go there any different to the rest of my squad," he told them. "I'm going to fight, not win a fashion contest!"

"You what?" Winston asked. "You don't want us? You haven't even heard what we're gonna say."

"I'm not saying that...." Michael protested.

"Good," Edna snapped. "Now, you'll be like a celebrity when you get there, so you're going to need to look the part."

"What do I need to change?" Michael asked her.

"Well, that haircut for one. When was the last time you cut your hair?" Edna asked, looking disgusted.

"A few months ago?"

"Ergh, we have to work on that. Now, if you don't want a costume, that's fine, but I'm sure we'll be able to make you look ... well, better," Edna said critically.

Michael looked at the four of them and sighed. "Fine ... just don't make me look a fool," he said quietly.

"Darling, we wouldn't dream of it," Carter said with a high pitched laugh.

Michael didn't feel reassured at all. He just prayed it would be over quickly.

* * *

"What have you done?!" Michael demanded, looking in the full length mirror. It was about an hour after. His hair was a lot shorter than it had been. He had been dressed in pale gold-coloured shirt, with a camouflage pattern and thin armour plating inside. In the centre, there was a red 'V' logo, the symbol of the Ancient Spartans. However, it didn't really feel like armour. Over the top, he wore a khaki jacket and khaki trousers. It was like a mash-up of ancient armour and the former British Army uniform. "And I thought I wasn't getting a special uniform?"

"It's not really a special uniform, it's protection," Winston replied coolly. "The Sheikh wants you to be safe. Although it looks like ancient armour, it's actually very light and very durable. It could potentially save your life."

"Why would someone want to kill me?" Michael queried, his eyes widening in alarm. He thought he would be safe in the USA. Had he massively misinterpreted the Coliseum? "We're all on the same side, it's not a war, right?"

"Darling, don't worry-" Carter reassured, but Winston interrupted.

"Because you're a threat. Everyone loves an underdog, except the favourites. The Americans always win. If they have a slight hint that they might not, you're in danger. There was a case of suspected food poisoning for a particularly strong Australian team one year. We don't want you to fall victim to a more direct attack," Winston said.

"I don't like this attack on my country, Winston," Carter said, looking disappointed. "America is the land of the free. But anyway Michael, you look dashing. The khaki is what everyone will be wearing. You can keep your jacket zipped up if you like, but we suggest for your first encounter with the public that you leave it open."

Michael was surprised. It didn't look that bad, and was quite comfortable. "Do I get a helmet too?" he asked jokingly.

"We're saving that for the actual event," Edna replied.

Michael laughed, then realised she wasn't joking.

"Oh, er, thanks," he told them all.

Edna nodded. "We'll see you in the States. In the meantime, don't let yourself go too much."

Michael nodded at Carter, who waved, Winston, who nodded back, and Mabel, who blushed and smiled a little.

"I'll try my best," he said, before walking out of the room.

In the lobby, there were a few other people from his squad, all wearing khaki jackets and trousers.

Jürgen, Sophie, Emily and Thomas.

"Oooh, check you out," Sophie commented with a smirk. "Had a haircut?"

"What gave it away?" Michael asked innocently.

Sophie laughed. "Don't worry, it suits you. Ready for your big day?"

"Well, the first of many," Michael remarked. "Not really."

Jürgen looked sympathetic. "Just don't panic. A cool head is very important," he advised.

Michael nodded. "I'll try. Is everyone doing okay? Someone mentioned Carl is gone?"

"Oh, yeah, he got in a fight with some macho guy from the Legionnaires." Sophie laughed. "Both of them were punished, but Carl's was worse because he started it."

Michael sighed. "Well, that's a great start," he commented.

One by one, recruits from the Institute team came down into the reception.

Elizabeth smiled at him, but Michael just nodded back. He was still a bit annoyed after the ball, but had more important things on his mind.

Joe was last to arrive, looking sullen as ever. Michael nodded at him, but Joe ignored him.

"Glad you're joining us," Dominic said with a chuckle.

Joe didn't reply.

"Is that everyone?" Thomas asked, looking around. Sure enough, there were fifteen people.

"Not everyone," a voice said as the lift opened. It was Darius Finch, in his exoskeleton.

"You're coming?" Raymon scoffed, looking at the boy's legs.

"Not competing, though," Darius reassured them. "Lieutenant Blackburn has requested my presence."

"What for?" Thomas asked suspiciously.

Darius shared a glance with Michael. "None of your concern," he replied, as Lieutenant Jones walked into the room.

The recruits all stood up straight.

Jones looked around, counting to see if everyone was there. "Alright, guys, just don't mess this up. People are expecting a lot this year, especially your sponsors."

Michael felt a few people's eyes on him. He didn't react, just nodded at Jones.

Jones sighed. "Listen, you probably think that I only want you to do well for my career. Which is partly true, but ... I want you to do well for yourselves. Some of you are nearly as good as I was. If you guys make an impression at the Institute, you can actually get a decent life from the military, and not get killed in some ditch in Germany, right Jürgen?"

Michael frowned. Jones must be exaggerating, right?

Even so, it didn't help Michael's nerves. He felt there was more pressure on him now. If the team didn't do well, would it be his fault if they all ended up dead in Germany? Why did Jones mention Germany, anyway?

He glanced at Jürgen. There was pain in the boy's eyes. Had something happened in Germany?

Jones clapped his hands together. "Yeah, well. You've gotta make an impression."

He waited for a few seconds, as though expecting a reaction, before shrugging and turning to leave. "We've got a jet for you all. I'll accompany you there, and the rest of the recruits will follow on to spectate."

Michael took a breath as he followed Jones out, walking through the chilly air towards a plane. This was it. They were going to the United States, the leading country of the Western Alliance. Michael had never even imagined getting a chance to go there, let alone to represent the Institute.

Michael was leader of his team. He would compete with only four other teams from around the world. That was an honour for him, and an opportunity to secure a better future as well as earn funding for the Institute next year with the prize money.

He just wasn't sure if he was ready.

62 -   **LAND OF THE FREE**

"We're here!" Michael announced, craning his neck to look out of the window of the plane.

Outside, he could see the Western coastline of the USA. It was huge, and stretched for miles. Michael smiled like a child. This was exciting.

"Yeah, *the land of the free*," Joe muttered from the aisle opposite them.

Michael looked at him. "What's your problem?"

"Them. The Americans. I want to beat them," Joe declared.

"Well ... we all do. But, we need to gain support and funding for the Institute," Michael reminded him.

Joe shrugged. "That's your job, right? I'm just here to ruin the Americans. Serves them right for what they did to my family."

"Exile, right?" Michael questioned, remembering Arthur telling him about Joe's grandfather's persecution because of his skin colour.

Joe nodded. "These games are rigged so they'll win. I'm gonna hit them where they won't expect."

"And where iz that, Joseph?" Sergeant Vellon's French accent interrupted.

Michael glanced up at him. Sergeant Vellon was standing over the boy in the aisle of the plane. Michael hadn't even been aware he was on this flight.

Joe glared at the instructor. "Why do you care?"

Sergeant Vellon stood up straight. "Excuse me?" he hissed.

Joe didn't say anything, just looked him in the eye.

Sergeant Vellon held his gaze, then smirked a little. "Alright Joseph, have your fun," he said as he walked off.

Michael raised his eyebrows at Joe. "What was that?" he asked him.

Joe shrugged. "I don't like bullies," he said simply.

"I mean, why didn't he punish you?" Michael asked him.

"Because I'm black?" Joe questioned.

"No, because he punishes everyone for like, the slightest thing," Michael replied, wondering why Joe was so defensive. "Why not you?"

341

Joe shrugged again. "Don't care."

Michael sighed. "Fine," he said, looking back out of the window as the plane touched down. He could see a crowd gathering around the plane. What was this place?

"Michael? The Sheikh wants to speak to you."

It was Dan. Again. Michael got to his feet, stretching and walked over to the first class cabin. Sure enough, Sheikh Bakir was there, lying back on a comfortable chair as two flight attendants waited upon him.

When he saw Michael, the Sheikh waved them away. They hurried out and closed the door.

Michael stood there awkwardly.

The Sheikh looked at him. "You know why you're here?" he asked, his voice surprisingly sharp.

"No, sir," Michael replied.

The Sheikh sat up. "Then, let me make it clear. I've put a lot of effort into you. I heard that, maybe you weren't quite so keen to promote your image. Think again. You *will* give this your all. I expect you to make an impression in the Coliseum. You'll need to become the role of Leonidas and challenge for victory."

Michael stared at him, shocked. There was no way the Institute could *win*, right? Their best position had been fourth, and any improvement on that would be a success.

The Sheikh looked at him seriously, a hard edge to his round face. "Otherwise, those food supplies your father is making such great use of might just be cut off."

Michael swallowed. "Sheikh Bakir, I promise, I'll try my best," he pleaded.

"You are still in my debt, Michael. There's more at stake than just you. My reputation among the sponsors is a bit of a joke. You're going to restore it. I want you to beat the American team. Otherwise, your career might just take a turn for the worse," the Sheikh warned.

Michael nodded. "I will, sir," he told the Sheikh, trying to hide his fear. Why was the Sheikh doing this? Did he doubt Michael's conviction?

The Sheikh beamed at him. "Wonderful! Now go outside and make the crowds love you! Lead your team well."

Michael nodded, and left the first class cabin, feeling a bit shaken. He took a deep breath, calming himself. How could the Sheikh expect so much?

He walked towards where the recruits were sitting on the plane. He stood in the aisle in front of them all. They were all talking.

"Guys?" Michael asked, but people didn't hear him. Nadia looked at him, and gave him a reassuring smile.

"Everyone! We're landing!" he announced. They turned their attention towards him.

Michael looked at them all individually. Thomas. Elizabeth. Jürgen. Emily. Raymon. Amelia. Joe. Nadia. Henry. Sophie. Arthur. Dominic. Dan. Paul.

A few weeks ago, he had never spoken to some to these people. But they had all fought in Norway. They were all strong and capable recruits. He had to be a successful leader.

"There will be people out there, expecting us. We've been talked up. They're expecting soldiers who've fought in Norway and beaten Fenrir. That's what we are. Forget being afraid. None of the other teams have fought in Norway. To them, we're heroes. So let's embrace that. Let's go out there and win over the crowd. Win over sponsors. Get everyone on our side. We've got the best chance the Institute's had in years. Let's make the most of it," Michael urged, feeling emotion well up in his chest. Was it pride or fear? He didn't know.

Michael gave a small smile then nodded, holding his khaki jacket in his hand, wearing his uniform, as he walked back down the aisle towards the plane exit.

This was it.

"Hey, Michael."

It was a quiet voice from behind him. He glanced back to see Thomas with him.

343

"We're with you," Thomas said. Michael nodded, glad to have support, and stepped outside.

The first thing that sprung to mind was how cold America was. It was mid-December, and the ground was a thick blanket of snow. This cold hit Michael quickly, making him want to put his jacket back on.

There was crowd of people around the plane, with security guards forming a passage towards a large compound.

The crowd was loud, many of them screaming. They, however, seemed wrapped up better than he was.

He smiled and began walking down the steps, wondering how much had been said about them.

"Someone's pleased to see us," Thomas remarked with a laugh.

Michael agreed. The crowd did seem very keen. This must be a big event in the USA.

Now, he needed to be professional, and win them over. He put on a smile, and waved to them as he walked down the stairs.

They cheered loudly, and as Michael got closer, he could hear what some of them were saying.

"It's Leonidas!"

"He's here!"

"We love you, Leonidas!"

"Sign my t-shirt!"

Michael glanced towards the speaker of that last shout. She was a girl, around his age. He gave her a smile and a nod, as he walked forward, trying to ignore the cold as he made eye contact with as many people as he could. His father had always said eye contact was important.

He carried on walking and smiling, as he saw flashes of cameras.

The compound was not so far away, about one hundred metres. Hopefully it wouldn't take too long before he could get to the warmth.

There were three figures waiting near the compound, with various security guards outside. It was quite large, with many different buildings.

Michael approached them, recognising the man on the right.

It was Captain Blackburn, his eyes scanning for someone.

The man in the centre gave a wide smile, offering a hand for him to shake. He was tall with tanned skin and blond hair.

"Leonidas, how do you do? I'm Lieutenant James Nicholls, and I'll be attached to your Institute's team while you stay here. You have any questions, you ask me," the Lieutenant told him as Michael shook his hand.

"Nice to meet you," Michael told the Lieutenant as the man moved down the line of recruits. Michael noticed the third man looked on edge.

Captain Blackburn looked at Michael. "Is Master Finch here?" he asked Michael.

Michael nodded. "He's at the back."

Blackburn nodded. "You did well in Norway," he stated, then began striding down the column towards Darius, who was last off the plane.

Michael faced the third man. "Shall I go in?" he asked, anxious to get warm.

The man opened his mouth to answer but was interrupted by screams breaking out from the crowd.

Michael whipped around.

There was a white van hurtling towards the recruits at high speeds. Security reacted quickly, opening fire on the van. One guard launched a concussive grenade at it, and it detonated underneath the van, toppling it and sending it hurtling towards Darius, who dived out of the way.

Michael ran forward, hoping to pull away whoever was in the way of the vehicle.

Captain Blackburn stepped smartly out to the side, as the van grounded to a halt in front of him. He leaned closer to look for a driver.

"There's no one in," Blackburn announced.

Michael ran towards him, thinking.

Why would someone send a driverless van towards a crowd? It would be hard to hit a specific target, if that was the intention.

Why a van? Vans were mainly used for storage.

Michael's eyes widened as he realised what might happen.

What if it wasn't just a van?

"GET AWAY FROM IT!" he yelled, grabbing Blackburn and pulling him away.

It was too late.

The van exploded.

Michael was caught in the blast, the force throwing him forward. He could feel the heat searing his back.

The blast threw him against the ground, sending daggers of pain up his right arm. He rolled onto his back, his ears ringing as people swarmed around him.

He gritted his teeth, dimly aware of Captain Blackburn being dragged away. Michael was placed on a stretcher.

"Keep calm, you'll be okay," a young medical orderly told him.

Michael felt faint, as his head lolled back and he closed his eyes.

63 -   QUESTION TIME

"Your heroics out there caused quite a stir."

Michael opened his eyes. Darius was standing in front of him, an eyebrow raised.

He was lying in a bed, in an unfamiliar room.

He flexed his arm. He felt alright, though he was a bit sore.

"Oh, don't worry, there's not much damage. Your uniform is incredibly resilient - it protected you from the blast and the impact on the ground," Darius explained.

Michael blinked. He knew it was special, but hadn't realised the extent of its protection.

He would have to thank the Sheikh's team.

"Was anyone hurt?" Michael enquired.

"Captain Blackburn was injured, but remains largely as he was," Darius clarified.

"Do we know who carried out the attack?" Michael asked.

Darius frowned. "No. But, there are a few suspects. I think you should know who they are," he decided.

"How do you know?"

"I ... ahem, *accessed* a digital folder containing various suspects and their political inclinations. I needed to know who the attack was targeting," Darius explained, referring to a tablet Michael hadn't noticed he was holding.

"The first suspect is anti-war protest groups. Most of them are peaceful, but there are a few radical ones, such as the self-proclaimed Social Revolutionaries. These frequently try to destabilise the Western Alliance military, and speak out against war games like the Coliseum. The attack could be to gain publicity, however they have not claimed it was their doing," Darius said.

Michael nodded. "So, they could have been targeting me to disrupt the Coliseum games?"

"It's unlikely, as the vehicle was driven into a crowd. The attack was more likely used to send a message to the military. If it weren't for you, Captain Blackburn would have been killed," Darius said.

"Who are the other suspects?"

"Well, there are two more. One is a lone Russian sympathiser with little strategy, seeking simply to kill military members. It's possible, especially given the current situation."

"The situation?" Michael queried.

"Ah, yes. I was also able to uncover that Washington isn't at its most stable. There have been a huge amount of anti-war protests and riots, with the military even being sent in to subdue them. Years of war have taken its toll on the American population, and a lot of people are calling for peace," Darius explained.

"All this is in a file?" Michael was perturbed by this news. The US had always seemed like a safe haven, with the war mainly being fought elsewhere.

"It's hard to keep this sort of thing quiet," Darius commented. "Now, the final suspect is just a rumour to the public, but is a very real threat to the military. A terrorist, nicknamed 'Techno', has been linked to several acts of violence against the military. This attack could have been orchestrated by him, but again, it's hard to see how the attack could have targeted anyone specifically."

Michael nodded. "I guess the US is more fractured than we thought."

Darius nodded. "I'm sure the Eastern Bloc is the same. No country is fully behind its leaders. In a democracy, there is always bound to be conflict. The United States has been a superpower for many years, but not without challenge."

"It's survived so far, at least."

Darius smiled slightly. "Oh, and you have an interview in twenty minutes. I think the Sheikh's people are coming to fix you up."

Michael sighed, but then remembered that it was their uniform that had protected him. He had to thank them.

"Cheers, Darius. By the way, what happened with that Trojan robot-thing that saved you? Did anything become of it?" he inquired.

"I assume you are asking of my role in its design?" Darius remarked. "I shall be working with Captain Blackburn beginning tomorrow. That unfortunately means we might not have as much contact in the future. I do, however, wish you all the best."

Michael smiled. "Thanks, Darius."

Darius turned and strode away. "Goodbye, my friend."

"See you," Michael replied, still getting used to Darius' formality.

The boy left, leaving Michael alone. He flexed his arms. He felt stiff, but was mostly alright.

He stood up, thinking.

This attack had been a huge shock. He had never realised how dangerous it might be.

"Leon-*idas*?"

Carter's high pitched sounded as the door opened. "Let's hope our war hero's not too cut up!"

"I'm fine," Michael reassured as Edna, Winston, Mabel and Carter all came in.

"I saw the video, Michael," Carter gushed. "You were *soo* good! Anyway, you have an interview now so you'll need to look your best!"

"An interview? What for?" Michael questioned.

"It's tradition. You have one before all the preparation starts. You know, just to get a sense of who the fans prefer."

Michael swallowed slightly. He remembered the Sheikh's threat. He couldn't mess this up, not if the Institute were to do well and his village was to keep their supplies.

"Oh ... of course, sure," Michael said, attempting to remain calm.

Carter beamed. "That's the spirit! Now, we won't do much, just make sure you look like your role."

"Alright .... let's get this over with," Michael said.

* * *

Eighteen minutes later, Michael was walking into a news broadcast studio.

He was feeling nervous. A man came towards him, with combed greasy black hair. He looked in his early forties.

"Leonidas?" the man asked.

"Yes?" Michael replied.

"My name's Charles Duggan. I'm the head reporter here. Nice to meet you," he introduced, offering a hand.

Michael assumed this guy would be interviewing him.

He shook his hand. "Nice to meet you," he told the man.

"Yeah, so, when you're in there, just be yourself, answer the questions honestly. There's no wrong answer," Charles reassured.

"Alright. Anything in particular I should avoid mentioning?" Michael asked him.

"Well, I'd steer clear on any speculation. If they ask you why that van with the bomb was sent, say you don't know. This, of course, is true." Charles raised an eyebrow.

"Of course it is," Michael replied carefully, knowing Darius wasn't supposed to be allowed to access those files.

Charles nodded. "Excellent. Head inside, and don't forget to smile for the camera. Sam will be interviewing you," he told Michael.

Michael was surprised, but nodded.

"Three seconds ... go in," Charles told Michael, motioning for Michael to enter through a glass door as he looked at a fancy watch.

Michael pushed it open and walked inside.

"Let's welcome ... Leonidas!" a blond woman was saying. She sat on a comfy red chair, with a large couch opposite her. They were in a studio with camera crews around.

The crowd applauded as Michael walked forward, a smile on him face. He hadn't expected Sam to be a woman.

"Sit down, Leonidas," she told him. Her hair was tidied back into a ponytail, and she was wearing a large amount of makeup.

Michael did so. "Nice to meet you," he said, slightly unsure.

She beamed. "Welcome to the Show!" she announced. "I'm Samantha. Now, obviously you're new here. For anyone that doesn't know, Leonidas is the leader of the Institute squad that's arrived here for this year's Coliseum. As you know, the

Institute has consistently finished fourth. Do you think you can do any better this year?"

Michael smiled. "I hope so. We've got a good team, and I think we've got as good a shot as anyone else," he replied.

Samantha laughed. "Do you think you could win?" she asked jokingly.

"Is there any reason why we couldn't?" Michael returned.

Samantha chuckled, and the crowd laughed as well.

"Well, you have a sense of humour, that's for sure," she remarked. "But, quite frankly, there's been quite an advertising campaign for you over here. A fair amount of support has been drummed up. How do you feel about that?"

"I'm very grateful for anyone who supports us, and the generous Sheikh Bakir who has been kind enough to endorse the promotions," Michael replied.

Samantha raised an eyebrow. "This level of hype for an Institute team has never happened before. What's changed this year? Apart from the extra funding and elite squad that's being introduced."

"I'm sorry, what elite squad?" Michael queried.

"You don't know? Well, this year the winning team from the Coliseum is being drafted into an elite team for the Western Alliance. Obviously, it's unlikely the Institute will make it, but it's an added incentive for the American team."

"Well, again, I think we have a very strong team. We have experienced real combat," Michael said, thinking it would be good to send a message of confidence.

"Oh yes, your time in Norway. Is it true that you killed Fenrir?" Samantha asked Michael.

He nodded, remembering the sadness of that day. The loss.

"Yes," he replied quietly, looking down.

"Did you lose friends?"

Jenny. Hans.

"Yes," Michael said.

"That must be hard," Samantha commented with sympathy.

Michael looked up determinedly. "It was. But it's made us stronger. All of us. We were able to survive the worst Fenrir could throw at us."

Samantha smiled. "Is your family proud of you? For being a killer?"

Michael raised an eyebrow, surprised at the question. "I haven't discussed it with them."

"Do you think they would be? Do you think that representing the Institute at these games is something they would want?" Samantha challenged.

"Yes," Michael told her without hesitating. Was she trying to unnerve him?

She seemed surprised. "Alright, thank you for this, Leonidas. What made you choose that name?"

"Leonidas? Well, my squad at the Institute was called the Spartans, and I was their leader, so I thought it would be good choice as, obviously, Leonidas was the historical leader of the Spartans," Michael replied.

"And, finally, what do you think was behind the attack on you this morning?"

"The attack on *me*? I don't think I was the target," Michael commented. "But, then again, I've just got here, I have no idea who was behind it."

Samantha smiled, though it didn't seem quite genuine. "Well, it was nice having you here, Leonidas. Good luck in the Coliseum."

She laughed, then shouted, "Give it up for Leonidas!"

The crowd applauded, as Michael stood up, smiled at the camera then strode back out though the door.

"Well, that was entertaining," he heard Samantha say as he left the room.

Edna was there, a look of pity on her face.

Carter looked sympathetic. "Don't worry about it," he told Michael.

"Worry about what?" Michael demanded.

Carter opened his mouth to speak, then closed it and shook his head. "I'll take you to your residence."

"Where is that?"

"The Washington Military Base. You'll love it," Carter told him, clapping him on the back.

Michael sighed. "I hope so. America hasn't been great so far."

64 -   PREPARATION

"Welcome ... to The Facility."

It was the day after his interview. Michael and his squad were being escorted by Lieutenant James Nicholls. He was leading them into a huge white room containing training equipment.

There were arrays of weapons, both ranged and melee. There were strange pieces of technology Michael had never seen before, like a robotic hand and electronic panels.

Within the room, there were several Western Alliance soldiers patrolling.

"And, here you'll find the other teams," Nicholls added.

Michael immediately scanned around. There were several red-shirted people training. A few of them stopped to look at the Institute members.

Michael locked eyes with a tall, bulky recruit that had a short beard and long blond hair. He smirked at Michael then strode away to some of his teammates.

"In red is the American team, in orange, the Dutch, in green, the Australians and in blue, the Canadians. You guys are of course in grey," Nicholls explained.

Michael would have preferred blue, but he didn't mind.

"So, train, get used to the equipment, ready for the tournament. You guys are being monitored by sponsors, so I wouldn't mess about," Nicholls warned.

"Thank you, Lieutenant," Michael told him.

"Also, don't fight anyone else. There are soldiers on hand who will taser you if you try anything. You can interact with the other groups, but no fighting. If you want to spar with someone, ask the soldiers on hand," Nicholls explained. "Any questions?"

Michael glanced around.

"Ja, I have one. In the Coliseum, are we allowed to make alliances?" Jürgen asked him.

Michael raised an eyebrow at Jürgen.

Nicholls laughed. "Not officially," he told Jürgen with a wink. "Anyone else?"

There wasn't. Nicholls nodded, then walked away.

Michael faced his squad.

"Train whatever you feel you need to improve on. Don't show off. We don't want the other teams knowing our strengths," he advised.

"I suggest we make friends with the other teams," Thomas stated.

"Which?" Michael wondered.

"The Dutch," Dan suggested. Michael laughed, knowing the Dutch were consistently the worst team.

"Dan's right," Jürgen spoke up. "Vhy not the Dutch?"

"They're always the worst team," Elizabeth remarked.

"But ve are always the second worst team. If we can do vell, so can other teams," Jürgen stated. "And, I think the fact that I am German might help us get along vith them better."

"Yeah, because Germany and the Netherlands have always had a *great* relationship," Joe muttered.

Michael listened. Jürgen had a point. How could they judge other teams when they were fed up of being judged themselves?

"Alright, Jürgen, you come with me," Michael told him. "Let's go say hello."

"Do you vant me to come too?" Nadia offered. Did she not trust Michael and Jürgen together?

"Sure," Michael said with a shrug, scanning around. There were some orange-shirted people at the far end of the training room.

Michael started walking, expecting Jürgen and Nadia to follow him. He realised he wasn't too sure what he was going to say.

He glanced back at his squad, who were now dispersing towards the various training stations. Arthur was heading straight for electronic panels, whereas Raymon was striding confidently towards an array of melee weapons.

Michael found who he was looking for. "Sophie?" he called.

She smirked then sauntered over to him. "Yes?" she replied coyly.

"You're good at making friends, right? We need to make the Dutch team like us, so hopefully we can team up in the games. I'm hoping you can help, er, persuade them to agree," Michael said, feeling a bit awkward, but realising as a leader he had to use his team's skills.

Although he felt that he was friendly enough, he knew Sophie was good with people. Especially males.

"So ... you need my help?" Sophie asked slowly.

"Yes," Michael said, with a sigh.

"Well of course I'll help," Sophie said, flashing him a smile. "Anything for you," she teased.

Michael rolled his eyes. "You head over, I'll join you soon," he told Sophie, noticing Jürgen and Nadia were deep in conversation.

He walked over, hoping to listen. However, they were speaking in German.

"You guys okay?" he asked.

"*I'm* fine," Nadia replied, looking pointedly at Jürgen.

"Ja, ve are ready," Jürgen told Michael.

"Good. I've sent Sophie over," he told them. "Is everything alright between you?" Michael didn't want any disagreements between them affecting their chances in the Coliseum.

"Yes," Nadia snapped. "Now, are ve going or not?"

Michael raised his eyebrows in surprise, then turned on his heel and strode towards the Dutch group. He would have to speak to Nadia about her attitude.

Sophie was already there, chatting with a blond-haired boy. The boy was a similar height to Michael, and had a lot of freckles on his face.

"This is Michael, our leader," Sophie told the boy.

"Greetings, Michael. I am Arjen. I lead this team. It is a pleasure to make your acquaintance," the boy said, offering Michael a hand.

Michael shook it. "It's good to meet you. I was hoping our teams could be friends," he told Arjen.

"Friends? That's a surprise. No one wants to be allies with the Dutch team, let alone friends," Arjen remarked with a dry laugh.

Michael smiled. "Well, we should probably change that," he commented. "We've got a better chance together."

Arjen raised his eyebrows. "How can I be certain you do not have ... ulterior motives?" he remarked.

"What motives could we have? We're both underdogs," Michael reminded him with a smile.

Arjen nodded. "Very well. But first, you must pass one test," he said with a grin.

"What's that?" Michael asked.

"Spar with me. If you beat me, we get an alliance," Arjen said, his eyes lighting up.

"We're not allowed to fight," Michael pointed out.

"They will if we're supervised," Arjen stated confidently. "So, will you accept?"

Michael thought about it. If he backed down, he might look weak. If he fought and won, he would earn respect and an ally. However, if he fought and lost, he might lose his reputation.

"I accept," Michael decided.

* * *

Ten minutes later, Michael and Arjen were facing each other, surrounded by a ring of American soldiers. A lanky officer explained the rules.

"Anything foul, and you're tasered. Anything that could permanently hurt the opponent, and you're tasered. Any use of weapons, and-"

"They're tasered, we get it," Sophie interrupted. "Can we just get on with the fight?"

Michael steeled his nerves. He watched Arjen calmly.

Jürgen stepped in front of Michael. "Don't let yourself get too close. That boy is stronger than he looks," he warned.

Michael nodded. "Alright," he said, stretching his arms.

The officer huffed. "The spar will be until submission, or first blood. I'm not having any of you badly hurting yourselves. Are you ready?"

Arjen and Michael nodded. The officer blew a whistle, and they began circling around each other.

It reminded Michael of his first fight at the Institute against Brooke, Raymon's friend.

Michael remained light on his feet. He decided to play this defensively. He needed to find out Arjen's strengths and weaknesses.

They circled each other, until Arjen lunged forward. Michael stepped back, and Arjen lunged again.

Michael kept backing up until he could feel the edge of the circle was near.

Arjen was clearly trying to test him.

Michael suddenly blocked his punch then ducked low and aimed one at his gut. Arjen blocked him but was forced to step back as Michael threw another punch.

Michael was now on the front foot, as he stayed light on his feet.

Suddenly, out of the blue, Arjen launched a powerful kick to his face. Michael recoiled but grabbed his foot.

Arjen tried to use this to his advantage but Michael threw him back, sending him sprawling on the floor.

Michael immediately charged forward, pressing his advantage, but Arjen dived for his legs. Michael dropped, grabbing the boy's wrist and twisting it, using the wrist lock Hans had taught him.

Arjen's face contorted in pain, but he used his other hand and launched a volley of punches to Michael's face.

Michael kept twisting, then let go, disrupting Arjen's balance. Michael then pressed his weight down on Arjen's punching arm, pinning him to the ground.

"Please submit," Michael said quietly. He didn't want to have to hurt Arjen.

Arjen sighed. "Very well. I submit," he told them, and Michael let go, standing up.

Arjen climbed to his feet and smiled at Michael.

"Well, it is decided. We are allies."

"Michael, have you seen this?!"

It was evening. Michael had left the training room after sparring with Arjen, and had taken a shower. Now, he was sitting at the table where his squad were supposed to eat.

Michael glanced up.

It was Elizabeth, her posh English accent prominent.

She handed him a newspaper, named 'The Daily Scribe'.

"Look at this page," she ordered, opening it.

Michael glimpsed news about some riots on the front page, but looked towards where Elizabeth was pointing.

LEONIDAS' EXPLOSIVE ENTRY

By Amanda Coleman

The Institute has always finished poorly in the Coliseum, but sources suggest that this year, things may have changed for the British team. We have already seen the powerful advertising campaign for their leader, Leonidas, but his arrival in the United States has certainly made an impression on the general public.

As Leonidas led his team off their plane, a van loaded with explosives careered into the crowd welcoming them. Fortunately, there were no casualties, but the Leonidas was injured whilst saving a military officer from the blast.

However, this did not stop the heroic soldier from carrying on his duties. See page 12 for an exclusive interview, televised last night.

Michael did not need to remind himself of the interview, he remembered it perfectly well.

"Seems you have a fan," Elizabeth commented with a raised eyebrow.

"Yeah," Michael agreed, surprised. He smiled slightly. "It's nice to have something going well."

"Don't speak too soon," Elizabeth warned. "But you fought well earlier. I'm sure the press will hear about that."

Michael gave a dry laugh. "Hope so."

"Can I see that?"

Joe walked over. Michael handed him the paper, and Joe flipped to where it was talking about riots.

"*Peace protests turn violent as police open fire,*" Joe read out. "I'm glad I don't live here. Not that I'd want to, anyway."

"Why not? America's our ally," Michael replied, not knowing much about the States.

"Because there are people starving back home while everyone here has more food than they need," Joe remarked. "I can't blame these protestors, wanting peace. The US spends more on this war than helping people."

"What can we do about it?" Michael asked.

Joe shrugged, then glanced up at the camera in the room. "I've got to go."

"Where?"

"None of your business," Joe retorted, standing up quickly.

Suddenly, the door burst open and American soldiers stormed into the food area.

Michael stood up as he, Elizabeth and Joe were surrounded.

"What's going on?" Michael demanded.

Sergeant Vellon strode in.

"Joseph King," he stated in his French accent. "You are under arrest on suspicion of betraying the Western Alliance."

Michael was shocked.

"What? What evidence is there of that?" Joe shouted indignantly.

"Sir, what does that mean?" Michael asked Sergeant Vellon.

"It means, garçon, that your friend Joseph is the traitor known as Prometheus," Sergeant Vellon declared.

Michael's eyes widened. "What?"

"What evidence do you have?" Joe repeated.

"Sensitive documents and materials have been found in your room, and several transmissions have been linked to you," Vellon said. "Please, come quietly, without resistance."

Joe looked around, but there was no way out.

He sighed, and raised his hands in surrender. He looked at Michael seriously.

"I'm innocent. You've gotta prove it to them," Joe said, as the soldiers put him in handcuffs.

"That's enough!" Sergeant Vellon barked. "Take him away!"

"When's my trial? Who's my lawyer?" Joe demanded as they pulled him away. "Am I not getting one?"

Sergeant Vellon remained silent.

Michael looked at him with alarm. "How did you find this evidence?"

"We searched his room," Sergeant Vellon replied simply. "Now, as Prometheus has been caught, you will no longer need to worry yourselves about him."

"But, he's not been convicted. We don't know that it's him," Michael pointed out.

Sergeant Vellon narrowed his eyes. "Focus on the Coliseum, Bakerson. When the press get wind of this arrest, things will be hard enough for you."

Damn. Vellon was right. If one of his team were arrested, then their chances of winning the public over would plummet.

Michael sighed.

"I'll need a replacement squad member then," he told Vellon.

Vellon nodded, a small smirk of victory coming to his face. "That will be arranged. The rest of the recruits from the Institute will arrive the day before the tournament begins to watch the tournament. A person will be selected from them."

Michael nodded, downbeat. He glanced up as Elizabeth spoke.

"Will the instructors be coming?" she asked.

Sergeant Vellon nodded. "Yes. Though you should be competent to know what to do by now. Instructors are forbidden from giving advice."

Michael nodded. "Thank you, sir," he said quietly. He didn't have any more questions.

Sergeant Vellon huffed, and then strode out.

Michael locked eyes with Elizabeth. He was completely stunned.

"I did not see that coming," she admitted, sounding surprised.

Michael shook his head in disbelief. Could it be Joe?

He bit his lip. "I'll have to speak to the team. It happened just when our luck seemed to be improving, too."

"Listen; don't let this get to you. Joe knew what he was getting into. Just think of what he caused in Norway," Elizabeth reminded softly.

"*It wasn't Joe!*" Michael snapped, annoyed at the mention of Norway. "I won't believe it until I see evidence. Joe fought alongside us in Norway, and he's my friend. Sergeant Vellon might think he's sure, but I'm not going to turn my back on my friend."

"But, Michael, it's no secret he hates the Americans," Elizabeth said.

"I hate the Americans too! That doesn't make me a traitor!" Michael retorted, frustrated.

Elizabeth's eyes widened.

Michael realised what he had said.

"I'm sorry. I don't hate them. But I don't get why they're arresting Joe," Michael said, looking down.

He activated the communicator on his wristwatch for his squad.

"Guys ... I have some bad news."

66 -   THE REPORTER

"So, Leonidas, what is this latest incident?"

Michael was back in the chat show, having an interview with Samantha again.

"I think you guys already know," Michael replied with a slight smile.

"Just, tell us again, for our viewers," Samantha insisted.

"Well, all that is happening is that we are bringing in a new squad member," Michael said.

"To replace whom?" Samantha pressed.

"One of our current members. Joe," Michael told her.

"Why?"

"Our instructor, Sergeant Vellon, thought it was best," Michael said.

"Is there anything that might have caused this change in strategy?" Samantha asked, clearly trying to get Michael to talk about the arrest.

"You'll have to ask Sergeant Vellon. As of now, nothing is confirmed," Michael maintained.

"Well, alright then. How do you feel this affects your chances?" she asked.

"Obviously, it's a hit, but there are plenty of capable recruits that can replace him," Michael said.

"And, what's this rumour of you fighting the Dutch leader?" she asked.

Michael smiled. "Well, I'm sure you guys can catch the video. Arjen and I decided to spar in a controlled manner, supervised by the guards there. No rules were broken, and it was a close contest."

"Who won?"

"He submitted."

"Do you not feel you've given opponents a chance to see your combat abilities?" Samantha wondered.

"I have. Let them take note. Everyone on my team can fight well," Michael told her.

"We won't go down easily."

Samantha smiled. "Have you seen your opponents fight?"

"I have not," Michael conceded.

"You seem to underestimate the American team, Leonidas," Samantha remarked.

"Well, I'm not afraid, if that's what you mean," Michael commented. "Samantha, which team do you want to win?"

She looked surprised. "Well, the American team, of course."

"But you're still an impartial interviewer?" Michael questioned.

She paused. "Yes, of course. Anyway, a few of our viewers have put questions to you, Michael."

Michael smiled. "Great."

Samantha looked at a screen.

"A. Coleman asks: *What quality would you say most defines who you are as a person?*"

Michael considered. He had never really thought about that. He knew he had to send a strong message.

"I'm loyal to my friends. If I'm supporting them, I won't back down. I won't give up. But, I think most important is that I don't let war, or anything else, change who I am," Michael stated firmly, looking at the camera.

Samantha laughed. "Er, alright. A.G. Phelps asks: *What was it like facing Fenrir in Norway?*"

Michael bit his lip. "It was tough. I mean, none of us expected combat, and we were thrust into the middle of it. Strategically, Fenrir had the upper hand. But we out-fought him. When you're in battle, you can't panic, because people's lives depend on you. You have to just trust your instincts, and back yourself. I took a risk there, and it paid off. But I knew that if it didn't, then a lot of lives would be lost because of me. And that was hard. That weighed on my mind. The deaths I did cause ... still weigh on my mind now. And I just deal with it," Michael said, forcing emotion out of his voice. He had to be seen as strong, not weak.

Samantha, for once, didn't reply, as she glanced towards the room Michael had come from.

"Well, thank you for that, we won't be having any more questions," she said curtly.

Michael waited with a charming smile on his face. "Are you sure? I'm happy to answer them."

"No, that will be all," Samantha replied coolly.

Michael smiled. "Well, everyone, I hope you enjoy the Coliseum," he said, standing up.

The crowd applauded, and Michael strode out. That interview had gone better than the last one.

This time, however, Michael had not been provided with any company. His team were nowhere to be seen and he was expected to make his own way back to the Facility.

Clearly, the Americans had little regard for him.

As he exited the studio, he heard his name called.

"Leonidas?"

It was a ginger-haired woman, hurrying towards him. She was dressed in a long coat and carried a satchel over her shoulder.

Michael looked up, tensing himself.

The woman was out of breath as she reached him.

"I'm ... Amanda Coleman ... I was hoping I could speak to you?" she asked him. Her hair was tied back in a ponytail. Michael noticed she was wearing a lot of makeup. He guessed she was in her early twenties, a few years older than him.

"You were the one who wrote the article about me. Sure," Michael said.

She smiled. "So, you read it. What did you think?"

Michael shrugged. "It was interesting, although you seemed to be very complimentary of me. A heroic soldier? What made you put that?" he asked curiously.

"Well, I did a bit of research, and by all accounts of the battle, your performance was exemplary in Norway," she hesitated. "Do you mind we go somewhere for a chat? There are a few things I want to discuss."

Michael frowned. This was an unusual request.

Was he allowed meet people outside the Facility? The interview had been organised by the Americans, but this would be unscheduled.

"Can't you talk to me here?" he asked.

Amanda glanced around. "There are things which I don't really want to discuss in public. Things that could help your friend Joe."

Michael's interest piqued. "You mean ... about Prometheus?"

Amanda nodded, biting her lip.

Michael nodded. "Alright, I'll come with you. I've got some time before my next meeting."

Amanda smiled. "Great .., you don't mind walking, do you? It's not too far," she reassured him.

"Where, exactly, are we going?" Michael wondered.

"Oh, just our editorial," she told him, beckoning for him to follow as she strode off.

Michael wasn't sure whether to trust this woman. It seemed strange to have her so willing to speak to him.

He followed cautiously, glancing around. He hadn't really paid attention to the streets of Washington before. They were bright, well-kept and overall, it seemed quite a nice place. It was quiet, as it was a working day, but there were a few groups of teenagers around, most likely enjoying the time off school.

It was a life alien to Michael's. He had never been in a city before.

As he followed on, he noticed the streets generally became more dilapidated, as they journeyed into a different area of town. They had been walking for about twenty minutes when Michael hurried up to Amanda.

"You said this would be quick," Michael accused. "Tell me what you know."

Amanda cleared her throat, fidgeting. "There's not much further," she reassured, but it was in vain.

Michael was not going any further until he knew she had answers. "What do you know about Prometheus?" he asked her, folding his arms.

Amanda fiddled with her bracelet, and then pulled a folder from her satchel. "Alright ... I was doing some digging last week, about your time in Norway. A friend of mine is in the military, he was able to access some classified files. So, the Ragnarok attack was supposedly organised by Prometheus, right? My friend sent me the data logs for the file transmission – I think your Sergeant Wallace mentioned it in his report. So, two signals were sent out on the night before the attack. One of them was encrypted, but the login was a secure one – I couldn't access it. Only an instructor, or someone who worked on the system could have sent that message," she explained.

Michael's eyes widened. "An instructor? Are you sure?"

"Yeah, the military knows it. That's what your Sergeant Vellon is investigating. So, basically, your friend Joe, if he was behind the attack, must have had help from an instructor, or a technician," Amanda said.

"Why are you telling me this?" Michael asked her, frowning. Something wasn't right.

"Because there's more. Your military is covering something up. Something big. The power grid in Oslo going down? Was that just a coincidence?" Amanda questioned. "I'm going to expose this. Just come with me. I have friends who can help."

Michael shook his head. "I have to get back," he told her. "Thank you for the information, but I'm not betraying the military. Not like Prometheus did."

"No, Michael, you need me. If you ever want Joe to get a trial, you need public support," Amanda insisted, grabbing his arm.

Michael held her gaze, and saw fear in her eyes. He glanced down at her bracelet. There was a flashing light coming from it.

She must have activated some sort of alarm.

"Please..," she whispered, but Michael wrenched his arm away, and ran off, hoping to get back to the Facility.

He turned a corner, and heard a car pull up in the street behind him.

He activated the alarm button on his wristwatch, and was about to speak into it when he heard voices talking behind him.

"Where is he? We need an inside man!" a man was shouting.

"He ran off, just now!" Amanda told the man. "You can catch him!"

Upon hearing this, Michael turned and hurried down the street, looking for a place to hide. Luckily, there was an alley to his left. He hurried into it, hoping that the people looking for him, whoever they were, would pass him by.

He squatted down, waiting, until he heard a laugh behind him.

He whipped around, as he saw a group of about five men facing him from within the alley. Michael saw the dim glow of lighted cigarettes.

They walked towards him, and Michael had a decision to make. Run, or fight.

He decided to run.

Michael turned and pelted out of the tunnel, glancing to his right. There was a man there, wearing a black cloak.

"Please," the man said. "We just want to talk."

Michael did not trust him. He backed away, still keen to escape the alleyway.

"I'm sorry," the man said.

Michael glanced at a car that was driving past, the blacked-out windows slowly being rolled down to reveal ...

A gun.

Michael covered his face as it fired. He felt a prick on his arms and immediately felt woozy.

The black-cloaked man ran over and caught him. His face was a blur, but Michael could hear his voice.

"We're on your side."

67 -   FRIEND OR FOE?

"Is he awake?" a man's voice asked.

"I think so," someone replied.

"Why did you tranquilise him, anyway? You could have just asked him nicely to come," the first man asked.

"We did try, but he didn't trust us," a third voice replied. This voice was female.

"Gee, I wonder why," he remarked.

Michael opened his eyes. He was sitting on a chair, in a dark room. There were several figures around. He couldn't see their faces.

"Who are you?" Michael asked.

"We're the Social Revolutionaries. We want to help you," the second person told him. "Michael, you're popular with the people. The military are not."

"What do you want?" Michael asked.

"We want you to fight for your friend," he said.

"Joe?" Michael questioned.

"Yes. If you can make a stand and prove the military wrong, it will make people question their integrity," the figure said.

"I can't do that," Michael stated, turning off the emergency button on his watch.

"You said you'd stand by your friend, no matter what. We just want to help you. Amanda can gather you support within the press," the voice said.

"I'm fighting for Joe, but not for you. You don't want to help me; you just want to attack the military. I'm not working with radicals," Michael replied.

"Radicals? We just want to make a difference. We want peace, not war," the man stated.

"I'm a soldier, not a politician. The Russians are brutal, and someone has to stand up to them. My focus is the Coliseum, and getting the best for my squad," Michael said, repeating what he had been taught at the Institute.

"Have you ever *seen* a Russian who isn't a soldier?" the man questioned.

Michael shook his head.

"No."

"Then, you can't really comment, can you? But anyway, we're not Russians. Instead of financing war, we want to help the people," the man implored.

Michael stalled. He hadn't seen any poverty here. He had always assumed that the US was a rich country. "What do you want me to do?"

"Go back to the base, pretend nothing happened. Amanda will publish an article about your friend's trial. Her last one was well received, so it won't be hard to gather support. The military will have no choice but to carry out the trial and you'll probably have to speak about it in an interview. We'll bring a lawyer in for Joe, don't worry," the man said.

Michael considered. Joe needed help. It was a plan. If only these Social Revolutionaries weren't radicals.

"Was the terrorist attack you?" Michael asked them sharply, intending to provoke a reaction.

"What terrorist attack?" the woman replied, sounding confused.

"You know, the van with the explosives," Michael pressed.

"That? That wasn't us. There were too many civilians there for it to be us," the man reassured.

"How do I know that's true?" Michael asked.

"Because ... we'd have no reason at all to do that. We're trying to win over the people, that would just turn them against us," the man said.

Michael listened. They did have a point. They seemed like they wanted to help Joe. Still, he couldn't trust them. They *had* tranquilised him.

"I'm sorry," Michael told them.

"You're not going to fight for your friend?" the first speaker questioned. "You said you were loyal."

"I am fighting for Joe. But that's not what I'm sorry for. When you captured me, I sounded the emergency button on my watch. The military know who you are, and they're coming," Michael said quietly.

"No one took his wristwatch?" the first man demanded. "Let's get out of here, now!"

Michael stood up. He felt a fist hit him in the face.

"Bastard," the woman muttered, before he heard people running away.

He heard shouting, and gunshots.

The military had arrived.

Two black-clad soldiers with helmets on ran over to him.

"Bakerson?" they asked.

Michael nodded. "That's me."

"You're coming with us," they ordered, leading him towards an exit.

Michael glanced back as he walked away. They were in a warehouse. There wasn't much resistance to the military. This must just have been a temporary location for the Social Revolutionaries.

"This way," the Western soldiers ordered, opening the door letting the bright outside light to flood in.

Michael adjusted his eyes, and was surprised by what he saw. A convoy of military vehicles were there, mainly trucks and jeeps, but led by an armoured car.

They had brought a lot of firepower.

Michael was led towards two officers who were standing at the back, talking. Michael recognised Lieutenant James Nicholls of the Coliseum, but there was also a woman he had not seen before.

"Here he is, sir," the soldiers told Nicholls, who looked up.

"Ah, Leonidas! This is Major Jones, she's in charge of dealing with ... revolutionaries," Nicholls explained.

Michael smiled and nodded at her. He was surprised that a woman outranked Nicholls.

"Well done, Bakerson. You led us right to them. I do, however, have some questions," Jones stated. She was in her forties.

Michael nodded. "Sure."

"What did they want with you?" Jones asked.

"They wanted me to work for them against the military. I said no, of course," Michael added quickly.

Jones nodded.

"And how did they capture you?"

"I was spoken to for an interview by a reporter, and then they ambushed me. I ran, but I was shot by a tranquiliser from a car," Michael explained.

"And they captured your near the recording studio?" Jones asked.

"No. The reporter had led me away from there," Michael told her.

Jones pursed her lips. "In the future, Bakerson, stick to your schedule. Only speak to those authorised by the military. Who knows what they could have done otherwise? Nevertheless, you helped us capture members of the Social Revolutionaries. Rest assured that they will be punished," she informed him.

Michael was conflicted. They didn't seem like bad people. But he knew his loyalties had to lie with the military. He couldn't afford for his image to be tarnished.

Although, he wondered if the reporter, Amanda, had been caught. He didn't feel she was an enemy.

He nodded. "Is there anything else?"

"You'll be given a ride back to the Facility. Try to stay there," Nicholls told him, sounding friendly, but Michael sensed an undertone to his voice.

Michael nodded. "Yes, sir," he told Nicholls.

Nicholls nodded, led him to a jeep. "Sit in the back," he said, getting in the driver's seat.

Michael did so, thinking.

He was going to fight for Joe. He just didn't know how. He would need to find someone who was more experienced than him. Someone who knew about Prometheus.

Nicholls drove back to the huge, hi-tech Facility, through several checkpoints.

372

"I couldn't help but hear what the Revolutionaries were asking you to do in the emergency message you sent," Nicholls commented.

Michael didn't feel the need to say anything.

"Listen, kid, you want the military on your side. Don't fight us. If you need help with something, we can help you," Nicholls said.

"Yeah ... actually, I think I would like some help," Michael told him. "You see, my friend Joe was arrested, but we haven't actually been shown any evidence against him."

Nicholls nodded. "Well, if it means you staying to your schedule, I'll see what I can do," he told Michael.

Michael smiled, satisfied, as the jeep trundled into the base. When it stopped near the entrance, Michael got out.

"Leonidas?" Nicholls inquired.

Michael looked back. "Yes?"

"If being leader is too much for you, you can always step down," Nicholls told him.

"I appreciate your concern, sir, but I think I've got this," Michael answered as he strode inside.

A feeling of annoyance and frustration welled up. Why did people think he wasn't capable?

He had this.

Michael returned to the training room, security guards searching him at the door.

"Where've ya been?" a bald guard asked him, tapping on a tablet.

"Interview," Michael replied, with a dry laugh. "They're a real pain."

"Ha, tell me about it! Before I joined the military, I was a football player! A real star and they always wanted me for interviews," he commented wistfully.

One of the other guards rolled his eyes. "Go in," he told Michael.

Michael grinned at the guard. "Well, maybe you can go to mine," he joked as he went in.

The guard chuckled. "You're a funny kid," he commented.

Michael walked over to where his squad was training.

Jürgen and Thomas nodded at him, as Michael went over to where the drones were stored.

He had been training hard the last few days, to understand the American technology.

"Woah, Michael, stop!" a female voice cried.

Michael looked over. It was Emily, a member of his squad, looking angry.

"You almost set off my trap!" she complained, annoyed.

"What?" Michael asked, as Emily pointed to the floor.

Wait, no, there was something there. A long, thin wire.

"A tripwire?" Michael asked her. "What would it have done if I'd crossed it?"

Emily grinned. "That's a surprise. But, I wouldn't recommend it," she told him.

"Why not?"

"Well, let's just say, your ability to walk might be affected," Emily told him.

Michael laughed, then realised she wasn't joking. "Erm, you might want to put a warning sign up or something," he told her.

She tilted her head. "Fair enough," she agreed. "I did tell everyone in our squad, but you weren't here."

Michael carefully navigated around the wire and headed over to where Arthur was training with a drone.

He was currently looking in a screen, at what looked like a camera.

"What is that?" Michael asked curiously.

Arthur looked up in surprise. "It's a recon drone," he told Michael, pointing in the air, to where a small black helicopter-like object was flying around the room.

"It's armed with flares, and has thermal vision. It's very useful for scouting," Arthur explained.

Michael smiled, and noticed Jürgen walk over to them.

"Michael?" Jürgen asked. "I, er, have heard rumours."

Michael glanced up at him. "What rumours?"

"Raymon is planning to take leadership from you. He's speaking to people privately, trying to intimidate them into supporting him," Jürgen said quietly.

Michael's eyes widened. "Who told you that?" he demanded.

"Raymon did. He tried to guarantee my support," Jürgen stated.

"What did you say?" Michael asked with suspicion.

"No, of course!" Jürgen exclaimed, frowning. "Listen, Michael, you're going to have to start off this Coliseum well, otherwise, the sponsors might demand a change of leadership."

Michael nodded. "Alright," he muttered. "Cheers, Jürgen. Thanks for letting me know."

Jürgen saluted. "You're welcome, *Leonidas*," he told Michael with a grin, as he strode off.

Michael sighed.

"No pressure," Arthur remarked dryly. "The Coliseum starts in two days. Don't underestimate Raymon. His father has a lot of influence in the military. And he won't be afraid to play dirty."

68 -   BEGINNING

It was time.

Time for the Coliseum.

Michael stood still in the reception area of the Facility. The area was huge, with easily enough room for two hundred people. All five teams were there.

His squad were, for the most part, silent. Everyone was feeling the tension.

Michael's breathing was shaky; his hands were cold and clammy. He clenched a fist, trying to control his nerves. This was worse than before Norway.

He glanced over as the automatic doors slid open.

Michael saw two familiar faces.

Sergeant Wallace strode in, by his side a small, squat recruit.

Steve.

Michael broke out into a smile as Wallace spoke to Lieutenant Nicholls, then the duo walked over.

Sergeant Wallace grinned. "Laddie, good to see ya! I came as soon as I heard, but we were only told two days ago. Details were very scarce, mind you. So, why is Steve here?" he asked Michael.

"Joe was arrested for supposedly being the spy. Prometheus. I need you here to help prove he's innocent. And we needed a recruit to fill his spot. I had no idea you would bring Steve," Michael told him, pleased.

Steve smiled. "I'm glad I can help."

Michael was grateful that Steve was still not holding a grudge from their argument at the ball.

Wallace was alarmed. "Joe? What? I mean, he was on my radar, but I didn't think he'd be the spy," he muttered. "What proof do they have?"

"None that they've shown us. Vellon arrested him," Michael said.

Sergeant Wallace frowned. "I'll 'ave to speak to him. I'll see what I can do, laddie," he promised.

"RECRUITS!" a megaphone blared. "Christ, this is loud."

The volume lowered. "Is this better? Yep, we're good." It was Lieutenant James Nicholls speaking. "Well, everyone, it's time for you to shine. Today, you'll travel to the White House, where the official opening ceremony for the Coliseum will begin. New technology will be showcased, the President will make an announcement, and you will all salute. It's standard format, but this year should be special."

"Why's that?" Arjen, the Dutch leader, asked as he stood near Nicholls.

"Well, the President will have to win the public's support," Nicholls commented, away from the megaphone.

"He doesn't have it?" Arjen asked.

Nicholls' eyes widened slightly. "Ah, that's not really important. Just make sure you don't do anything weird. This ceremony is formal, and means a lot to the American people. I don't expect you to understand it," he said.

Michael frowned.

"So, you'll be sent out in the trucks in your teams. Good luck," Nicholls said, glancing around.

Michael clenched a fist, then relaxed it. He was nervous. He didn't feel like he had been provided with enough information.

"Well, good luck, laddie. Oh, I almost forgot. Sergeant Raines sent you a message. He said, 'Remember Sun Tzu,' whatever that means," Wallace informed him.

Michael nodded. "Okay," he replied, unsure himself on Raines' meaning. Was there a hidden message or something?

He remembered learning about the famous Chinese strategist, but wasn't sure how useful it would be in the Coliseum.

"First off is the American team. Oh, and you'll all be given a chance to meet with your sponsors once you get there," Nicholas announced, and the American team began to leave.

Michael noticed Raymon talking to Sophie. He decided to go over.

"Come on, Sophie, I'm a much better leader," Raymon was saying.

Sophie remained silent, glancing at Michael. She smirked as she looked between them.

"Everything okay?" Michael asked with a friendly smile.

"Yes, *Leonidas*," Raymon sneered.

"Let's hope this Coliseum goes well, eh?" Michael remarked.

"Yeah, let's hope so," Raymon said with a slight grin. "We wouldn't want anything to ruin it, would we?"

Michael held his nerve. "Course not," he agreed.

Sophie rolled her eyes. "*Boys*," she muttered, walking off.

Raymon narrowed his eyes at Michael. "If you don't smash this first task, I'm taking control. The sponsors and recruits both want me. Lieutenant Jones' judgement won't stand over here," he told Michael.

Michael shrugged. "We'll see," he replied nonchalantly, as he turned and walked away from Raymon.

No pressure then.

Michael went over to where Steve was. "You okay?" he asked his friend, hoping everything was alright between the two of them.

"Are you?" Steve raised an eyebrow. "There's a lot more pressure on you than me."

"I know," Michael commented, sighing.

"Listen, Michael, I'm sorry for being an idiot at the ball. I was just annoyed that I didn't get in this squad and you did," Steve apologised.

Michael smiled. "It's okay, Steve. I know how you felt. When your name was read out in the Selection, I was envious," he admitted.

"So we're okay now?" Steve asked.

Michael grinned. "Yeah. We're good. We'll stick together," he said.

Steve laughed. "Then let's smash this Coliseum," he declared, punching Michael lightly on the arm.

"Hope so," Michael agreed.

The Institute was called next. Michael walked over to the entrance of the Facility, where early morning sunlight shone down.

"What is it with the Western Alliance and calling everything 'the'?" Steve mused. "I mean, we have The Institute, The Selection, The Facility. It's like they can't think of actual names so they just call it general terms."

Michael laughed as they boarded the trucks.

There was a small amount of chatter on the journey there, but Michael didn't join in. He was wondering what might happen when they got there. Would the Sheikh have anything to say?

After about forty minutes, the trucks arrived at their destination. Michael glanced outside at the large stately building as the recruits climbed out.

"This is where the parade begins. You'll march out from here to the White House," Nicholls remarked. "Your sponsors are inside."

The building was enormous. Michael was led to a set of double doors, where a large amount of cameramen and staff were standing around. Recruits were quickly snatched away by their sponsors.

Michael saw the large figure of the Sheikh sitting down on a large sofa in a corner, his eyes closed.

He made his way over to the large man and cleared his throat.

There was no response. The Sheikh's two burly bodyguards narrowed their eyes at Michael.

"Sheikh Bakir?" Michael asked.

The Sheikh slowly opened his eyes. He shook his head a little, his chin wobbling.

"Ah, Leonidas!" the Sheikh exclaimed when he saw Michael. "I was wondering when you would show up!"

"Yes, we just arrived," Michael told him.

The Sheikh nodded. "Well, Michael, let me ask you something," he said slowly. "Are you fully committed?"

"Committed?"

"Will you do whatever it takes to win?" the Sheikh asked.

"Yes," Michael told him. "Within reason, anyway."

The Sheikh nodded. "Then you will instruct your squad that my team will prep them," the Sheikh said.

"But don't they all have their own sponsors?" Michael asked.

"I will deal with the sponsors. You order your team to follow you," the Sheikh told him.

Michael's heart pounded. He was nervous. What if his team didn't agree?

"Yes, sir," he said.

"I'll help you, Michael."

Dan, the other recruit sponsored by the Sheikh, was there. "Let's make this work."

Michael took a deep breath. "Yeah."

"Looking good, Michael!"

Michael looked in a mirror. He was wearing a gold coloured t-shirt, padded out with protection. He wore a red cape, and a golden Spartan helmet that covered his head. Everyone else in his squad, by comparison, wore a black helmet but a similar uniform.

His team had taken some convincing, but he had persuaded them to wear the uniforms.

Sophie was first to agree, and most members decided to after she did. Jürgen and Nadia were reluctant, but agreed.

Even Steve decided to give it a go, despite repeatedly commenting how stupid they would all look.

Once everyone was in a Spartan uniform except Raymon and Henry, they sullenly got changed as well, not wanting to be the odd ones out.

Raymon insisted on being different, painting three slashes of red across his black helmet.

"Thanks, Carter," Michael told the man. The Sheikh's team had worked quickly and efficiently, taking no less than twenty minutes to get everyone sorted.

"Try not to be embarrassed out there," Carter reassured him. "The helmet will hide your face. Everyone in your squad has one. And all the squads dress up. It's a tradition."

"It is?" Michael demanded. "Why had no one told me this?"

"I assumed everyone knew." Carter spread his hands out. "It's on television every time."

"That explains it. Well, great. I thought we were the only ones wearing these. Do you know what the other squads will be wearing?" Michael asked him.

"No," Carter admitted, "but you'll be the most charming by far."

Michael nodded. "Cheers, Carter."

He heard someone wolf-whistle behind him. He turned around, expecting to see Sophie.

It was Sophie, but she wasn't looking at him. Jürgen was there, wearing a similar uniform to Michael, but without the golden helmet.

"Looking good, Jürgen! Amelia will be loving it!" Sophie teased. The girls wore the same uniforms as the boys, but wore black leggings.

Jürgen smiled a little, and was about to reply when Michael interrupted.

"Are you guys ready?" he asked curtly, striding towards the door. "We don't want to be late."

"Ja," Jürgen said. "I am ready."

"Okay, I'll be a minute," Michael said, wanting some privacy to prepare himself.

The floor seemed to swim unsteadily as Michael opened the door and stepped out. He found himself in a large illuminated corridor, still in the stately building where the Sheikh sat downstairs.

Michael knew the parade to the White House would begin soon, but didn't want to be the first one to go back to the reception wearing uniform. He turned left and walked down the corridor. At the end was a polished oak door, with gold plated lettering on, reading 'PRIVATE'.

Michael glanced behind him, before slowly twisting the doorknob. It swung open smoothly, revealing a well-furnished office. In front of Michael was a window, giving a view of the street below. To his left was a desk with various assorted objects on. There was a beautifully crafted wooden eagle which stood upon it. Its lifeless eyes seemed to stare at Michael. In front of the wooden eagle was a golden nameplate. It read 'SEBASTIAN GREY'. He wondered if it was the name of the eagle or the owner of the office.

Behind the desk was a chair, and behind the chair was a huge bookshelf. He went over and glanced at the titles. *A Modern History of the World. The Great Constellations. The World's Greatest Wonders. Rome – the Eternal City.*

Michael picked this latest one out. It was an old book, he could tell by its smell. The pages were thin and seemed to be about to crumble as flicked through them. He saw a photograph of an amphitheatre, with hundreds of arched windows. He looked at the caption and smiled.

It read: 'The Coliseum, one of Rome's greatest landmarks. Here, gladiators would fight each other as well as savage beasts, with their lives at the mercy of the Emperor. Now, the monument remains as a symbol of the majesty that was once the Roman Empire.'

Michael closed the book and placed it carefully back onto the shelf. He didn't know the Coliseum was a real place. He thought about the words. Was he about to become a gladiator?

He walked over to the window and looked outside. There were crowds there, huge numbers of people, either side of a white paved road. The road led up to a white building in the distance.

It reminded Michael horribly of when he had arrived in the USA, when the trucks had careered into them.

"Bread and Circuses."

A voice emerged from behind Michael, making him jump. He whipped around, seeing a middle-aged man with bright blue eyes and grey hair standing in the doorway. The man slowly walked over to the window, peering out.

"That was a saying in Ancient Rome. That was how they kept the plebeians happy. Governments nowadays have not changed. Only the medium has. Television, the radio, mobile phones. They all spew out lies for the people to believe. The government keeps them so preoccupied with minor events and worthless celebrities that they fail to see the truth," the man said quietly.

"What is the truth?" Michael asked him.

"That they are fools. That society is fragile. That this war will not end. There are many truths, Leonidas. I wonder, how many have you discovered?" he mused, turning his piercing gaze towards Michael.

Michael looked at him. "Is this your office?" he asked him worriedly.

383

"This is my house," the man said with a smile. "Sebastian Grey. The Coliseum games were my initiative, a little over thirty years ago. Ever since the Olympics and all sports stopped, we needed a way to entertain the masses."

"That's all this is? A way to keep people happy?" Michael questioned.

"Of course that's not all it is. Every canvas is made from many different threads," Grey remarked. "There is never solely one reason for an action. Chains of cause and consequence, action and reaction can be traced back to the origins of the universe."

"Why do you hold the Coliseum games?" Michael asked him.

"Why? Because it is the only way to prevent the collapse of order and society. Also, it pays well. Also, it is excellent training for military recruits and raises a lot of money for the military," Grey commented, slowly clasping his hands together. "You see? Never just one cause."

Michael nodded. "This Coliseum ... has anyone ever died?" he asked the man.

The man tilted his head to one side. "People die every day. One death is a tragedy. A million deaths are a statistic. But in answer to your question, yes."

The man sighed. "Leonidas, I am a scholar. I seek to acquire knowledge. The Coliseum is merely a hobby for me. A game of chess, if you will. I wish you luck, but remember – there is no way you can win. You cannot beat the game itself. The USA must win, especially at this critical time," he told Michael.

"The USA has lost before," Michael pointed out.

The man sighed. "Yes. A fluke. And the team that beat them were sent on a stealth raid in Eastern Europe three months later. They were never heard of again. The rules of the game are very simple, Leonidas. The Americans win. Canada and Australia fight for the next two spots. Britain is fourth, and the Netherlands are fifth. Don't get your hopes up," the man said.

"What would happen if we did win?" Michael asked him.

The man raised an eyebrow. "Well, then you would have beaten the game," he said, smiling a little to himself. "If you do not mind, this is my office, and I do have to prepare for the parade."

Michael apologised and left quickly, returning to the changing rooms. His squad were there, all ready.

"Took your time," Steve remarked.

Michael looked at them all. Was there any chance they could come higher than fourth? He wasn't sure. But they had to try.

"This is it," Michael announced, taking a deep breath. "This is the parade. After that, the Coliseum. We're going to give our best. No one expects anything of us. We have nothing to lose. Let's show everyone! We've come fourth every Coliseum, but this will be the time we don't. They're all reliant on technology, but we're not. We know how to fight. We've beaten Fenrir's hunters! Let's show them what real soldiers can do."

Sophie grinned. "Great speech, Michael. Now, come on. We've got a parade to go to."

70 -   THE PARADE

The ornate double doors were flung open. Cool air flooded in. Trumpets played, the recruits stepped out, the crowd cheered. The parade had begun.

The American team were at the forefront of the parade. They all wore smart navy-blue uniforms, like officers.

Then followed the Canadian team, wearing white snow gear which covered their whole bodies. They reminded Michael of Fenrir's Hunters.

"Canadian Snow Troops are some of the best marksmen around," Arthur remarked. "And they're the only ones who are actually dressed for this weather."

"Isn't Canada pretty much all snow?" Michael inquired.

"Of course not," Arthur replied. "It does have seasons, you know."

Next up were the Australian team. They wore khaki hunting clothes, similar to how Michael imagined a typical Australian. Their prep team clearly didn't have as much imagination.

"Ready, Leonidas?"

Michael glanced to the side. A uniformed Spartan was next to him, and although he couldn't see who it was under the helmet, he knew it was Jürgen.

Michael nodded. He glanced at his team.

"Follow me!" he ordered, and then turned to face the crowds.

Michael strode forward, the cold air biting at his legs. He could feel the wind stinging his eyes.

The crowd was applauding, perhaps. His helmet muffled the sound.

He didn't turn to the side, though. He walked straight on, eyes ahead.

Michael had an irrational fear that his team weren't following him, that he had gone out of turn, that he would have to go back inside.

He felt an arm brush past his. He glanced over to the side.

Nadia's brown eyes looked back at him, filling him with reassurance.

Michael smiled slightly to himself as he looked ahead. He had support. He knew his friends would stand by him.

Onward he walked, scanning ahead. Their destination, a grandiose white structure, lay ahead with a lawn of frost-covered grass either side of the entrance gate.

Military guards lined the route, armed with rifles, several with rocket launchers. They clearly did not want any trucks crashing into this parade.

There was a balcony on the building, upon which several figures were standing. As Michael advanced closer, he saw a large person standing in the centre, with two people either side of him.

The American team stopped. They had been walking in two ordered lines, unlike the rest of the teams.

The Canadian team stopped behind, then the Australian team. Michael stopped as well, stepping back. His team hastily ordered themselves into two lines.

Michael looked up at the man in the centre. He was tall, and broadly shouldered. He looked to be in his forties or fifties, with short black hair. There was a gravitas about him. He wore a smart suit, in contrast to the military uniforms the people around him.

Michael knew that this was the President of the United States and the Leader of the Western Alliance.

On his right side was a round faced man with a white moustache and bald head. He wore a military uniform weighed down with medals of service.

To the President's left was a man Michael recognised. Sebastian Grey stood there, looking at his watch.

The President cleared his throat. "Hello, fellow Americans! I am stood here today with the honour of opening the Coliseum games. For those recruits do not know me, I am the Elliot Hudson the President of the United States of America," he spoke clearly and confidently, with a strong American accent. There was some applause.

"The Coliseum is an amazing event, and where we Americans can rally together in support of our soldiers, who give their lives for our country. I would like to thank Sebastian Grey, for once again hosting the event, as well as the various sponsors who have endorsed our recruits," the President continued.

"I would like to take this opportunity to reinforce the ideals of patriotism within our people. This is a country where everyone is free. Everyone has a voice. No one is above the law. Everyone has a right to defend themselves. Our military is there to defend us. I'm asking for everyone to honour them, and to honour the soldiers of the Western Alliance, now, more than ever, as we sing our national anthem," the President stated, striking a hand to his chest.

Music played, and people sang loudly.

Michael ignored the words and instead focused on the people of the balcony. The President was singing heartily, as was the military general. Sebastian Grey, however, looked distracted.

When the song was over, Michael shivered slightly, the cold getting to him. Could they get on with the ceremony?

The President smiled. "Thank you, everyone. Now, as tradition, this is the time of the year when we unveil a little surprise for everyone. And, it is my pleasure and my privilege to inform you, that *this war is on its way to its end!*" he announced.

The crowd cheered, and Michael looked up sharply.

"Ladies and gentlemen, citizens of America and the Western Alliance, I am proud to present to you ... the Trojan!" he roared, gesturing to a stage on Michael's right.

The crowd looked over, as metallic humanoid machines moved up into view. They stood straight, upright. Michael saw there were about twelve of them.

"Made with the finest artificial intelligence, these robots will bring us the victory we deserve without the sacrifice of our soldiers! Developed by the Technological Integration department, I can tell you that by this time next year, there will be a new sight on the battlefield, taking this war to Russia itself!" the President continued.

The Trojans all saluted, robotic arms going up. The crowd cheered and applauded, as cameras focused on the President and the robots.

Michael noticed Lieutenant Blackburn standing near the stage, with Darius Finch nearby.

After a few minutes, the crowd descended into silence.

The President cleared his throat. "Everyone should be familiar with the Coliseum. The first round is designed to push the bodies and minds of the recruits to their limits. I cannot reveal what the tasks are yet, but all will be clear in a few hours, when these recruits are fighting for the ultimate prize. Yes, this year, the winning team will be selected to work with Technological Integration as a new Special Forces team, leading us to victory alongside these Trojans."

The President looked down at the recruits, and seemed to lock eyes with Michael. "Let the Coliseum begin!"

71 - THE COLISEUM

"Welcome to ... the Coliseum!" a speaker blared. Michael and his team had been taken to an outdoor amphitheatre. Crowds and camera crew surrounded a huge, circular arena. On the ground was green grass, too green for this time of year. The sky was a cloudy grey.

The grass ran in a circle around the edges of the arena. On it were five equidistant flags near the edge. Michael recognised the American flag, but there were others there he did not recognise. Next to each flag was a metal rack that was about waist height. The racks were all empty.

In the centre of the arena lay an island of sand. It was about fifty metres in diameter, and had a few obstacles upon it. Concrete barriers. Bushes. Even a few small trees.

In between the island and the grass was a fast flowing river which surrounded the island. Michael could hear it from where he was. He looked towards the river. There seemed to be platforms floating on it, but they were moving quickly. Michael wouldn't want to fall into it.

"Follow me," a black-clad soldier ordered Michael and his team. Their squad had been led from the parade to a preparatory building, where they were made to change back into plain grey clothes, to avoid any competitors smuggling in weapons. The American team wore red, the Dutch wore orange, The Australians wore green and the Canadians wore blue.

They followed the soldier, Michael looking around the arena. They were taken to an unfamiliar flag. "Here's yours," the soldier told them, then strode off.

Michael glanced at the flag. It had a blue background, with a red cross on top of a white one.

"It's the Union Jack," Arthur said. "It used to be the flag of the British Empire, before it became Occupied Britain. Now, we just have the Western Alliance flag."

"Oh," Michael said, surprised. "Wonder what the task will be."

"I expect ve'll soon find out," Jürgen remarked.

Right on cue, a speaker blared into life. "Welcome to the first round of the Coliseum!"

There was applause from the crowd, which sounded faint to the recruits, as they were quite far away.

"This round will test the competitors' endurance, strategy and risk taking. The rules are as follows." A voiceover then began to play.

"*The Coliseum - round one. In the centre of the arena, there are fifteen golden discs which have been placed on the island. The object of the round is to obtain as many discs as possible. A player must take the disc and return it to their flag. Once placed on the rack next to the flag, the discs will change colour to match that team.*"

Michael glanced at the rack. It had eight slots.

"*If any team collects eight discs and fills their rack, the round ends and their team is victorious. Alternatively, if, after forty minutes, the round has not ended, then the round will cease and the team with the most amount of discs will be victorious. Discs can be taken at any point from another team's rack. Every ten minutes, the direction of the current of the river will reverse.*"

Michael tried to remember all the information. It seemed simple enough.

"*Rules - the racks, flags and discs are not to be used as weapons. If any player does this, the result will be a foul and the player will be disqualified. The discs are not to be thrown. Physical force is allowed, as all recruits should know how to fight.*"

There was a pause.

"*Good luck recruits, and may the best team win. The round will begin in three minutes.*"

Michael was full of nerves, but he looked at his team. A large timer began counting down on the screen.

"I'd say we rush the discs," Sophie said.

"Not all of us. We'll split into three teams of five. Raymon, you lead the Offensive group. You'll try to take discs from other teams, but defend if necessary. Jürgen, Henry, Sophie, Dan, you go with him," Michael decided, speaking quickly.

Raymon nodded, seeming satisfied with his role.

"Thomas, I want you to lead the Defensive team. Protect our discs and any injured players. Steve, Arthur, Elizabeth, Amelia, you go with him. You are not to abandon the base," he commanded.

Thomas frowned, but nodded. Michael guessed he was unhappy at being forced to defend.

"Emily, Nadia, Paul, Dominic, you're with me. We'll rush the unclaimed discs and try to take them off individual opponents," he said, looking at them. His team nodded.

"Anything to add?" he asked everyone.

"There are fifteen discs," Paul said. "That works out three per nation. How many are we aiming to get?"

Michael looked at him. "We get as many as we can. We're not here to play it safe. We have to make an impression on the sponsors."

"Are we staying clear from the American team?" Arthur asked.

"No. We're targeting the American team," Michael said with a slight grin. Steve rolled his eyes.

Michael glanced at the timer. Ten seconds.

"One more thing. Our alliance with the Dutch team stands. Don't take their discs, but keep our guard up," Michael ordered. "Now, let's give this all we've got."

"Five .... four ... three ... two ... one ... BEGIN!"

Michael sprinted for the river. He had always been a fast runner, and he knew his team were with him. Hopefully they could get there before the others.

Emily overtook him and reached the edge of the river first. Michael looked around. The platforms were moving quickly along with the river. One went past them before Michael could jump on board.

He had to time this right. He didn't fancy falling in that river. It was at least ten metres wide, too big to jump. Luckily, the platforms were large.

He eyed the next platform, and took a run up.

He hesitated, and it passed him. Emily, however, had no such qualms. She didn't even run up, springing onto the platform and landing nimbly on her feet.

Michael needed to get the next one.

It came closer. Ten metres. Five metres.

He ran forward and leapt, controlling his jump.

He landed, tumbling forward and rolling towards the edge of the platform. He twisted, throwing himself away, and eventually steadying himself in the centre.

The platform seemed to be moving faster when he was on it.

He clambered to his feet, keeping his balance. He looked behind him. His platform was moving around the river, and was now nearing the Dutch team.

He took a breath, and then dived onto the island, scrambling to his feet.

Emily sprinting towards a disc. Michael could see another disc nearby, and he advanced towards it.

Canadians, Australians and Americans had now arrived. For now, they were avoiding each other as they attempted to get the unclaimed discs.

Michael hurried over to the disc, but heard a loud yelp from his right.

Emily had grabbed the disc, but a large American boy was grabbing the collar of her shirt. The boy was ignoring the disc. He was tall, muscular, and had a goatee of facial hair. Michael recognised him as Gideon, the American team leader.

Michael had a decision to make. Get the disc, or help his teammate.

He didn't hesitate.

Michael ran towards Emily, tackling Gideon to the ground. He let go of her, and Michael scrambled up, keen to get away and avoid a fight.

"Not so fast, Leonidas," Gideon seethed, leaping to his feet. "You run, and I hunt you down."

Michael turned and faced him, light on his feet. He didn't say anything, trying to stay concentrated. Hopefully, he was buying time for his team to get disks.

"You know, I've trained for this my whole life," Gideon snarled. "I will destroy you."

Michael smirked slightly. He kept quiet still, hoping that would annoy Gideon.

It did. Gideon lashed out, a lightning-fast attack. Michael instinctively leapt back.

Gideon laughed. "Scared?" he sneered.

Michael feigned a lunge forward then turned and sprinted away, back towards the Dutch team.

He could hear Gideon behind him. He saw a figure rushing towards him from the front, and stepped out of the way.

The figure thundered into Gideon, spearing into him and knocking him to the ground. It was Arjen.

Arjen smashed his elbow into Gideon's chest. "Let me have this one!" the Dutch leader commanded. Michael acquiesced, ran back to the discs. He could one see one left.

Unfortunately, there was an Australian girl also eyeing the disc.

They looked at each other for a split second before they both raced towards it, trying to get to it first. Michael dived for it, closing his fingers around the circular object.

THUD. Pain shot through the top of his head, making him bite down on his tongue.

She had kicked his head!? Michael lurched towards the Australian girl's legs, knocking her to the ground.

He recoiled as she swung a fist towards his head. She was quick.

Michael scrambled back to his feet. Instinct took over. He had a disc. He had to get out of there.

He turned and ran once again, pelting towards the nearest platform. There was just one problem.

There was someone already on it.

72 - HIGH-DISC STRATEGY

On the platform stood a tall, lanky Canadian boy. He was deliberately blocking Michael's way of returning the disc to his team, in the hope of taking the disc for the Canadian team.

Air rushed passed his ears as Michael ran, keeping pace with the current of the river and staying alongside the platform.

He was being chased by the Australian girl. He needed to get on the platform, get round the Canadian and make it back to the Institute's rack of discs.

He needed help.

His fitness was good, so he hadn't yet broken a sweat. Michael ran quickly, although he suspected that she would catch him eventually.

The Canadian on the platform waited, knowing he had the advantage. Behind him, Michael could see the maple leaf flag of Canada.

That was good. It meant if he kept following the platform round, the next rack he would pass would be his own.

Michael's breath was heavy as he ran. He glanced back over his shoulder. Now there were two Australians chasing him.

It made sense. With only fifteen discs and five teams, there would be numerous recruits going for the same discs.

Michael accelerated. The Institute flag was getting nearer. He needed to take his opportunity.

He saw a grey clothed teammate running on the grass outside, towards the platform. Michael took his chance and leapt, from the island onto the platform.

The Canadian boy grinned, thinking he could snatch the disc from Michael. Suddenly, the platform rocked. The Canadian swung around.

Raymon Collins had jumped onto the platform. As Michael landed, Raymon calmly swung a punch to the Canadian's head, sending him crashing into the water.

Michael steadied himself. The Canadian wasn't moving.

"Cheers," he told Raymon, then leapt back onto the grass, jogging back towards their flag.

Thomas nodded at him and Michael passed them and placed the disc in the rack. Emily's disc was already on there, so now they had two.

He looked up, hoping get a third. Out of his small team, Emily was here, but Nadia, Paul and Dominic must still be out there. Henry, Jürgen and Dan were wrestling with some Canadians near their base.

Steve, being on the defensive team, looked at Michael. "How're we doing?" he asked Michael.

"Okay, for now. We'll need to raid the discs from another team." Michael stated.

"Is that Nadia?" Steve called, pointing to the island.

Michael looked up. Nadia was surrounded by three Americans, as she held a disc in her hand. Raymon was charging over.

Nadia stayed light on her feet, daring one of them to attack.

Michael began running, wanting to help.

But it was unnecessary. As one recruit lunged for Nadia, she sidestepped, using the recruit's momentum to throw him over.

Raymon threw a punch at one American, who ducked. The American launched a kick at Raymon, but Raymon caught his leg, and threw him to the ground like a ragdoll.

Michael was surprised by Raymon's strength.

The last American was female, with blond hair tied back in a ponytail. She calmly circled Nadia, unperturbed by her fallen teammates.

As the first American got up, Raymon kicked him back onto the ground.

Nadia, no longer surrounded, turned and ran. The American girl lunged after her, but Raymon blocked her path. Nadia leapt onto the platform and ran back towards the flags.

Michael smiled as Nadia reached him. They now had three discs.

He looked at the clock. They were eighteen minutes in, almost halfway.

"Get everyone in!" he ordered, wanting to regroup.

Every ten minutes, he knew the direction of the current would reverse. He wanted to use that to his advantage.

By now, he guessed most of the discs were in various teams' racks. To take them would need a lot of people.

"Emily, can you scout around?" Michael asked her. "I need to find out how many discs the other teams have. They should ignore you as long as you don't threaten them."

She frowned. "Just me?"

Michael put a hand on her shoulder. "You can do this," he told her. "And if you see anyone from our team, send them back here."

Emily sighed, then turned and jogged off. Michael hoped she wasn't injured.

"What's your plan, Michael?" Steve questioned.

Something had caught Michael's attention. "What are the Americans doing?"

There were about ten red-shirted opponents in a pack, going towards the Australian flag. However, the American flag seemed unprotected.

"They've abandoned their flag!" Steve exclaimed. "We have to attack!"

"No," Michael said. "We wait. We need to hear from Emily before we make a move."

"There isn't time for waiting. We have to act, now!" Steve urged.

"Steve," Michael said firmly. "Why would the Americans leave a rack full of discs unattended? Either the rack is empty, or it's a trap."

Steve went quiet. "Good point."

"And if we did make a run for it, the Dutch would get there first, being closer. If we leave our rack unattended the Canadians will not hesitate will to strike," Michael remarked.

Steve sighed, holding his hands up. "Okay, okay, I get it!"

Michael waited, as Raymon came back, along with Sophie, Jürgen, Henry and Dan. Emily was last to arrive, panting. "The Dutch have two discs. The Americans have four. They're going around in a pack, keeping the discs on them instead of putting them on the rack. The Australians have three which the Americans are trying to take. And the Canadians have three, but they're keeping to themselves."

Michael acknowledged her. "Thank you, Emily. Our right flank is secure. The Dutch are our allies, and Arjen hates the Americans. They will go for them," he told them.

"So what do we do?" Elizabeth asked.

"We either attack the Canadians, or bypass them and try to take what we can from the Australians and Americans," Michael told them.

"Or do both," Arthur said quietly.

Michael looked at him. "How?"

"We could send in our quickest people to snatch a disc from the Americans or Australians, whilst keeping most people around here to pressure the Canadians, as they're nearest us," Arthur suggested.

Michael nodded. "Okay. Thomas, Nadia, me and Elizabeth will attack. The rest of you, try to take the Canadian's discs, but keep an eye out for the Dutch in case they betray us."

They nodded.

"If anything goes wrong, just focus on protecting what discs we have," Michael told them.

He gave a slight smile. 'It's just like Capture the Flag,' he thought.

"Now, let's go!" he ordered.

He jogged towards the platforms. One of them had just past, but Michael glanced at the clock.

The digital timer reached twenty minutes, and the platforms slowed down as the current direction reversed.

"Everyone on, quick!" Michael ordered, taking advantage of the slow moving platforms. He leapt on, Nadia following him, then Elizabeth. As the platform began to pick up speed, Thomas mistimed his jump, but Michael caught his shirt and pulled him on.

They passed the Canadian base without any incident. Emily was right, they were playing it defensively.

They circled round, getting closer to the Australian flag. "Okay, Nadia, get off now, try to sneak around them. Us three will distract them by running directly at them," Michael told her.

Nadia nodded, leaping from the platform and landing on the grass with a roll.

Michael waited; they got closer to the flag. "Now!" he shouted, leaping off. Elizabeth and Thomas followed, and they all ran for their rack.

The Australians had created a human shield around the rack, and were trying to hold off the Americans.

Michael saw Gideon punch an Australian girl, knocking her to the ground, her face covered in blood.

Michael raced for the rack, and a few Australians noticed him and faced towards him. A boy got ready to tackle Michael in case he got close, and Michael sidestepped him.

However, another Australian took Michael to the ground. They wrestled, but the boy pinned him down with his elbow.

Michael struggled, but the Australian was on top. He glimpsed Nadia sneaking towards the rack and inwardly smiled. Their ploy had worked.

A shout went up as Nadia snatched the disc from the rack and began pelting back towards the platform.

The boy on top of Michael elbowed him in the gut then got off, sprinting after Nadia. Michael was winded. He lay there for a few seconds, catching his breath, before clambering to his feet. Nadia was running away, with three Australians pursuing her.

Michael saw Gideon circle around the Australian defence and charge for the rack. He bounced one Australian over, and then snatched a disc for himself.

A few Australians went for him, and the whole line descended into chaos. Michael saw his chance, lunging and grabbing the last disc from the rack.

As his fingers curled around the cold metal, he noticed something which made his heart sink.

Elizabeth was lying on the floor, her face covered in blood. She was in no fit state to move. Michael turned and ran, looking around for Thomas.

Thomas was hovering away from the fight, looking for an opening. Nadia was at the water's edge, having been caught by the Australians. Michael hoped she got away.

"Thomas, get Elizabeth out of there! We've got enough discs!" he shouted as he ran.

An American and an Australian who had been circling each other took off after Michael.

Michael sprinted, not going for the platforms but running the long way around. The American flag was unprotected and empty, so he could get past that.

However, to get to his flag, he needed to get past the Dutch team, running right past their flag. Would their alliance hold?

Michael felt someone catching up to him. They were fast, but luckily he had a lead.

As he ran past the American flag, he noticed a few Dutch people standing and guarding the rack. They must be waiting for any successful Americans to return so they could rob them of a disc.

Michael ran, approaching the Dutch team. His heart pounded in his chest. His legs were burning at the fatigue, but he carried on.

He noticed Arjen standing with the Dutch team, dried blood on his face.

He raced forward, and noticed some of the Dutch move towards him.

Come on, Arjen, stick to the alliance.

Arjen shouted something in Dutch, and his squad began running towards Michael.

Damn.

They were coming for him. They had the advantage. He couldn't outpace them all.

Michael increased his speed, veering away from them, waiting to be brought down by the Dutch team...

But it never came.

A large Dutch boy ran past Michael and took down his pursuers. Michael grinned in relief.

"Cheers!" he shouted to Arjen, and the boy nodded.

He had stuck to his word.

Michael reached his squad, and Steve cheered. "You made it!" he exclaimed. "Thought you'd get clobbered!"

"Is Nadia back?" Michael asked, looking around as he placed the disc on the rack, turning the blue disc to grey, the colour of the Institute.

"No. She got caught by the Australians; they took her disc and left her. Except for the Americans, four discs are more than any other team at the moment!" Steve said. "If we hold onto this, we'll be finishing second."

Michael smiled. "Assuming the Americans get another one," he remarked.

"Well, I imagine they will. The Australians went for Nadia as she stole a disc, and their defence fell apart. It seemed to descend into individual fighting," Steve said.

"You've been watching a lot," Michael commented.

"Well, it's all quiet on the western front here, the Canadians haven't got close. Raymon led a charge for their rack, and tore two of their best fighters to pieces. He's freakishly strong, it's like he's been injected with the Russian stuff," Steve laughed.

"Did he take any?"

"No, Canadians have put all fifteen people around their rack," Steve informed him. "Still, I think we've done pretty well."

Michael grinned. "Yeah, we have," he agreed, walking towards the platforms. He could see Thomas carrying Elizabeth on a platform. "Just hold the fort."

"Where are you going?" Steve asked.

"I'm seeing if Elizabeth's alright, and then checking up on Nadia," Michael told him.

"Ay, you sure that's all?" Steve teased, winking at him.

Michael rolled his eyes and shook his head, then hurried over, back towards the river.

* * *

Ten minutes later, the round ended. Little happened for the Institute team and they finished the round with four discs. The Canadians finished with three, the Dutch with two and the Americans with five. The Australians only finished with one.

Michael was at the Institute flag, having found Nadia lying on the ground, beaten, and brought her back. She seemed alright, having been bruised but not badly hurt. Thomas had brought Elizabeth back, and had found she had a cut on her cheek. Dominic, a member of Michael's squad who he didn't know very well, had showed up, telling them he had fallen in the river.

As a loud honk blared, everyone breathed a sigh of relief. The round had been a tough test for their nerves.

Michael grinned, looking around. Steve shrugged.

"Not bad, Leonidas," he commented casually, giving him a light punch on the shoulder.

"Well done, Michael," Elizabeth said. "You got us that last disc."

"Not alone," he reminded them, flustered at the attention. "I wouldn't have been able to get it without Nadia."

"Vell done, Michael," Jürgen told him, patting him on the arm.

Michael was saved from the embarrassment by the speakers sounding.

"The round is over! Now, let's get the scores. The winning team is ... The United States of America!" the speaker roared, the crowd cheering. After about a minute of cheers, the speaker continued in a monotone.

"Second place is Occupied Britain, third is Canada, fourth is the Netherlands and fifth is Australia," he stated.

Michael looked at the screen, as a large table was formed.

PLACE - TEAM - POINTS

1 - USA - 10 points

2 - Occupied Britain - 5 points

3 - Canada - 3 points

4 - The Netherlands - 2 points

5 - Australia - 1 point

Why was the United States so far ahead? They had only won one more disc!

Michael frowned, remembering Sebastien Grey's words:

'You can't beat the game.'

Michael was slightly indignant, but was grateful to be second, with his team mostly in one piece.

'Now, the next round will commence tomorrow, so the recruits have time to rest. No details can be given to the recruits at this time, but, it will push them to their mental limits,' the speaker announced. *'The recruits will now return to their residence. The first round of the Coliseum ... has been completed.'*

73 - CHALLENGED

"Leonidas, can we speak to you?"

"Leonidas, how do you feel?"

"Leonidas!"

Michael smiled as he walked through a corridor, news crews taking photos of him. After the round had finished, the squad members were taken back inside, whilst the team leaders were taken to speak in a 'news conference'. Before the first task, only one news station had interviewed him, and now there were many.

"Leonidas are you happy with this result?" a man asked, holding a microphone towards him.

"I'm proud of my team," Michael replied. "It's a good start to the Coliseum."

"The Institute has never finished second in any round before. What has changed this year?" a woman asked him.

"I think this year we've realised the places aren't set in stone. We've got a great team, and there's nothing stopping us from doing as well as we can," Michael told her as he was led into a large room. There were several reporters and cameras facing five seats behind a stand. Arjen was on the far right, and Gideon was in the centre.

"Go up there," a soldier told Michael.

Michael felt a pit of nerves open in his stomach. He had to speak in front of everyone?

He walked up slowly, the world in eerie focus. There were rows of seats of reporters in front of him. He could see his reflection in the black glass of a camera. A bald man sat on the front row, wiping his glasses.

Further back, there was a woman with a ponytail. She was looking intently at Michael. Their eyes met, and he recognised her.

It was Amanda Coleman, the reporter working for the Social Revolutionaries. What was she doing here? He hadn't seen her since running away from her about a week ago.

Michael was astonished the military hadn't caught her, then realised they probably weren't sure who she was. She was probably just here to report on the Coliseum.

Even if she had tried to get him to betray the military, it was nice to see a familiar face.

Michael went and sat in the seat beside Arjen, where a golden nameplate read 'MICHAEL BAKERSON'.

Arjen nodded at him. "Well done, Leonidas. You're better than I imagined," he commented.

Michael shrugged. "I think I was a bit lucky," he admitted.

"Don't tell them that," Arjen advised, motioning his head towards the reporters. "Any show of weakness, they'll rip you to shreds."

Michael nodded. "Thanks. And thanks for sticking to our alliance," he told Arjen.

"If a man has no honour, he has nothing," Arjen stated.

Michael laughed. "I wish everyone thought like you."

Arjen smiled slightly. "So do I."

Michael glanced to his left. Gideon, the American leader, was there, ignoring them both. Michael felt slightly intimidated by the larger boy, but was glad to be next to Arjen.

The Australian team leader, a long haired wild-eyed boy, sat next to Gideon. Last to arrive was the Canadian leader, a tall, dark haired girl.

Lieutenant Nicholls was standing at the side. He nodded to the press, and they began asking questions.

The first was addressed to the American leader.

"Gideon, you went for an unusual tactic of waiting until the end before claiming any discs. What prompted this ingenious strategy?" a journalist asked.

Gideon smiled slightly. "Well, I listened to the rules at the start, and nothing forbade it. I thought, why risk spreading out our forces when we can stay as a pack and protect each other? I just went for the most logical option, and it worked," he said cockily.

"Arjen, you seem to hold your team back from taking a disc from Leonidas. Was there an alliance agreed beforehand?" a man asked Arjen.

Arjen glanced at Michael then looked at the reporter. "I make strategic decisions for reason of my own. I felt Michael had earned that disc, and it would be dishonourable for us to take it from him," he stated calmly.

Michael noticed he had not answered the question, and was glad, as he had no desire to be accused of cheating.

"Leonidas?" It was Amanda Coleman with her hand up.

"Yes?"

"Do you feel that the unexpected results of this round marks a change outside the Coliseum?" she asked boldly.

There was some muttering among the reporters, and they waited for Michael's answer.

"I do," Michael said. Arjen raised an eyebrow. There was whispering.

"Can you clarify?" a reporter asked.

Michael glanced to his left. Lieutenant Nicholls looking intently at Michael.

He had to be careful; he didn't want to be seen as incendiary.

"Well, up until now, there hasn't been a team of recruits that have fought on the frontlines before. We have. We were real soldiers before we came here, unlike the rest of the squads. I'm no politician, I don't know how it affects anything or what it means, but this Coliseum has the potential to surprise a lot of people," Michael stated.

Lieutenant Nicholls seemed satisfied. Michael was relieved. He didn't want to undermine anyone, but at the same time wanted to make an impression.

Amanda Coleman smiled slightly, as another reporter posed a question to the Australian leader.

It continued for a while. Question. Answer. Question. Answer.

Michael lost track of time, but after what must have been half an hour, the news conference ended.

The five team leaders stood up, and were escorted out of the room.

"Get some food, get some sleep, and get ready for tomorrow," Nicholls told them. "And please don't fight. We don't need any more complications."

They were all escorted to residence for the recruits.

"Institute is floor 5," a guard said, and Michael stepped in the elevator. Arjen joined him.

"Well, I think you made an impact," Arjen remarked.

Michael smiled slightly. "Cheers. I kind of owe you after that," he admitted.

Arjen shook his head. "No, you don't. You would have done the same for me."

Michael smiled slightly, but deep down he wasn't sure if he would have.

"Leonidas? This is your floor," Arjen told him.

Michael smiled. "Thanks. And, er, our alliance stands for the next round, right?" he asked Arjen.

Arjen gave a pained smile. "Provided I am still leader. I imagine some of my teammates will question my actions," he stated, as the elevator closed.

Michael's eyes widened. He would feel awful if Arjen lost his leadership because he had helped them.

Michael took a deep breath then began making his way to the communal room. He passed wall paintings of various historical battles Americans had fought in.

When he got outside the room, he hesitated, listening.

"Michael did well, yes, but that was luck! We all know I'd be a better leader!"

Michael knew it was Raymon speaking.

"Are you saying you would have beaten the American team?" someone remarked sceptically. It sounded like Sophie.

"Yes!"

"Vhat vould you have one differently?" Jürgen challenged.

"That doesn't matter now. I need your support for when Michael comes back!" Raymon urged.

"You feel threatened by him, don't you?"

"Shut up, of course I don't!"

"Nadia's right. You don't want him getting recognised for the team's successes."

Was that Thomas speaking?

Michael pushed the door open.

Raymon was standing in the middle, with everyone else sitting on sofas around.

They all looked around to face Michael.

Raymon scowled, balling his fists. He flexed his neck, then folded his arms.

"Michael, I challenge you to a fight. The winner gets to lead this team," Raymon announced.

74 -   SECOND CHALLENGE

After Raymon's bold proclamation, there was silence.

"No." Michael was calm and spoke clearly.

"What?" Raymon barked.

"You're not challenging my leadership," Michael said clearly.

"Yes, I am. I should have always been the leader," Raymon stated, narrowing his eyes.

"Raymon, no one wants you to lead. Give me one reason why you should, other than your father wants you to," Michael replied coolly.

"I'm a stronger fighter," Raymon stated.

Michael's fists clenched almost imperceptibly, then he relaxed. He looked up at Nadia.

She gave him a small smile, rolling her eyes.

Michael returned it, then looked at Raymon. "Listen, Raymon. We've come second in a task. We've got one tomorrow. You should be using your time to rest and recover, not try to break down the team," he stated.

"You don't get it, do you?" Raymon growled. "We're gonna fight, and the winner leads the team."

Michael ground his teeth in annoyance, fed up of Raymon. There might have been a time when he would have tried to compromise, but he wasn't in the mood at the moment.

"I don't think you get what *I'm* saying. I'm saying no. We will not fight. Yes, you're the strongest fighter in our squad. But it doesn't make you the best leader. Raymon, I was chosen to lead us by the instructors. I'm not going against that. If we do well, I'll make sure you get credit. If we don't, then it's just the same as the Institute has always done," Michael appealed, looking directly at him.

Raymon didn't say anything, so Michael continued.

"I know you want to make your father proud. So do I. Being leader is not about fame, or glory. I don't want the interviews, or the press conferences. I just want our team to do the best we can. And that means we have to stay united. I'm not having feuds cause a rift in the team," he said.

Raymon remained silent. "Alright. I'll give you another chance, *Leonidas*. But if you mess up this next task, it'll be a different story," he warned Michael, and then walked out.

"I'll ... get some rest too," Henry muttered, before following Raymon out.

Once they had left, the room broke into chatter.

"Michael, I'm impressed," Steve remarked. There was a broad grin on his face. "I could never keep my temper with that jerk for as long as you did."

"Yeah, he's been looking to take over for a while now," Michael informed Steve.

"You dealt vith him excellently," Jürgen commented with a nod. "Although it means there is a lot more pressure on doing vell in this task."

Michael sighed. "Yeah, I realise that," he said. "But, for now, I'm hungry. Let's deal with the second task when we get to it."

"Let's hope we survive it," Steve muttered.

Michael laughed. Steve had a tendency to be over-dramatic.

Michael was relieved the first task had gone well, though was worried about the second. Was there anything he could do before the next task?

"Sophie," Michael said.

Sophie was laughing at something Thomas had said. She made no reply.

Michael walked over to them. "Sophie," he repeated.

She turned and smiled sweetly at him. "Yes?"

"You made friends with the Dutch team, right?" he asked her.

Sophie nodded slowly. "I did."

"There's something I need you to do. It's possible the Arjen might no longer be leader of his team after this task. If that happens, we need to try to keep them as allies," Michael stated.

"Why?" Thomas asked. "Surely, it would be an excellent opportunity to make an alliance with a decent team, like the Canadians."

Michael glanced at him. He had a point. The other teams might expect cooperation between the Dutch and Occupied Britain, but it would surprise them if they allied with the Canadians.

"No," he decided. "If we ally with the Canadians, they'll betray us. For them, it's a golden opportunity to get second place, now that the Australians have fallen down." Thomas nodded.

Sophie smiled. "So what do you want me to do?"

"I'll leave it up to you how you get your information, but I'll need to know before the second task whether the Dutch are our allies or not," Michael told her.

Sophie smirked. "And what do I get in return?" she teased.

"A sense of achievement?" Michael suggested, raising an eyebrow.

Sophie laughed. "Alright then, Michael, I'll do this one for you," she said, winking at him before slipping out of the room.

Michael glanced after her, before noticing Thomas was looking at him.

"You're good at making friends, aren't you?" Thomas mused.

"I guess so? I mean, I just try to be friendly," Michael admitted.

"Of course you are. But you're the leader; you shouldn't pander to people's wishes. You don't have to be nice to people to get them to follow you. It's better to be respected than liked," Thomas advised.

Michael cocked his head to one side. Thomas had a point.

"Maybe I can be both," Michael remarked. "Come on. We've got a big task tomorrow. I'm getting some food."

* * *

"WELCOME TO THE SECOND TASK OF THE COLISEUM!" a deep voice boomed.

Where was he? The last thing he remembered was going to bed the night before.

Michael's eyes snapped open. A mixture of green of brown hit him. He was in a forest, with tall, bushy trees around.

He could see the sunrise in the distance, and early morning light shone through the trees.

The flowing of a river could be heard faintly, but it was quiet, eerily quiet.

There was no one else in sight.

"You have been placed in a simulation." The sound reverberated around; Michael couldn't tell where it was coming from. *"Your task is to make it to the clearing in the centre of the forest. This will test individual squad members' resourcefulness, intelligence and logic."*

Michael scanned around. He couldn't see any clearing.

"This simulation is a replica of the forest immediately to the north of the simulation building. Once the simulation is over, you will wake up there," the voice spoke. *"Remember, recruits, your objective is to find the clearing, and reach it."*

Michael frowned. This wasn't what he had expected at all. Why would a simulation be a test of their resourcefulness?

He set off, heading for the sound of the river. Hopefully, he could meet someone else there.

He jogged forward, remembering the practise simulation in training, which seemed so long ago now. There would be distractions, but he had to focus on the task at hand.

First things first. Where was the clearing?

The rushing of the water became louder, and Michael soon found himself overlooking a fast-flowing, wide river. He could probably swim across, but there wasn't any need.

Or was there?

He looked across, and his eyes widened. On the other side, after a few small trees, was a large, open clearing. The grass was much greener there, and air in front of it seemed to shimmer.

Well, that simplified his objective: he had to cross the river.

He looked to either side. There wasn't anyone in sight. That could mean that everyone was in their own simulation, or that he was the first to arrive.

Michael looked at the water, and tentatively dipped a hand in. It was warm.

Too warm for this time of year.

It was a simulation, but why would the makers of the simulation make it so easy for any competent swimmer to get across?

No. This task was about resourcefulness.

He picked up a stone from near the river, and tossed it in. There was a loud 'plop' sound, signifying it must be deep.

Michael remembered the river in his own village, the one that he had swum in as a child. Once, he had fallen in while trying to jump across. His father had scolded him, warning him that rivers were treacherous. The narrowest parts were the fastest-flowing.

This river, though, was different. It was wide the whole way across, and smooth. There weren't any rocks that he could step on.

He looked around. There was a large tree to his right, with a branch that leaned over the river. It seemed quite sturdy, but not too thick. Michael jumped and grabbed hold of it.

The branch leaned under his weight, but held.

Michael let go, unsure what to do. He needed a second opinion. Did he try to swim across?

No. This wasn't a physical test.

He retreated back, away from the river, scanning around. There were a few stones and the base of trees, and a few small bushes.

Michael squatted in front of the nearest bush. The branches were thick, with long, glistening thorns sticking out all over them.

That ruled them out then.

Michael walked along the side of the river, assessing the trees. A tall, leafless tree, its branches spreading far. A thin tree with spindly branches. A small tree that looked like it was about to fall over.

That seemed perfect.

Michael rammed his body against it, hoping it would topple.

He wasn't so lucky. The tree swayed slightly, but did not move. Michael tried again, this time wrapping his arms around it and throwing his bodyweight against it.

It groaned, slowly uprooting and tipping over.

He smiled to himself. This might work.

Ten minutes later, Michael was ready to cross. The tree was on the ground, reaching to about two-thirds of the way across the river. He had taken off his trousers, and used them to tie the end of the tree to the root of a larger tree.

He had decided he would go across like he had crossed the beam in the Slog, all those months ago. He didn't was to risk standing up, and falling in.

He went to the trunk and hugged against it, straddling it with his legs. He could do this.

Gradually, he inched his way forward. He was sore, his thighs rubbing against the dry bark. After several minutes of pushing forward, he reached the end. He could feel the tree threatening to tip over.

He was still about five metres from the opposite bank.

Michael held onto the log tightly, as he pulled his feet up onto it, trying to stand up.

His heart pounded in his chest as he stood there, preparing to make the leap.

He took a breath. He could do this.

He leapt forward ungracefully, splashing into the water.

Immediately, he felt his legs suddenly burn in pain. He felt something brush past him in the water as the fast current tried to drag him away. Something was definitely wrong with this river.

He thrashed, forward, desperate to reach the other side. His hands reached wet reeds, and he pulled himself towards the bank.

Suddenly, something slimy wrapped around his ankle. It was strong, and was tugging him.

Michael gritted his teeth and didn't let go. He threw himself forward, kicking his leg and reaching dry land.

As he made it out, whatever had grabbed him retreated. He looked back, but there was nothing there, only a few ripples in the current.

Michael let out a sigh of relief as he walked forward towards the shimmering air in front of the green clearing.

He was about to reach it, when abruptly, the simulation changed completely.

75 - BACK TO REALITY

"Simulation has ended!" a soldier was saying, as Michael found himself strapped into a seat with a headset on.

"Forget about the Coliseum, we're under attack!" a wild-eyed soldier said, ripping off Michael's headset and unclicking him from the seat.

Michael looked around. He was in a dark room, illuminated only by dim emergency lights. To either side of him, his squad was all in seats, looking equally surprised.

"GET TO IT!" the soldier roared, before storming out of the room.

"Vhat is going on?" Jürgen demanded.

Michael had no idea.

"What do we do now?" Dan questioned uneasily.

"We find out where we are, and who's attacking," Michael said determinedly, standing up. "Let's go explore."

"Did anyone make it to the clearing?" Steve asked.

"I did," Michael told them. "Anyone else?"

No one else replied.

Michael opened the door, blinking a few times as they entered a brightly lit corridor.

An alarm rang out shrilly, and lights in the corridor began flashing. Soldiers ran down the corridor, weapons drawn.

"What's going on?" Michael asked, running alongside them.

"Revolutionaries," the soldier replied, as though that was a suitable explanation.

"Where's the armoury?" Raymon demanded.

The soldier pointed. "Go to the end of the corridor, turn right and follow it until you see the store room. If you've got clearance, the thumbprint scanner should work," he instructed.

Michael nodded. He glanced back and saw his squad were behind him.

Raymon started off towards the armoury, and Michael followed. The alarm was still ringing.

Arthur caught up with Michael. "Michael?" he said hurriedly.

Michael didn't slow down. "Yes?"

"Don't you think, well, it's a coincidence there's an attack whilst we're in a task?" Arthur panted.

"What do you mean?" Michael asked.

"Do you remember coming here?" Arthur asked, gesturing around, as they reached the door the armoury. "This place?"

Raymon scanned his thumbprint and a robotic voice sounded.

Unauthorised personnel - denied.

Michael frowned in annoyance.

Arthur was still talking. "What?" Michael asked him curtly.

Arthur took a breath. "The last thing I remember before the simulation was going to bed last night. I can't remember this morning."

Michael scowled. "I don't care!" he told him. "That's not our issue at the moment."

"Why won't the door open?" Raymon demanded, scowling.

"I don't know. We mustn't have clearance," Michael stated, pacing up and down.

"Michael, what if this is a task?" Arthur asked.

"No, Arthur, this is real life. The task ended when I reached the clear- "

Michael stopped his pacing. He hadn't actually reached the clearing, despite having crossed the river.

"I didn't actually reach it. I was about to get there, when the simulation ended," Michael brushed off. "But that doesn't matter. We need weapons before we can help with this attack."

"But Michael, we don't have any orders," Elizabeth said quietly.

"We can't just stay here," Michael said resolutely. He glanced away from them, his heart pounding. It seemed he had to make every decision.

Someone cleared their throat. Michael looked back to see Sophie there, along with a soldier in a standard grey uniform.

"Whilst you guys were busy debating, this soldier kindly agreed to open the door for us," she told them, smiling sweetly.

417

Michael recognised the soldier as one of the security guards from the door. He walked forward and scanned his thumbprint on the door. It swung open and Michael's squad hurried in.

"There you go, you guys. You're on our side, so make sure these revolutionaries don't get too far," the soldier said.

"Is this a simulation or something?" Michael asked him seriously, looking at the soldier.

The soldier raised his eyebrows. "I hope so, but it's the first I've heard of if it is. I'd suggest you treat it like it's real," he advised.

"Thanks," Michael replied quietly.

"No problem. Though I gotta say, these revolutionaries are a lot better armed than anything we've seen before. I'd watch out if I were you," he warned, before striding off.

Michael went into the armoury. "Let's get ready to fight," he announced.

* * *

Ten minutes later, his squad was armed with weapons and equipment. Michael had chosen an assault rifle, the same model as the ones he had fired back at the Institute.

"What's the plan?" Steve asked Michael. He was lugging a heavy machine gun stubbornly.

Michael nodded. "We don't have any orders. Let's head out, assess the situation, and try to make sure these revolutionaries don't have any success," he decided.

"So, kill as many as we can?" Raymon suggested.

"Well, try to suppress them and cause a retreat. But if necessary, yes. These aren't Russians," he told them.

"They're still the enemy," Raymon said. "But whatever."

Michael nodded. "Everyone ready?" he asked.

"Michael?" Nadia said, brushing hair out of her face. "Vhat if the task is still the same?"

Michael glanced at her. "What do you mean?"

"Vhat if we still have to reach the clearing?" Nadia suggested.

Michael felt his temper flare up in annoyance again, before recalling Sebastien Grey's words.

You cannot beat the game itself.

He swore to himself, realising what might be going on.

"They don't want us to win," Michael realised, looking around. "This is still the Coliseum. The task hasn't ended. The Americans control the games. We're second, so they'll fix it up against us. That's why we didn't have clearance for the armoury door. In fact, we were never meant to go in the armoury. We just wasted time," he said urgently.

"Michael, you're babbling." Thomas folded his arms. "Get to the point."

"The task never ended. We have no orders. We simply have to follow the last orders that were given to us," he replied. "We complete the original task."

"If this is still the Coliseum, then what's our task?" Steve scoffed. He laughed. "It's not like there's a clearing we have to get to around here."

Arthur muttered something.

"Arthur?" Michael asked him. "Got something to say?"

"In my sim, the voice told me that the clearing was north of the simulation building. I'm guessing that this building is the simulation building," Arthur explained, fidgeting.

Michael nodded. This was taking a risk. If they didn't assist the military, he could be accused of cowardice. But the Coliseum was his priority.

He looked at his squad, trying to block the prospect of what a wrong decision might mean.

"Right, we go north, to the forest, and find the clearing," Michael decided.

Raymon shook his head. "No way," he said. "I'm not running away."

"We've wasted time already, Raymon. We're completing our mission. This is about the Coliseum," Michael urged.

"For what it's worth, your logic seems sound," Thomas interjected. "I say we go to the clearing."

"In which case, Leonidas, I'm not following your orders," Raymon replied coolly, and walked outside. "I'm going down fighting."

Henry cast the group an apologetic look, then went out after Raymon.

"Anyone else?" Michael demanded, looking around.

"Ve have wasted enough time already, Michael. Let's go," Jürgen barked.

"For the Institute!" Steve mocked sarcastically, shaking his fist.

"Not the time, Steve," Michael replied, heading out of the door. "We're going to complete the task."

* * *

"Michael," Steve panted, as they jogged into the forest. "How are we going to cross the river? Last time, I tried swimming, but it was impossible, the current was too strong."

"We'll cross that bridge when we come to it," Michael told Steve, focusing on navigating his way to the clearing. Their wristwatches had an advanced compass on them, which gave them a basic map of the nearby area.

"But there isn't a bridge!" Steve exclaimed, chuckling to himself. He was quite red in the face, having insisted on bringing his heavy machine gun.

"Wha- oh. Very funny, Steve," Michael replied dryly.

Soon, they reached the river. Hopefully, he could cross it with a similar tactic to last time, by using a fallen tree.

However, as they neared the river, a sinking feeling formed in his gut. There were no small trees by the river he could knock over. In fact, the only tree that seemed capable of reaching to the other side was huge, firmly rooted into the ground.

Real life was different to the simulation.

Michael stopped dejectedly, trying to think of ways to cross.

Thomas went over to him. "You alright, Michael? This was your idea, to come here. I'm sure I can think of a way to cross this," he said, clapping Michael on the shoulder.

"I'm all ears," Michael replied, half-glancing back at Thomas.

"Thank you. Jürgen, do you still have those explosives from the armoury?" Thomas asked.

"Ja," Jürgen replied, raising an eyebrow as he unhooked a wad of C4 from his belt. "You're not suggesting ve ..."

"Precisely. Just like Norway, eh?" Thomas said, striding over and looking at Jürgen. "Plant the explosives at the base of the tree, all around it. After that, we detonate a concussive grenade on our side to make sure the tree falls towards the river."

"We'll be using a lot of explosives," Michael remarked.

"I don't suppose you have a better idea?" Thomas replied, glancing at Michael. His tone was jovial, but Michael thought he sensed a hint of aggression.

"It's the best we've got," Michael acknowledged.

"Leave us to it, then. Sophie, help me set it up," Thomas said briskly, whilst Michael watched silently.

Soon, Thomas was ready. It hadn't been very long, but it had felt like forever as Michael waited, ever conscious of time ticking steadily onwards. His only comfort was in the fact that maybe the other teams hadn't worked out that completing the task meant coming to the clearing, but this was undermined by the sickening thought that he was wrong.

"Stand back, everyone. Emily, are you ready?" Thomas asked. "Jürgen, detonate as soon as Emily has armed her grenade."

Michael backed away a few steps, watching.

"Three ... two .... one ... go!" Thomas ordered. Emily pressed the button on her concussive grenade, triggering the countdown before it would explode.

Jürgen pressed a button on his belt, detonating the explosives that surrounded the tree. The blast ripped the earth upwards, sending dirt flying in all directions. The tree wavered dangerously.

Emily, meanwhile rolled the concussive grenade towards the tree. It stopped, and the group waited for one agonisingly long second before it too exploded, the force of it knocking the tree over. The tree fell, slowly at first, then gathered speed and thudded into the ground across the river, bouncing slightly as its branches snapped.

Michael watched, stunned for a second, then realised he was meant to be in charge. "Right, over we go," he told his team.

"Just like the Slog, eh, Michael?" Steve reminded him with a grin. "Only there, you got to crawl along the beam right behind Alexandra, giving you the perfect view of her –"

"Shut up, Steve," Michael snapped, his face reddening as he clambered onto the fallen tree, going over first.

He went forward with a mechanical fury, not looking to see how far he had left but repeating the same technique again and again, gripping with his legs and pulling himself forward with his arms.

When he reached the end, there was no relief. He walked forward, towards the clearing, and what he saw made his heart sink.

Fifteen Canadian squad members, ten Americans, and three Australians were already there in the clearing, waiting.

Michael noticed Gideon, the American leader, smirk, as he said something to one of his squad mates.

One by one, Michael's teammates from the Institute joined him. He didn't look at anyone else, but kept his eyes firmly focused on a small black box in the middle of the clearing.

A speaker crackled into life. "Now that everyone who was on their way is here, that task is over! Teams will be scored based on how many members reached the clearing, the time they took to get there, and how well they responded to the threat of the attempted revolution," it said.

The message sunk in. Michael had been right; they were supposed to be at the clearing. The other teams had just worked it out more quickly.

"Just to clarify, the revolution was purely staged, and there has been no threat to any recruit's life during this task. The scores will be counted up shortly. Meanwhile, the recruits will be escorted back to their barracks, where they will have a final meeting with their instructors before the third task," the speaker sounded. "Good luck, recruits."

"Michael Bakerson!" Sergeant Raines announced. "Congratulations!"

Michael couldn't help but smile. His squad had been taken to a room where they were reunited with their instructors from the Institute, for the first time since before the Coliseum. This was in order to prepare for the final task, which was as yet unknown.

Sergeant Raines, Sergeant Wallace and Lieutenant Jones were in a meeting room, sitting at the end of a long table.

"Thank you, sir," Michael said, nodding to his instructor.

"Alright, sit down!" Lieutenant Jones said, waving a hand. "All of you. Now, first off, you've done okay. First task, you came second, which is decent. This reflects well on my training, so well done. Now this task you've just had, not so much. It's hard to see how they'll score you, but you will certainly not be winning."

Michael already knew this, but the confirmation made him look down.

"Now, I do have some very important advice, but I'll let Sergeant Wallace and Sergeant Raines speak to you first," Jones said, gesturing to them, before taking a sip from his coffee.

Sergeant Wallace cleared his throat. "Sergeant Vellon would be here, but he's busy with his Prometheus case," he told them.

"Any news on Joe?" Michael asked him.

Sergeant Wallace sighed. "Some ... transmissions 'ave been found that have been attributed to him. They're bringing some technicians in from the Institute to verify," he told them.

"Is he getting a trial?" Michael asked.

"I don't know," Wallace said. "But, he ain't your concern right now. You deal with the final task, and let Sergeant Vellon handle Joe."

"Yeah, get back on topic, Private," Jones told Wallace. "No one cares about the kid who got caught betraying the Institute."

"With respect, Lieutenant, it's Sergeant Wallace, not Private. And, as Prometheus may have led to the deaths of both my regiment and many recruits that could have

424

been here, I'd say it is bloody important," Sergeant Wallace retorted, as he glared at Jones.

Jones rolled his eyes. "Raines, you speak. I bet you've got some decent advice," he remarked. "And Wallace, don't address me like that again."

Michael shifted awkwardly.

"Lads," Raines said seriously. "Ye've done good so far, and ye've got a chance here, but the final task is always the toughest. We don't know what it is, but Sergeant Albrecht suggested it will be something to do with technology, as they haven't had one like that so far. He said to make sure the equipment is configured to what you're used to, as they like toying with the settings. Expect something you've not seen before, and remember, everything will have some sort of weakness, some sort of power supply. Only use what yer comfortable with. The most important thing for yous, is that ye stay united as a team. Collins, Blake, I don't want you wandering off again. That could have cost us."

Henry nodded slightly, but Raymon didn't say anything.

"Make sure you figure out what they want ye to do early, but keep yer minds open. They like making recruits squirm, throwing in new obstacles in the middle of a round, anything to test ye," Raines explained, then looked back to Jones.

Jones carried on drinking his coffee, nodding, before realising Raines was looking at him.

"Oh, yeah, Raines is right, he's covered it all pretty much," Jones agreed. "One more thing though, Bakerson, are you capable of leading? I've heard reports of division within the team. Can you handle it?"

He looked over towards Michael. Michael's heart pounded. There would be less pressure on him if someone else led. It would mean he wouldn't be blamed for defeat.

But there was something driving him. Admitting he couldn't handle it would mean he lost the respect of his peers. He had to do this for himself. He was capable. He had proved himself, and could do it again. If he stepped down and they didn't win, he would always be thinking 'What if...'.

"Yes," Michael said firmly. "I can."

Jones nodded. "I'm glad. Well, team, you've done better than I expected, and hopefully, if you do well enough in the last task, you might even scrape third place."

Michael looked down. He could do better than third, surely.

"Now, your sponsors will be having a chat with you, so go along to them, they're in a room upstairs," Jones said, waving a hand. "Dismissed."

The recruits stood up, and Michael looked towards Wallace, who caught his eye and mouthed 'LATER'.

Michael nodded, standing up.

"Sir?" a voice said. Michael glanced over, to see it was Steve.

Jones glanced up. "Yeah?"

"I don't have a sponsor," Steve stated, looking determinedly at Jones.

Jones shrugged. "Get one then? Listen, Green, I don't care what you do, as long as we don't mess up the task. Now go."

Michael exited the room with Steve, wanting to help him, but not sure what to do.

"Michael!" Dan's loud voice called him. "You ready to see the Sheikh?"

"Er, yeah, sure Dan," Michael said, casting an apologetic look to Steve.

"See you?" he said uncertainly.

"Yeah, sure," Steve replied, giving a small smile. "Go on."

Michael felt guilty, but went over to Dan.

"I wonder if the Sheikh has lost weight," Dan mused.

"I wouldn't ask him that," Michael advised.

Dan laughed. "Yeah, he might eat me," he commented.

"Or he might simply cut your sponsorship and have his bodyguards beat you up," Michael remarked.

"Michael, has anyone ever told you what a barrel of laughs you are?" Dan said, raising an eyebrow.

426

Michael let out a dry laugh. "I suppose I'm not particularly in the best mood," he admitted.

Dan shrugged. "Well, it might help with your mood if you relax a bit," he suggested as they entered a large room with several different sections, one for each sponsor.

"Here's ours," Dan said, indicating to a sign that read: 'SHEIKH BAGIR'.

"They spelt his name wrong?" Michael questioned.

"Yeah, must be a mistake," Dan brushed off. Michael suspected it was intentional, seeing as Sheikh Bakir was seen as a joke amongst the other sponsors.

They entered the area, and Michael was unsurprised to see the Sheikh sitting on a large golden couch, with his two burly bodyguards standing either side of him. Sat on a chair in front of the Sheikh, was a girl with pale skin and dark curly hair.

"Mike-al! Dan!" the Sheikh boomed. "Sit down! Cath-er-ine, you may leave."

The girl stood up, and Michael saw she was wearing white leggings and a pale blue t-shirt.

She smiled when she saw the pair and walked past them. Michael could have sworn she winked at him.

"Wh-who was that?" Michael asked the Sheikh, sitting where she had been.

"That was Cath-er-ine, a Canadian recruit that has decided to be sponsored by me," the Sheikh said very slowly, treating each syllable as if it were a word on its own. "Is that not wonderful? She defected from Ellen Payne."

"I wonder what caused that," Dan wondered.

"Me, of course!" the Sheikh exclaimed, and then beamed at the pair. "And you two have done well. Sales of cars from Bakir Motors have gone up since the first task, which is ex-cell-ent..."

The Sheikh trailed off, and then looked back up, his chins wobbling. "Now, you must be memorable this last task. Especially you, Leonidas," he stressed. "You have been good, but there is room for im-prove-ment."

Michael nodded.

"You must try to mention me, of course, if you have the opportunity to, and try to win the games," the Sheikh told him.

Michael looked up. "Sir ... we can't win the games ... the Institute has never won the games. We've never came higher than third," he protested, feeling himself go pale.

The Sheikh recoiled his head slightly, and then shook it, raising his eyebrows. "But you must. This is why you receive the food for your village. You have to make a name for yourself here, and so you do that by being the leader of the winning team, or by pulling off something spec-ta-cu-lar..," Sheikh Bakir decided.

"Now, after the final task, we will meet again before the ceremony. Edna and my team will prepare you, and then I will introduce you to some of my associates. Some of them are large supporters of these games, so you may assist me in securing a contract with them," the Sheikh finished, and looked at his bodyguards.

The Sheikh waved his arms around in some bizarre motion, and his two burly bodyguards immediately hurried over and pulled him to his feet.

"Mike-al, Dan, it has been ... a pleasure," the Sheikh said, beaming at them. "You may leave."

Michael nodded awkwardly. "Thank you, Sheikh Bakir," he muttered as he left the area, followed by Dan.

Outside the door, however, he was surprised to see the Canadian girl, Catherine, waiting. She was leaning against the wall, and gave a slight smile upon seeing him.

"Well, Leonidas," she remarked. "I must say, it's an honour to meet you in person."

Michael nodded. "Thank you," he told her. "It's Catherine, right?"

She laughed. "Yes, Katherine with a 'K', but please, call me Kat," she replied.

Michael smiled slightly. "Sure," he said, although he was actually feeling quite unsure about this conversation.

"Anyway, Leonidas, let's get down to business. Your team did decent in the first task, and not so good in this last task. Your team needs an ally, and I'd like to propose an alliance on behalf of my team, the Canadian team," Kat stated, looking him in the eyes. "Do you accept?"

Michael frowned. What would the Canadians have to gain from an alliance with Occupied Britain? Even so, this was an important decision, and he couldn't squander the opportunity.

"I'll consider it," he replied evasively, glancing at her.

"Aren't you giving me an answer?" Kat queried, raising an eyebrow.

"Not now. I need some time to think," Michael said, pursing his lips slightly. "Is that alright?"

Kat smiled slightly. "That is alright, Leonidas. Get back to me with an answer before tomorrow. My room is number 13C, on the second floor," she reeled off, still looking at him.

"We can be powerful friends, but you don't want us as your enemy," she warned.

"I'll take that into account. Now, if you'll excuse me, if have my own squad to attend to," Michael replied, following where Dan had gone and striding back towards his team's floor.

"I'll be waiting," Kat called after him.

"I'm sure you will," Michael muttered to himself.

* * *

"The scores for the second task are being broadcast at seven o'clock, which is five minutes away," Amelia told the squad as they sat in the common room.

Michael nodded, watching the screen, where news coverage of the Coliseum was being shown.

He didn't particularly want to re-watch any footage of the second task, but was interested to see what the other teams had done.

He was sitting near Arthur. He still hadn't mentioned Kat's offer of an alliance to anyone from his squad.

"Arthur," Michael said quietly. "Do you think we have a chance?"

Arthur glanced at him. "You know we do," he replied simply.

Michael didn't reply, watching the screen, as a lively commentator talked about how well the US team was doing, and how they were set for yet another victory.

"Why don't people get bored of the same team winning each year?" Michael asked, more to himself than anyone else.

Arthur looked up. "Well, pride is a powerful weapon. The Americans try very hard to instil patriotic feelings within their citizens, and these games are just another way of showing how America is supposedly the greatest country in the world," he explained.

"So, the Americans buy into propaganda, then? They believe they are the best country in the world?" Michael laughed.

"Supposedly. I can't speak for all Americans, but they do believe that their democratic government, their capitalist economy and their constitution make them great and superior to all other countries," Arthur replied.

"Do you think we can beat them?" Michael asked him.

Arthur smiled slightly. "I've never really understood national pride. Who we are is not defined by where we are born; every person is just a random mix of genetics from their parents. Americans aren't superior in any way. Of course we can beat them. Our only problem is that the games are designed so as to favour them," he said.

Michael nodded. He agreed with Arthur, but still doubted whether they were good enough.

"And Michael, no one expects us to win," Arthur reassured him.

Michael let out a dry laugh. That wasn't true. Sheikh Bakir expected him to win.

"Hey, everyone, it's on!" someone called.

Michael looked up at the screen, keen to hear how they had done.

"Now, it is time to announce the scoring of the second task of the Coliseum. Both the recruits and our viewers are waiting with anticipation to find out how well they have done in this task. This task was judged on a variety of factors, and the scoring system has reflected how well each team has performed," the commentator spoke.

"Without further ado, we will reveal the scores of the second task, as well as the team's current total score. The results are in no specific order.

First, we have the United States of America. As we know, they won the first task, scoring ten points. In this task, they achieved another very high score, scoring six points and giving them a total of sixteen points!"

Michael realised that the Americans hadn't won the second task, but the news were still portraying it as a victory.

"Next, we have the Canadian team. They scored twelve points in this task, making their total fifteen points.

Occupied Britain scored four points, making their total nine points.

Australia scored three points, making their total four points.

The Netherlands scored two points, making their total also four points.

Here is the leaderboard, where we see the American team sits once again comfortably at the top! Occupied Britain has moved down and has been replaced by the Canadian team, who has taken over second place.

LEADERBOARD:

TEAM - Overall Score

1. USA – 16 points

2. Canada – 15 points

3. Occupied Britain – 9 points

4. Australia – 4 points

5. The Netherlands – 4 points

Soon, we will reveal how the final task will be scored, but for now, let's review the team's performances. Let's begin with the American team..."

Michael zoned out. He was still looking at the leaderboard. They were so far behind the top two teams.

He looked around at his squad. "Well, I better say this now. The Canadian team has offered us an alliance. I'm wondering whether to accept. What do you think?"

77 - THE NIGHT BEFORE

"An alliance with us? That's great!" Steve exclaimed.

"Ve say no, of course," Jürgen said. "Ve already have allies. The Canadians are not our friends."

"Who offered the alliance?" Sophie asked.

"A girl named Kat - Katherine, from the Canadian team. I don't know if she's their leader or not," Michael informed them, standing up to face the group.

"Yeah, she's their leader," Sophie confirmed. "Curly hair, pale skin, green eyes?"

Michael nodded. "That's the one."

Sophie smiled slightly. "Seems you're popular," she remarked.

"That isn't the point," Thomas said. "We just need to decide whether to accept or reject the alliance. Personally, I think we should accept, as it might mean we can work together and prevent the American team from winning. It's quite close between them, and I think the Canadians could win."

Michael looked towards the screen. "Have they released how the last task will be scored?" he asked Arthur.

Arthur shook his head. "They're doing it now."

"We need to know if we have a chance of victory before we agree to anything," Michael stated.

"Victory?" Raymon scoffed. "We were never going to win, Michael. Best we can hope for is holding onto third place. The Australian team aren't a pushover."

"That isn't the issue, though," Sophie said. "Michael has she said how long you have to deliver your answer?"

Michael frowned. "Yeah, she said to give it her tonight," he said, not seeing why that was relevant. "Why?"

"I think she's manipulating you," Sophie guessed.

"How?" Jürgen asked. "Ve haven't agreed to anything."

Sophie shrugged. "Michael, when we allied with the Dutch team, how did you go about doing that?" she asked.

"I had a fight with Arjen," Michael replied, unsure as to what she was getting at.

"No, before that. You sent me over to talk to him and befriend him, as you put it. It seems like she's doing a similar thing," she said, leaning back on her chair.

"What's your point?" Michael demanded.

"My point, is that I don't think you should go to her tonight when you deliver your answer. You'll be going to the Canadian floor, and there's no telling what they might do," Sophie replied, glancing around. "Oh come on, I'll put it bluntly. A pretty girl bats her eyelashes at Michael and asks for an alliance. She says, come to my room later with your answer. Michael, being a gentleman, feels the need to deliver the answer in person. It's at night, and Michael's alone, and outnumbered. See what I'm saying?"

Michael felt himself flush in embarrassment. "I can handle myself, Sophie. I think you're exaggerating," he said. "We don't even know what our answer is, yet."

Sophie raised her eyebrows. "That's for you to decide. But I advise against delivering the message in person," she remarked.

"Fine, I won't," Michael replied.

"Also, I forgot to mention, Arjen's still in charge of the Dutch team," Sophie replied. "The Dutch alliance is still on, according to them."

"Will you accept?" Thomas asked Michael.

Michael didn't answer. He wasn't sure himself.

"Guys, they've just released how the last task will be scored," Arthur said, writing something down in a notebook.

Michael looked over.

"The winner gets 14 points. Second place gets 7 points. Third place gets 5 points. Fourth place gets 4 points, and fifth place gets 3 points. This task is a step up from the last round, and it's worth the most points," Arthur explained.

"Well what does that mean?" Steve asked. "Can we win?"

"Well, conceivably, yes. If either the USA or Canada wins the last task, then the best we can come is third. However, if we win, Canada come second and USA come third, then we'll be on 23 points, Canada will be on 22 points, and the USA will be on 21 points. That's the only way we could realistically win," Arthur said, looking up.

"So we need to win the last task, and make sure the USA doesn't come second, for us to win?" Michael asked Arthur.

He nodded sheepishly. "Yes," he admitted.

Raymon laughed. "Well, there you go. It's impossible. We've never even won a task, and the USA have finished in the top two each time. We should just settle for third," he declared.

"And should we ally with the Canadians?" Michael asked.

"For us to win, we do need the Canadians to come second," Arthur admitted.

"And if they don't?" Michael asked.

"Then, well, we and the USA would be tied on top points. I have no idea what would happen then," he said, shrugging.

Michael nodded, pacing up and down as he thought to himself. If they allied with the Canadians, it could help them guarantee that the USA didn't win. However, it would mean that the Institute would definitely come third.

"We won't ally," Michael decided, looking around. "We can do this ourselves. I'm not relying on the Canadians to be our only hope. We're going to try to win the task outright, and we can't do that if we're allied to the Canadians."

"It does depend on the task," Elizabeth pointed out.

"I know. But we'll focus on keeping our team up. We can't afford to be distracted by any alliance," Michael said.

"Surely, you realise we won't win, though. You're fooling yourself if you think we even have a chance of winning," Thomas said. "Coming third is a success in itself."

Michael nodded. "But this is the first year the Institute has ever had a chance of winning. Before this year, there was no way in hell we could win. Finishing fourth was all the Institute could ever achieve. If we're the first year that has a remote chance of finishing top, then we're going to give it all we've got," he announced.

He noticed Nadia smile slightly.

"Sophie, you can be the one to tell the Canadians we're declining their offer," Michael said. "Room 13C is Katherine's."

Sophie smirked. "Very well," she replied, getting up from her sofa.

"And Sophie? Make it quick," Michael advised her.

Sophie didn't reply, just smiled to herself as she left.

Michael looked at his team. "Right, let's focus. Let's go through the last tasks and see where we went wrong. We need to communicate and remember what we've learnt. As Raines said, we have to stay united," he told them.

The group descended back into conversation, as they began planning the last task.

* * *

That night, Michael could not sleep. Despite the coolness outside, his room was uncomfortably hot. In the end, he got up and went into their team's common room, and sat down.

At his village, a fire was sometimes kept going on the colder nights, which Michael liked to look at. Here, there was no such comfort, and Michael had to be content with looking at the electric heater in the corner of the room.

"You cannot sleep?"

Michael looked up. It was Nadia, standing there in grey pyjamas.

He shook his head. "Nope. What about you?" he asked.

"I thought you might be feeling nervous," Nadia replied, walking over and sitting opposite him.

"What? No, of course not. I'm fine," Michael brushed off, waving a hand. "Well, maybe a little."

"You'll be fine, Michael," she told him, looking at him.

He looked up. Her eyes were very dark brown. "You really think so?" he questioned.

"Yes. You are a good leader. I don't know anyone who has the same respect amongst the squad that you do," she reassured. "You have proven yourself so many times, you should not doubt yourself. I have faith in you."

Michael smiled slightly. "Thank you, Nadia," he said. It seemed hotter in this room than before. He would have to turn down the heating.

"I think you overthink," Nadia remarked.

"You don't?" Michael replied, raising an eyebrow.

She laughed. "No, I do as well. But I'm not the important one here," she replied.

"You're always important, Nadia," Michael told her seriously. "All of my team is."

Nadia smiled. "You're always putting your team first, Michael. You vorry too much about vhat people think of you. You try to make people proud, but sometimes neglect yourself," she said.

Michael considered. She was probably right. He did worry he wasn't good enough far too often.

"How do you suggest fixing that?" he asked her curiously.

Nadia bit her lip slightly. "Relax?" she suggested. "Concentrate on something else for a while."

"Like what?" Michael asked.

She glanced at him. She opened her mouth to say something, and then shrugged. "I don't know. I'm not sure. I just didn't vant you to vorry about the Coliseum," she said, standing up.

"I'd almost forgotten," Michael said with a smile.

Michael thought he saw her blush slightly as she walked over to turn down the heater.

"I'll see you tomorrow, Michael. I hope you sleep," she said.

Michael stood up and faced her. "You're going?" he asked, somewhat disappointed.

"I have to sleep now, Michael," Nadia replied with a smile, leaving the common room.

Michael stood there, unable to quite fathom what he was feeling at that moment. He smiled to himself and shook his head, returning to his room to sleep.

This time, he found himself thinking about something other than Coliseum.

78 -   THE BRIEF

"I hope this gamble pays off, Mr Grey," a deep, clear voice spoke. "Releasing the scoring system early means we have to accept the winner."

"As do I, Mr President," Sebastian Grey replied. As Head of Logistics at the Coliseum, it was down to him to ensure the final task went smoothly. "Although, I must say, the times aren't as settled as they have been in previous years."

He was standing in the Oval Office, face to face with Elliot Hudson, the President of the USA. Visitors always stood when facing the President. It was a small thing, but the message was clear: he was superior.

"The tapes are off, Grey. Speak what you will," the President ordered, sitting down, his body relaxed and his fingers intertwined together. His face gave nothing away, but the look in his eyes was inviting, challenging almost.

Grey sighed. "I'll put it plainly. You and I both know that the establishment is unstable. Revolutionaries, riots, terrorists ... a spark could set things off. War weariness is overwhelming the people. There's no end in sight," he stated, glancing at the bookshelves in the office.

"Spare me the lecture, Sebastian. I know where we stand. I've seen the reports. The Trojan Initiative will do its part, all we need is time. A few months, maybe a year, and we'll be able to churn them out onto the battlefield. Now we can't do that if there's a lily-livered democrat in power, who's promising to end the war. I need to win the election this year, and for that, I need the Coliseum to go as smoothly as possible," the President stated clearly, looking at Grey.

"The Trojan Initiative?" Grey raised his eyebrows slightly. "You believe it will end the war?"

"We have to believe it," the President replied. "Otherwise, there might be no option for peace with honour. The only way we can agree to an armistice is if we're on top."

"You believe the Russians will ever accept an armistice? From what I hear, their soldiers are fanatical believers in the Russian regime. They would rather die fighting than give up their ideals. The Trojan is a medical android. Militarily, we'll still be outmatched on the European Front," Grey pondered, looking pensive.

"Sebastian, you and I both know that we won't win through a medical unit. Blackburn assures me that by next year, they'll be ready for mass production and combat duty. Then, we just have to hope that our government is re-elected and we can end this unrest," the President declared, looking firmly at Grey.

"It seems that time is not on our side," Grey mused, then slid a confidential document onto the President's desk. It contained exactly how the final task would play out.

"The Coliseum will finish similar to usual, with a few minor tweaks," Grey informed him.

"Minor tweaks?" The President flicked though the document. "I see that the order has changed? The Institute are finishing third this year?" His tone was questioning.

Grey cleared his throat. "I felt it would be apt to give some success to a team that was popular with the masses."

"Popular with the masses? Grey, the point of this is to inspire *American* patriotism, not to give in to the whims of the people," the President said, frowning.

Grey didn't reply. The President continued. "And the task itself? It seems to be unusual?" the he remarked, clearly expecting an answer.

"Ah yes, I'm hoping, by forcing the teams to work together, we can send a message of unity," Grey replied. "It's what we need."

"Hmm. I concede that we do have to keep the people on our side. This decision is on you, as are all others. This year has to be the cleanest yet. No hiccups, no controversy. You understand?"

"Perfectly," Grey replied.

"You're dismissed. I have other matters to attend to, now is a busy time," the President told Grey.

Sebastian Grey raised an eyebrow. "Another incident?"

The President looked hard at Grey. "Dismissed," he repeated.

Grey nodded, and withdrew from the room, deep in thought.

He could not allow anyone to mess up the Coliseum this year.

79 -   **FINAL MESSAGE**

"It's finally here! Rise and shine! The Institute is gonna win the Coliseum!"

"Shut up, Steve." Michael lay in his bed, wishing he didn't have to get up. He wished he could just feign an illness, or say he was injured. The pressure of this final task was getting to him. He had been awake, but hadn't yet moved.

"Leonidas, it's your big day! Don't mess it up by not looking your best," Steve's voice reminded him.

Light flooded in as the curtains were thrown back. Groggily, he forced his eyes open.

"Steve, okay, I'm good from here," Michael told him.

"I'm pretty sure that as soon as I leave the room, you'll go back to sleep," Steve remarked, raising an eyebrow.

Michael stretched. "Of course I won't!" he protested, smiling slightly. "But come on. Give me some time to think. I need to rehearse my motivational speech."

Steve laughed. "I know you're just going to wing it anyway," he decided, leaving the room. "Good luck!"

As soon as Steve had left, Michael sank back down into his bed.

The final task was here.

He took a deep, shaky breath.

He had dealt with nerve-wracking situations before, yet it didn't seem to get any easier. His stomach twisted, and he forced himself up.

There was no going back.

* * *

The Sheikh breathed slowly, looking at a screen. His two burly bodyguards stood either side of him, as he had placed himself on a large sofa. The last task of the Coliseum was due to start in one hour.

The Sheikh was more nervous than he was letting on. He had spent a lot of money on the Coliseum, including the hiring of the prepping team for Leonidas. He was hoping for a large sales boost to recuperate the money spent and expected the Coliseum sponsorship to provide the necessary exposure.

However, the Coliseum was more than that. He needed to enhance his reputation amongst the other sponsors. He did have pride, despite what the others might think.

"Sheikh?" one of his deputies entered, a small Middle Eastern man. "I have news. Firstly, a government branch has contacted us about the acquisition of a warehouse and some of our production lines..."

The man trailed off, as the Sheikh waved the news away.

"Erm, also, the prep team have just finished with Leonidas. Shall I send him in?"

The Sheikh nodded slowly.

* * *

Edna peered at Michael. He was in his Leonidas gear, ready to face the crowds before the final task. He fidgeted with his shirt slightly; making sure it was all even.

"Leonidas," she said quietly.

Michael looked up at the head of the Sheikh's team.

"It's been a pleasure working with you. Whatever happens out there, just know, that there are a lot of people supporting you," the woman stated, her face twitching into a slight smile.

Michael smiled and nodded awkwardly. "Thank you, Edna."

She pursed her lips. "Now go. The Sheikh wants to see you," she ordered, shooing him away.

Michael turned and left. He was in Sebastian Grey's mansion, where the recruits would soon have to parade out one last time, before the announcement of the final task.

"This way," one of the Sheikh's security guards led him. He was huge, both in height and in muscle mass.

Michael followed him, not saying anything. The Sheikh's men, from his experience, didn't speak much.

They went down a set of stairs, and then into a large room, which displayed several different screens. They broadcasted news channels, cameras and some were even playing footage from the first two tasks.

"Leon-idas!" a familiar voice boomed. The Sheikh was sitting on a sofa in the centre of the room, a tray of food next to him.

"Sheikh Bakir," Michael replied, nodding.

"I will make this brief, Leonidas. I am sure you are keen to get to the final task. But I want to impress upon you the importance of my name. If you succeed, it is down to me, and so you shall tell the world what a good sponsor I've been. I expect results," the Sheikh said, speaking more quickly than usual.

"Of course, sir," Michael said, surprised. Did the Sheikh doubt his commitment?

"I do not know what the task is. No one does. But I do know that it will be fixed so the Americans win. I expect you to stop this," the Sheikh informed him.

"How? If it's fixed, then I can't do anything," Michael protested. "We can only do our best in the competition."

"Expose it, then. Make it so they have no choice but to accept the true winner. This is no time to back down, Mike-al," Sheikh Bakir advised.

Michael frowned.

The Sheikh took a sip of water. "Do not play their game. If you play by their rules, the American team will win. Do what you have to do. These are more than games, Mike-al. You will give me recognition," he stated.

Michael nodded. "Yes, *sir*, I will," he replied, clenching his jaw, and then striding out decisively.

Did the Sheikh think he wouldn't give this his everything? He wanted to beat these Americans more than anyone!

He took a deep breath. It was time.

80 -   THE FINAL TASK

"These are troubled times. But now, more than ever, it is a time to stay united," the President of the USA addressed the nation, as the recruits stood down below his balcony.

Michael waited impatiently.

"We are all one people of the Western Alliance, standing together for our beliefs. For our values. For our ideals. These games represent our unity, our perseverance, and our patriotism. We are all proud to be Americans, and we are proud of those who give their lives for us so that we can live without fear. In supporting these games, we are honouring our heroes and their memories," announced the President.

"Ladies and gentlemen, welcome to the final task of the Coliseum!" he roared. The crowd cheered and applauded, the President's speech striking a chord with many Americans.

He continued. "Now, let me pass over to the head of the Coliseum games, Sebastian Grey, to describe the task."

* * *

Sometime later, Michael was striding towards the American team, flanked by Sophie and Jürgen.

"So, the Dutch team are no longer our allies?" Michael asked her.

"No. Last time I checked, Arjen was no longer their leader. So, I'd play it safe and assume that the alliance has gone down with him," Sophie replied, flicking back her hair.

Michael nodded, frowning slightly. He had expected it, but it was still an upset to his plans.

Jürgen cleared his throat. "Michael, you don't seriously expect that the Americans will ever agree to an alliance? They have nothing to gain from it. They're in first place, they only care about keeping their position," he stated.

"I'm hoping they'll humour us, and we can get a chance to check out what they're up to," Michael replied, glancing at Sophie.

She smiled slightly. "Let's hope your plan works."

* * *

Sebastian Grey smiled wearily as he stepped up onto the podium. The crowd quietened down, keen to hear what he had to say.

"As you know, the scoring system has already been released. The tournament is wide open, and soon, we will find out which team will be victorious," Grey spoke eloquently, like he was addressing himself rather than a crowd.

"Today's task is unusual. Over the years, the final task has always brought an extra challenge to competitions. Teams have had to adapt to rapidly changing circumstances, utilise what resources are around them, but they have never had to work together. Today, they will have to unite, and fight a common foe, together."

Sebastian Grey let this sink in.

"I know what you're thinking. This is a competition; they're competing against each other. And that's true. That will be accounted for during the tasks. But it is important to remember that this is not a war against one another, it is a time for both national and international unity. These recruits are putting the Western Alliance before themselves, as should we all," Grey pronounced, then gestured to a large screen, where the briefing for the final task played out.

* * *

The fifteen-man American squad was situated around a small base camp, which contained various weapon racks, crates of supplies and technological equipment. In this final task, recruits had been given the opportunity to utilise the gear they had trained with during their training time at the Facility.

As Michael, Sophie and Jürgen approached, they were confronted by two Americans. They wore red clothing.

"Who are you?" a shaven-headed American recruit asked, with a prominent accent.

"Leonidas," Michael replied. "I'd like to speak with your leader, if possible."

"Wait here," he grunted, before turning back towards the group.

Michael didn't wait; he and Jürgen followed the recruit.

"Don't be so polite," Jürgen advised Michael quietly, before they reached where Gideon was flexing a pair of robotic gloves.

The American leader ignored Michael and Jürgen, clearly wanting to show his superior status by making them wait for him. In the meantime, Michael looked around, taking in which items of equipment the American team were using.

One of them brandished an odd-looking heavy machinegun, whilst a small group of others were assembling a small mortar.

"Why are you here?" Gideon demanded, and Michael glanced at him.

"Well, I was hoping we could come to some agreement. After all, this task we have to work together," Michael stated with a smile.

Gideon narrowed his eyes. "No."

Michael raised his eyebrows.

Gideon stepped forward, his dark eyes glaring as he towered over Michael.

"You still think you've got a chance, don't you?" Gideon mocked quietly. "This whole thing is scripted. Every last detail. We know exactly what we have to do to win, and that does not involve your team. I don't care what your team does, as long as it stays out of our way. Got it?"

Michael smiled. "So that's a no on the alliance?"

Gideon laughed to himself. "You think you're funny, don't you? You think this is a game? Well, it isn't to me. My career depends on this. Maybe you don't give a damn about your future, not that you have one, but my team do. So go."

He looked at Michael firmly, his jaw clenched. Michael heard the whirring of one of the weapons behind him.

"Alright," he replied simply, turning and walking away, his head down. Jürgen followed him.

"Don't be too disappointed, ja?" Jürgen reassured him. "You knew it vas a long shot. Vhere's Sophie?"

"Here!" Sophie called, hurrying up to join them, a little breathless.

Michael glanced at her questioningly. She winked, providing Michael with all he needed to know.

* * *

"The objective of this task is simple," a loud voiceover announced, as the screen displayed a 3D image of a military base. "The teams' objective will be to infiltrate the base and extract captured prisoners, the locations of which are unknown within the base. All of the teams will be entering the same base, but from different starting positions."

The screen showed five flags around the massive complex, indicating where each team would start.

"Each team is expected to rescue as many prisoners as they can. For every prisoner killed, all teams will lose points, so cooperation is in their best interests. The five teams are free to work together or against one another, however the only aspect of the task that matters is the number of prisoners rescued alive. Each team will have their own, separate checkpoint outside the base where the prisoners are to be escorted."

The voiceover sounded over a video of computer generated holograms carrying out the task.

"To assist the teams, they will be provided with the finest Western Alliance technology. They will be up against trained personnel, who will be guarding the prisoners. Live rounds will not be used. This task will not be easy for the recruits, and is their biggest challenge yet."

The video ended with the Western Alliance logo, and Sebastian Grey resumed.

"That is all the information the teams will be provided with. They will be taken to the location, wherein they will have until dawn tomorrow to complete the task. The task will commence at dusk, with the sound of a siren. The time before is for the recruits to prepare. Good luck."

* * *

Michael, Jürgen and Sophie returned back to the Institute camp, previously located on the screen, where they would begin the task at nightfall. It was early evening.

It had taken a few hours to be transported to the location of the final task from the parade, and Michael had used the time to come up with a plan. Having attempted the first part of his plan with a visit to the American team, he was now almost in position to start the task and commence the infiltration of the base.

Arthur looked up sharply as Michael arrived. He had figured out where the American base camp was, using a sonar function on his wristwatch.

"Who's back?" Michael asked him.

"All except Emily's group, they're on their way here now. The Canadians said yes, though Thomas doubts their authenticity. The Dutch said yes, I've been told, and the Australians said no," Arthur replied, biting his lip. "What did the Americans say?"

"Take a guess," Michael remarked with a wry smile. "Did everything go smoothly?"

Arthur shrugged. "So-so. The Dutch seemed wary of our intentions; they wanted us gone as soon as possible. The rest didn't see us as much as a threat."

Elizabeth had wandered over to join the conversation. "It's ironic; the Australians still looked down on us, despite being in last place. They think that we're getting cocky, and it's an insult to offer them an alliance."

She pursed her lips, and then glanced at Michael. "But an alliance of three in five isn't bad. I hope you've got something more to your plan than just that," she commented pointedly.

446

Michael raised an eyebrow. "Why the lack of faith?"

"Because you seem to be too much of an idealist, Michael," she stated. "You have morals, that's all well and good, but other teams don't. You won't win this task by being a gentleman."

Michael smiled confidently, masking the doubts that were plaguing him. "You're absolutely right. Now, allow me to show you how we're going to win this task."

81 - KNIGHTFALL

It was dark, the sun finally having set. Michael and his squad were ready to enter the military base, rescue as many prisoners as they could and bring them back to the extraction point.

Michael, like the rest of his team, was wearing all black, but he carried a silenced submachine gun. He had opted to travel lightly, as opposed to carrying heavy equipment which would slow him down. He was on a hill, about two hundred metres away from the base.

He could see the complex below. It looked even bigger up close.

He spoke into his radio. Emily and Jürgen were beside him, and the rest of his team had split up into separate groups, each in different places.

His breathing was irregular.

"Team ... whatever happens ... do what you think is right ... whatever it takes out there. Follow the plan where possible, but trust your judgement if things go wrong. If I'm down, then Thomas is in command..."

Michael trailed off. There was no reply. He spoke again.

"Keep the communications open."

Arthur's voice crackled to life. *"American team is moving out fast, heading towards the facility. Leonidas, go now. Raymon, Canadians are moving, but at a slower pace. They've spread out, staying hidden."*

Michael acknowledged, checking his wristwatch. It showed a live update of an aerial view of the base, thanks to Arthur setting up a drone in the air. Heat signatures were visible down below as tiny dots, but Michael's real source of information came from bugs that his team had planted on the opposition.

Earlier that day, as Michael, Jürgen and Sophie had visited the American team; Sophie had been able to plant a bug on one of their members. Overall, the squad were able to track every team except the Dutch.

Arthur had remained at the camp to fly the drone and monitor the bugs. He was vital to Michael's strategy.

Michael scanned the area below with his visor. He could see the Americans descending the hill slowly, and stopping in positions where they faced the base. He waited for them to make a move, but they remained still, waiting themselves.

Michael could count at least ten of them. The sentries patrolling the complex were few and far between, and they hadn't spotted the Americans. So much for trained personnel.

"Vhat are they waiting for?" Jürgen whispered.

Michael didn't have an answer. He listened. There was a faint popping sound in the distance.

All was quiet.

"The Canadians have made it into the compound, still undetected. The Australians aren't far behind," Arthur updated them.

Then, in the distance, explosions erupted in the far side of the base.

"That's mortar fire, near the Dutch team! The alarm will be sounded any time now!"

The Americans reacted instantly, collectively sprinting down the hill. The mortar must have been their signal.

Michael was impressed, as he sprung to his feet. "Team, go loud!" he announced down his radio. Stealth might be working for the Canadian team, but once the alarm sounded, all hell would break loose.

Michael glanced at Jürgen and Emily. "Come on!" he told them, and the three of them pelted down the hill after the American team.

* * *

On the opposite side of the base, Raymon stood with Steve and Dan. Armed with heavy weapons, they intended to keep any guards and rival teams suppressed as long as possible.

They heard explosions, then a loud, ringing alarm which filled the air.

"The Canadians have been spotted, and they're near the barracks. They won't stand a chance," Arthur spoke quickly from the radio.

Raymon clenched his jaw.

"If I get shot here, then Michael's gonna have hell to pay," he muttered, unhooking some flashbangs from his waist as they jogged down into the base, through the hole in the fence the Canadians had cut.

"Don't get shot then," Steve replied, lugging a minigun in with him.

Raymon checked his wristwatch. On their right was the main road through the complex. They would be vulnerable out in the open.

He looked at Steve and Dan. "You guys heard Michael. We go loud."

Steve grinned, and Raymon threw his flash grenades towards the barracks. Their visors protected them as they walked round the corner, opening fire at the guards streaming out.

The defenders were met with a hail of gunfire, and could not leave the barracks without getting hit. Other sentries in the complex were attracted to sound of the gunfire, as Raymon and his squad mates found themselves dangerously exposed.

* * *

Sophie, Amelia and Thomas were also in the complex, although had seen much less action. Having entered the complex before the chaos had started; they had been searching building by building for any sign of the prisoners.

"Guys, I've got info from the bugs. There's a group of prisoners in a building, off the main road. Sophie, it's about a hundred metres east of your position," Arthur told them.

The group began sneaking quickly through the shadows towards their destination.

"Who found them?" Thomas asked.

"Canadians," Arthur said, a trace of nervousness entering his tone.

Sophie peered around a cabin, scanning ahead. "I see them. Five prisoners are being shepherded by about eight Canadians, back towards their side."

She spoke into her radio. *"Raymon, Steve? They're going towards you and the barracks now. Are you still there?"*

There was no response. She listened. The sounds of the minigun had ceased.

Sophie swore.

"The Canadians will get cut down on their way out, they're practically walking into the guards that way," she muttered, then glanced at her teammates. "We need to take these prisoners off the Canadians to stop them from being killed."

"They're our allies," Thomas said quietly.

Sophie's eyes flashed. "We all lose if the prisoners die. The alliance was never meant to last. We all knew that."

Thomas nodded. "Let's go."

The three of them hurried towards the fence, steering clear of the main road.

"Down!" Thomas yelled suddenly, and they flung themselves to the ground. Bullets whizzed over their heads, thudding into the wooden cabins. Thomas turned and returned fire, his visor letting him see the targets clearly. There were two guards, and his silenced pistol took them down with ease.

Sophie scrambled to her feet, not looking back as she headed towards the Canadians. By now, the guards from the barracks had spotted the Canadian team and opened fire.

"One hostage down," Arthur said. *"I suggest getting out of there. It's no use if everyone gets killed."*

"Raymon played his part, we have to play ours," Thomas panted as they ran towards the group.

Sophie unhooked a smoke grenade from her waist and threw it towards the guards. Thick, grey fog began spewing out quickly, masking the soldiers who defended the base. One of the Canadians glanced back towards Sophie, but they continued heading for the exit.

Thomas, meanwhile, aimed to cut them off. He ran towards the fence, throwing a flash grenade as his visor would protect his eyes.

It exploded with a bang, temporarily blinding the Canadians, one of whom accidentally fired a burst on his rifle with the shock.

When they had readjusted, both Sophie and Thomas had each grabbed one of the prisoners, and were holding them hostage, holding a gun to their neck.

Katherine, or Kat, glared at them. "We're on the same side!" she seethed, pulling her own pistol.

"Shoot us, and we shoot the hostages. Everyone loses points then," Thomas replied, his expression steely.

A small Canadian spoke urgently. "We don't have time for this, we can discuss this later, those guards will be on us any second now, we have to move!" he rushed out.

Thomas nodded, and grabbed his prisoner roughly, pushing him towards the exit. Sophie followed him, giving Kat a wide grin as they passed.

The Canadians carried on with their two prisoners, and the teams hurried out of the base, conscious of the enemy at their backs.

Bullets whizzed over their shoulder as they ran, sending one of the Canadians sprawling.

"Arthur, can you distract those guards?" Thomas shouted down.

"I thought you'd never ask."

Arthur's drone was still high in the sky, out of sight of the defenders at nightfall. It had been equipped with two small flares as a precaution.

It flew over the corner of the base nearest the American team and shot one down, a bright, green flare lit up the night sky as it rocketed down towards the compound below.

BOOM!

It exploded before it reached the ground, the sound louder than the alarm that had woken up the base.

452

The gunfire stopped, as defenders travelled towards the source of the sound, and the recruits were able to disappear into the night.

Once they had made it into a nearby wood, Sophie stopped. Thomas followed suit, looking at her.

"Where's Amelia?" she asked quietly.

Thomas glanced around, and then shook his head. "She must have gotten shot earlier. I didn't hear her cry out."

The Canadians had stopped now too, and Kat, their leader, once again spoke up.

"You absolute *idiots*," she spat. "You realise we could have all gotten shot because of you? Then the Americans would have won for certain. And speaking of that, we were allies! You need us to do well to have any shot at winning! We're meant to be working together against the Americans, not fighting each other for prisoners!"

Thomas looked at Sophie, silently asking who should answer, then looked at her. "We're allies. We take some prisoners each, not let you have them all. You know who kept the guards at bay for so long? That was our team. We take half the prisoners each, two and two. That's fair."

"*Fair?*" Kat retorted. "I don't give a damn what's fair, I give a damn about winning this task! And you've just taken my prisoners!"

Sophie snorted. "Calm down, kitty-kat. We don't want to work with you either, let's just take our prisoners and be off. Our extraction points are in different places."

Kat narrowed her eyes. "You're outnumbered. There's two of you, and seven of us. We should have more prisoners."

"No," Thomas said bluntly. "If you fire at us, we will fire on you and your prisoners. It makes no difference to the overall score if everyone loses points, only your team will have lost the potential rescues."

Kat looked at her teammates. "What if we can neutralise you before you get any shots off?" she remarked casually.

"Then our sniper, will pick you off as soon you get close to your extraction point, targeting the prisoners first," Sophie boasted.

"You're bluffing," Kat decided.

"Test us. But if you do, then it will be on you if the Americans win," Thomas told her, then nodded to Sophie and began walking away with their two prisoners.

His body tensed up, expecting to be shot at or tasered from behind, but nothing came.

He and Sophie smiled at one another.

Now all they had to do was make their way to the extraction point.

* * *

BOOM.

Michael squinted as the flare lit up and exploded over the building the American team had entered. He still hung near the entrance, watching and waiting for them to come out.

Guards heard the sound and came rushing over. He heard gunfire from within the building.

Genius, Arthur.

Now the Americans would be discovered and suppressed, hopefully ruining their chances of a victory.

He glanced at Jürgen with a slight smile.

Jürgen though, was frowning. "Look," he muttered. "They're not stopping."

Ignoring the glowing remains of the flare, the defenders of the compound moved right past it, not even checking the building.

Why weren't they checking it?

Michael's breathing grew faster. Did the guards know the American team was in there?

He clenched his jaw.

Of course they knew. They just wanted the Americans to win. But now the guards were in between Michael's team and the American team.

Arthur's voice crackled to life once again. *"Michael, you won't believe this. The American team are coming out of a back entrance from that building, and they've got about ten more people with them."*

Michael swore.

Ten people? If the Americans could rescue that many prisoners, the other teams wouldn't stand a chance. The Americans had made a beeline for that building, and it hadn't even been guarded.

"They're making their way out of the base now, where another group of them are going to cut the fence. I'm listening out for any mention of the extraction point now, because our only chance here is making sure they don't reach it," Arthur spoke frantically.

"Aren't their extraction points at vhere they started?" Jürgen asked.

"It might be, but we don't know for sure," Arthur replied.

Michael took a deep breath. He had to make a decision, fast.

"How long until dawn?" he asked Arthur.

"About six hours. But we don't know how far away their extraction point is. We don't know how long we've got."

Michael nodded, and then spoke into his radio again, but this time, he wasn't speaking to Arthur.

"Nadia? It's time for Plan B. The game has changed."

82 -   "THE GAME HAS CHANGED"

Earlier

Michael approached to Nadia. The siren hadn't yet signalled the beginning of the final task.

She was standing alone, in a lightly wooded area on the top of a small hill. She looked through her visor down at the base far away. She adjusted a setting slightly with her hand, whilst an advanced sniper rifle was strapped to her back.

"That's a nice rifle you've got there," Michael remarked, his heart beating slightly faster in his chest.

Nadia took off her visor and raised an eyebrow at him, making Michael realise how dumb his conversation opener had sounded.

"It's more capable, but I prefer the old-fashioned one," Nadia replied. "What weapon will you be carrying?"

"I haven't decided, but probably a submachine gun. I haven't really found a weapon that suits me yet, to be honest," Michael admitted, cracking a slight smile. "It's funny; you'd think with all this training, I'd have found what I'm looking for."

She nodded. "You've probably had other things on your mind," she commented, her mouth twitching slightly.

Michael laughed for a moment, looking out across the sky. The sun was beginning to set. "We'll have to be in position soon. But before this begins, there are some things I have to tell you."

Nadia raised her eyebrows. "Go ahead."

Michael pursed his lips, and then looked at her. "This task is different. We can't win just by trying hard."

She remained silent, knowing he wasn't finished.

"When I spoke to Gideon, the American leader, he said this was all scripted - and before you say anything, I know he was trying to get in my head. But it's not just him. The creator of the Coliseum pretty much told me that we can't win. At least, not by playing by their rules. If they're going to manipulate the Coliseum to ensure they win, then so can we," he stated resolutely.

456

"You're going to cheat?" Nadia demanded, her eyes flashing.

"No! Well, maybe ... no. These games are not a level playing field, Nadia. If we just do what they expect us to do, then we will not win. I don't know how much they've planned, but so far, it has all gone their way," Michael declared.

"Not in the second task," Nadia reminded him. "They did not win that."

Michael nodded. "I know. Maybe they were trying to make it close. But I don't know who to trust anymore. Was I intentionally made leader of the Institute team because they thought I would play by the rules? I don't know. But Arjen headed straight for Gideon, the American leader, in the first task, and now Arjen's no longer in charge of his team. This is our *only* chance to do the unexpected," he said.

"And you think you can get together a coalition of some sort? To unite against the Americans?" Nadia replied. "You put too much faith in human nature, Michael. Our *allies* are out for themselves, just as much as we are. We just have to get in the base, and get as many prisoners as we can. You have a plan for how we can do that. We play our own game, not go off what the other teams do. If we lose, we keep our heads held high. We won't let ourselves down."

Michael shook his head. "Nadia, I'm not going just focus on our team. Everyone has fought on their own so far. That's what has kept the Americans winning every year. They play the dirty tricks, the controlling of the games, and they win. But not this year. I'm going for them, Nadia. We're making the playing field even. If they don't play by the rules, neither will we."

Nadia looked at him in the eye, a long, hard gaze. Michael's eyes flickered away and back to her. She let out the smallest of breaths, and seemed somewhat disappointed.

"Michael, I do not want to see your integrity sacrificed for these games. As your friend, I advise against going down this spiral of revenge, or whatever it is ...”

She shook her head, then continued. "But as your teammate, I will follow whatever orders you give me. What is it that you want me to do?"

Michael grimaced. "Well, you won't like it."

457

* * *

"Nadia? It's time for Plan B. The game has changed."

Nadia waited in a wooded area near the American camp, hidden in foliage. Nadia had sniped the one American left guarding the camp earlier.

Back at the Facility, she and Emily had practiced making traps. Now, Michael had ordered her to sabotage the American camp before the rest of them returned. She had done so, and now waited and watched.

She sighed upon hearing Michael's words, and checked her sniper rifle once again. It was fully loaded.

Suddenly, she froze, hearing movement.

Footsteps.

Shouting.

She wasn't alone. The Americans were coming back.

She remembered her orders. She would obey. Michael had known she would.

"Where the hell is Arnold!?" an angry American voice was ranting. "He was meant to meet us here!"

"Maybe he fell asleep," another, female voice said with a laugh.

"If he HAS, I am going to-"

The string of obscenities that followed made Nadia wince slightly. She saw two figures walk towards the American base.

She waited.

Three ... two ... one.

The first American, still ranting, crossed the invisible laser beam that Nadia had set up. With a small click, it triggered a concussive grenade, which detonated directly under the two Americans' feet.

Powerful shockwaves of energy sent the Americans backwards onto the ground. Nadia witnessed one of them fall, his head hitting the floor with a thud.

She heard more shouts.

"What the hell!"

"Who was that?"

"Are the guards pursuing us?"

"No! All of you, shut up!" Nadia heard Gideon's voice restore silence. "It was the other teams, probably the Dutch. They're out for us. We've got enough prisoners now; we have to get to the extraction point immediately. Then, the guards will take out the remaining teams."

There was murmured assent.

"I'll lead the front. Clinton, Hunter, you take the rear. Divert any pursuers, use fire if necessary. The rest of us, we'll take the prisoners and get them out of here. I'm fairly certain they'll be taken out of here as soon as we get to the extraction point. Once we reach it, it's game over. We win."

"How far away is it?" one of the Americans asked.

Gideon didn't answer. "Follow me, and fast. Let's finish this Coliseum."

Nadia waited until their footsteps had faded away, and then leapt to her feet. She was her team's only chance. She would have to pursue them to the extraction point.

* * *

Michael opened his comms link. "Henry, are you still with the Dutch team?" he asked, as he pursued the American team.

"Er, yeah, but they're getting impatient. Half of them have gone towards the base, but Arjen and the rest are with me."

"Well, we need you now. You've got heavy weapons, right? Take them with you, and follow the American team. Promise the Dutch team any American prisoners we capture," Michael commanded.

"And if they don't believe me? Or if they refuse?"

"Then head back to our extraction point. We still have to defend our captured prisoners until dawn," he told Henry, as he ran after the American team.

"Arthur, how are we doing?" he asked.

"Michael, you're about half a kilometre behind the Americans, but you're moving at a slightly faster rate. But, there's movement from the main base."

"What's happening?" Michael asked.

"The guards. They've got vehicles. I think they're planning to get back the prisoners."

"So we're chasing the Americans, but the guards are chasing us?" Michael asked, slowing his pace slightly. "We're completely vulnerable."

"You'll have to choose who to fight."

"I know that. Alright. Henry? Change of plan. Bring the heavy weapons to us. We'll take down the guards, and then chase down the Americans," Michael decided.

Jürgen looked at Michael. "But there are only three of us! We won't stand a chance against the guards. They'll just take us out then, then ignore the Americans and go for the rest of our team."

Michael nodded. "Do you have any other suggestions?" he asked Jürgen, genuinely.

"Ve could try to get the guards to fight the American team," Jürgen suggested.

"How?"

"Vell, assume they are in a column, and are looking for us. We could hide, and take the back of the column, then use their vehicles and go with them until they reach the American team," Jürgen said.

"So we could try to pit them against each other?" Michael questioned. "But aren't the guards on the side of the Americans?"

"They von't make it obvious that they are. This task is being viewed live," Jürgen reminded him.

Michael nodded. "Well, it's the best plan we've got. Let's give it a shot."

* * *

Hunter, the shaven-headed American recruit, stalked up and down, his annoyance clear to see.

"Why is it that we have to stay behind?" he demanded. "I mean, you're good with traps and stuff, but *me*? I should be with the front, leading the extraction out of here!"

Clinton, the other recruit assigned to the rear-guard, was looking at a tablet, connected to an infra-red camera that had been set up. They were on the road, and the American team had just left them. He didn't reply to Hunter's rant, feeling any comment would aggravate him further.

As soon as someone got close to the American team, he would know. Every second, his team got closer to victory.

"Why couldn't he leave Jenson here? Or Miller?" Hunter carried on, picking up his assault rifle and checking it.

"Can you shut up?" Clinton said quietly, still watching the tablet.

"What did you just say?" Hunter challenged, his eyes flashing in anger, as he stood up.

"Please, just be quiet!" Clinton protested, looking at Hunter. "We're both in this situation, and we gotta deal with it!"

Hunter narrowed his eyes at the other recruit, and Clinton lost his nerve, his eyes flickering back down at the tablet.

"Holy-" he exclaimed, before he heard the roaring of an engine in the distance. He picked up a detonator, and activated it, before picking up his weapon.

"What is it?" Hunter demanded, picking up the tablet and looking at it. "Oh..."

A small column of headlights was moving up the road, with four motorcycles surrounding a troop transport.

"Have you detonated yet?" Hunter asked Clinton, who nodded, a slight smile crossing his face.

"Yeah."

* * *

"How hard could it be?" Michael muttered to himself as he climbed onto the motorcycle, glancing at the discarded body of the guard.

"Ready?" he heard Jürgen call from the other motorcycle.

"As I'll ever be," Michael replied with a nervous smile.

The three team members of the Institute had ambushed the back of the guard convoy, taking out two motorcyclists that had lagged behind the rest of the group. Luckily, so far no other guards in the convoy had noticed anything, but they would have to catch up with them quickly.

Together, Jürgen and Michael revved up their engines and pressed on after the guards.

He hoped the plan would work.

* * *

BOOM.

The chain of explosions detonated, creating a roaring blaze amongst the trees. The front two motorcyclists of the convoy were thrown backwards.

In the centre, the troop transport caught fire and the soldiers packed into the back began, hurrying out. They were greeted with the smell of smoke as fire spread throughout the trees.

Clinton watched as an officer began trying to maintain order, before looking up as the man heard a creaking sound.

Exactly as Clinton had planned, a tall, flaming pine tree began tipping over towards the troop transport. The vehicle reversed, not willing to risk getting crushed, as the tree landed, blocking the road with a wall of fire.

"It'll take some time to get through that!" Clinton declared triumphantly.

Hunter exhaled. "Means we won't get any action though," he muttered.

* * *

"What the ..."

Michael rounded a bend to see a huge, flaming tree on the road, with the troop transport having stopped in front of it. He had heard the crack of explosions.

He glanced at Jürgen, who signalled to go around it.

Michael did so, and peeled off to the right of the road, whilst Jürgen took the other side. He drove among the trees, feeling the heat around him as he got closer to the flames.

He tried his best to steer the motorcycle, but it was only luck that prevented him from crashing.

I could die.

The sobering thought reached him amidst the chaos. He dismissed it quickly, focusing on the task. He had signed up to be a soldier, after all.

Once he was past the burning tree, he returned to the path. He glanced to the side, and Jürgen wasn't there. He was on his own.

He slowed his speed slightly, speaking down his wristwatch.

"Arthur? I'm gonna need some news. Is my route clear?" he shouted.

"Your route ... no, it's not clear. Two hostiles around the next bend, presumably Americans. You can circumnavigate them by going straight on, through the boggy area just ahead of you," Arthur informed him.

"Where is everyone else?" Michael asked.

"We've got four prisoners at the time being, two from the Canadians and three of our own. Henry and Emily are with the Dutch team, moving to intercept. And ... oh no..."

"What is it, Arthur?" Michael demanded, accelerating into a mudflat straight ahead. His motorcycle slowed, kicking up dirt as he pressed on.

"An aerial transport is flying in, about two kilometres north. It must be here to extract the Americans," Arthur said. *"What should we do?"*

Michael swore.

"Tell Henry to head to wherever that transport lands. Try to ground it if they can, if not, just take down as many Americans as they can," he ordered.

"Ground it? Is that allowed? They're on our team..."

"They're not on our side. We're winning this on our own," Michael told him, gritting his teeth as he pressed onward, making it out of the mudflat and back onto the rough track.

"Nadia?" he asked into the microphone.

There was silence for a few seconds, before she replied.

"Ja?"

"How are you doing?" he asked her, swerving to avoid a stone on the road.

"I'm tracking them. But ... Leonidas, do you want me to capture the prisoners from the Americans, or take them out?"

Michael frowned slightly. She didn't usually call him Leonidas. He had thought about it before. Capturing the prisoners from Americans was a risky strategy; it would increase the Institute score whilst lowering that of the American team. However, it would be much harder to pull off. On the other hand, taking out the prisoners would hurt the American team, but it wouldn't help his own.

Michael wasn't a natural risk-taker, but he knew that he wouldn't win this task by playing it safe.

"Shoot the Americans, but not the prisoners. We'll capture them, we've got until dawn," he ordered. "And if you can ... take out their leader, Gideon."

* * *

"Hurry up!" Gideon roared at the prisoners. "We've rescued you! We're trying to get you out of here!"

"We're tired..." one of them complained. He was very skinny, making Gideon wonder if the prisoners had been starved.

He had been lagging behind the rest of them for some time.

464

Gideon pulled out his gun, ready to shoot him, but one of his teammates grabbed his arm. "Gideon, we need them to win," he reminded him.

"We've got ten. One less won't make a difference," Gideon remarked coolly.

"What about if we let him tag along, but behind us?" the teammate, a tall, lanky recruit suggested. "You say we'll have enough to win regardless, so it won't do any harm to leave him. If another team finds him, they'll have to go all the way back to their base."

Gideon cocked his head to one side, still walking. "Alright. Everyone, carry on."

One of the female Americans looked up sharply at the group of trees in the distance. She put on her helmet, flicking her visor down.

"What is it, Casey?" the tall American asked, noticing her.

"I saw something ... we're being followed!" she said urgently. "There's a heat signature coming from the forest there!"

A flash emitted from the forest, and Casey was thrown to the ground.

"Sniper!" the tall American shouted.

"Really, Darren?" Gideon muttered, pulling out his gun. He aimed, and fired a concussive grenade towards the forest.

It exploded, masking the air between them in smoke.

"Did you get them?" Darren asked.

"I hope so," Gideon replied. The prisoners were huddled together in obvious fear. He squatted down, taking off Casey's helmet and tossing it to Darren, before putting his own helmet on.

"She's out cold; we'll have to carry on without her. Seems Clinton wasn't as good a rear-guard as we thought," he remarked nonchalantly, looking up at the sky.

"Don, pass me the Javelin," he ordered, taking a small electrical device with a long barrel, and aiming it at the sky.

"If the other teams are targeting us, then they'll probably be using the drones we were all given," Gideon guessed, looking at a small screen on the device.

"As I suspected," he remarked, squeezing the trigger on the device. It blasted an electrical wave up into the sky towards the drone, frying it. The broken shell of the drone dropped to the ground, out of sight.

Gideon smirked. "They can't follow us anymore. The other teams will be on foot, so if we maintain a good pace, they won't be able to catch us."

"I wonder why they're so aggressive," Darren commented.

"If they play dirty, the people in charge will even the odds," Gideon assured him. "Let's just get to the extraction point."

* * *

Nadia watched the American team move onward, leaving a prisoner lagging behind them. Luckily, the concussive grenade had missed, but she couldn't afford to give away her position again.

A voice crackled into life on her radio.

"Everyone, it's Arthur. The drone is down. We're blind."

He sounded nervous. Nadia replied.

"I've still got eyes on them. Jürgen, there's a prisoner that they've left behind. Can you pick him up?" she asked.

There was no response.

Then, she recognised Henry's voice, with the Dutch team. "Leonidas? We're under attack! It's by either Americans or guards, I can't tell, but we're outgunned here! You're on your -"

There was no more.

"Henry?" Michael demanded, but there was no response. "Right. Well, team. Change of plan. Go all out to disrupt the other teams. Shoot the American prisoners. We can't afford to rescue anyone else, we don't have the time."

Nadia clenched her jaw, glancing away, and then spoke into her radio. "Ja."

466

She slung her sniper rifle onto her back and took off after the American team, intent on finishing her task.

* * *

"Citizens of the Western Alliance, welcome back to this live broadcasting of the Coliseum games. This year, we have had record viewing figures, as the five teams are attempting to rescue prisoners from a hostile base."

On television screens across the country, viewers were witnessing the cameras showing the landing of a transport helicopter, to pick up the prisoners that had been rescued.

"The first transport to arrive is for the American team, who currently have nine prisoners with them that they have rescued. Let's see what happens."

Gideon led four Americans, along with nine prisoners, towards the transport helicopter. He was tense.

"Hurry, come on. Just get inside," Gideon ordered his team, now that they were in eyesight of the helicopter, which had landed in a large, open clearing.

Exposed, was the word that sprung to mind.

Gideon stopped, to face back. "I'll guard our backs. Don't stop for anything," he instructed his teammates, checking his gauntlet and staying back amongst the trees. "You'll be sitting ducks out there."

He drew out his assault rifle, fixing the concussive grenade launcher onto the front.

One of his teammates hesitated. "What should we do when we get there?"

"Just leave. We've got enough prisoners to win," Gideon ordered. "Now go!"

They ran off, getting closer and closer to the extraction point. Gideon waited; his gun ready.

* * *

Michael increased his speed on his motorcycle, heading for Nadia's location. He didn't like checking his watch whilst driving, but he had no choice.

He powered onward, entering an area of densely packed trees. He was forced to slow down, circling around them.

He looked up beyond the trees, and a large clearing was in sight. In the distance, a huge transport helicopter had landed. He could see figures running towards it.

He smiled. The end was in sight.

Finally out of the wood, he began accelerating towards them. Adrenalin shot through his veins as he sped up.

He heard a bang from behind him, and time seemed to slow down.

A grenade exploded next to him, the blast throwing the motorbike off course. Michael was thrown off as the vehicle spun away.

His head hit the ground, hard. Groggily, amidst his blurry vision and ringing ears, he looked up. The motorcycle was about ten metres away. He needed to get back on it.

He crawled towards it, forcing his body to obey him.

Then, heart-stopping, another bang. Michael froze, looking at the motorcycle, before another grenade landed. It exploded, destroying the vehicle before his eyes.

He stared for a second, and then looked at the American team, mere silhouettes in the distance. There was no way he could catch them.

He turned his head behind him. Gideon was striding towards him confidently, a metallic glove on his hand.

He was pointing it at Michael.

Michael reached for his rifle, but it had come off his back in the explosion. He drew his pistol and fired, as Gideon fired some sort of taser.

Agony ripped through him, making him miss his shot. His muscles convulsed and he clenched his teeth, shaking.

He dropped his pistol, unable to help himself writhing in pain.

Gideon kept the taser pointed at Michael, his expression hidden beneath his helmet. Michael's vision seemed to fade.

Michael had taken a gamble, and lost. There was no way he could catch up with the Americans on foot, and his motorcycle had been destroyed.

CRACK!

A bullet smashed against the side of Gideon's helmet and he fell to the ground. There was another crack, and another shot thudded into Gideon's body on the floor. Michael tried to pull the barbs of the taser out of him, but couldn't move.

A figure ran over and kicked the taser away. Michael flopped to the ground limply, still twitching.

He opened his eyes and looked up. Nadia was crouched over him, a sniper rifle in her hand. Her eyes were full of concern. She was saying something. She was shaking him.

"Michael ... can you shoot?" she was asking. She rolled her eyes, picking up Gideon's assault rifle and pressing it to Michael.

"N-nadia... the Americans, we can't catch them," he murmured, gripping the gun tightly and rolling onto his front.

"But we can still shoot them," Nadia replied, determination in her eyes, as she knelt and aimed her sniped rifle at the Americans, who had almost reached the transport by now.

"We'll take them together. Don't panic," she advised, as she squeezed her trigger. Michael saw someone tumble.

Michael nodded, holding his rifle against his shoulder, his hands still shaking slightly. He flicked the setting to a three-round burst, and steadied his breathing.

He fired at the figures, hoping one of his shots found their target. He loosed off a whole magazine towards them, and then looked around for ammunition.

"Come on, come on..." Michael muttered. He could hear the sound of the rotor blades in the helicopter picking up.

"We're too late," Nadia replied. "They're all in, except for the ones we hit."

Michael didn't listen, attaching a second magazine and firing at the helicopter. The rubber bullets bounced off harmlessly, and Nadia grabbed his arm.

"Michael!" She pushed his gun down. "There's nothing more we can do! They're safe now."

Michael was too weak to resist. He watched mutely as the helicopter moved up in the air, taking the American team and their prisoners with them.

His radio crackled into life.

"I've got another drone in the air guys!" it was Arthur's voice, optimistic. *"I see the transport ... it's leaving ... they've ... got away."*

Michael watched it fly off.

"How many of them did you get, Michael? Was it enough to win?"

Michael swallowed. How many prisoners had they managed to stop the Americans rescuing?

Not enough, a voice in his head warned him. *Not enough.*

Nadia place her hand on Michael's shoulder. "Let's go, Michael. We have to get back to our own extraction point before dawn. The other teams might have done enough."

Michael exhaled, blinked a few times, and then glanced at Nadia. "That taser really hurt," he admitted.

He clambered to his feet, and then looked towards the taser, which lay on the floor. Gideon was still out cold.

"Are you going to shoot him with it?" Nadia asked, cocking her head to one side.

Michael picked it up, toying with the idea. It would certainly make them even.

He shook his head.

"No. We're on the same side, really. We fought each other in the Coliseum, but that's over now," Michael stated, tossing the taser aside. "He's not my enemy."

Nadia smiled at him. "I was beginning to think we'd lost you to Leonidas."

Michael grimaced. "I just hope it was worth it," he remarked, picking up his original weapon.

Nadia nodded, her smile fading. "Me too," she replied. "Let's go."

Michael sighed, and began gingerly walking back, his muscles occasionally contorting in pain. "Can I ... lean on you? I'm still a bit sore," he asked Nadia.

She raised her eyebrows at him. "Just this once," she replied, steadying him. They began walking back together.

Despite his exhausted body, Michael's mind was racing. One question stood out though, amongst all his thoughts.

Had they done enough?

83 -   THE RESULTS

"Sir, here are the results from the final task."

A short-haired man confidently placed a sheet onto Sebastian Grey's desk. His name was Herbert Crane, and he was the Managing Director of the Coliseum games, subordinate to only Sebastian Grey himself, who had the full backing of the US government.

Grey examined the sheet intently. It confirmed what he had already deduced.

"Well, this puts us in a predicament," Grey mused when he was finished.

"Absolutely not. The American team won fair and square. The British team is obviously disqualified for cheating, so we're miles ahead of the next team," Crane said jubilantly.

"However, the British team technically did not cheat," Grey pointed out.

"We're in the right here, sir. We should deduct points; they shot the prisoners they were supposed to be rescuing," Crane suggested.

"Are we?" Grey asked him. "If we start any mention of cheating, Director, then it becomes very easy for the blame to point towards us, as the organisers of the Games."

"Well, if not cheating, then perhaps, improper conduct?" Crane tried.

"Improper conduct? In war games? No, such an accusation would be hypocritical," Grey remarked.

"Are you suggesting that the Brits go unpunished?" Crane asked, shocked.

"On the contrary, Director. The Institute team exploited a weakness in the rules. They are at fault, but so were we. As to the overall scores, hope is not lost. We have a contingency plan, in case such things happen. But I shall consult with Lieutenant Blackburn, in case he requires anything more from the outcome," Grey informed, clasping his hands together.

Crane stood up straight. "Very well, sir. It seems you have made your decision," he stated, clearly restraining himself.

Sebastian Grey smiled. "Don't worry, Director, I'm sure you'll have my position soon enough. It might even be next year, if the President doesn't like our performance for this Coliseum. In fact, he might even fire the whole leadership team," he contemplated, slightly amused at the flash of panic in Crane's eyes.

The Managing Director regained his composure, nodded at Grey, then turned on his heel and walked out, not closing the door behind him.

Grey sighed. *The ambition of the young.*

He looked down at the document and smiled slightly.

Leonidas *had* somehow managed it.

* * *

"How many prisoners did we rescue?" Michael asked his team.

He was relishing a well-earned breakfast. Scores were to be announced at midday, and Michael had just caught up on a few hours of much-needed rest.

"By the end of the task, our squad had rescued a total of seven," Arthur responded. "Three ourselves, two pinched from the Canadians, courtesy of Sophie and Thomas, one Jürgen picked up, and one from you and Nadia."

Michael nodded, satisfied. At the end of the task, he and Nadia had searched the people they had fired upon. There were five bruised bodies. One American and four prisoners. However, amongst them, Michael had found a prisoner who had fallen over whilst running, but hadn't actually been shot.

When he and Nadia returned with the prisoner, they found Sophie, Thomas, Arthur, Jürgen and Paul waiting there. Less than half of his squad had made it back.

"Do we think that's enough?" Michael questioned.

Arthur grimaced. "Not exactly. It might be sufficient to secure the third task, but to win the tournament, we'll need the Canadians to have beaten the Americans in this last task, but not done as well as us," he explained.

Michael took another bite of some toast, and then raised an eyebrow. "Do you remember the points table? Can you do a prediction for the final result?"

Arthur shrugged. "I could, but I don't want to get anyone's hopes up. It's likely they'll change something if we're ahead of the Americans," he remarked.

Michael nodded slowly. "Yeah ... and thanks, Arthur," he told his friend.

Arthur looked at him. "For what?"

Michael smiled, thinking it should be obvious. "For the task, of course ... it wouldn't have been possible without you. I just want you to know that I'm grateful," he said, somewhat awkwardly.

Arthur frowned. "Okay," he said, then glanced up as someone approached.

Michael looked around, to see Raymon had entered the canteen. He wore a long-sleeved shirt with a collar, which Michael found unusual.

They made eye-contact, and Raymon nodded briefly. Michael nodded back, surprised. He hoped their feud was over.

One by one, members of Michael's team entered the canteen to have breakfast. As they had also been up all night, they all looked very weary.

Steve and Dan had many bruises, as did Amelia. Michael hadn't really considered the pain that getting shot might cause, even if they were just rubber bullets.

Sophie smiled at Michael warmly as she entered, and Michael couldn't help but return it.

Thomas entered, chatting with Paul and Dominic, no doubt asking them what happened at their part of the Coliseum. Michael had sent Paul, Dominic and Elizabeth to try to rescue prisoners from the base, like any other team, to increase their score. However, it meant that Michael had very little idea of how they'd gotten on. From what he'd gleaned, Elizabeth and Dominic had gotten shot, and so Paul had rescued three prisoners on his own.

Emily and Elizabeth then entered before Henry, who had a black eye.

Nadia and Jürgen were last to enter, their faces not giving much away. Nadia avoided Michael's gaze, but Jürgen nodded at him.

Michael nodded back, and then addressed his team as a whole.

"Well, guys, I'm not sure what to say here, but ... I want to thank you all. Every one of us put in the effort, and gave it everything. Whatever happens today, I'm proud of you all. Almost every other year, the Institute has come fourth. This could be the year where we don't. We're not sure of our final position, but we gave it our all," Michael announced.

"You weren't a bad leader in the end, Leonidas," Steve remarked. "I wonder what will happen to this squad after the Coliseum."

"Who knows," Thomas replied, sitting down. "But we have more important matters now. What are we doing about Joe? Is he still accused of being that spy, Prometheus?"

Shame burned through Michael. He had forgotten about Joe.

Sophie spoke up. "I say, after the Coliseum, we speak to the press about it. We just want a fair trial for our friend, and to see what evidence there is that he's guilty," she replied. "They can't refuse us that, if the public are on our side."

Michael nodded. "I was thinking of that too. Joe is our priority now. He's one of us. We've got to do what we can to make sure he's given a fair chance in this country," he said determinedly. "But for now, enjoy your breakfast. It's been a long night."

* * *

"Welcome to the final announcement of the Coliseum! Here, we will tell you, which team has been victorious in the final task, and the overall winner of the Coliseum! Here is the Head of the Coliseum to tell you more."

Sebastian Grey stepped up. "I'm sure you will agree; the last task was an exhilarating one. Not only did the teams have to contend with the guards, they also had to watch out for betrayal from each other. We must all appreciate the magnitude of these challenges, and the skill with which all the teams performed. Without further ado, I shall now read out the Scoring of the final task, starting from the bottom.

Finishing fifth place in the final task was the Australian team, who rescued one prisoner.

Next, the Dutch, who rescued two.

In third place, the Canadians, who rescued four.

In second place, the American team, who rescued six.

And, winning the final task was the British team, who rescued seven prisoners!" Grey announced. The crowd applauded.

Michael smiled, pleased. He didn't dare to hope.

Grey cleared his throat. "And now, we will display the final scoring table of the Coliseum. The overall winners are ... the Americans!"

The screen displayed the points table, and the crowd roared. The American national anthem blared loudly, and Michael looked up in outrage.

USA – 23 points

Occupied Britain – 23 points

Canada – 20 points

Netherlands – 8 points

Australia – 7 points

Grey smiled, and it seemed he looked down at Michael. "In the event of a tie, we are forced to award the victory to the team with the highest aggregate positions, and in this case, the Americans were victorious. They won one round, and finished second in the other two. In contrast, whilst the British did win the last round, they came third in the round two and second in the round one. The rulebook states that, therefore, victory is awarded to the Americans. However, I must say, all sides fought valiantly, and this is the closest top three we've had for a long time," he finished, and stepped down.

Michael saw the screens showing the triumphant smile on Gideon's face, and boiled with anger. The Americans didn't deserve to win! Michael's team had won the last and most difficult task!

He noticed another familiar figure step up to the podium. Lieutenant Blackburn, Head of Technological Integration was there, his pale face looking down at the teams.

"In light of the ... outstanding performance of the squads in this Coliseum, we have decided to make a change the reward for winning. Originally, we planned for the winning team to be drafted into an elite squad, trained by my own department. However, with so little to separate the top two teams, we have decided to instead make two elite squads, to reflect the skills of the recruits. Those who work hard will succeed, and be granted better opportunities. Let it never be said America is not a meritocracy," he drawled, then turned and left the podium.

President Elliot Hudson then stood up, with much cheering from the crowd.

"This does not take way from the victory of the American team. They won, folks! America is once again victorious! But, healthy competition is always to be promoted. I think I speak for the all our viewers when I say we will be happy to see more of the leaders, Gideon and Leonidas. The military really do make 'em strong. It is important that we stay united in these times of war. The real enemy is still out there. However, I pity the enemy that has to face our soldiers!" the President roared, causing tumultuous applause. "Let the celebrations begin!"

Michael didn't move. His team remained silent, standing to attention. He tried not to let any emotion show on his face. He saw the press swarming over the American team, snapping pictures of them, asking questions.

The points tally remained on the screens, showing the world how close it had been.

Steve broke the silence.

"Well, like that's fair!" he complained. "What now?"

Before Michael would respond, a journalist came up to him with a cameraman.

"Leonidas, how are you feeling?" she asked him.

"I'm, er, proud of my team. To be level with the top side was more than what we'd hoped for, and this was definitely a success for us," he replied.

"Are you disappointed that you didn't win?" she asked.

"To a degree," Michael said. "But the American team also fought well, I wouldn't want to take away from their victory."

"Leonidas, what do you-"

"That's enough!" Lieutenant Nicholls interrupted the reporter. "You can speak to him later." American soldiers escorted the journalists away.

"Recruits, follow me," Nicholls ordered, and he took them away from the crowds, back towards Sebastian Grey's house. He beckoned Michael towards him as they walked.

"What is it, sir?" Michael asked him.

"Tonight, your team will attend a formal reception, at which there will be sponsors, politicians, foreign dignitaries, and even the President might show up - so your squad better look the part. It could be your chance to get a deal of lifetime," Nicholls spoke quickly. "Now, I'm gonna take you back to your old instructors. They're in charge of you now, until you sign the forms to join whatever squad you want. Are you eighteen yet?"

"No," Michael replied.

"Right, you'll need one of your instructors to sign it for you. The "elite" squad that you've been invited to is part of Technological Integration, which Lieutenant Blackburn is charge of. It's up to you what you do. But, if you ever want to join the Marines instead, a friend of mine is looking for members. They're the real special forces."

Michael nodded. "I'll think about it," he replied noncommittally.

"Yeah, yeah, I know. But kid, you did well. Even if I don't see you again, I wish you the best of luck," Nicholls told him. "It seems I underestimated you. You're an American at heart."

"Is that supposed to be a compliment?" Michael replied with a grin.

"It was." Nicholls smirked a little. "You'll learn to know that."

Michael nodded. "Is there any update on Joe's case?" he asked Nicholls pointedly.

"Yeah, it's complicated ... the evidence is kept quite securely, you know, sensitive materials and stuff, they can't have anyone accessing it." Nicholls glanced away uncertainly.

"Well, if the President's going to be there tonight, I'll be sure to speak to him. I'm sure he'll appreciate you forcing me to bring the case to his attention," Michael replied.

Nicholls laughed. "Kid, don't get cocky. You're a soldier. You should not get involved in the messy world of politics. My advice is to keep your head down, and do your job."

"That's what Joe did, and it didn't go too well for him," Michael replied.

Nicholls grimaced. "So that's how you're playing it? Well, it's your call, but if you start getting other factions involved, your career will suffer. We heard what the Social Revolutionaries offered you, Leonidas. Don't be fooled by them. Joe will get justice, but not through them," he warned.

Michael smiled. "I'm glad you think so, sir. Thank you for agreeing to cooperate," he told Nicholls. "Is there any more messages for my squad?"

Nicholls frowned. "No, there isn't. But we're all soldiers here, Leonidas. We're all on the same side," he reminded him.

"I'm glad you're on Joe's side too, sir. May I re-join my squad?" he asked.

"Yeah, dismissed," Nicholls remarked, as though they weren't all walking in the same direction anyway.

Michael slowed down to walk alongside Elizabeth and Thomas. It would seem they were in for an interesting evening.

84 -   THE LAST TIME

"Well Leonidas, that might be the last time we dress you," Edna remarked, her face tight as she surveyed him critically in the mirror.

Michael smiled. "I'm very grateful, to all of you," he told them, looking at the emotionless Winston, an energetic Carter and a shy Mabel. "You made such a difference."

"I should hope so, we aren't paid for nothing," Edna replied. "But you were one of our more successful recruits. I must say, the ones from the other nations were not as compliant as you."

Michael shrugged. "I thought you knew best."

Winston smirked. "We did," he replied simply.

"Michael, hun, we will really miss you!" Carter exclaimed. "Wherever you go, I just hope you're safe!"

Michael smiled. "In my profession, there's not much chance of that," he remarked. "But I'll try my best."

There was silence.

Eventually, Edna coughed. "Well, the Sheikh wants to see you. It's best we don't keep him."

Michael gave a single nod, feeling emotional for some reason. "Yeah," he agreed quietly, looking away.

He turned and left the dressing room, where a dark-skinned security guard waited, as usual.

"You ready?" the guard asked him.

"Yep," Michael replied, and the guard led him away.

As they walked, Michael noticed the guard kept glancing at him. Eventually, the man spoke.

"I, er, thought you did well out there," the guard said quietly. "The Americans aren't so popular, you'll have probably have gained some friends."

Michael raised an eyebrow at him.

"Yeah, I should probably stop talking now," the guard admitted with a nervous laugh.

Michael gave a slight smile, sympathising with the guard.

"What's your name?" Michael asked him.

"Me? Erm, Zain Zaman. Been working for the Sheikh a little over a year now. It's my first Coliseum, though," he informed, inclining his head. "I know who you are, of course. *Leonidas.*"

Michael let out a laugh. "Seems everyone does, unfortunately."

Zain Zaman laughed. "It can't be all bad though, ha? It bet it helps with the girls, am I right?" He gave a toothy grin.

Michael frowned, laughing awkwardly. "I've been a bit preoccupied, to be honest. How ... old are you?" he asked, surprised at the turn of conversation of this security guard. The Sheikh's men didn't usually speak to him at all.

"Hmmph, twenty-four now. You're making me feel old, ha," Zain remarked. "I've got a woman myself, actually. She enjoys watching the Coliseum, though the signal isn't great in Arabia."

Michael raised his eyebrows. He wasn't really interested, but tried to stay polite.

"I didn't know Arabia supported the Western Alliance," Michael stated.

Zain raised his eyebrows. "Course they do. All British Empire territory was taken over by the Western Alliance. Virtually, anyway. We still have our monarch. So do you, now I think come to think of it," he mused.

"A monarch? Britain doesn't have a king - there's no Empire anymore," Michael said, confused.

"No empire, no, but still a Commonwealth. King George, I think he's called. Lives in Canada. Of course, most of the original royals were killed, but I think he's descended from a cousin or something." Zain shrugged. "History's not my forte."

Michael was surprised. His isolated existence had always led him to believe that there was nothing left of what was the British Empire, except for Independent Britain.

"Does Independent Britain have an embassy here?" Michael asked Zain.

"Yeah, yeah, of course. They're practically a part of the Western Alliance, though; just no military bases are allowed to be stationed in Independent Britain. That doesn't stop soldiers like yourself going south to Western Alliance territory."

They had reached the Sheikh's room. Michael wasn't sure how to reply to Zain.

"Erm, thanks," he told the guard.

"You're welcome." Zain grinned. "Good luck!"

Michael blinked, and then pushed open the door. He entered a dimly lit room, wherein the Sheikh sat, as usual in between his burly bodyguards. There was a scantily-clad young woman sat on the Sheikh's lap. She looked barely an adult.

"Leon-idas!" the Sheikh boomed. "What a pleas-ure!"

Michael smiled, going slightly red. "Sheikh Bakir," he said respectfully.

"Yes, yes, we must talk. Crystal, leave us," the Sheikh commanded, shooing away the girl.

"I can be very quiet," the girl, 'Crystal', whispered, pouting.

"Go!" the Sheikh insisted, his chins wobbling as he turned his head away from her. "But not too far!" he called as she left.

Michael had been looking at his feet the whole exchange, bright crimson.

"Ah, Mike-al, how well you have done!" the Sheikh exclaimed. "*You* have helped me. Yes, you have."

"I thought you were aiming to win?" Michael replied, raising his eyebrows.

The Sheikh laughed throatily. "Ha, no, no ... you were never going to win, Mike-al. There was no chance of that. But by aiming so high, you achieved much more than if you had aimed to avoid fourth place."

Michael sighed. "So it was all for nothing?" he questioned.

"No! Because of your efforts, you earned the rest of your squad a place in the Technological Integration team. But most of all ... you made an *impression*. Tonight, at the ball, there will be many well-connected people interested in you. You have the chance to tell them the reason for your victory was me," the Sheikh said, with a satisfied smile.

Michael frowned, standing up straighter. "Hold on ... what do you mean I earned *the rest of my squad* a place on Blackburn's team. Are you saying that it doesn't include me?" he demanded.

Sheikh blinked. "You are indebted to me, Mike-al. Whilst I sponsor you, you will join no team. I intend to use you on my next visit to the Emirates. You will be very popular there," he replied.

Michael breathed out, looking at the Sheikh. "Not a chance. I'm staying with my squad," he told the Sheikh.

"Nonsense! You no longer need your squad to prosper! You can do much better without them!" the Sheikh exclaimed. "Your future is not tied to them."

"Except in the military, it is. I trained with them, I fought with them, and I've competed with them. I'm not leaving them to go with you," Michael retorted.

"Mike-al, you owe me. I am your sponsor. Your village currently receives food supplies from me. Imagine how they would cope if they stopped," the Sheikh said slowly, looking at Michael.

"Sheikh Bakir, I am not your pet, to be paraded around. You sponsored me in return for recognition. I will honour my word, and sing your praises tonight, but if you attempt to force me to leave my team, then I'm sure I can find a new sponsor," Michael snapped.

The bodyguards stepped forward, but the Sheikh held up his hand.

"Mike-al, stop this. You would not have done so well if not for me and my team," he said. "And very well. I will not send you away. You will remain with backing from me. But I will not forget this slight, Leonidas. Remember, it was I who gave you that name."

Michael nodded. He was about to say thank you, but he didn't want to seem as if the Sheikh was doing him a favour. "I'm glad that's clarified," he told the Sheikh. "Is there anything in particular I should be saying to these well-connected people tonight?"

Sheikh Bakir shook his head, his chins wobbling. "You need only introduce me. My own charisma will do the rest," he assured Michael.

Michael restrained his smile, assuming by charisma, the Sheikh meant money.

"Am I dismissed?" he asked.

"Yes ... and Leonidas ... I am proud of you," the Sheikh said.

Michael nodded. "Thank you," he said briskly, before striding out.

Outside the door, Crystal was waiting, a coy smile on her face. She winked at Michael.

Michael ignored her.

The Sheikh was a businessman above all - he only wanted personal profit. Michael was a soldier, not the Sheikh's marketer. The Coliseum had blurred the lines between the military and the outside world. Maybe that was what the Americans wanted.

He returned to the team's conference room, where they were due to be reunited with their instructors from the Institute. He took a deep breath, straightened his hair, and then went inside.

"Nice outfit, *Leonidas*," Steve snickered.

His fourteen squad members were sitting down, and there was an empty seat at one end of the table. At the other end, Lieutenant Jones sat, along with Sergeant Raines, Sergeant Wallace and Sergeant Vellon.

"Nice of you to join us, Bakerson!" Sergeant Raines announced, slamming his fist on the table. "You might think you're a big shot now, but yer still a Private, and that means you answer to me!"

Michael didn't know what to say, shocked by the outburst. He stammered an apology, but Raines burst out laughing.

"I'm just kidding, laddie. As I was saying, ye did a bloody good job out there. Ye took a risk, with the foul play, but ye got away with it. Everyone single one of ye deserved to be on this team and you proved us right for picking you. So, it's not often I say this, but well done," Raines told the team.

Michael smiled, as he took a seat at the end of the table. There was still one more empty seat.

"Yeah, yeah, well done and all that," Jones drawled in his American accent. "You guys were good enough to get me out of this job, and up for a promotion. This ball tonight will hopefully be the last time I see you guys. I'm glad you were able to apply what I taught you to this Coliseum, and that's why you did so well."

"In fact, Lieutenant Jones, you were so good, we might have to keep you here," a posh voice stated. A tall officer had entered the room. He had a wispy moustache. Michael recognised him from somewhere, but he couldn't quite place him.

He had an amused smile on his face. "An eight-year contract, perhaps?" he suggested to Jones, his eyes twinkling.

Jones stood up, saluting. "Major Cunningham, sir," he said, quickly. "I will do whatever is required of me, sir, but I was hoping to move to a sunnier climate, sir. For health purposes, sir."

Michael couldn't help but grin.

"We'll discuss this another time, Jones. I was invited here on more pressing concerns," Cunningham replied, looking around.

"Invited here, sir?" Jones repeated. "By who?"

"By me," Sergeant Wallace stated. "You may we wondering why there's an empty seat here. Well, that's for our good friend Joe. Joseph King, who was arrested and held *without* trial."

"But for good reason!" Sergeant Vellon exclaimed. "I have seen ze evidence!"

"Funny, that. Yer not so keen to let anyone *else* see the evidence," Sergeant Wallace mused.

"Very well, then. I will show it to you all. It is very convincing," Sergeant Vellon assured them.

"I'm sure it is. But, I've uncovered evidence of my own. Now, before Vellon was on the case of the spy, Prometheus, I was the one trying to establish the identity. The night before we left for Norway, there were two radio messages sent from the Institute to Norway. One was sent with official encryptions, and its contents were completely bland. I'll read it out now."

"What is the meaning of this?" Vellon demanded. "This was before we found the culprit."

"Let him continue," Cunningham ordered.

Wallace spoke. *"Ruth, I accept that going to norway was a grave risk, I object to killing innocents. Privately, if rescuing hostages overcomes guilt, must you endanger yourself trying to help innocents. Even though u are safe Now. Your Second brother André."*

"At the time, I discounted this message, thinking it was useless; the Polish technician had simply used the system to send a letter to his sister. That was all we concluded."

"We?" Cunningham questioned.

"Bakerson was with me at the time. He searched the location of the other transmission. He found nothing," Wallace clarified. "Now, that was all I thought of the matter, until a recent tip-off from an anonymous person, signing himself simply as 'The Reporter'. He told me to check the official communications from that night. I found that message, once again. This time, I had a closer look, and it was there, plain and simple."

"It was a code?" Arthur guessed.

"Exactly. Take the first letter of every other word, and there you have it. *Ragnarok. Prometheus. Now,*" Wallace stated triumphantly. "It was simple after that. I questioned the Polish technician. Turns out, he was told to send the transmission ten minutes earlier, but there had been a delay. Giving whoever sent the transmission enough time to get out of there. For some reason, the CCTV from that evening was unavailable for *that* transmission, but it *was* available for the other location, where I had sent Bakerson."

Michael remembered. He had seen someone there.

Jürgen. And Jenny.

"What happened there, Bakerson?" Wallace asked Michael.

"Is this really relevant?" Jürgen interjected.

"Yes," Wallace said. "Bear with me. Go on, Michael."

"Well, it was a while ago, so I don't remember perfectly, but I had gone looking for the place where the transmission was sent, and I saw Jürgen there. I thought he was the spy, so I ... attacked him. But, it turns out, he was meeting Jenny there. I was pulled off him, and we had to leave."

"Who pulled you off, Michael? Who told you that you had to leave?" Wallace asked him.

Michael tried to remember. "Vellon," he said. "It was Sergeant Vellon, he saw us fighting."

"That's what the CCTV confirmed. Now, the transmission, my tip-off reminded me, was sent with official encryptions. So, that had to be someone of rank."

Michael's eyes widened. Amanda Coleman, the reporter with the Social Revolutionaries, had told him the same thing.

"How did this tip-off gain access to classified files?" Vellon demanded. "Zhat is a serious breach of security!"

"Not as much as Prometheus, Sergeant. It turns out; the Polish technician's name *wasn't* André, as the message suggested. It was Klaudius. And when I asked Klaudius to identify the officer who gave him the telegram, guess who it was, Vellon? Who then arrested Joe, and took control of the Prometheus investigation himself? Who falsified evidence against one of our recruits? And who remained in Oslo during the attack by Fenrir, at the *same time* the power grid happened to go down!"

"This is preposterous!" Vellon slammed his fists on the table, standing up. "You cannot accuse *me* of this!"

"Yes, I can, Sergeant Vellon! Yes I bloody well can! The technician is here, to give evidence, and I have the CCTV of you being witnessed at the site of the transmission centre. And in the first ever transmission we found from Prometheus, it mentioned that he was going to the Coliseum. Now that's must be someone in this room, isn't it, Vellon?" Wallace accused, standing up. "*You* are the reason that the Royal Scots were ambushed! You are the reason that so many bloody recruits were killed!"

Vellon glared at Wallace. "If you hadn't claimed zhat Fenrir had been located, then Ragnarok would never have been triggered! It was your desire for revenge about zhat Scottish team that got the recruits killed! Not me!" Vellon spat.

"Sergeant Vellon, stand down," Cunningham ordered sternly. "You are hereby under arrest for treason and collusion with enemies of the Western Alliance."

Vellon cried out in anger, advancing towards Major Cunningham. "Sir, this man eez framing me! I have done nothing! It was Joseph, I heard him plotting on ze plane to bring down ze Americans!"

"Sergeant, that is an *order!*" Cunningham shouted, drawing his pistol and pointing it directly at Vellon.

Vellon growled, and halted, glowering at the rest of the room.

"Nothing to say for yerself, eh?" Wallace remarked. "No confession? Yer a rebel without a cause now, aren't you Vellon? You were Fenrir's man, but now he's dead. Yer a lone wolf, alone, and friendless. It's nothing less than ye deserve."

"Well done, Wallace," Sergeant Raines exclaimed. "But Vellon ... I never suspected ... why did ya do it?"

Vellon clenched his fists. "My country was conquered by ze Americans. So were so many others, in the name of America. My countrymen fight the American's wars, and *die* for them, whilst they play their war games. I am a freedom fighter, not a traitor. The real traitors are-"

Vellon lunged, forcing Cunningham's hand up. The gun went off, and Vellon wrenched it out of his hand.

Michael stood up, as did other recruits, but Vellon pointed the gun at Cunningham and shouted, "ZIT DOWN!"

Cunningham smiled. "Recruits, do your country proud. Stand tall in the face of adversity. This Frenchman has nowhere to run," he announced, seemingly oblivious to the pistol pointed at his face.

"SILENCE!" Vellon shouted, sweat running down his forehead. "I am not going to rot in an American prison! You let them take your country, but I will not let them do the same to mine! I am not the first, and I will not be the last! Vive la France!"

Wallace walked towards Vellon, his hands up. "Vellon, it's over. Yer gonna get exactly what's due to ye."

"Don't move!" Vellon told him.

Raines stood up. "Sergeant, there's no way yer gonna get out of the building. The Americans will be coming for ye. Better surrender now."

Vellon fired the gun at Wallace. Michael threw himself at Vellon, going for the gun in his hand. Vellon fired again at Michael, as Major Cunningham smashed his elbow into his face. Michael barrelled into Cunningham and Vellon, sending them to the floor. Vellon kicked him away, sending Michael sprawling.

Michael blinked, looking down at his right shoulder as the rest of the recruits took down Vellon. He had been shot, but the bullet hadn't penetrated. Even so, it was agony, the sheer force of the shot having shattered something. He looked up at Wallace.

The ginger-haired Scot had sunk to his knees. A pool of red stained his shirt. His eyes locked with Michael's registering some emotion before he collapsed forward.

"Wallace!" Michael shouted, rolling Wallace over to look at the wound. "Someone, get help! We need to save him!"

Wallace coughed blood, and it was clear to see it was too late. The bullet, at close range, had ripped a hole in his chest.

Seal the wound. Prevent his lung collapsing.

His training ran on autopilot. He didn't think, and didn't want to.

Emergency medics arrived, taking over. He was dimly aware of soldiers arresting Sergeant Vellon. Michael remained on his knees, looking at the glazed expression on

Wallace's youthful face, at the expanding pool of blood seeping through his uniform.

He didn't move.

85 -   OVER AND OUT

"He was gonna go back to Scotland, after all this," Raines revealed, taking a shot of whisky.

Sergeant Wallace had been pronounced dead. Major Cunningham had ordered them all to continue with their duties and not to speak of the matter. Raines had summoned Michael to his quarters.

"Did he have a family?" Michael asked him.

"He wasn't married, but had two older brothers. One of 'em was killed in the Royal Scots. His body was never found," Raines answered. "Now ah'm gonna have to tell his family the bad news. Wallace was a good lad. I never mentored him, but he was a recruit ... about five years before you, I reckon," Raines said, taking another drink.

Michael felt empty. Wallace had been more than just an instructor to Michael, almost a friend. He hadn't known him closely, but had respected him. He had been the last Royal Scot still alive after the Fenrir's ambush in Norway, and was wounded trying to track down the agent in Auli. He was a brave man.

"He had a friend ... Jack, he mentioned," Michael told Raines.

Raines nodded. "Aye, I'll let him know. Don't you forget this, Michael. It could quite easily 'ave been you that got killed today. Wallace's sacrifice will not be in vain. He gave you a chance ... don't you waste it," he looked at Michael, and then dismissed him.

"Go. Ye've got that formal event to go to. Do yer duty, Michael, just what Cunningham ordered. Do yer duty."

* * *

Michael was fuming.

He was angry at Vellon, he was angry at himself, he was angry at the Americans.

But, he couldn't show his anger. He had to hide it, behind fake smiles and forced politeness, as he and Sheikh Bakir were introduced to yet another prestigious businessman.

It was whilst Sheikh Bakir was chatting about a contract with the head of an American energy firm; a bald man with a terrible cough, that Michael was approached by a tall, brown-haired man in a military officer's uniform. He looked youthful, and had a lot of vigour in his manner.

"Leonidas," the man remarked with a slight smile. "Congratulations."

"Sir." Michael saluted. He was unsure who this man was, though his medals showed he was of high rank.

"I must say, I'm glad we made it so close this year. The Americans always like to brag about their military. I say, ours is just as good. When it is hosted in Britain, then we will show them who the best is!" the man declared.

"Are you British, sir?" Michael asked curiously.

"My, my, do you not know who I am?" the King looked at a smartly dressed man who cleared his throat.

"May I present King George the Seventh, Emperor of India, and Head of the Commonwealth!" the man announced.

The King smiled "I'm surprised, I've always felt a connection with the people of Britain, being my mother's birthplace."

Michael forced a smile. "Are you the King of Britain … your Highness?"

"Your Majesty, actually. And yes, I am; my mother was cousin to the Windsors, and we emigrated to the safety of Canada during the war," King George replied with a smile. "When the royals were killed, the burden of the monarchy fell to me, and I took the name George VII."

"I haven't seen you before at this Coliseum," Michael commented.

"No?" King George asked, raising his eyebrows.

"What are you doing to help Britain, Your Majesty? We've been severely damaged by this war," Michael remarked.

King George smiled. "Yes, the Empire has seen better days, but the President has assured me that the Commonwealth will have independence and aid money once the war is over. It's my hope that Britain can rebuild itself, we just need the resources."

Michael smiled, feeling weary. "Well, speaking of resources, it might be prudent to strike up a deal with the Arab Sheikhs, I hear they have a lot of oil," he told the King, as he saw Sheikh Bakir bumbling towards them. "Your Majesty, might I introduce you to my sponsor, Sheikh Bakir? This is the man who has given the chance for recruits like me to rise up and do your nation proud."

The Sheikh shook the King's hand with both of his flabby ones. "King ... George ... it is ... an *honour..*," Sheikh Bakir enthused, much to the horror of the smartly-dressed man beside him.

"Ah, a pleasure, sir," the King replied, looking thoroughly alarmed at the interruption. "I must say, this is unexpected..."

Michael smiled. "Well, I'll leave you two to get acquainted!"

He retreated, seeing the King furrow his eyebrows as he tried to decipher what the Sheikh was telling him.

Michael took a deep breath, relieved to have the Sheikh off his back.

"It seems you did try to beat the game, after all."

Sebastian Grey had appeared next to Michael.

"Mr Grey," Michael nodded respectfully.

Grey's mouth twitched. "I must say, you surprised me. There aren't many teams that finish above where we want them to," he remarked.

"We almost won," Michael pointed out. "That would upset your plans."

Grey looked at him piercingly. "Did you? I can see why you might think that. Leonidas, I don't think you realise how little impact you really have. Soldiers are ultimately just pawns in the grand scheme of things. Do you really believe it was your influence that caused your team to finish where it did? Men always seem so important in their own perspective, whereas in reality, they're just another piece in the puzzle."

Michael shook his head. "No. That's ridiculous. You didn't expect me to attack the other teams, you couldn't just plan what would happen," he argued, frowning.

The man's mouth twitched again. "You think it was chance? You didn't think that I considered that by telling you that you couldn't beat the game, you would try to?" he questioned.

Michael looked at the man, unsure. "I think your system is very fragile, and that you were shaken by us becoming so close. You can't control what people do. I shot the Americans as they boarded that helicopter. It wasn't you who decided who I shot. You can plan all you want, but what happens in war is down to the soldiers."

Sebastian Grey shook his head slowly. "You could never have won the Coliseum, Leonidas," he replied.

Michael frowned. "Because you fixed it?"

Grey smiled, giving Michael a look of pity. "You have a lot to learn, but I admire your spirit. There are a lot of soldiers like you, Leonidas. You want to do the right thing, but you don't want to make tough choices."

Michael sighed. "Spare me your lectures, Grey. You don't control me."

Grey sighed. "Leonidas, when President asks you, you must accept. Otherwise you will have made an enemy."

"Asks me what?" Michael retorted.

"ALL RISE FOR THE PRESIDENT!" a uniform-clad guard announced, even though everyone was already standing up.

Michael looked up.

President Elliot Hudson had entered, secret service bodyguards on either side of him, a large grin on his face, as he shook hands of various businessmen.

Once he had finished, he made his way to a small platform with a microphone on. He smiled at the crowd, and then began speaking.

"Well, once again, I'm making a speech," he announced. "But this time, we are all gathered in celebration, of what has been an incredible showcase of the skills of recruits from all over the Alliance. I'm going to make this brief, as you've heard a lot of me recently."

He smiled, and looked around, his gaze settling on Michael.

"We've often said in the United States, that if you work hard and serve your country, you will be rewarded. Well, I'm here to reward those that deserve it today. In the Coliseum, our American team truly outshone the rest. Therefore, I'd like to personally congratulate their leader, Gideon Knight, on his success. Come on over here, son," President Hudson announced.

Gideon confidently walked up, an easy grin on his face. He shook the President's hand.

"Thank you, Mr President," Gideon told him.

President Hudson clapped him on the back, smiling with one side of his face as cameras flashed.

"And, Mr Knight is not the only one I'd like to congratulate. The leader of the British team, Leonidas, created quite a rivalry. Of course, Gideon triumphed, but Leonidas will not be going home empty handed. Leonidas, as a reward for serving the Western Alliance, I'd like to grant you the honour of an American citizenship." President Hudson smiled.

Michael felt everyone's eyes on him. A citizenship? Being American as well as British? *Reject it.*

The thought appeared out of nowhere. He couldn't turn down the President! Could he?

It would show them they couldn't control every outcome. He would be doing it for Joe, and for Sergeant Wallace. For Jane, back in the village. For all of Britain, that had been ravaged by the war that the Americans had started.

But no. He couldn't make an enemy of the President. He had to be a good soldier, to do his duty. It wasn't up to him to make political statements.

He glanced at Sebastian Grey. A pawn, was he? Did everything have to go according to his plan?

Michael smiled at the President.

"Thank you, Mr President, but I unfortunately cannot accept this honour. As the leader of my team, I must remain the same nationality as them. I am proud to be British, just as I'm sure Gideon is proud to be American," Michael stated.

The President's gaze hardened for a half-second, and then he grinned. "That's an impressive answer, son! Everyone, look at this recruit! He sticks by and supports his nationality, just as all we Americans do. Whilst he might not be American, there's certainly the spirit of one in him," he proclaimed, as the crowd laughed.

"Now, friends, please, enjoy the evening! Celebrate the successes of our nation as victors, and the successes of the Western Alliance!" Hudson announced, stepping down.

Michael's heart was pounding. He stood still, waiting for some repercussions. Sebastian Grey had disappeared.

"That was quite a brave thing, you know."

Michael looked back to see Darius Finch, a slight smile on his face.

Michael grinned, embracing him. "It's good to see you," he enthused.

Darius grew quite flustered at the contact. "Likewise. You performed excellently in the games, just as I thought you would. Lieutenant Blackburn is here, and he invited me to accompany him here," he informed. "It's been an interesting evening. I thought you'd accept the President's offer, but I understand why you did not. I spoke with Steven earlier, he told me to let you that they're going for a meal in celebration with Joe, if you would care to join them?"

Michael laughed. "That'd be great; I'm dying to get out of here. Are you coming?"

Darius looked uncertain. "I imagined only the recruits who competed would be invited," he remarked.

Michael smiled. "You're one of us, Darius. You're coming. Besides, Arthur will be interested to hear about the Trojan programme you're working on. It'll be great."

Darius nodded. "As you say. I'll make my way there. Are you finished here?" he asked Michael.

"No, *he's not*."

Sophie had sauntered over, a coy grin on her face. "If you don't mind, Darius, I'd like a word with Leonidas," she said sweetly.

Darius raised an eyebrow, and then looked at Michael.

"I'll join you in a sec," he told Darius, nodding.

"Or he might not," Sophie suggested with a grin, as Darius briskly moved away.

Michael looked at Sophie. She wore military uniform, which was usual for a recruit, but for Sophie it hugged her figure well. Her dark hair was tied back loosely, as though she didn't care how she looked, a strand in the way of her face.

"To what to I owe the pleasure?" Michael asked her, trying to remain confident.

Sophie smiled. "Well, officially, I'm here to *persuade* you to change your sponsor towards my one, Julian Quinn. But ..."

She moved closer. "I'm really just doing it as excuse to hang out with you."

Michael laughed, feeling flustered. "Sophie, please. You've never wanted to just 'hang out' with me before," he replied, raising his eyebrows.

His heart was still beating fast. He remembered when he'd first met Sophie. How she could still make him feel like the awkward, nervous recruit he had been, he didn't know.

She smirked. "We've never got a chance to be alone before."

"We're not alone now, Sophie. We're in a room full of people," Michael said with a smile.

Sophie played with her hair. "Maybe we should go somewhere we can talk privately," she suggested, biting her lower lip. Her blue eyes sparkled slightly.

"What do you want to talk about?" Michael asked quietly, looking at her.

"You were very brave, Michael," she remarked.

"With the President? Well, it was more of a-"

"Not *just* with the President," she interrupted, giving a half smile.

"Oh." Michael felt hot, his mouth dry. "Thank you."

He looked at her face. It was perfect, really. They were standing close now. She smelled nice. He resisted the urge to brush the hair out of her face.

He cleared his throat. "Well, I mean, maybe you should go ..."

Sophie grinned. "What?" she teased. "Are you afraid?"

Michael laughed, looking away. "No ... I'm not afraid."

He looked backed at her again, and realised. Sophie would always get what she wanted. She would always be able to make him feel like the awkward recruit that didn't know what was going on. But he wasn't that person any more.

"I'm sorry, Sophie, but I'm busy at the moment," Michael told her with a smile, stepping away. "Tell your sponsor that I'm taken, unfortunately, and that I'm not so easily ... persuaded."

Sophie's eyes widened. She laughed. "It wasn't about the spon-"

"I know," Michael interrupted, looking at her. "I'll see you around, Sophie."

He turned, and strode away. "Darius! Wait up!" he called, jogging to catch up.

Steve, Jürgen, Arthur and Nadia were all outside, waiting, along with Amelia, the girl whom Jürgen had been seeing a lot more of lately. Joe was there, looking a bit thinner than he had done, but otherwise fine. He was smiling, which was unusual.

He nodded at Michael. "Thank you, Michael," he said, clasping his hand in his.

Michael grinned. "It's good to have you back, Joe."

Steve clapped his hands together. "Glad you could make it! Thought you'd never come out of that snobs' nest!" he exclaimed.

Michael laughed. "I'm out, alright. Out for good."

Nadia smiled warmly at him. "I'm glad the squad's back together."

Michael smiled. "So am I," he agreed. "Now Steve, what are you cooking for us?"

Steve began walking off. "Nothing that you can afford. Anyway, I was chatting to one of the guards, who told me some great places to get some food, which even we can afford..."

Michael zoned out, glancing around at the group as he walked. He fell into step with Nadia.

She looked at him. "What was it like in there?"

Michael met her gaze. "Exhausting," he admitted. "I'm glad it's behind me."

He knew it wasn't behind him for good, and that he'd always have duties to perform, but for now, he was happy to live in the present.

86 - EPILOGUE

Arthur liked routine. He liked stability. Each day, he would wake up at military barracks, eat breakfast, and then come aboard the truck which took him and five other recruits down to Technological Integration. They would be searched at the checkpoint, and made to go through the metal detectors, and show their ID passes. They would enter the building, taking the first left, and go down the door marked 'Project Juggernaut'. They would once again scan their ID passes, whilst a friendly female guard ticked them off her list.

"All clear," she would say, opening the door. "Have a good day."

"You too," Arthur would reply, as he and the other recruits entered a computer laboratory, and logged on.

Today was different.

The security guard had been replaced with a burly man in a grey uniform, who said nothing as the recruits walked in. Arthur and Darius sat next to each other, as always, and waited for their project leader to enter.

They could hear raised voices long before the door slid open.

Alberto Morales, a Mexican inventor and designer, entered. He was the genius behind 'Project Juggernaut', and the creator of the first Trojan robot. The project was the first step in the mass-production of the Trojan. Under his guidance, Arthur, Darius and the other recruits had been learning to program and improve the machines.

Alongside Morales was the military presence in the room, Lieutenant Blackburn's second-in-command, named Solomon. He had been sent to oversee the project, keeping Morales' genius in check and making sure that he did not waste the their funding.

There was an unusual power dynamic between the two men, and Arthur was never quite sure who was in charge. Morales could be very stubborn, particularly when it came to the ethics of the programming, and resented any military control over his machines. On the other hand, he was completely dependent on the military for his resources and funding, and knew they could take away his Trojans at any time they wished.

Morales was firmly against the Trojans being weaponised, whereas Solomon envisioned them eventually replacing humans on the field as mechanical soldiers.

Darius had commented on the relationship a few weeks ago, stating that the more developed the Trojans became, the less the military would need Morales, and the only way for him to maintain his position was to become indispensable to the project.

Darius had suspected that Morales would be resentful of the recruits' presence, fearing they would replace him. However, Arthur had experienced only consideration from the inventor, as the man had taken the role of a mentor for the group.

"This is the last straw! I have told you many times, you cannot change the source code!" Morales exclaimed. "It could change the whole function of these machines, and I could not let anyone run riot inside them. Who knows what irreparable damage they might cause?"

"Morales, you need to trust your recruits! You trained them! They will have ideas too, they will improve the Trojan. If you are killed or captured, who will continue your work? What is your legacy?" Solomon pleaded.

Morales seemed to consider this, as he looked around at the recruits. "Darius Finch will be my second-in-command. He shows the most promise. The encryption to the source code will be granted to him, and only him."

Solomon looked at Darius, and nodded. Darius was recognised as the recruit with the most aptitude for programming, and this only confirmed the unspoken consensus that he was the best of the recruits.

The group was small; Morales had asked for only two apprentices. The military had given him six, to spread the risk.

There was Frederick, an overweight Canadian boy. He had been found by the NSA after hacking into bank software to pay for a video game currency. He didn't speak much, often engrossed in his computer.

There was Antony, the most extroverted of the group, a lively South African. He was easily distracted, and frequently stayed up late programming, powered by exceptionally strong coffee.

There was also Takumi, a Japanese-American boy who Arthur hadn't seen smile once. He kept to himself a lot, though Arthur felt him watching the rest of them sometimes. When he did contribute, he was straight to the point.

And finally, there was Jess, a quick-witted Australian girl. She was relaxed about the work, making it seem effortless. She had a nice smile, Arthur thought.

"Darius, Lieutenant Blackburn will want to speak with you. I'll schedule a meeting for later today," Solomon decided, scanning over the group. Arthur suspected that Solomon didn't actually know his name.

"How are they doing?" Solomon asked Morales.

"Better than expected," the inventor replied. "At current rate of progress, they'll complete the next update before the Trojans are even shipped out."

Solomon nodded. "I hope so. The President has high expectations for this program, as much as for propaganda as anything. They'll be a symbol of hope to the American people."

Morales raised his eyebrows. "I'm not American. The Trojans will be sent out only when they're ready. We can't have risks when lives are at stake," he remarked.

Solomon shrugged. "Lives are at stake every day. The longer it takes - the more of our soldiers die out in the field. I'm just the messenger here, Morales."

Morales looked at him. "Thank you, Solomon. Is there anything else?"

Solomon looked at the recruits. "Just – keep going," he told them.

As he left the room, Solomon smiled to himself.

Soon, the Trojans would be ready. Their potential was revolutionary.

ABOUT THE AUTHOR

A student with a love of history. I am a keen sportsman, one of four close and competitive brothers who enjoy gaming, reading, travel and adventure.

I hope to make the Institute into a series, and continue writing in the world of Michael Bakerson.

Printed in Germany
by Amazon Distribution
GmbH, Leipzig

18420763R00303